THE CRIMSON RUN

THE Crimson Run

Book 1 of *The Crimson Articles*

YASMEEN SALAMA

THE CRIMSON RUN

Published by
Illumify Media Global
www.IllumifyMedia.com
"Let's bring your book to life!"

Paperback ISBN: 978-1-959099-70-3

Illustration 13650076 © Dmstudio | Dreamstime.com COMPASS
Illustration 70173993 © Tanya Borozenets | Dreamstime.com KEY

Typeset by Art Innovations (http://artinnovations.in/)
Cover design by Debbie Lewis

Printed in the United States of America

For my brother Laith, the man who invented comedy.
His sense of humor has sent me to an early grave on more than one occasion.
Cause of death: lung failure due to incessant laughter.
His creative audacity spawned the backbone of this story,
and our all-night, super smart, very serious,
not-one-bit-of-it-spent-playing-video-games,
conversations brought it to life.

Prologue

(BECAUSE EVERY BOOK WORTH READING HAS A PROLOGUE)

Sometime during the Industrial Revolution, early nineteenth century, somewhere in Spain.

"**B**ut the Crimson thieves are far more infamous than the Informant," declared the accountant, Diego's fifth appointment of the day. "Besides, if this so-called Informant is such an infamous crime lord, how come I never heard of him until my lord mentioned your interest in him?"

Diego Del Castillo sat behind his dark wood desk in his study, sharpening a knife (because that's what bad guys do). He drew the blade over the whetstone, counted two seconds, then drew it over the stone again. Precisely every two seconds.

Whisk . . . whisk . . . whisk.

The fidgety accountant's shoulders tensed with each whisk. Diego wasn't sure why.

"My interest in him is precisely because no one has heard of him," Diego said. "A crime lord worth his salt is subtle, careful, clandestine. This man is clearly skilled."

"But—"

"While I appreciate your input, bookkeeper, the matter is settled. I care nothing about a couple idiot, petty thieves, regardless of their fame. The Informant, on the other hand, has proven himself quite capable. Your lord is to leave him be. Let him build his criminal empire without our interference, and without knowing of our existence."

The accountant swallowed, nodding. "Yes, sir."

Diego raised an eyebrow. The man had no reason to fear Diego. He had always welcomed the perspectives of those who supported his evil plan (not that *he* thought his plan was evil).

He shook his head, glancing at the three clocks on the mahogany mantel above the roaring hearth, its flames the only source of light in the room.

The first clock ticked 7:59:23.

The second clock ticked 7:59:23.

The third clock ticked 7:59:23.

"Anything else to report?" Diego asked.

"No, sir. I'll report your orders back to Lord Isaac."

"Very good. Thank you for your time, bookkeeper. Dismissed."

The man hurried out as though a viper were on his heels. Diego shook his head again.

As soon as he closed the door, all three clocks chimed eight o'clock.

Diego glanced around his austere study, habitually confirming everything was in its proper place. The tomes on the mahogany shelves were perfectly aligned, ordered alphabetically and categorically. They all wore black coverings. No one book diverted attention.

Despite the multitude of exotic artifacts, books, shelves, tables, and historic artwork, not a speck of dust could be spotted anywhere. The maps and files on Diego's desk were studiously placed in piles according to their size.

Perfection. Life was about order. Without order, the world would crumble. Why was Diego the only one in all of Europe who understood that?

As soon as the clocks on the mantel completed the eighth chime announcing the hour, a knock sounded at the door. "Come in," he called.

The short, stocky, pale-skinned man with a natural tonsure who entered was not what one would expect from the most competent manager Diego had ever known. Intelligent, organized, precise, and extremely well connected, Rodger Jolliman was a London-born erudite that had been supporting Diego's evil plan from the beginning (okay maybe a small part of him knew his plan was evil).

Rodger approached Diego's desk and bowed as well as a man with his profound gut could.

"Good morning, my friend."

"Mornin' General." Rodger plopped into the black leather chair before Diego's desk with a jovial chuckle.

Diego set his knife and whetstone down carefully on the desk before him, then leaned forward, resting his elbows on the desk. "Report."

Rodger continued his snickering as though remembering a good joke as he flipped through a ledger. "Item one: I just got word that Garnet is poking around for any information he can find about you. He's also been filing an absurd number of patents into a private holding you aren't supposed to know about."

"Have you located this holding?"

"Of course. Already got eyes on it too. All things considered, he's actually doing fairly well. Sly chump, that one. You sure you don't want to keep him around?"

"He can remain until he digs his own grave."

"And you're certain he's going to?"

"Yes."

Rodger laughed. "All right then. Well that's that. I'll just keep an eye or two on him. Item two: Garnet successfully discredited Professor Brass. Is that going to be inconvenient?"

"Have you secured a replacement?"

"I've *identified* a replacement and sent Isaiah to—" Rodger paused to smile—"*secure* his loyalty."

"Who is it?"

"A Spanish weapons specialist stationed on the coast of Pamplona. Goes by the name Antonio Condello."

"I've heard of him. His weapons are said to be revolutionizing warfare."

"Indeed they are. But there's a problem. He actually doesn't want to make weapons. He wants to fight in the war. Some kind of idealism about how other men fight for king and country, and he's safe in the forges making weapons for them to die by."

"What war is this?"

"I . . ." (Actually I have no idea. Pretend he didn't ask that question.)

"So he's a man of honor," Diego said, leaning back in his chair. "What's your play?"

"Isaiah already made it. He'll do it. Just a matter of time."

"Good. Very good. Now that Garnet thinks he's our primary source of capital, he doesn't need to know about Condello. And Condello doesn't need to know about me. Have Isaiah hire him directly. And be sure he understands discretion is paramount. Garnet is not to know of, nor interfere with this one."

"May I pose a question?"

Diego raised his eyebrows.

"Isaiah's been nothing but loyal to the cause, and has proven himself a valuable asset. Why not bring him in a bit more?"

Diego leaned back, quiet for moment. "It's not Isaiah. It's his wife."

"Isn't she the one who introduced you to Isaiah in the first place?"

"Yes." His former relationship with Isadora could prove problematic at some point. He suspected she still harbored some fondness for him. He also suspected her husband knew it.

And that, unfortunately, was a problem he could not afford.

Liverpool, England

Rejected!

This piece of gout is worthless, they said.

Try inventing something what actually works, they said.

But it *did* work. Constable Alexander Corbin fidgeted with his "better mousetrap," standing ankle deep in mist on the busy cobblestone street. It was always misty in Liverpool. So ghastly. All the time! Just like his mood.

Well if the courts wouldn't patent his work, then maybe Garnet Industries would. They were, after all, the leading patent holders of just about anything steel. The criers were always making a splendid time of how they'd patent their own toes if the courts would allow. Perhaps Alex had a chance there.

Hence why he stood ankle deep in ghastly mist on a ghastly cobblestone road on this ghastly morning. The multi-storied building before him was state-of-the-art, two stories short of being the tallest building in England but nothing short of intimidating. In there, through those ominous ten-foot doors, was his future.

And he was *definitely* going to blow it.

With a deep breath, his shaky hands betraying him, Alex shuffled inside. He approached the receptionist and cleared his throat.

"May I . . . um . . . s–s–see lord, sir, Lord Morgan G–Garnet? Please?"

The woman laughed. "Mister, the Queen herself has to book an appointment three weeks in advanced to see Lord Garnet. What makes you think you—"

The door to the lift screeched open, and a group of five important-looking men in suits, top hats and cravats walked out. They were immersed in turbulent discussion but Alex knew the one at the front was Lord Morgan Garnet himself. His likeness had been featured in the papers often enough. There was no mistaking that sharp jawline.

Before he could reason with himself, Alex swallowed his crippling fear and jumped right in front of Lord Garnet.

The men cut off abruptly as Garnet silenced them, looking Alex over.

Well he hadn't expected that. He opened his mouth to speak but Garnet beat him to it. "It's about time, constable."

Oh right. He was still wearing his uniform. These men likely wouldn't have given him the time of day otherwise. But . . . "What?"

"I called for you over an hour ago. I've been robbed."

"Oh. W–well I'm certain the chief is s–s–sending men over right away. I'm actually h–here on p–p–personal business. Sir. Lord Garnet . . . sir."

"Personal business? When I've an entire building in chaos?"

"Well I invented this, um, mousetrap and I thought . . ."

"Oh rubbish! If one more would-be inventor brings me yet another worthless pile of pathetic hopes and dreams, I'll pay Paul to rob Peter!"

"I . . . what? B–b–but it works, sir! Look." He played with his invention for a second. "See the mouse goes in r–r–right there, and when this little . . . uh . . . p–piece here senses m–movement, it—" The mousetrap zapped his finger, and he recoiled with a yelp. Great, that was it. He'd made a fool of himself, again. Cheeks afire, he hesitantly looked up at Garnet. The legendary man of industry looked at him flatly. "What's your name, constable?"

"Um . . . Corbin. Alex. Er . . . Constable Alexander Corbin. Sir."

"Well. *Constable* Corbin. To be frank, I don't have time for you. Escort this halfwit out of my building."

"But—" was all Alex got out before he was roughly tossed out on the wet street.

"The thief didn't break in, Lord Garnet," Chief Brighton said as he scrutinized the window frame on the third floor of Garnet Industries. He clapped his hands together, killing some sort of flying bug and wrinkled his nose at the viscous innards now splayed on his palms.

"Of course he did," Morgan insisted. How this dunce . . .

He swatted away a fly.

How this dunce of an old . . .

He waved his arms around wildly to clear away the cluster of bugs swarming around his head. Mr. Barrington, his chief administrator, a tall, willowy, dark-skinned man feebly attempted to help swat the bugs away from Morgan.

How this dunce of an old ruin became chief of the constabulary, Morgan would never understand. The only reason he called the man in was because his private investigators were stumped. He'd hoped against reason that this Chief Brighton could shed some light on the situation.

"There is no other way to—" He yelped as a stick that was apparently alive climbed over his shoe. Mr. Barrington kicked it away. It whacked the window with a *thunk,* then crawled off in indignation. "There is no other way to get onto this floor!" Morgan fumed. "Mr. Barrington, would you kindly stop slapping me!"

"Except by special access through your private lift, granted only to special people, that you granted access to, yes?"

"Precisely. So if you are actually suggesting any of my people—" He yelped again as Mr. Barrington swatted a large beetle off Morgan's shoulder. It thunked against the wall. That thing was big enough to have a personality.

"Oh no, Lord Garnet. Your people are clean, that's for sure, no doubt in my mind, or your mind, or anybody's mind."

"Then get on with it!"

"Have you looked through the list of everything that was stolen from you? Everything you're missing?"

"Has a list been compiled?"

"Constable Terry."

The young constable accompanying Brighton stepped up hesitantly, wiping his neck in discomfort. Morgan openly sneered at him. Keepers of the peace indeed. This lad was about to soil his trousers in the presence of near-royalty.

Or he had a bee crawling up his neck.

In fact, there it went, flying away into the rafters. Morgan had already been stung once and he was two stings away from having a mental breakdown.

"Read off all the missing items."

"Yes, Chief. Ahem. Three window screws, door knob, a length of chain, a woman's handbag, the wheels of one chair, two pulleys from the main lift, a set of pliers, a table leg, and several draft tubes."

Morgan blinked. "Excuse me? The entire floor is in chaos. My workers are panicked, claiming they've been robbed, tables, chairs, equipment and the like have all been vandalized, and you're telling me the only things missing are random rubbish? I don't buy it. Not for a moment. It's all a cover up. It's—" Bee sting number two. He swatted his leg, killing the infernal creature.

"We've spoken to all your attendants," Brighton continued, not nearly as put off by the infestation as Morgan was. "Nothing is missing. Your men went through every inventory and made it quite clear to me that *nothing* is missing."

Morgan couldn't believe it. This was not possible. What thief broke into a highly secure facility and stole a table leg? It was almost insulting considering the treasure trove Morgan possessed here. Unless, the draft tubes stolen weren't empty . . . .

He gave Mr. Barrington a pointed look. Barrington took the hint and went off, fighting his way through a swarm of some sort of tiny flying insects, to investigate the one thing on that preposterous list of items stolen that could bode ill for his plans.

Shifting his attention back to the weathered chief, Morgan frowned. He did not look remotely concerned.

Waving an indignant hand at another UFB (unidentified flying bug; it's an industry term), Morgan sighed. "All right. You have my attention. I want it straight from the horse's mouth."

Brighton raised an eyebrow. "What?"

"What do you know, that I do not?" Morgan snapped.

Chief Brighton chuckled. "Do you read *The Times*?"

"Not if I can help it." That was a lie. Everyone read *The Times*. But if everyone *thought* he didn't, then they assumed he was out of the gossip loop, which always gave him a social advantage.

"I thought not. Well Lord Garnet. No sign of a break in, nothing of apparent value stolen, no one hurt, lots of chaos . . . I'm afraid you're just the latest victim of a Crimson run."

"A what?"

"You might consider reading the papers, sir," Chief Brighton said as he collected his men to leave. The lads couldn't have assembled faster if their lives were in danger. "The Crimson Run column is printed every Saturday," he explained as his eyes followed a flying bug carefully. He prepared his hands for a clap. "Every Saturday without fail. It's very popular. And based on the heists of the notorious Crimson siblings." He clapped another. The idiot was actually satisfied at his accomplishment.

"The Crimsons? This is their doing? How can you be sure?"

Chief Brighton raised an eyebrow. "Bugs?"

A valid point. Insects of every sort, some they'd never seen in England before, had somehow gotten loose on the floor and wreaked havoc. They'd managed to kill or sweep out a lot of them but they'd likely be coming face to face with praying mantises and hairy spiders the size of his hand for weeks to come.

"So what? There's nothing that can be done?"

"What do you want me to do?"

"Arrest them, of course!"

"For what?"

"Vandalizing my property!"

"Your own people did that in their panic to get away from these infernal pests. And you have no proof the Crimsons released the bugs, or caused any of this damage. I can't go against the law, no I can't. I got to follow the law, plain and simple."

"You do as I say," Morgan threatened darkly. "Or I'll bite the hand that feeds you. And I say arrest them."

Chief Brighton blinked, trying to make sense of the expression—no one ever appreciated a good expression these days. "Been trying for years, to be honest," Brighton said with a sigh. "If you have any leads, send them our way." With that, the old ruin left, leaving Morgan to fight the army of insects alone. Sometimes, he wished money *could* solve all his problems.

Chapter 1

𝕿𝖍𝖊 𝕿𝖎𝖒𝖊𝖘

THE CRIMSON RUN: ARTICLE 64
THE CIRCUS HEIST SPECTACULAR

THE NOTORIOUS CRIMSON DUO STRIKES AGAIN!

"The Circus Heist Spectacular," Lady Isabelle Viece read aloud in her best mock theatrical voice, spreading a hand out to the side in a grand gesture. That was the headline of this week's episode of the Crimson Run column. Needlessly melodramatic, if you asked her. As heir to the Viece family fortune, it was not particularly seemly for her to be reading such mindless entertainment, but . . . well frankly she didn't care. She had work to do.

On the illustrious opening day of The Great Cedric McFlavin's Circus Extravaganza: Featuring Molly the Dancing Bear, The Beardless Man and the Flavin Trio's High-Flying, Death-Defying Exploding Nitroglycerin Grapefruit Act, Sponsored in Large Part by Garnet Industries, the citizens of

13

Liverpool gathered in earnest before the ticket podium. "Step right up ladies and gentlemen," the ticket seller cried, "And behold such wonderful curiosities, such fantastical creatures, such amazing feats of impossibilities, that you'll never again believe your eyes!"

As families, wealthy and common alike, gathered before the main entrance, unable to contain their enthusiasm as they gazed at the magnificent tents of all garish colors laid before them, a lone sinister figure crept in amongst the oblivious crowd. The master of masquerading, the inventor of insanity, the king of cons, this dark delinquent was none other than the notorious Jasper Crimson himself. God save us all! And the Queen too!

Isabelle smirked, holding *The Times* newspaper steady against the trundling coach. The inventor of insanity? Honestly, The Crow, the author who penned the Crimson Run column for *The Times*, was quickly depleting his warehouse of clever alliterations describing the notorious thieves.

Jasper Crimson sneered at the ticket seller. "He takes such advantage of the common folk," Jasper opined. "They'll pay a shiny penny to enter this emporium of curiosities, and what will they see? All manner of ill-conceived falsehoods, designed to trick them into handing over their hard-earned wages? Well he will surely not prevail. For I, Jasper Crimson, shall have the last laugh."

Though Isabelle hoped to have the pleasure of being so close to the unorthodox thieves some day to slap cuffs on them herself, in her years of tracking the Crimsons, she never once heard them speak. If she *had*, she reserved the highest level of doubt they would say anything akin to this drivel.

> *A keen mare hauling a wagon behind her stood just beside the charming thief. He unhooked her from the wagon and gave her a solid slap, sending her racing right into the crowd waiting to enter the circus. The mare's zeal startled the crowd out of her way. She pranced right to the archway entrance, and promptly kicked its wooden supports. A loud crack echoed through the chill morning air, and the fine archway collapsed. Such was the chaos that ensued, it was a matter of tea and cakes for Jasper Crimson to sneak past the ticket seller and into the circus proper, not a single penny leaving his pocketbook. With a skip of delight, Jasper made his way through the Market of Exotic Vendors, past Monster Mayhem Square, and into the main pavilion, where his pernicious plan proceeded perniciously.*

Isabelle rolled her eyes. Though she'd already read the story a half dozen times since the event took place the day before, she still hoped to find a new crucial detail hidden within its ridiculous, overdramatized prose.

> *The pavilion revealed a magisterial Moorish camp of exotic things, strange people, and unimaginable creatures. The handsome Jasper Crimson smoothly swam through the crowd of amazed onlookers, taking a look himself at what occupied their undying attentions so. THE CLOWN HOUND OF THE NETHERWORLD, read one sign beneath a*

cage containing the most demonic abomination you've ever seen. THE DEAD RAT THAT LIVES, read another sign, containing the shocking, decaying carcass of a rat brought back to life with the new clockwork technologies. The Clockwork Doctor, who gave life anew to the rat, boasted many more creatures could come back to the world of the living by virtue of his prodigious talents with gears, steam and clockwork.

So many curiosities! A multitude of cages holding such horrifying creatures as to inspire fear and excitement alike.

"Ah ha!" declared Jasper. "I shall free these poor beasts and let them run amuck within this degenerate crowd, so easily seduced by such an evil business. In the chaos that will surely pervade henceforth, I shall seize my prizes and be gone from this dreadful place."

At Jasper's behest, thus chaos in abundance erupted within the pavilion. The abominations, once seemingly docile and subdued within their cages, now bared their teeth and gnashed at the crowd. Throats were ripped, entrails were spilt, and a river of blood gushed through the pavilion, washing the people's feet in red. Women screamed and children wailed, while their brave men tried to rush them to safety.

Isabelle cringed. There was just so much wrong with that paragraph, she didn't know where to begin.

Jasper Crimson laughed with mischievous glee, picking pockets as the frightened people ran for their lives. He burst out of the pavilion into a scene of chaos, he alone standing confident, dashing in the soft glow of the gas lamps. To his side he glimpsed his buxom sister, a lovely English jewel who dared show off her luscious form at a place as humble as a circus. She arrived at her brother's side covered from head to toe in the most lavish jewelry, having taken her cut of the spoils created by her brother's mischief.

Buxom? Isabelle had never gotten very close to the siblings, but even from distant, brief glimpses, the Crimson sister was clearly a tiny little twig of a girl.

"Ah, my dear sister," exclaimed Jasper. "Have you discovered the information I requested of you?"

"Yes, I have brother," Scarlet replied. "The despicable man you seek sits wallowing in self-pity in his painted wagon."

"Then let us be after him."

Jasper and Scarlet dashed to the ringmaster's wagon, easily scaled up to the top, and descended inside through the skylight. The ringmaster recoiled at the sight of the dangerous Crimson siblings. Jasper approached the cowardly man. "You've been naughty, I dare say," he chided. The ringmaster could do nothing, could not speak, had nowhere to go.

"I cannot abide the likes of you," Jasper Crimson declared as he put a knife to the man's throat. "Cease this deplorable theft and let the people decide where they will spend their coin.

How they will spend their coin. Lay aside your wicked ways of big business. This shall be your one and only warning. For the next time my knife touches your neck, it will spill blood."

Isabelle chuckled lightly. Hardly The Crow's best Crimson article. Apparently he'd abandoned subtlety about his ulterior political motives. Still, she would always give him a nod of respect for sheer entertainment.

"Time is against us, brother." Scarlet had been keeping watch and just then, the constabulary arrived to arrest the Crimsons. Alas, such a feat is not so easy. And so the chase began. The Crimsons left in a hurry, leaping over the back fence, and quickly scaled the city buildings beyond. Over the rooftops they went, pursued by the constables, leaping from one rooftop to the next, flying.

But lo! Scarlet tripped and fell into an alley, unbeknownst to Jasper, who continued his rooftop run. Will Scarlet be caught by the constables? Will Jasper ever notice she'd fallen behind and return to her rescue? Will—

The luxurious coach bearing Isabelle to the crime scene lurched abruptly. She hastily gripped the window casement beside her with a gloved hand. They must've entered the District of Poorly Maintained Roads . . . or they had arrived.

"We've arrived, Lady Viece," called her coachman as he pulled the coach to a stop.

Finally, Isabelle thought, a smile creeping onto her lips despite her efforts to contain it. She'd been bounced around enough to have strands of her curly black tresses fall out of her pristine braided updo.

The coachman opened the door and offered Isabelle a calloused hand. Delicately tucking the papers into her leather satchel, Isabelle accepted the coachman's offer and stepped out. Her laced, knee-high boots squished in the mud. Her mother would have a fit over that, but Isabelle practically danced in it as her eyes devoured the wonder of the circus before her.

At the circus entrance, Constable Chief Brighton led a small squad toward her. Hiking up her bulky brown skirts, Isabelle trudged through the mud as gracefully as a lady trudging through mud in thick white petticoats could be expected.

"Chief Brighton," she exclaimed with a smile, nodding graciously.

"Lady Viece," replied Chief Brighton with an even more respectful bow of his head. "Sorry for dragging you all the way out here, I am."

"Nonsense. I dare say I'm glad you did. Your telegram spoke of another Crimson run?" Gracious, she was giddy as a schoolgirl. She barely kept her hope that it was indeed a Crimson run out of her voice. She took a subtle breath to contain herself. Marginally better.

"Yeah. S'got their signature all over it, just like the bugs fiasco a couple weeks ago. Looks just like something they'd do." He gestured at the aftermath of a hurricane. Circus rubbish littered the misty streets, everything from smashed, stomach-churning greasy foods, to lost articles of clothing, carelessly discarded in the mayhem. The archway that clearly labeled the circus entrance surely did not begin this day lying on the ground and cleaved in two. The entire scene proclaimed chaos, mayhem, and mischief.

Isabelle grinned.

Chief Brighton yawned. "No doubt about it. Clearly a Crimson run. Big expensive mess and nothing of value stolen."

"Nothing of value *apparently* stolen." Chief Brighton was aware of Isabelle's theory regarding these Crimson runs, though she hadn't managed to convince him of it. Isabelle insisted he inform her of every Crimson run he investigated. Eventually, the Crimsons would turn sloppy, opening the door for Isabelle to prove her theory, and thus irrefutably connect the Crimsons to a series of thefts, slandering, and suspicious deaths. She'd been investigating for a couple years now. Theories were abundant. Hard evidence elusive.

Despite Chief Brighton's skepticism, he supported Isabelle fully. And not just because she paid his salary. Why a former military man had such faith in her was something she didn't quite understand, but appreciated nonetheless. Anyone else wouldn't have dared indulge a high born lady's unseemly hobby.

The two strolled toward the circus entrance, where disheveled workers cleaned up the mess. Several men lifted the broken archway even as Isabelle approached.

"Stop!" she shrieked, hiking up her skirts and bolting over. "You're soiling the evidence! Leave everything untouched. Spread the word throughout the circus grounds that *nothing* is to be moved, touched, or otherwise disturbed. Pray you haven't already contaminated the evidence beyond pragmatic use."

The workers shared confused looks, but obliged without comment.

"Thank you." Isabelle softened her tone—these men were simply doing their jobs—but quickly moved on as she noticed the archway was broken from the bottom, and lay facing the street, *not* the circus.

"We found two dead here next to that arch," Chief Brighton said.

"Cause of death?"

"Trampled. Saw the bodies myself, poor souls."

"Do you remember which direction they were facing?"

Chief Brighton considered for a moment. "That way." He pointed away from the circus. "And both flat on their stomachs."

"Trampled as they tried to leave then." Isabelle bent down gracefully next to the archway, removing her lace glove and running her fingers over the wood.

. . . Such was the chaos that ensued, that it was a matter of tea and cakes for Jasper Crimson to sneak past the ticket seller and into the circus proper, not a single penny leaving his pocketbook . . . .

"This archway collapsed from the bottom. As though forcefully pushed down. Not hit with a sudden jarring force such as a horse's hoof. Was the mare ever restrained?"

"The mare would be long gone by now and nowhere in sight, that's for certain sure, Lady Viece," said Chief Brighton.

"Hmm. Or there was never a mare involved. I see no hoof prints. This archway toppled as citizens tried to escape the chaos ensuing from *inside* the circus. The two dead were trampled during the same mad dash for the exit. Besides, if such a raucous occurred so early in the day, wouldn't someone have reported hindrances to the circus's accessibility?"

"So . . . how did the Crimsons get inside then?

Isabelle stood up and dusted her knees. "They likely paid."

"What?" Brighton exclaimed with a barked laugh.

"It's not uncommon for them, from what I've been able to surmise. The Crimson Run column is decidedly inflated, obviously. But I've often found the ridiculous explanations provided for their heists are precisely that. Ridiculous. The simplest, and most obvious explanation is usually the correct one. Either they paid, or they climbed over the back wall."

She paused, then muttered to herself, "people honestly believe the nonsense printed in the Crimson Run column." The usually respectable and informative national newspaper, *The Times*, upheld a largely progressive viewpoint, promoting anything the publishers deemed "forward and in favor of socio-economic revolution". At times, it even subtley lauded acts of apparent criminality, provided said act unabashedly declared anti-government sentiment.

Hence why the Crimson articles were so popular.

Of course, it was also quite thoroughly entertaining, which likely had far more influence on its popularity.

A spring crept into Isabelle's step as Brighton led her past the archway and into the—what had the article called it? The Market of Exotic Vendors?—where carts lined the street, their owners trying to salvage all the inconceivable rubbish they had intended to sell to the masses. Only the cart owners furthest from the entrance had suffered any damage. They collected their wares and forlornly fixed their wagons. Collateral damage. Not deliberately caused by the Crimsons, but rather a byproduct of their mischief.

Monster Mayhem Square was another matter entirely. The large multi-colored cage wagons had not been touched. The strange beasts hunkered inside the cages appeared bored.

Moving past the square, Isabelle and Chief Brighton passed several constables, and a few haggard circus workers to reach the main pavilion—a gigantic red- and black-striped tent with a towering pole jutting out from the middle and reaching for the sky.

Chief Brighton held the entrance flap open for Isabelle. She ducked in . . . and was immediately assaulted by a bombardment of scents, sounds, and lights. The stuffy air stank of body odor, feces, and feet. But that wasn't enough. No. Then they thought making cheese pies was a splendid idea. No one had keeled over dead yet, and they just couldn't have that, so why not add a line of Mediterranean lamps overhead and have them burn rancid oil?

"I wish I could say you'll get used to it Lady Viece, but I ain't going to lie to you."

"To think it was filled with even more people than this," she remarked as she pulled out her kerchief and held it up to her nose and mouth.

In addition to the stench, the entire pavilion was a complete disaster. Row upon row of attractions packed the pavilion, which had the look and feel of a gypsy encampment. Circus workers and volunteers did their best to corral various animals back into cages that each had some sort of booth to display them in. Isabelle passed a cage to her left and peeked in. THE CLOWN HOUND OF THE NETHERWORLD, the sign above its cage said. It was a dog. Someone had dressed the poor mutt up as a clown and put a red nose on it.

With a frown, she moved on and glanced into yet another cage. *THE PLATYPUS FROM THE AMERICAS,* said the sign hanging above the cage. *This frightening creature is the result of the sadistic Americans' scientific experiments to breed a duck with an otter, a wasp, and a chicken.* Isabelle looked at the creature. It was an otter. Someone put a bill on its face. The droll look she gave Chief Brighton earned her a chuckle.

"Careful miss," said its handler in a distinct Scottish accent as he approached her and the chief, a broom crooked beneath his arm. "He'll sting you if you get too close."

Sting? And what of the chicken part? Someone had placed three eggs in the corner of its cage. She shook her head again. "You can't be serious? People actually paid money for this?"

"Lots miss. We made triple profits today."

Isabelle glanced sidelong at Chief Brighton, who merely smiled and shrugged. Shaking her head, Isabelle reached into her satchel and pulled out her leather-bound journal, scribbled a few notes, and moved on to note any helpful oddities.

The next exhibit was labeled THE BEARDLESS MAN. Chief Brighton bellowed a full laugh at that one. A smirk was about all Isabelle spared for the silly exhibit. Her eyes took in the entire platform. She circled it, went around the back between the dais and the tent wall and noticed some loose dirt right where the thick tent fabric hit the ground. "Chief Brighton," she called. "The column reported the pavilion collapsed in the chaos."

"Yes, Lady Viece," Brighton said as he came up beside her. "Many of the stakes holding the tent in place were missing after the animals got loose."

"Missing. No doubt stolen."

"Stolen? Why would anyone . . . ." He trailed off with a grimace. It was common knowledge the Crimsons stole anything and everything. Even items of no apparent value. Isabelle postulated that all this chaos, and their tendency to steal worthless objects, created a reputation for them that hid a more sinister motive. Thieves usually had a penchant for a particular type of item. Therefore, by varying what they stole, the Crimsons could:

One, make it supremely difficult to anticipate where they would hit next.

Two, hide their true target within the assumption they didn't have one.

And three, keep themselves mysterious and interesting to the public, which obliged them to revel in their own fame. All master criminals had an element of publicity written into their plans.

So the question becomes clear, Isabelle thought. *What are the Crimsons hiding with this run?*

Pulling out a brush from her satchel, Isabelle knelt down and examined the loose dirt.

"All right, girl," Isabelle said to herself. "What do you see?"

These were definitely new stakes holding the pavilion down from here. So the Crimsons must've stood on this very spot at some point. This was not a walkway, meaning the single set of vague footprints were of note. Fine gentleman's shoes by the looks of it, and a completely intact imprint, signifying a hard step. Isabelle frowned. The siblings rarely left footprints at all, preferring to climb their way around the city. Isabelle followed the footprints backward, on hands and knees, to the side of the dais.

"Do you see something, Lady Viece?"

"Someone crouched here. A heavy fellow, if I'm not mistaken."

"Hiding from the evil Clown Hound of the Netherworld?"

Isabelle smiled. "I can't imagine a fate worse than being mauled by the Clown Hound of the Netherworld. But, honestly, I think this man was likely wealthy. These prints are from the sole of a fine loafer. I was unaware of any wealthy soul in all of England who would dare be caught in this rubbish yard."

"Except you?"

"Acquitted. No one was ever able to prove my presence."

Brighton laughed again. "What does it matter?"

"The stakes just behind me were among those the Crimsons seem to have stolen. So the Crimsons were here. At this exact spot. Along with an unknown corpulent man of wealth. At the same time perhaps? And what is this?" Isabelle reached beneath the dais at a shadow that caught her attention and pulled out . . . "A briefcase?" Isabelle's eyes glittered.

Finally a decent piece of evidence. What was in this case? Why was it hiding beneath the dais? Who was the wealthy man, and why did he put his briefcase here? Was he leaving it for the Crimsons? Were the Crimsons leaving it for him?

"Lady Viece?"

Isabelle blinked, coming back to the moment. "Too many questions. I need this opened. Your pistol."

"I . . . what?"

"Your pistol. If you please." Isabelle carried one in her satchel, but Brighton was unaware she had it. Best to keep it that way.

Brighton blinked, then merely chuckled and shook his head as he unholstered his pistol.

"Stand back, Lady Viece."

Isabelle obliged as Brighton took aim, cocked the pistol and—

"Wait," she exclaimed.

Brighton turned around and eyed her curiously.

Crouching down in front of the briefcase, Isabelle held the lock up for Brighton to see what caught her attention. The lock was already open.

Brighton frowned. "Looks like they were interrupted before they could finish their business."

Isabelle nodded, frowning. She pulled off the lock and delicately opened the briefcase. Inside were stacks of paper, each showing signs of use, from pristine to tea-stained and crumpled.

"Rather kind of the Crimsons to steal all the shiny stuff, but leave the important evidence behind."

Isabelle grinned at Chief Brighton, who graced her with a knowing look. This could be the find that turned the tides in her investigation. She picked up a crumpled sheet of paper. A list? She handed it to Chief Brighton, then picked up the next one. Another list. List upon list upon list, and finally a set of strange blueprints at the bottom.

"A briefcase filled with lists," Isabelle said to herself. "Each list contains seemingly random objects with no connection to each other, but they lay out much like ingredients."

Brighton nodded. "A few of these could be instructions."

"And then there's this blueprint for some sort of mechanized contraption. Our affluent gentleman is building something."

"Something advanced, by the looks of it. Any idea of who the git might be?"

Isabelle smiled triumphantly. Finally, after two years of digging into this conspiracy, she had an iron lead. "Many of these lists are counting down, which is decidedly unusual, unless you happen to know a particularly large nobleman with a sturdy step, who is not only fond of lists, but tends to count everything from top to bottom. Highest to lowest."

She got to her feet and dusted off her dress. "Chief Brighton, you have my sincere gratitude for escorting me through this crime scene. I wonder if I can repay your good services by extending you an invitation to my family's banquet this evening? There is a certain Count Upton Downey, quite the renowned businessman who I'd be most honored to introduce you to."

Brighton scowled. "Does that mean I gotta wear my fancy suit?"

"If I have to wear a corset, heels, and petticoats, you can certainly bear to wear a cravat for a few hours, my dear Chief Brighton."

Brighton laughed. "I'll inform the missus. She'll be delighted to dress me up like a bloody fool."

Isabelle smiled fondly. "Be grateful it's not my mother dressing you up like a bloody fool. She may very well wax your mustache."

Brighton graced Isabelle with his hearty, infectious laugh, and she found herself beaming at their progress today. A most invigorating breakthrough indeed.

Chapter 2

COUNT UPTON DOWNEY ARRESTED AT VIECE ESTATE, CONSTABULARY UNDER FIRE

VIECE HEIR BRINGS HEAT UPON FAMILY REPUTATION AND CONTROVERSIAL CONSTABULARY AGAIN AFTER FACILITATING PUBLIC APPREHENSION OF TEXTILE MOGUL.

"**. . .** is going to be lavender. It'll match the wedding cake, which will also have a dash of rose pink of course. Lavender and roses. Such a lovely combination." Lady Catherine (because there's always a Lady Catherine in a circle of English elite) had been going on about her wedding plans, and Isabelle was already on the cusp of death.

Probable cause: boredom.

Isabelle had only bothered listening to a fraction of the conversation. She stood in the midst of the next generation of peerage, sipping wine in the center of her family's ornate ballroom, a massive crystal chandelier sparkling above them.

Her companions were not precisely her friends, but Isabelle was obliged to be amiable anyway, as these were likely the people she'd be politically maneuvering around for the rest of her life. Being amiable for

Isabelle usually meant observing and deducing their secrets while they prattled on about nothing.

Which served as her entertainment until she could locate Count Downey.

"It's going to be a beautiful wedding, Catherine," preened Lady Sarah. "Oh, I just love weddings."

Sarah seemed quick to jump in the conversation today. Isabelle noted the diamond on her wedding ring faced down, indicating she'd been fidgeting with it. Not a typical habit of hers. *Trouble in the young marriage, it would seem,* Isabelle thought. Her husband's conspicuous absence tonight suggested that he was likely the one displeased with Sarah, as he wouldn't miss a Viece party for the world.

"I hope you are not planning to hold the wedding ball in your own estate, Catherine," said Lady Marion in her characteristic monotone. With her long limbs and longer neck, vertical pink and plumb stripes were probably not the best idea for a dress, but given its fashionable cut, it was apparently excusable. "Those new electric lights your father installed are dreadful. I simply can't tolerate them. My headaches, you see."

Leave it up to Marion to dampen everyone's mood. She looked particularly sallow this evening. The woman collected ailments, which Isabelle pitied her for, but honestly, everyone had ailments. Marion's need to remind everyone of hers every chance she had elicited more eye rolls out of Isabelle than sympathy.

Marion casually scratched at her arm for the fifth time this evening. Isabelle leaned forward as though to sip her wine to get a good look at Marion's eyes. Unusually wide and slightly dilated. She'd gotten a hold of the needle again. Such a shame.

"It will be at *my* estate actually," said Lord Hugo, Catherine's groom-to-be. He, along with the other gentlemen present, wore smart suits with satin vests decorated with pocket watch chains, cravats of varying colors, and slicked back hair that would still maintain shape after removing their top hats in the foyer. A quick scan of the evening's gentlemen did not reveal Count Downey.

"Once the renovations are complete, of course," Lady Catherine continued. "The first attempt at it was a nightmare. First, we couldn't . . . ."

Lady Catherine considered herself at the cutting edge of all things "in", but Victorian fashion was her first love. She was often the first to be seen in colors and cuts passed along from the royal family. Her entire self-worth depended on it.

The other ladies standing in the circle each wore the exact same fashion as Catherine, but different colors and patterns: hair up in intricate braided buns, extravagant dresses with tight bodices and thick skirts that just touched the floor in the front and had a longer train in the back.

Honestly, Isabelle could barely tell them apart.

Hence her irritation that Mother dressed her in the exact same thing. Mother did allow Isabelle to pick the color though, and so naturally Isabelle selected a deep, borderline scandalous shade of red. Fortunately, Mother found it fitting for the purpose of this particular party.

Isabelle glanced around the room again. *Where is he*, she thought, frowning.

"Oh that is splendid. Your father has the most beautiful estate," said Sarah.

"If you think it was beautiful before, you should see the new . . . ."

The conversation continued on its inevitable route to boring. It inevitably turned into gossip, which was inevitably where Isabelle stepped off the "I'm politely listening to this drivel" ferry in favor of boarding her much more entertaining "lost in my own thoughts" train.

"Does it really matter?" asked Jonathan, as he brazenly joined the conversation. The group turned their eyes to him, suddenly quiet. That piqued Isabelle's attention. "Who cares who Theodore wants to court? If he fancied a married woman, I could understand, but Anna is just . . . well Anna. Besides what does it matter to you?"

Jonathan was new to the peerage. While most of Father's guests had inherited their titles the traditional way, the new wave of industry sweeping England bore a small, yet formidable faction of tycoons, moguls, and industry leaders who were reluctantly allowed to join the exclusive hierarchy. Reluctantly by all except her shrewd father.

The Mayberry family acquired their wealth recently through . . . (um . . .) The Mayberry family acquired their wealth recently, and so the young man had a basis of comparison between wealth and disparity. Isabelle found his rural influence refreshing, though she pitied him for it as well.

She was rolling out her pity carpet for the masses today.

"Well I suppose we should expect nothing less from the farm boy," replied Catherine evenly. "Hasn't quite gotten used to the idea of civilization."

Jonathan reddened as the others snickered. He had grown up feeding pigs on a farm.

Catherine's fiancé joined in the fun. "From what I hear he's more comfortable sleeping with the pigs than in his own chambers." Hugo Bothers. That was actually his name. Prophetic, in Isabelle's estimation. "At least in the barn he has company. Sometimes even females!"

The louder the others laughed, the deeper red Jonathan's face turned.

Isabelle sipped her wine, eyeing the portly youth with barely masked condescension. No, it was readily apparent condescension, but for the record, she tried. "Well you would know best Lord Bothers, considering whom you will soon be sharing your chambers with." She shot a pointed glance over the rim of her glass at Catherine.

The group silenced. Almost as one, they understood the implications and Isabelle basked in their reactions. Marion was not amused, but Jonathan blurted out a laugh, and Sarah buried her face in her wine glass to cover her mirth. Catherine and Hugo's look of utter humiliation was the cherry on top.

"How dare you!" roared Hugo.

Isabelle eyed him coolly. "You mean you were not aware of the true nature of your fiancé? My, my Catherine. Shameful. You should have informed him."

Jonathan was practically on the floor and Sarah could no longer contain her mirth.

Isabelle didn't need to say more as Hugo and Catherine stewed.

"Ah yes," cooed Marion. She looked down her nose at Isabelle. "Ever crass, aren't we, Isabelle? I do tire of your childish tongue and I pray that our Lord would expedite your maturity."

"Just as soon as He answers my prayer to finally lay you to rest. It must be exhausting to have to come into society from the morgue everyday. Curious, how do you manage to keep your decaying limbs from falling off your body?"

Isabelle had officially crossed the border of Clever into the land of Mean, and knew she needed to reign it in. Her peers were fools, but stooping to such insults was equally foolish.

"Why don't you investigate and learn my secret for yourself?" Marion snapped.

"I would, except that your case is hardly worth pondering. Clearly you were murdered and now seek revenge on your murderer, since the magistrate considered it an accident." She flicked her eyes toward Hugo. "But I personally agree with the magistrate. Poor Hugo can hardly help his lethal stench."

Jonathan and Sarah renewed their laughter, with Sarah still trying and failing to control it.

Marion gave Isabelle a nasty smile. "Enjoy your misconduct while you can, Isabelle. How much longer do you think your betters, or even the common people, will continue to ignore your unseemly, crude, masculine pursuits? Go ahead. Make your witty comments and have the last laugh while you can. I need not indulge you. You'll surely hang yourself before the year is out." With that, she turned and swayed away with as much dignity as she could muster.

Isabelle shook her head. It was the needle causing Marion's sallow appearance, not her ailments, but nevertheless, Isabelle pressed her lips together, a bit of guilt touching her conscience. It was time to cease fire.

"Y–you," Catherine spluttered. "Are the most horrid, degraded, unimaginable—"

Isabelle's tongue was locked and loaded. "Cat, dog, horse . . . Careful Catherine. You're dangerously close to using all the words you know."

"How dare you—" Hugo butted in, but Isabelle didn't give him any more leeway.

"How dare I *what*? Insult a guest in someone else's home?"

Hugo, to his credit, actually hesitated at that.

Isabelle smiled mirthlessly, content that she'd made her point. "Then I hasten to apologize. Please continue regaling us with your wedding plans. If you'll excuse me, however, I shall take a turn about the ballroom to greet my father's *other* guests. Pray, enjoy the evening."

She glided away before her tongue could do any more damage. Besides, she had a job to do tonight and hopefully it wouldn't ruin her parents'—

"Lady Viece!"

Isabelle turned around to see Jonathan Mayberry approaching. Lean, with curly sandy hair, he looked quite smart in his gentleman's suit. His vest was unbuttoned though and he was missing a cufflink. "Lord Mayberry?"

"I . . . ah, that was quite an impressive display."

Isabelle cocked her head, but Mayberry's smile indicated it was a compliment. Curious, that. "I've no tolerance for untoward insults such as those Lord Bothers tosses about," she said. "That fool looks to insult only because it absolves him of occupying the butt of everyone's jokes."

Jonathan blurted a genuine laugh. "It's a wonder he continues to set himself up for it."

Isabelle smiled, glancing around the room. Still no sign of Downey. "I've come to rely on him for that particular skill. Few are as adept at it as he."

Mayberry grinned and nodded, but didn't seem to know where to go from there. Isabelle was used to that.

"Enjoy the rest of the party, Lord Mayberry," she curtsied and moved to leave.

"But . . . wait. Lady Viece."

Isabelle raised her eyebrows.

"Would you perhaps care for a dance?"

Well that was unexpected. Isabelle pursed her lips, trying to decide how to deflect his attentions. He stiffened, swallowing, uncomfortable. Men always did that when she was considering how to get rid of them. She had yet to deduce why.

"I am flattered," she replied. "But alas I have business to attend to. Enjoy your evening, Lord Mayberry." With that, she left the young man spluttering behind her and sought . . . there he was.

Count Downey was an awkward man, able to make a fine gentleman's suit look ridiculous. Large, squat, and round in every way, the man pretty much embodied the physical definition of gluttony.

Isabelle moved through the ballroom, passing the elite of society, nodding graciously to her father's guests. She shot a quick glance around the room and spotted Chief Brighton speaking with an older gentlemen who served in the military with him. She nodded to him and he began to slowly draw his companion toward Count Downey, as though they simply went for a stroll while chatting. Good man.

Isabelle's heart pounded its way out of her chest. She shoved it back in as she came upon . . . "Count Downey."

The ridiculous man looked at her and smiled. "Why Lady Viece. Ah, what . . . ahem . . . what a lovely reception your family has prepared this evening. You look quite lovely, as always."

Certainly nothing eloquent about him either. Isabelle nodded graciously. "Why thank you, Count. I am pleased the festivities are to your liking. How is business these days?"

"Quite well, quite well."

"I hear you have been considering expanding your family's industry?"

"Quite right, quite right. The textile mills are of course a fine living but in order to maneuver within this changing age, one must explore other options."

"Certainly. Though I should think exploring options closer to your specialty would be more viable. Why the interest in building machinery specific to metal fabrication?"

Count Downey hesitated. "I beg your pardon?"

"It's quite brilliant actually. I must commend your business acumen. Delving into a rival industry and upsetting the balance? But"—she leaned in conspiratorially—"I don't understand something. How ever were you able to invent something so profound in an industry you do not specialize in?"

Count Downey narrowed his eyes. "How do you know about the weapon?"

Weapon? Is that what that contraption in the blueprints was? "Well you did patent it."

"No I did not. No one is privy to that information Lady Viece. I ask you again, how did you know about the weapon?"

"Oh bother," Isabelle plastered a wince on her face. "He told me not to say anything but I didn't think he meant you too. After all, you are the one who invented it." She had no idea who *he* was, but hopefully Downey would oblige and relinquish another name for her to investigate.

"He? You mean . . . ." Downey began to sweat. "That fool. Look Lady Viece, I assure you, this is a simple business matter and warrants no concern for you."

"If I was not supposed to be privy to this information then perhaps you should exercise more discretion in the people you confide in."

"Indeed. Well Mayberry is still fairly new to this business world, so I suppose I can hardly fault him." He chuckled, trying to make light of the situation.

So Mayberry was involved too? Isabelle wondered if his son was involved, considering his recent attempt at courting her.

"Well there's no harm done. No one will hear of it from me. Did you invent it all by yourself?"

"Forgive me, Lady Viece, but I am not comfortable speaking of it just yet."

"I apologize. You will hold a presentation of your fine invention, will you not? When you're ready, of course."

He relaxed visibly. "Oh yes, of course. When it's ready."

"Can we expect an invitation in the next couple weeks then?"

"Next couple . . . no, no, no Lady Viece. It's still a work in progress. I don't expect it to be ready until some time next year."

"But Lord Mayberry explicitly said it was already finished."

"He . . . gets ahead of himself. Far too excited about the progress we've made."

"Even though the blueprints say the invention was completed last week?"

Downey froze and Isabelle matched his panicked face with an icy grin. Verbal proof the blueprints were either fake or stolen. The date in the top corner of clearly completed blueprints placed the invention at last week. It was already stamped with a patented seal from the magistrate.

"Count Upton Downey," Chief Brighton said. He'd been loitering just behind the count, nonchalantly listening in and narrowly managing to remain within the new laws of apprehending suspected criminals. In fact, Isabelle herself was playing a dangerous game, since she had no legal jurisdiction to investigate the count without a proper appointment in the constabulary. Perhaps this victory would finally be the tipping point that allowed her to investigate crimes as a detective.

"You are under arrest for theft and corruption," Brighton declared, cuffing the stunned Downey with his hands behind his back.

"What is this?" he demanded.

The other guests began to take notice of the disturbance, turning refined heads and frowning.

"This is what becomes of a man who breaks the law," Isabelle said smugly, taking a sip of her wine.

"This is preposterous. You . . . you can't arrest me. I didn't steal those blueprints." He licked his lips as constables armed with batons filed in. Two constables flanked him and grabbed either arm, hauling him forward. Downey stared fireballs at Isabelle. "How did you know of the blueprints?"

Isabelle sipped her wine.

"Take him away, lads," Chief Brighton declared, darting Isabelle a covert, triumphant look.

"How did you know of the blueprints!" Downey yelled as the constables towed him away. "Do you have any idea what you've done? You think yourself clever? You have no idea what you've gotten yourself into! You are dead! Do you hear me! You and your house! YOU'RE ALL DEAD!"

He shouted that last part from the foyer as Brighton's constables closed the massive double doors to the ballroom, leaving an entire party in stunned silence. Except for that baby crying in the background.

"Well now." Father finally broke the silence, moving to the center of the room and demanding everyone's attention. "I dare say that was decidedly . . . unexpected. I must apologize for the spectacle ladies and gentlemen. I'm sure this was all just a misunderstanding and we'll have Count Downey properly exonerated by morning."

Isabelle's jaw dropped. "Father!"

"Alas, my daughter has always enjoyed reading crime stories and often fancies herself something of a detective."

Isabelle reddened as her family's guests chuckled at the comment.

"We'll have this cleared up soon enough. But please, do not let the disturbance ruin our revelry. Eat, drink, be merry. Enjoy the rest of the evening." He tipped his wine glass to them as the excited gossip began, and moved to his daughter.

Any euphoria over making her first big breakthrough of a case she'd been working on for years faded with her father's scathing comment. She clenched her fists, controlling her ire, as he approached her.

"You've been busy this evening I see," he said evenly. He too contained his emotions for the sake of their guests, but Isabelle knew he was furious.

"You insulted me in front of everyone," she replied through gritted teeth.

"It is getting late, darling. And you look quite weary after your exertions this evening. Perhaps it would be well if you retired. Your mother and I will entertain our guests in your absence."

"I'm quite well, thank you," she said. "The night is still young."

"Isabelle," the name he only used if she was in trouble—otherwise he called her some term of endearment—"you are very weary and need your rest."

Matching that stern gaze had never been difficult for Isabelle, much to her father's chagrin. Tonight, however, there was something a little more intense about his eyes. It was the same look he'd given her when she was nine years old and came home with a swollen face and broken arm after challenging a couple of street urchins bullying a stray dog. There was no arguing with that face.

With a petulant huff, Isabelle glided out of the ballroom with as much pride as she could maintain. She glided all the way through the main entryway of her family's manor. She glided across the white marble tiles of the staircase. She glided down the carpeted hallway toward the west wing. She glided to the doors of her quarters, and slammed them shut behind her.

And then she stomped all the way to her bed, threw herself on the luxurious blankets, and most definitely did NOT sulk. She was just . . . gathering her thoughts. That's all.

Chapter 3

GARNET INDUSTRIES RAISES TOAST, QUESTIONS WITH 100TH SECURED PATENT

AS FORMIDABLE STEEL COMPANY CHEERS TO RECORD PATENTS, CELEBRATIONS REACH BOTTOM OF GLASS AS CALLS POUR IN FOR INCREASED REGULATION ON NEW PATENT SYSTEM.

Questions. That was the secret to solving problems, crimes, dilemmas . . . life itself. You had to ask questions. Unanswered questions had always itched at Isabelle worse than when she had fallen into an English ivy bush while spying on a boy she was convinced stole her music box as a child.

Hours after she had retired from the benefit ball, Isabelle had mostly recovered from her embarrassment. She wore black satin robes and sat primly on her bed, deep in thought. Her quarters were dark. The windows that dominated the west wall framed a beautiful, cloudy night sky.

The fire in the hearth provided most of the room's light, though several oil lamps scattered on her side tables added their eerie glow. In this lighting, her skin looked lightly tan, but it made no difference with her deep, silky black hair. In fact, lighting often gave it a silvery cast. Her curls—courtesy of her mother's Spanish-Moroccan heritage—hung below her shoulder blades, and framed a narrow face with high cheekbones, a wide mouth and strong, thick brows.

With a sigh, she stood up from her canopied bed, which was by far the most obtrusive furniture in the room with its heavy red drapes and thick comforter. Her father's wealth came from savvy investing. He was always vague with the details whenever Isabelle inquired, but everyone in the city respected Lord Viece for his financial competence.

A desk took up most of the space on this side of the room. The only other furniture was a chalkboard on an easel.

And then there was the wall.

Isabelle glided over to her wall. She crossed her arms and looked it over with a quizzical frown, slowly pacing the length of the wall, back and forth.

Notes, newspaper clippings, evidence bags, the wall was an organized map of information. Tables and graphs and calculations on the left near the window, notes and deductions organized on the far right, news articles specifically placed next to the numbers and notes, according to date, and finally, at the center, a piece of paper with a question mark on it, signifying who was behind her investigation.

She'd been working on this particular case for some time now. When a local, esteemed inventor had contacted her several years back, desperately asking for her aid, she had been caught off guard as to why he sought her out and not the constables.

He was dead now, unfortunately, by way of suicide. Apparently, no one believed him as he had been discredited by four prestigious officials at the patents office, raked over the coals by the press, and jeered publicly by . . . well as of yet, her best guess was that *that* group of idiots had been hired to make a fool of the poor inventor in the public's eye.

Though admittedly, Isabelle hadn't believed him either. Securing patents was a bit of a rat race these days. Everyone wanted to be responsible for the next big invention that changed the course of society.

Only after three other innovators—a doctor and a chemist among them—had suddenly been found insane, indiscreet, inconceivable, or in . . . corrigible? (sure, incorrigible), that Isabelle's suspicions aroused. She took the case and had since found everything listed on her chalkboard in numerical order:

1. *Nine inventors or innovators conspicuously discredited over the last two years*
2. *All nine had their reputations smeared in the newspapers*
3. *Four allegedly committed suicide and two met with unusual deaths*
4. *All nine on the brink of a new discovery but not yet published (discoveries still unknown)*

Those were the facts. Oh she had other little tidbits here and there, but most of it didn't correlate. They were isolated concepts that, though applicable and likely accurate, did not lead her to the common thread. The one she had labeled the Puppet Master because he or she would be working behind the scenes, orchestrating the show but likely would not be implicated if the conspiracy failed.

With a click of her tongue, Isabelle glided to her desk and picked up her leather journal, held closed with a metal lock. She opened it and sat gracefully upon her chaise, crossing her bare legs in front of her and reading her notes.

> *I have noticed a strange but clear pattern tenuously linking the Crimsons to my suspected patent scandal. The last four*

incidents involving these unfortunate innovators contained evidence that something of their most recent inventions had been stolen, despite the fact that the papers did not cover it. How can something be stolen if no one was aware of its existence in the first place?

The Crimsons have long built a reputation for stealing anything and everything, regardless of value, and though the papers have made quite the successful column telling of their entertaining heists, I have long suspected they do in fact have more nefarious motives.

Perhaps it is conceivable they began their unsavory occupation with this reputation holding a modicum of accuracy, but no criminal who can boast such talent at larceny and evasion would even consider maintaining such humble pursuits. They will, inevitably, graduate to a higher level of criminality.

I believe this has already happened. The thefts have involved the Crimsons on several occasions now, but the objects missing are not accounted for in order for anyone to notice their absence. These objects have also not appeared on the black market according to my contact, which means the Crimsons themselves may be the fence, delivering these stolen goods to the Puppet Master whom I seek.

Conclusion: The Crimsons are at the heart of this patent scandal, and could potentially lead directly to the Puppet Master. Find the Crimsons, find the Puppet Master.

Leaning her head back, and setting the journal on her lap, Isabelle sighed, lightly biting her bottom lip.

Having Count Downey in custody was her biggest breakthrough yet, and the contents of the briefcase represented the first piece of useable evidence with a clear direction.

"All right, girl," she said to herself, crossing her left arm under her breasts, and raising her right hand to her chin. "What do we know?"

She narrowed her eyes, tapping her index finger to pursed lips. "One, his fortune was built from the cotton trade, inherited by his father.

"Two, he's very nearly run it into the ground with his frivolous spending and lack of business savvy. He couldn't possibly have created the blueprints. So why did he have them? Why drop them at the circus? Or was he picking up the briefcase and the Crimsons dropped it off for him?"

She considered that for a moment, then shook her head. "No, those lists are a clear indication that it was *his* briefcase. The briefcase lock was open, implying some sort of trade had been in the works, but was interrupted. The Crimsons failed to retrieve the contents. Perhaps their clever distraction backfired on them. For once."

Standing again to look over the notes on the wall, she considered what she already knew of the rest of the case. "This is far too sophisticated to be run by anyone without considerable resources."

To that end, Count Downey was clearly a puppet. He was likely offered a piece of the pie once the Puppet Master acquired whatever he was after. He would've been fairly easy to bribe, given the disastrous state of his affairs. She still suspected the Crimsons to be fences or middlemen of some sort. The Puppet Master was never seen, orchestrating his marionettes from above the stage, hidden from the audience. The Crimsons, on the other hand, were too public.

The blueprints were already pinned up to the wall, next to the list and background of the inventors she'd found in the newspapers. A weapon. Powerful. She had long since investigated what the inventors had in common in terms of specialty but that had quickly perplexed her. Perhaps now that she had an actual invention, that piece of the puzzle would come together.

"Doctor Albers, specializing in the creation of medical equipment. Tommy Addison, said to have been experimenting with making light. Hah! That one likely was actually insane. Wade Marrow, supposedly working on a more efficient printing press. A.J. Forsight, renowned for patenting fulminate gunpowder. Joshua Shawshank, known for his percussion cap, which apparently changed the arms race significantly. But what do any of these things have in common?"

She studied the blueprints. The gun they depicted used percussion cap technology. But she had no idea what that meant—something to research tomorrow, she supposed. But other than the gun specs . . . .

"It's a weapon. So Shawshank and Forsight make sense, but not Marrow or Albers. Or Addison, or any of the others. It is a firearm, and so would need gunpowder and perhaps operates on some other kind of substances? Which could perhaps add Dr. Albers to the equation but it's a stretch. Addison doesn't fit into any of this at all, trying to *invent* light instead of something remotely useful. And then there's James T. Morthanstern. Holder of the steam engine patent. He was one who died mysteriously, presumably because discrediting someone who invented something that profound would be a trick indeed."

Isabelle yawned. She had another piece to add to the puzzle but it merely demonstrated the puzzle's daunting size, not what image it would eventually depict. She found that annoying, monochromatic piece that fits down there in that insignificant corner of the puzzle.

A knock at the door interrupted her thoughts.

"A moment," she called, while she properly did up her robe. "Come in."

She knew it would be Father—he had a distinct rap when he knocked—even before his tall, authoritative figure slid into the room, closing the door behind him.

"I suppose I should not have been surprised to see light coming from your quarters at this late hour." Isaiah Viece exuded authority in his very bearing. He wore his gentleman's suit, coat, and cravat so perfectly pristine and sharp that one would expect him to be an austere, taciturn individual. His dark hair slicked back without a wayward strand in sight, exacerbating his gaunt, distinct features. He stood with his hands behind his back, looking down his beaked nose at Isabelle.

"Forgive me Father," Isabelle said stiffly as she began her rehearsed speech. "It was not my intention to cause any embarrassment to you or our name this evening. I hope our guests continued their revelry unencumbered."

"Indeed. The party was a success, as always." Father approached her, but then glanced beyond her at her wall of notes and frowned.

Father did not often come to her quarters directly, usually preferring to summon her to his study, or take a stroll about the estate with her where they would chat amiably. She couldn't say how he'd react to her extensive notes.

Striding over to her wall, Father scanned it over, his face impassive, a direct contradiction of Isabelle's growing anxiety. But she matched his expression nonetheless. It wasn't as if Father didn't know what she spent her time doing. But seeing it up close . . . .

Finally, Father turned around. "Care to explain what happened this evening?"

No, Isabelle thought. With a deep breath, she laid out the circumstances of Count Downey's arrest. She mentioned the briefcase, and where it was found, but left out the part where she found it. In fact, she omitted any mention of her personal presence at the circus.

When Isabelle finished, a short silence rested between them. Father cracked the first smile. Which gave way to a fond chuckle, which released the palpable tension between them.

"Could you not have at least outed the Count in a more private setting? Was it really necessary to embarrass him in front of our peers?"

Isabelle smiled and Father simply shook his head. He had always been bewildered by her unseemly interest in law, and though he had never been supportive of it, Isabelle had always had the distinct impression he wished he could be.

"Well, I can't say it displeases me that it was Downey. Watching that ridiculous man splutter his way out of the ballroom was nothing short of brilliant." He paused. "As is all this," he added, gesturing to the wall.

While Isabelle couldn't help but beam at the unexpected praise, she remained on edge. Father would be chastising her any second now.

"You have quite the case before you here. These are grave crimes indeed, and if Downey was part of it somehow . . ." Father shook his head again and turned back to Isabelle.

Here it comes, she braced herself. *Come on, let's get this over with.*

"Isa," he said more seriously. "I know I cannot dissuade you from this . . . unseemly hobby of yours, but you must know you crossed a line today. Downey is very influential, despite his shortcomings. And while this display of yours today amused many of us, it will not bode well for our family."

There it was. Although not quite as harsh as she had expected, which was odd. "You assume he is not guilty of the charges I've laid against him?"

"It doesn't matter what he's guilty of. You embarrassed a powerful man today. And the assumption is you embarrassed me. In front of our peers. I know you meant no harm in your actions, but that is the problem. You are part of the Viece family. Everything you do represents our name."

"I know Father. I didn't—"

"Do you? Do you know?" There was a strange tension in Father's voice that silenced Isabelle. "Because every time we have this conversation, the very next day I read your name in the papers in connection with yet another Crimson run investigation. This has to stop, Isabelle. For the sake of our family."

Isabelle didn't respond, trying her best to cool the rising heat in her cheeks.

"Father, the Liverpool Constabulary is reliant on me to—"

"Oh I am aware. I commend your financial support of local societal organizations. This speaks well of you, of our family, and frankly it can only benefit us all in the end. But you will not directly involve yourself anymore. Read the papers as you like, and I'll even allow Chief Brighton to consult you. But you will not involve yourself personally. Am I clear? No more arrests on my estate, understood?"

"Are you certain? I had Lord Garnet next on my list of influential boars to incarcerate on charges of boorish idiocy."

Father burst into laughter. "I would pay my entire fortune to see that."

"Father, setting jest aside, you can hardly expect me to cease in the middle of such a high profile investigation. I'm so close!"

"And you've done well. Now pass it off to Chief Brighton and be done with it."

"Would you be able to simply extricate yourself from a new promising business deal without seeing it through?"

"Oh don't play that game, Isa," Father replied, amusement upon his face. "You're far too skilled at it. Have mercy on your poor father. And I have made up my mind on this matter. I will have no further arguments this evening." Father turned to leave.

"But—

"Isabelle," Father turned back to her once more, but this time, his amusement vanished, replaced with stern reprove. "That is enough. Our family's reputation is strong, but it is merely a reputation. And reputations are fragile by nature. Do you realize how many would seek to bring our family to ruin? All it takes is a single incident, a single lie, a single breath breathed against our family and—"

"Nothing would happen," Isabelle interrupted. "Our family has stood for generations against such foolish gossip. There's nothing I can do in the span of ten minutes that will undermine it."

"And the fact that you think that worries me," he said in a low, dark voice.

Isabelle let her entire list of irrefutable arguments die on her lips. Something about the way he said that implied a hidden meaning. After a moment of consideration, Isabelle decided not to push it with Father tonight. He was being very gracious with her after her actions this evening, and if there was something else weighing him down, she certainly didn't wish to grieve him further. She'd ask him about it another time.

"Forgive me, Father," she said instead. Besides, he was right. As an investigator, she had set the perfect trap. But as a Viece, she had compromised her family, a family with a lot to lose and many enemies who'd happily exploit any whisper of a weakness. Perhaps finding the balance between those two identities would be a case she could crack some day. But for now, the heat rose back up in her cheeks at her own oversight.

Isabelle took a deep breath. "And I am sorry for my actions tonight, Father. Truly."

Fortunately, Father smiled. "Might a loving father steal a hug good night?"

Smiling, she slipped over to give her father a hug, they bid each other good night, and Isabelle allowed him to leave without any further argument. She'd figure out a way to appease him without giving up her pursuit.

The clock chimed midnight.

Tomorrow, she thought with a jaw-cracking yawn. Blowing out her oil lamps and curling into her plush, canopied bed, Isabelle actually felt good about her work today, despite her embarrassment. Though she was relieved that Father's wrath had been short, his words at the party, and his resolute decree gnawed at her all night.

Chapter 4

COUNT DOWNEY COUNTS HIS BLESSINGS

AFTER SCANDALOUS APPREHENSION AT VIECE ESTATES, COUNT UPTON DOWNEY FLEES TO COUNTRYSIDE, COUNTING ON LIVERPOOL CONSTABULARY INCOMPETENCE TO COUNT HIM OUT.

Isabelle scowled as she stepped out of her fancy coach before it even stopped rolling up to the constabulary precinct. Her carriage driver cried out in alarm at her most undignified exit. Honestly, he should be used to it by now. She stomped up the cracked steps to the front of the edifice that stood in the middle of the busiest part of Liverpool.

Her dark brown skirts were fashionable despite their pragmatism, topped with a white lacy blouse, her waist cinched with an under-bust corset.

After hearing the crier shout the latest gossip that morning, Isabelle had crafted her attire to exude a ladylike authority, tying her hair back in a utilitarian ponytail rather than taking the time to do it up in a proper braid. No jewelry, no accessories, though she did have her satchel and a simple hat. She meant business today.

Barging into the precinct, Isabelle ignored the outcry from the constables in the main room. Her eyes scanned through the collection of dark blue uniforms for Chief Brighton. "Where. Is. He."

One of the constables pointed hesitantly toward the chief's office. Isabelle barged in there too. "Chief Brighton!"

Brighton (no, he doesn't have a first name) sat at his desk and eyed her from behind this week's issue of *The Times*. "Lady Viece?" he said calmly. "Are you well?"

"Do I look well?" she snapped, closing the distance between them in a heartbeat. Judging by his casual tone, he already knew why she was there. As well he should. "You let him go."

Brighton sighed. "No, I didn't. I didn't *let him go*. Being under house arrest is not the same thing."

"A most secure house arrest you placed him under indeed, seeing as how he fled to his family's estate in the back country not two hours ago!"

Brighton grimaced. "Nothing I could do about that."

"Of course not. It would've been far too inconvenient for you to put the ridiculous cow in a proper pen rather than allowing him free rein of the grassy fields in the country. Is this how we treat criminals these days? We serve them tea with honey and a side of cakes?"

"Now, now, there's no call for that. You don't gotta insult me or call me names or nothing. What did you expect me to do?"

"Your job. You had my full support and financial backing to keep Downey subdued until due process could be carried out."

"Yeah, well, it wasn't enough. Your patronage is generous, Lady Viece, but once Downey pulled the *I-have-friends-in-parliament* card, and I had no choice. I had to oblige him."

"I see. So it's not ineptness that led to this travesty, but cowardice."

Brighton looked as though he'd been slapped. "Cowar—how dare you imply I'm unfit for my position."

"Imply? I dare say that was as blunt a declaration as I could've managed. Unless you'd prefer I simply state *you are unfit for your position.*"

"I-it-You. Watch. Yourself," Brighton spluttered, a dark cast in his eyes. "Lady or not, you don't get to barge into my precinct and insult me. I did all I could do. I followed the law, and that's that."

"You," Isabelle declared, leaning forward over Brighton's desk and holding his insulted eyes with her smoldering ones, "are charged with serving the law for all citizens. Not to favor the elite. What precedent does it set for the constabulary that you would allow someone to be placed on house arrest simply by virtue of his wealth?"

Brighton rubbed his eyes. "Are you truly that naïve, Lady Viece? Look around you. Just take a bloody look. We ain't in a palace. We ain't got lots of money to spare. We're the constabulary. An experiment. Our wages are fragile as it is and our positions are unstable for damn certain. One little wrong step and we break our bloody necks. You want me to serve the law? I'll do my absolute best, but I can't be going after the likes of old Count Downey and other bureaucratic bastards. Your own high-do-to friends won't allow it and you know it. The quickest way to get myself and my men fired, imprisoned, or dead, is to start arresting lords."

"The law does not discriminate—"

"Bah! Perhaps it doesn't discriminate on paper but the truth is if you got money, you write the law. And if you write the law, then you're above it. It's just the way it is. It's the way it's always been."

"And you had your chance to change that when I delivered Downey to you on a silver platter!"

"And I did my best! But there was nothing else I could do."

"Nothing else you *could* do, or nothing else you *would* do?"

Brighton's eyes widened at the challenge and the two stared fireballs at one another until the room caught fire . . . .

. . . Once the fire brigade put out the fire before the whole building went down in flames, Brighton and Isabelle continued their staring match as though nothing happened.

AND THEN SOMETHING HAPPENED!!!

"I'VE BEEN ROBBED!"

Finally breaking away from the staring contest with Brighton, Isabelle glanced out of the window to see a man scrambling up the constabulary steps.

"I've been robbed! Where's the chief?" The frantic man was a constable, odd as that was. He wore his navy uniform unbuttoned and wrinkled, with the hems of his trousers looking like he'd run through the mud to get here. He was missing his conical hat, exposing a matted mess of sweat-soaked hair.

Brighton gave Isabelle a *we'll-continue-this-conversation-later* look and went to see what his constable was raving about. "What are you raving about, Corbin?"

"I've been robbed, sir!"

"Yes, we heard you. What happened?"

"It's my . . . well . . . . So I w–w–went home last night and my tenement was a mess. Like a rabid, you know, a rabid dog had been let loose in there. I didn't think anyth–th–thing was missing at first, but then . . ."

Isabelle listened with a frown, leaning back against Brighton's desk with her arms crossed. Out of the corner of her eye, she noticed one of Brighton's drawers was open, revealing a number of office supplies. There were several newly minted detective badges in there. Few people were privileged to have those as of yet. They were still a new concept, meant to appease the public's concern about officers not wearing uniforms and therefore not being readily identifiable as constables.

"Relax, Corbin," Brighton said with his hands out before him. "They stole your invention?"

Isabelle perked up.

"That's right."

"And what exactly was it?"

"It was . . . um . . ." Constable Corbin glanced around him, wiping his hands on his coat. "My . . . mousetrap."

Amusement rippled through the room, and Isabelle frowned at the strange reaction. There was more to the story here. But Isabelle was keener on the story unfolding before her. He had an invention stolen. With a surge of excitement, Isabelle was about to move into the room to speak to the man herself, but hesitated when Brighton spoke first.

"It was stolen?" he asked almost paternally.

"Right from my home, sir."

"Are you all right?"

"NO! I . . . well, I'm not hurt, if that's what you're asking. But—"

Brighton nodded, obviously containing his amusement. "I'm glad you're all right, Constable. Brooks. Rivers. Go and investigate. Come back with a full report."

Brooks and Rivers grumbled at the assignment.

"Did I ask for your opinions boys?" Chief Brighton snapped at the two constables. "You're officers of the law, and we've got a crime. Someone's been robbed. Go. Check. It. Out!"

Brooks and Rivers leapt to obey, following Corbin out. Isabelle found herself shaking her head at the lack of discipline. That young constable who had pointed Isabelle toward Brighton's office stood in the corner and made a quiet comment to a friend, and they both snickered at Constable Corbin behind their hands. The entire room was against the poor man. He had come here for help and they treated him like a tavern joke. Even Chief Brighton was reluctant to send anyone to investigate this crime, though he handled his men's dissent admirably.

Isabelle's eyes narrowed, but she set her jaw. It didn't matter what inside joke these men were privy to. Everyone deserved justice. If Chief Brighton wouldn't do what was necessary, then Isabelle would.

With that, Isabelle snatched one of the detective badges, stuffed it into her satchel, and followed the constables out of the precinct.

"Constable Brooks! Constable Rivers!" she called from the top of the steps. Brooks, Rivers, and Corbin all stood at the bottom and turned as one to look up at her. "I insist you take my coach. It will be much faster. Anything I can do to aid the constabulary is my pleasure."

"You can't come with us, Lady Viece," said Constable Brooks. "I don't think you're allowed."

"Oh rubbish." Isabelle waved her hand nonchalantly. "Not allowed to offer my carriage in the name of serving justice? Ridiculous. Come now. In you go." Her coachman groaned as he opened the carriage door for the constables. The three men shared uncertain looks but who were they to refuse a lady? They got in. And thank goodness for that, because Brooks was right. She had no legal jurisdiction to go on the investigation with them as no one had specifically hired her for it. Fortunately, these men didn't know that.

Constable Corbin's tenement was positively pitiful. Not just because it was barely fit to house mice let alone humans, but this cigar box, such as it was, had been ransacked. What few possessions Constable Corbin could boast were ripped, torn, tattered, desecrated, shattered, bludgeoned, and battered. It smelled like a stable and suffered the stuffy aftermath of poor ventilation. It certainly had Crimson written all over it.

Stepping over the remains of a table, Isabelle took in the scene herself, from the torn curtains to the missing planks in the wooden floors. The Crimsons had been quite thorough.

"Th–th–they broke in th–through the front door," Constable Corbin said, shuffling into his tenement. The two constables were hardly listening. In fact they looked bored. One even yawned. Fools.

"Over th–th–there is my workshop," Corbin continued. "That's where they s–stole my invention." Corbin went *over there* and tenderly picked up the sad remains of one of several contraptions. Isabelle had no idea what that strange hodgepodge of gears and brass tubes used to be. She suspected it didn't *used to be* anything.

"Well this here looks to me like a break-in," declared Rivers.

"I think you may be right," Brooks replied. "Definitely a break-in. A Crimson run, likely as not. Lots of chaos. Big mess. Random selection of goods stolen."

"You say they took your mousetrap?" asked Rivers.

"I . . . yes. My prototype mousetrap. Ah–a *better* mousetrap, mind you. It—"

"Yes, yes." Rivers waved a dismissive hand as he pulled out a notepad and began studiously writing. "So your mousetrap is missing and so are the mice?"

"The . . . mice? N–no. No I haven't used it yet, it j–j–just—"

"I see." Rivers furiously wrote some more on his pad. "And what is that?" He pointed his pencil at some strange pile of cogs and gears in the corner.

"Well I was working on making a clock that could also predict the weather. They . . . um . . . d–d–destroyed that too."

"Ah," Brooks exaggerated the sound as though that were the missing piece of the puzzle. "A clock what tells the weather. Brilliant that. Why didn't they steal that?"

"I don't know. It didn't work. Just, you know, just something I was experimenting—"

"I think I have it! Brooks you old fool, we've done it. We've solved the most important case in the history of the constabulary. Maybe even all history."

"They'll knight us for certain."

"And grant us lands and gold and what have you."

"At least a promotion."

"And a fine woman on each arm."

"Drinks on the crown?"

"Drinks all around!"

Isabelle rolled her eyes. She stood in the doorframe—the door itself had been ripped off its hinges and lay off to the side—with her arms crossed and her eyes narrowed reprovingly at the inept constables. There was no way her patronage was paying the salaries of such worthless, insincere buffoons.

Rivers showed Brooks his notes. "All we have to do now is show this to Chief Brighton and we'll have medals round our necks before the day's out."

Brooks looked at the note. The two men burst into laughter.

Peeking over their shoulders, Isabelle could make out the pathetic scribbles Rivers had drawn. It depicted a crude representation of a mousetrap trapping a human (not really; it was far more vulgar than that, but this book is rated PG).

"Well that was a bloody waste of my time." Rivers again declaring his brilliance with every passing comment. "Come on Brooks. Let's get back and get the paperwork over with. Maybe the chief'll let us go home early."

"I doubt that. Never does. Blasted man thinks we all like to work like asses just because he does."

"Of all the mindless prattle you've concocted today, Constable Brooks," Isabelle chimed in. "I dare say insulting your superior officer might've been the most foolish."

Brooks frowned. "I ain't done nothin' Lady Viece. I was just saying'—"

"Nothing remotely interesting, witty, nor wholesome. Might I suggest taxidermy as an alternate profession? That way when you grow unbearably tiresome, your customers won't keel over dead, because they already are."

Brooks stuck out his bottom lip, wilting under the insult and eventually sniveling. With a huff, Rivers put an arm around his sobbing friend and led him carefully around Isabelle. "There, there Brooks. Your father would be proud of you for joining the constabulary. Taxidermy didn't suit you anyways." He darted a hard glare at Isabelle as the two left.

Isabelle closed her eyes and grimaced. How could she possibly have known his father had been a taxidermist? But that certainly didn't excuse his uncouth behavior. Complete idiots, both of them!

Shaking her head, Isabelle forgot the buffoons for the moment and watched the morose Constable Corbin drag his feet through his tenement, oddly fidgeting with a pocket watch while he kicked at the remains of his meager possessions.

"Are you well, Constable Corbin?" Isabelle asked.

Corbin turned around. "Oh, Lady Viece. I didn't know you was still here."

"Of course I am. Your case is hardly solved, after all."

"What, you m–m–mean you actually think my invention is worth g–g–getting back? Please. Just . . . just leave me be. I should have known no one would listen to me. They never do. And why should they? Me? I'm . . . I'm nobody. Just a miserable lout what thinks he's an inventor."

"Are you quite finished wallowing in self-pity?"

Corbin looked up at her sharply, taken aback by the comment.

"Because as soon as you are, I'll begin my investigation."

"You're . . . g–going to help me?"

"Why do you think I'm here?"

"Well . . . it's just . . . I mean can you? I took this to the constables already. Don't they have jurisdiction?"

Isabelle studied him for a moment. The man wasn't much to look at. Not ugly, per se, just . . . plain. Maybe only a few years older than Isabelle herself. Sandy brown hair poking his blue eyes and making him blink incessantly, pasty white skin with lots of freckles, a tiny nose perhaps a smidge too low on his face, a mouth perhaps a tad too wide. In fact the man looked perpetually startled. Not to mention a bit scrawny. He certainly didn't seem like the type who would catch on to her ruse. This could work. But it would have to be done carefully.

Decision made, Isabelle stepped over a broken table toward Corbin. "Did all of this not seem a little staged to you?"

Corbin frowned.

"Or rather, too convenient. Brighton has been covertly investigating a series of thefts very similar to yours. The current theory is that those responsible are highly intelligent with ample resources to watch the constabulary's every move. Hence, discretion is paramount. In order for us to bring these reprobates to justice, we need the best detective in the constabulary."

"Who?"

Isabelle gave him a flat look, then pulled out the detective badge she stole. She didn't explicitly state that she was a detective, nor that she was the detective Brighton sent, narrowly obeying the laws of jurisdiction. But when she solved this case, that wouldn't matter.

Narrowing his eyes suspiciously, he glanced from the badge to Isabelle. "You're a detective?"

"Is there a problem?"

"You're . . . um . . . rich. Can't you just hire someone to do this for you?"

"That doesn't imply I'd find a competent substitute."

"But—"

"Every second we waste is another second the Crimsons have on us. If it's all the same to you, I'd very like to be on with this investigation. The question is, are you going to help?"

Corbin nodded eagerly.

"Good. Now be silent whilst I look around."

"But—"

Isabelle gave him an intense look and he clicked his teeth shut.

Ok, Isabelle, she thought. *What do you see?* A big mess, for certain. The Crimsons enjoyed destruction. But this was taking it too far. Chaos as a diversion was one thing. Destruction for the sake of destruction? Something wasn't adding up. "The Crimsons took nothing other than your mousetrap?"

"It wasn't the Crimsons."

Isabelle looked sidelong at the constable. She was about to contradict him, but something about the way he said it . . . . "Really. How so?"

"Well–I–It . . . they only use chaos and destruction to, you know, distract people. There was no one here to distract, so why destroy the place? And it's a bit . . . um . . . overdone. You know? Too much of a mess, like they went out of their way to make a m–m–mess. Makes me think whoever did this was trying to make it *look* like a Crimson run. But–but–but see over there?" He pointed out a dusty set of footprints. "I found four different sets of footprints. Boot prints, all men. The Crimsons never leave signs and I–last I checked it was a man and his sister what made up the Crimson siblings. Not four gorillas. Um . . . Lady Viece." He looked at his toes and blushed.

Isabelle blinked. She looked back over the tenement, and blinked again. The constable was right. She glanced at him with a frown as she glided over to the desk, cleaved in two. *Split in half,* she thought. *Crudely. No clear cuts and a great deal of splintered wood. It must've been done with something blunt. A mallet perhaps? And it must've required a great deal of strength.*

"I think that was done with a mallet," Corbin chimed in. "Huge thing. Would've taken a big fellow to handle that."

Isabelle's frown deepened. "Street toughs then. Hired by another to do his or her dirty work. We'll start there."

Kneeling down, she noticed the footprints Corbin had spoken of on the wood amid the dust. Large, just as he said, and likely a boot. A factory or construction worker perhaps? She pinched her lips together in masked irritation at the constable's observation, and contented herself with noticing that something was off about the dust itself. Most of the dust and debris in the apartment was dark or grayish, but everywhere there was a boot print, it was mixed with something finer and whiter. With a self-satisfied grin, she looked up at Corbin. "Do you have any vials or empty packets I might use?"

"Well I already collected some of that dust, if that's what you want."

Isabelle raised an eyebrow.

"It looked different. Whitish but only where the fellows' boot prints are. I figured that might, um, give me a clue? You know, like where to look."

"You intended to look yourself?"

"I was gonna give it to the constables but . . . ."

"I see. Well excellent," she exclaimed, trying to hide her embarrassment. Perhaps her self-gloating should've waited until she knew whether everyone in England already noticed the same thing she had. "Kindly fetch it for me please."

She spent another twenty minutes looking around but the dust was really the only clue she could find. She stood up from the corner she had been inspecting. Her brown skirts glistened with all the dirt and dust she'd collected from bending and sitting on the floor and brushing up against broken furniture, but she was much too excited to do more than haphazardly brush it off.

"This dust provides a unique opportunity I doubt your true assailants considered. With the right instruments and expertise, it may be possible to determine its origin. I have a . . . contemporary who can analyze it for us. Meet me at the corner of Uptew Boulevard and Nogoud Lane tonight at nine o'clock sharp. Don unassuming attire and bring a notebook. I'll need you to take detailed notes."

Constable Corbin just stared at her. "What? You mean . . . Brighton wants me on the case too?"

"You are the closest thing to a witness we have on this case. Your knowledge is invaluable. Those two buffoons going by the pseudonyms Brooks and Rivers,"—she spared a grimace for them—"were meant to discredit you in the same way other inventors in this case have been discredited. Then, I would remain behind, brief you on the case, and we would proceed together. As partners." That time she barely stifled a grimace. She did not want a partner on this case, and she certainly was *not* an advocate for lying, but what choice did she have? She couldn't risk Constable Corbin innocently asking Chief Brighton how the case was going, or telling him that Isabelle was investigating illegally. Besides, he *was* a valuable witness to this case—on account of being the only witness she had.

What she did not expect was skepticism. Constable Corbin narrowed his eyes. "I . . . it seems a bit . . . elaborate, don't you think? Why would the chief go through so much drama just to assign me to a secret case? Besides, I didn't, well, I didn't think he liked me much."

Blast. A solid argument. She opened her mouth to retort but fortunately, he answered his own question. "He must finally be seeing my talents. After so many years of trying to be a good constable, he's finally giving me a chance." He grinned broadly, but Isabelle stiffened. This . . . could very well backfire in her face. But she'd come too far.

"Yes, well . . . ." She cleared her throat. "You have deductive skills I take it?"

"I know I don't seem like much, 'specially to a lady like yourself. But I promise I won't fail you. I can do this. I know I can."

"All right then. Prepare for this evening."

"Wait . . . Y–you're not going to . . . you know . . . brief me?"

"All in good time. I shall see you tonight."

Chapter 5

SHOCKING ACCUSATIONS SURFACE CLAIMING VIECE FAMILY INVOLVEMENT WITH TREASONOUS PLOT

RENOWNED INVESTOR AND BELOVED PHILANTHROPIST LORD ISAIAH VIECE STUNNED AND DISAPPOINTED AT UNFOUNDED TREASON ACCUSATIONS, CLAIMING LACK OF EVIDENCE INDICATES "THIS IS A DELIBERATE POLITICAL ATTACK ON MY HOUSE, MY FAMILY, AND MY REPUTATION."

Constable Alexander Corbin dutifully scouted the streets as he approached the intersection of Uptew Boulevard and Nogoud Lane, dissecting every detail, determined to demonstrate his deductive dexterity with dogmatic diligence . . . Anyway, Alex was a bit obsessed. He slowly made his way through the streets, passing all kinds of unsavory characters. He could hear their colorful curses muttered under their breaths, or in most cases shouted quite rudely in his face. The flies buzzing around scattered rubbish added to the cacophony of sounds but Alex could isolate each and every one.

That child crying hoarsely, the woman yelling at her husband to his left, the screeching exotic birds coming from out of sight just up ahead. Likely a black market hub.

There were also the smells: salt from the sea just out of sight, body odors of every sort clashing with cheap perfumes, cheap food, animal feces, that wet dog running around somewhere.

The cool damp in the sea air clung to his skin and pasted his sandy mop of hair to his pale forehead. And the slight tremor in the ground announcing the eruption of a volcano somewhere Northern and cold. Definitely Iceland. And there was also the indigestion from his improvised meal last night and then there was that fellow with the long black coat coming up behind him and—

Alex jumped, picking up his pace, trying to make it back to where he started. Shifting his eyes from side to side, he searched for something useful. Why didn't he bring his truncheon, or a pistol? Idiot! His tail drew closer.

Men with scraggly beards wearing moth-eaten autumn coats and loose shirts over dirty trousers.

Women in their colorful, tattered skirts, and scandalous corsets, hair sloppily put up in ranging hair styles, topped with tiny hats.

That cockroach feasting on someone's fallen paper bag of half-rotted vegetables. Judging by how few vegetables littered the ground, it must've fallen a short distance, meaning a child must've dropped it. AND THAT MEANT . . . absolutely nothing useful.

He finally reached the corner where he was to meet Lady Viece, the weathered street lamp casting an eerie glow on the cobblestones. A flagpole was the only other thing on this particular corner, which was an absolutely pointless piece of information. Lady Viece was not there. Alex's pursuer was almost upon him.

"Constable Corbin?"

With a yelp, he jumped onto the flagpole, wrapping his arms around it tightly. But it was just Lady Isabelle Viece herself, brow furrowed with concern.

"Constable? Are you well?"

He hastily climbed down, and cleared his throat. "Apologies, Lady Viece. I d–d–didn't recognize you in that coat."

"That's the point. Best not to draw attention to yourself in this part of the city."

"Yes well . . . wh–why are we . . . here?"

"We're meeting my associate."

"Here?"

"Not exactly." She smiled mysteriously and began striding toward the more populated area of the port, that long, black coat trailing behind her. She wore fingerless gloves, fine laced boots, and a silver-buckled corset over her dress, and coming up just below her bosom. The dress itself, had several layers of black and silver fabric making up the bustle skirt, while a shorter layer was scrunched up in the front by two, silver buckles to about mid thigh.

Her unusually dark hair was braided to hang over her shoulder and she wore a small top hat. No jewelry, and though it was clearly fine attire, it didn't have that haughty air of wealth common of the upper class. Rather than looking salacious the way the other women in this quarter appeared, it gave off an air of authority. As though she had earned her right to be there and was well-off for it.

In fact it looked quite contrived, perhaps to convey the very message Alex had deduced from it. If that was the case, it certainly worked.

Lady Viece didn't say anything as she led Alex through the dark, misty streets of the infamous pirate port. People here generally gave Lady Viece a respectable distance, and Alex found himself somewhat self-conscious of his own attire. Trousers, a dark blue coat over a white shirt and brown vest. Suspenders to keep everything in place. Nothing remotely remarkable to remember.

He sighed, already feeling a fool. Despite Lady Viece's unassuming confidence, Alex couldn't help but feel as nervous as an untried adolescent feeding a raw steak to a starving lion with his bare hands. The chilly coastal breeze stirred up a fishy smell and a ghostly sound and OH MY GOD IT'S A MONSTER . . . no, wait. It was just a scraggly mutt.

Why Lady Viece would choose such an unsavory place to meet an associate, he couldn't quite fathom.

He swallowed hard, but held his tongue. This woman was strange.

And brilliant.

And a living legend in her own right, despite her youth.

He couldn't believe she actually let him come along. The famous Viece heir. And he had the chance to not only meet her, but work with her? If he could prove to her he was not a worthless, pretend inventor, a coward afraid of his own big toe—if you had seen his gout, you would've been afraid of it too—, perhaps that would improve his life AND OH DEAR GOD A GHOST!!!

No wait. It was just the royal colors rippling in the wind.

Get ahold of yourself Alex! he chided himself. *Courage!*

They approached a massive warehouse of some kind. Shipyard? Yes, it was definitely a shipyard.

Courage.

Alex wrung his sweaty hands as he followed Lady Viece through the back door.

Courage!

Alex nearly wet himself as she led him down a dark, damp, creepy staircase.

Of course it was going down. Into the pits of hell where a fire-breathing dragon awaited.

Courage?

Managing not to trip on his way down, Alex made it to the bottom only to find a long, narrow, underground tunnel, barely lit with torches along the way. All this beneath the shipyard . . . .

C–c–courage?

Alex almost passed out, but seeing Lady Viece stride so confidently forward, well his masculinity just wouldn't have any of that. So he forced himself to stand up straight, gritted his teeth, and followed.

"Have you . . . b–b–been here? Before?"

COURAGE YOU FOOL!

"Once or twice."

"W–what is this place?"

"It's a medieval smuggling tunnel. The Royal navy thought they'd properly sealed it off. It's an ideal route through which to smuggle merchandise in and out of the country, as well as sell goods on the black market without arousing suspicion."

"Is that who your . . . um . . . associate is? A s–smuggler?"

Lady Viece glanced at him curiously as they came upon a heavy, bolted doorway. "Not precisely." She knocked on the door. The biggest, broadest, bludgeoning, bloke Alex had ever beheld filled up the doorway. In fact, his head was hidden by the top of the door frame so that all Alex could see was his mind-numbingly muscled chest and biceps.

AAAAHHHH COURAGE!!!

Alex yelped, leaping backwards, placing a startled hand on his racing heart as he took in the implications of a man achieving such monumental muscle.

Once again, Lady Viece was hardly fazed. "Tony," she said casually, nodding familiarly to him. She assumed a street accent. "That's some God-awful julking going on in there. Who's making all that racket?"

Well that was brilliant. Start off a conversation with a man-eating man-beast by insulting the night's entertainment? The girl could be his fancy for all they knew. They'd surely never get in now. It—

The mountain stepped aside.

Lady Viece nodded curtly, gesturing for Alex to follow her in.

. . . *Ahem. Courage.*

With a deep breath, Alex followed Isabelle into a lounge of some sort. If not for the machinery taking up half the room in the back, it might've even been considered fine. There were pockets of sofas and chairs with tables hosting finely dressed people conversing amiably. The men's suits, though fine, did not match their hats, or fancy vests. It seemed haphazardly assembled. As did the women's attire, but the gowns they wore were clearly originally made from a finer cut and cloth. Their accessories were a random collection of objects, none of it matching, and all of it expensive. The result was a strange mix of high-class glamour and low-class apathy.

Fine and sloppy all at once. This was a den of thieves.

"Who might you be, darling?"

The man who had spoken approached Lady Viece with obvious interest. Ok, that's putting it lightly. The rogue openly ogled Lady Viece until she said, "I'm here for Monty."

All interest faded from the man's eyes, replaced by disappointment. "I see. He's over there." The man pointed to the far corner of the lounge, just past a stage featuring the aforementioned singer. The melody was actually quite lovely, if inappropriate. Alex decided *not* to notice what she was wearing.

"Thank you," Lady Viece replied coolly, already making her way toward . . . who did she say? Monty?

Alex hurried to catch up. "Monty?"

Rather than reply, Lady Viece nodded to a table straight ahead of them. Four gentlemen in those characteristic mismatched suits sat laughing good-naturedly. They were of various nationalities. One tan-skinned fellow looked Arab, while another even darker fellow was one of the rare Africans seen in England, though they were more common here closer to the ports. The other two were your average pasty white Englishmen. Well, one of them was. The final looked more Irish, especially with that bowler hat and green cravat. At a gesture from the African, the Irishman turned, saw Lady Viece, and froze, still half-smiling from whatever joke they had been laughing at.

Lady Viece stopped just shy of the table and crossed her arms. "Matthias Monaghan. Just the man I wanted to see."

Matthias's friends frowned, sharing confused expressions.

"Boys," the unperturbed Mathias said smoothly. "Give me and the lady some privacy, will you?" Well if the name didn't give him away as Irish, the accent certainly did.

Matthias's companions carefully withdrew, eyeing Lady Viece like they would a viper. Strange. Was it because she called Matthias by his full name? She had, after all, referred to him as Monty before.

Matthias gave no sign of the caution his companions displayed as they left the three of them in relative privacy.

"Isabelle Viece," Matthias said smoothly, leaning back in his chair. "Please, sit. Wine, as usual?"

"Yes, thank you," she replied as she gracefully sat across from Matthias.

Alex wasn't invited to sit, so he politely remained standing behind the chair between Matthias and Lady Viece.

The Irishman waved to a barmaid and ordered wine for Lady Viece. He didn't even look at the girl, even as she tried to stand just so to accentuate her figure. Matthias' eyes were locked on Lady Viece. In fact, Alex disregarded his original assessment that he wasn't uncomfortable with Lady Viece's presence. It was just a different kind of discomfort.

And Lady Viece . . . was that tension around her mouth? These two clearly did not like one another.

After an awkward silence, Lady Viece finally spoke. "How is business these days?"

"Excellent. Profits are as high as ever. A sort of . . . industry boom, you might say. And how's the view from the top of the world?"

"Distant. Boring. Unremarkable."

"And that's why you sought me out? Looking for a good time, would you say?" He smiled mischievously.

Alex's eyes widened. How dare he speak so inappropriately to a lady.

But Lady Viece actually gave him a genuine smile back. "If I wanted a good time, I wouldn't be here."

"Of course not. No proper beds in this establishment. But next door . . . ."

"Monty," Isabelle cautioned him, though she clearly wasn't upset.

Matthias smoothly backed off. "Very well. Suit yourself. Out with it then. You used my real name. I assume that was a sort of sign to tell me what you want is important? But just for good measure, you're lucky I don't really care if those fellows know my name."

"If I thought for a moment those men did not know your name, I would not have been so careless."

"And what makes you think they already knew?"

"The Englishman is actually the Scottish-born Alastair McFlapjack who made a name for himself as a skilled bounty hunter. He simply goes by Jack now but I've never heard of him working, nor sitting for that matter, with anyone he hadn't already thoroughly investigated."

Alex gaped. This was a very bad idea.

"The Arab is Ahmed Abdul Aziz," continued Lady Viece. "The son of a wealthy spice merchant, who has had more luck making his own fortune in dealing with the underground. His set of skills are particular to intelligence. Hence, it's unfathomable that he did not know more about all three of you than you know about yourselves."

Alex nearly pulled his hair out. What. Was. She. *Doing?*

"Finally, the African. Davis Miles. I didn't recognize him at first, but that laugh of his was unmistakable. Rather fond of his little trademark, isn't he? A man rivaled only by the Crimsons in the art of escape, the way he's so successful—and the only reason he will always be second to the Crimsons themselves—is because he studiously learns everything about an environment, the people, and anything else he deems important before pulling off a job. That's also why he's only ever hired for jobs rather than pulling them off himself. He's limited to escape, and therefore is reliant on the masterminds of heists to make his fortune. Why, pray tell, should I assume anything other than these men know precisely who you are?"

They were dead. Alex was sure of it. He began planning his funeral arrangements.

Matthias stared at Lady Viece. And stared. AND . . . stared.

AND THEN FINALLY . . . Matthias burst into laughter, giving Alex a heart attack. "Clever as always, Lady Viece. I always enjoy hearing your spot-on assessments of the fools who walk in here." Matthias shook his head. "You missed the part about Alastair's brother picking up work in the shipyard to get information on me. A sort of leverage, you might say. It's been fun feeding that fool all sorts of lies and then hearing Alastair try to use them against me the next day."

Huh. So this Mathias Monaghan was very well-informed himself. Alex glanced at Lady Viece, but she merely smiled.

"Of course you knew."

"Of course I knew." Mathias smiled. "But still, don't be blurting my name out like that. Even if you know exactly what you're doing. For good measure."

"As you wish. Matt Monty."

Matthias smiled at her.

She smiled back.

So Alex smiled too.

Alex looked from one to the other, shifting uncomfortably, and feeling a fool for plastering a grin to his face in a pathetic attempt to appear part of the conversation. Something about this situation was not quite . . . .

Oh. He really was a fool. It wasn't disdain he was looking at. Poor Lady Viece. Fancying a crime lord. It could never be anything more than a scandalous affair. And that was if Lady Viece dared indulge it.

When it became clear they were going to stare into each other's eyes until Mass, Alex let the smile slip off his face. When the barmaid brought over a cup of wine, Alex asked for a glass of water and was given a snarl in return.

This was, in Alex's estimation, the worst place a man could be, awkwardly standing between two would-be lovers intent on staring their eyeballs dry. He wasn't sure how much time elapsed before Matthias—or Monty, as he preferred to be called—cleared his throat. "So, what can I do for you, love?"

"Do you remember the patent scandal I came to you about last year?"

Monty nodded, narrowing his eyes.

"I have a new lead. This is Alexander Corbin, Constable of Liverpool."

Monty glanced at him.

Alex held out his hand. "It's a pleasure to—"

"You brought a constable here?"

"Relax. He's trustworthy." The glance she darted Alex's way as he awkwardly lowered his hand was clearly a challenge, but she had nothing to worry about. Every great bounty hunter had connections to the underground. Perhaps the constables would be more effective if they did too. It was a little startling that Lady Viece had such connections though, being a lady and all.

"Constable Corbin's invention was recently stolen from his tenement. We have ample reason to believe,"—she eyed Alex as she continued slowly—"that it was not the work of the Crimsons."

Monty grinned. "What did I tell you, woman? It ain't their style, I said. But you wouldn't believe me. I—"

"It was staged to look like a Crimson run."

Monty cut off with a frown. "All right. You have my attention. Someone is *staging* Crimson runs?"

"Now let's not get ahead of ourselves, Monty. First off, I still have ample reason to believe the other invention thefts were indeed Crimson runs. This particular theft represents a sudden and unexpected shift. As though more players have been added to the game. Constable Corbin's tenement was apparently ransacked by a group of men with considerable strength."

"And how does this play into your patent scandal theory? Sounds like an honest robbery to me."

Lady Viece smirked. "Only his invention was missing. Everything else remained. His invention had not yet been patented, it was still an untried prototype, and had no obvious connection to the other inventions stolen. Now, one of the signs clearly exonerated the Crimsons from this crime is that our perpetrators left evidence." Reaching into her satchel, Lady Viece pulled out the vial of dust they'd collected from Alex's tenement. She placed it carefully on the table.

Monty picked it up, his eyes still locked on Lady Viece's. He too wore fingerless gloves, though his were the worse for wear. Lady Viece's were made of delicate black lace. "Where did you find this?" he asked.

"In the boot prints of the p–p–people who robbed me," Alex offered.

Monty wriggled his mouth and nose as he studied the vial's contents. "There was nothing to—sit down, boyo." He gestured to Alex, who hastily plopped into the chair. "No need to be standing like a sort of butler or something. There was nothing in your tenement that these fellows could've stepped in? To make prints with . . . whatever this stuff is, do you think?"

"Nothing," Lady Viece replied. "That's why we came to you."

Monty smiled. "Aye. Right. Well, if that's the case, then I'll need my apparatus. I'll have to conduct a sort of . . . experiment, you might say."

Monty and Lady Viece stood up at the same time, leaving Alex to scramble to his feet as they began to leave the table. "Wait here, Constable Corbin," Lady Viece ordered.

Alex stood dumbfounded for a moment while Lady Viece walked away with the Irish crime lord. Feeling foolish for standing there with his mouth slightly agape, he hastily sat back down and did his best to look not-quite-so-out-of-place.

He failed. So what else was new?

Those had to be the silliest pair of goggles Isabelle had ever seen. She stood with her arms crossed, watching Monty study the whitish dust under a strange contraption he called a microscope. He claimed it was nothing new, but Isabelle had never seen one before. The vault of a room Monty had taken them to was little more than a box with a worktable covered in torture devices. Monty's "apparatus" was a mess of brass piping, glass tubes, gauges with needles pointing every which direction, and large metal cylinders that spewed steam out of tiny chimney-looking pipes sticking out of the top. It took up most of the room.

It looked pointlessly dramatic to Isabelle, but Monty claimed it all served a purpose. She suspected that purpose was to disguise how it actually worked, lest the invention fall into the wrong hands—Monty couldn't patent it without proper identifying paperwork, which he was averse to providing to the government. Besides, he hadn't actually invented the thing, though he'd likely be appalled to find out Isabelle knew that.

Monty had taken his coat off to handle the instruments, rolling up his sleeves, and revealing a powerful chest beneath his white shirt and dark green vest. With his short, dark hair, and imposing features, he couldn't be considered handsome, but he did have a certain tempting masculinity that held its own appeal. It never failed to make Isabelle uncomfortable. Not that she was attracted to him, of course. Certainly not that. It was just a bit . . . distracting. That was all.

Watching with practiced patience, Isabelle couldn't help but admire the man's precision. He was so still as he handled his tweezers with care, poking the dust about, and adjusting a few knobs and spokes near the gauges, making the needles change position. Isabelle dared not venture a guess as to what any of it meant. Nor did she care. She just liked watching Monty. Work that is. She liked watching him work. For purely educational purposes, of course.

Finally, Monty stepped back, pulling up the ridiculous goggles to rest on his bowler hat. "The lads that robbed your friend—Corbin was it?—were construction workers. Likely welders of a sort. They're working on an extensive project, top-of-the-line materials. Over the top, you might say."

Monty wriggled his mouth and nose, considering his discovery (which was 100% scientific, and represents exactly how actual science is scientifically done). "Check the eastern quarter, I'd say. Used to be a run-down pit of vermin, but Garnet Industries just purchased a large plot of land over there and there's been a lot of construction. Some really tall structures are going up. Your best bet, I'd say."

Isabelle smiled fondly. Say what you will about Matt Monty, he was the best chemist around. And the best smuggler. Unfortunate that he had to use his exceeding talents for crime. "Thank you, Monty. You cannot know how much this means to me."

"It's nothing at all, love. But one last thing you should know. There're traces of some kind of metal here. Fulminate, I'd say. Some gunsmiths have been using it to make stronger, more reliable bullets and barrels, but it hasn't hit the mainstream market yet. T'would break the bank, you might say. The only man I know who's managed to get enough of it that it might find its way onto some git's boot is Thomas Brass."

Isabelle raised an eyebrow. "Professor Thomas Brass? As in the Brass Company founder?"

Monty nodded. "His enterprise has been the most successful with it, so either your construction workers are working for Brass, or they paid him a visit shortly before Corbin. And whatever this powdery substance is, it must be everywhere in order for all of your miscreants to be tracking it all the way across town. Sloppy of them not to notice, and to leave so much evidence behind. They're clearly amateurs."

"Hmm. Could Brass be the one behind all this? Ever since he left Garnet Industries, he has been building himself a handsome profit from his multitude of ingenuities. Too many actually. It is quite plausible many were illegally procured."

"He's known for making medical equipment," Monty replied, frowning. "In fact, that's all he's patented, and his instruments have been used in hospitals across the country. He's sort of an obscenely altruistic git. Makes me sick."

Isabelle chuckled. "Indeed. So why steal inventions? He's been pioneering medical devices for over ten years and these thefts only began two years ago. I suppose it is a tenuous assumption for the now, but still . . . I dare say it's worth at least looking into."

Monty nodded again. "I'll keep my ears open on the docks."

"Thank you."

"Any time, love." He smiled at her, then collected the remnants of her evidence back into its vial and handed it back to her.

"Well," he cleared his throat as she stuffed the vial into her satchel. "You'd best get going. It gets more dangerous by the hour. My word on it."

"Yes . . . of course." With that, Monty escorted her back to where the normal, insufferably boring people dwelled.

Alex couldn't wait to get back to where the normal, insufferably boring people dwelled. Sitting on a stool at the far end of the bar, he was forced to endure the sight of a busty barista who bustled boisterously while bestowing beer upon the bearded buffoons babbling about brandy (hah! That's ten, a new record!).

In the time he'd been sitting there, minding his own business, he'd been knocked over, ignored, pushed, spilled on, barfed on, and even fancied by a severely inebriated woman.

His brothers would've laughed till dawn if they'd seen him there. He'd never been very good at being social, especially when drinking was involved. Beverage of the devil, if you asked him. Nothing good ever came of drinking that vile stuff.

At least from this position, he had a good vantage point of the entire room. He figured it was the safest place to be. There was so much going on in this lounge, he had a difficult time sifting through it all. The chair that lanky fellow precariously wobbled on was likely to give out at any moment. That pretty young lady had been flirting all night with the biggest fool in the room who somehow still didn't notice her advances.

That frustratingly handsome fellow with the long black coat and multitude of clinking metal objects hidden all over his person stood out among the crowd, and not only because of his unique attire. He had robbed practically everyone in the room and yet everyone in the room acted like his best friend.

And then there was that cute little doll who looked too young to be here, who had somehow managed to change accessories—hat, gloves, parasol, belt, jewelry—four times in the short time Alex had been sitting there, having snatched each piece right off some unsuspecting—

"Ready?"

Alex yelped, practically falling out of his creaky stool. But it was just Lady Viece.

"What happened to you?" she asked, eyeing the vomit and beer staining his shirt and trousers. She wrinkled her nose. "You smell of inebriation. And vomit. Are you well?"

Alex looked away in embarrassment. "I'm all right."

Lady Viece frowned, leaning closer. "Are you certain?"

Alex was a bit startled by Lady Viece's genuine concern, and for a moment he considered actually confiding in her. But no one ever really cared what happened to useless Alex, and so he looked away again. "I'd rather not talk about it."

Lady Viece eyed him for a moment, as though she intended to pry. Instead, she nodded politely, and then motioned for him to follow her. "Come. Let us be gone from this dreadful place."

Thank God! "Did you find anything out?" He asked as he hurried after her.

"Yes. I hope you didn't have plans for tomorrow. It seems we have a need to visit one Thomas Brass."

Chapter 6

BRASS ESTATES, REPUTATION UP IN FLAMES

ECCENTRIC MEDICAL EQUIPMENT INVENTOR AND MILLIONAIRE BLOWS UP OWN MANSION, DEMONSTRATING INCREASINGLY FLAMMABLE BEHAVIOR, ADDING FUEL TO RUMOR FIRE ABOUT 'RETIREMENT INTO ASYLUM'.

"Well, this is—"

"Terrible!" Constable Corbin exclaimed. "Awful! An absolute travesty, is what that is!"

"Inconvenient," Isabelle finished, through gritted teeth.

"I hope no one's hurt."

A part of Isabelle was beginning to regret bringing this squeamish coward along. How had he become a constable when he started at every bug that flew by, yelped at every imposing character he met, and wet himself when the night became too dark to see his toes?

Be that as it may, she needed him. She needed someone to legitimize what she was doing, and he was a key witness—and proof—in her case-of-a-lifetime. This was her chance.

And it was on fire.

A thick plume of smoke curled up in the air above the fine estate that belonged to the wealthy hermit and ingenious inventor, Professor

Thomas Brass. He was well known throughout England and he'd made his fortune selling medical equipment. Most of his days were spent cooped up in this estate alone, but not today.

Today, dozens of men from the district fire brigade gathered around the smoldering home, dousing it with water buckets and slowly taming the raging flames. Isabelle kept her distance for the moment, considering her next move. Even from here, the intense heat drenched her in sweat beneath her chocolate-colored, brass-buttoned bodice. At least she'd put her hair up in a bun today, topped by a tiny, fashionable top hat. A long sleeved white blouse proved to be a poor idea though. But how was she supposed to know her appointment location would be up in flames?

Curiously, the rooftop appeared to have a large hole in it off the eastern side. Had one of Professor Brass' experiments exploded?

"Looks like an explosion," Constable Corbin said. "You see the eastern wing there? No fire what started from a burning cook pot or tossed pipe would cause that. And all the windows on that side are blown out too."

Isabelle eyed him sidelong. She hadn't noticed the windows. With a prideful renewal of determination, Isabelle huffed, and stalked forward.

"Lady Viece? Where are you—w—w—wait!"

He caught up of course, but Isabelle got a childish satisfaction at seeing the awkward man scramble to keep up with her. She—

"Oh no you don't," a raspy voice said.

Isabelle glanced to the side just in time to see a broom approaching her face at a most unsettling pace. Instinctively, she ducked. The broom swept right over her head, and then came back for a second swipe. "What is the meaning of this?" she demanded as she leaned back away from the blow. Losing her footing with the awkward bend, she plopped onto her rump with a grunt.

"I won't be having no more of you damn writers slandering my good name!"

Isabelle could feel her cheeks burning with indignation. Her rump was already a bit wet with the dew glittering on the perfectly cured grass lawn.

"Writers?" Constable Corbin asked. "But–but–but we ain't writers. W–w–we're constables. D–d–detectives. Come to investigate your case."

Isabelle groaned.

"My case? The one where I'm a crazy loon? I don't think so!"

"No no no!" Corbin said quickly, before Isabelle could intervene. "The patent scandal. With all the stolen patents. You know. The ones that were . . . s–s–stolen? Maybe?" He looked at his feet. "Sorry."

Isabelle groaned again. This was quickly turning into a disaster.

"Well that's a new one. At least it makes me sound marginally intelligent. But I, to be clear, am NOT part of any scandal! Besides, the constables have already been here," the gangly old man said, leaning on his broom. "Said nothing about detectives and nothing about a scandal. They dismissed me for a quack. Said I blew my own estate up. Fools, the lot of them. Who needs you, you imitation peelers!" He shouted that last one to the air.

"You're Professor Thomas Brass, I presume?"

"That's Sir Professor Doctor Thomas E. Brass III Esquire to you! What of it?"

Isabelle blinked. "Your pardon. Clearly you've been through something dreadful, and we've no desire to exacerbate matters further. We would merely like to pose a few questions, if you don't mind."

"And I'm just supposed to believe you? Who ever heard of a girly detective anyway? You're writers for *The Times*. Admit it!" He lifted his broom to strike once more.

That does it! Isabelle reached into her satchel and pulled out the detective's badge. Catching the broom in her left hand, just above her head as it descended upon her, she thrust the badge in the boorish old man's face.

Startled, Professor Brass stared at the badge for a moment, then narrowed his eyes. "You really are a detective?"

"I'm an impatient investigator who is increasingly considering withdrawing from this ridiculous case altogether and agreeing with *The Times's* sentiments regarding your apparent lunacy."

Brass bristled.

"Look, Dr. Brass sir, ah, Professor . . . ahem," Corbin chimed in. "We just want to ask a few questions to, ah, you know, get to the bottom of this. W–w–won't you just maybe hear us out?"

"And put that infernal stick down before you fracture your hip."

Corbin gave Isabelle a suffering look, but Isabelle ignored it. *He wasn't the one with a wet bottom because of this old prune.*

"Fine!" Throwing up his hands, Professor Brass stalked away, settling down on a simple wooden bench in his gardens. With a cleaning-device-turned-weapon threatening her dignity, Isabelle hadn't really looked at the old inventor. The bags under his eyes, the crows feet at the corners of his eyes and mouth, his lips pressed together in obvious distress, this poor man looked as though he hadn't slept in weeks.

Blushing, Isabelle took a deep breath as she approached the bench. A briefcase rested in the grass beside it, and yesterday's newspaper lay crumpled in a heap beside the professor.

"How about we begin with your estate? Do explain why it's up in flames."

"Bah!" The professor threw his arms up in the air, standing up once more and pacing back and forth. "Crazy tinker, they're calling me. Almost blew himself up, they say. Best lock him away in Bedlam before he hurts someone. Bah! I've never hurt anyone. I'm not crazy! I didn't cause this mess and I swear on my mother's grave—as soon as she kicks the bucket—that someone did this to me!"

Isabelle exchanged a perplexed look with Constable Corbin. Brass didn't seem entirely stable. "The constabulary is calling you crazy?"

"Not just the constables. Them!" He nodded toward the fire brigade, pacing back and forth and fuming. "And them too!" he pointed at the bench he'd been sitting on. Constable Corbin picked up the crumpled newspaper and looked at it with a frown.

"Says right here he's crazy."

Isabelle rolled her eyes. "That's yesterday's paper. And this happened this morning. What evidence does it present to support such an aspersion?"

"Says he hasn't been out in public for weeks. He hosts masquerades for . . . ." He frowned.

"CATS!" Brass exclaimed. "Of all the ridiculous nonsense printed in that infernal paper, they pick cat masquerades!"

"I'm certain no one actually believes this, Professor. You needn't fear for your reputation."

"Mr. Brass, sir?" A young man from the fire brigade approached tentatively. He was holding a tiny black cat. "We rescued him from the fire, sir. We know how much they mean to you, so we made extra certain he was treated well." He handed the cat to Brass, who refused to take it, fuming at the unfortunate young man. The cat dropped to the ground and scurried off. "Sorry, sir. I'm sure he'll come back. Just a bit scared after the fire and all." The young man retreated quickly.

Brass gave Isabelle a flat look. "See?"

Isabelle rolled her eyes again. "Oh for goodness sake. Professor, I am sorry to inform you that you are but one of many innovators to have come under attack in recent years. Someone is clearly attempting to discredit you. I am not here about your alleged feline festivities. I am here to inquire after a certain group of construction workers. Welders, to be precise. I believe they paid you a visit recently?"

"Do I look the type to entertain visitors?" He hesitated. "Who are you, anyway? A woman come to investigate a crime. Who ever heard of such a thing?"

"Forgive me. Where are my manners? I am Lady Isabelle Viece. This is my comrade Constable Alexander Corbin."

"You're *the* Isabelle Viece? The one chasing after the Crimsons in the Crimson articles?"

"Ah—yes that would be me," she said with a grimace.

"Jolly good. I'm a big fan of that column."

"Are you," she hissed.

"Well, it's a pleasure to meet the famous Lady Viece, but alas, as you can see, I've a bit of a quagmire to clean up. First all these outrageous stories, and then this explosion, and now I must quell this rumor already spreading about me trying to blow my profoundly intelligent self up. Well let me ask all of you imbeciles!" he shouted to the air. "If I caused the explosion, then why am I standing here perfectly whole without a scratch on me!"

He had a point. If he were conducting experiments capable of such destruction, he wouldn't have left them unattended even for a moment. If he had, it would be out of negligence, in which case he likely would've had a history of it. The most logical conclusion was that someone wanted it to *look* as though he had exploded his own estate. Likely to cover something up. If she dared venture a guess that aligned with her current theories, perhaps a theft?

Looking exceedingly drained again, Brass sank to the ground and stared at the grass in front of him as it gently blew in the breeze. He still wore his nightclothes and slippers.

The poor man was clearly at his wits end, and was the precise reason Isabelle had such a penchant for justice. No one should be able to get away with causing such pain to others.

With a sigh, Isabelle swallowed the pride she lost at the hands of this unfortunate professor, and sat down beside him, gracefully arranging her skirts and folding her hands in her lap. Justice could not be served by harboring personal grudges against the unfortunate. And it certainly could not be served with displays of sympathy and heart-felt affection. Justice was cold, candid, and absolute, and she would serve it whole to the culprits of Brass's melancholy.

"Were you in the mansion when this happened?"

"Stepped out onto the porch for some air. Otherwise I wouldn't be standing here with all my parts intact."

Isabelle simply nodded. "If this explosion was indeed deliberate, then it's possible someone attempted to use this explosion to cover their true motives."

"I knew it! Someone wants to ruin my life's work!"

"Steal it is more likely. Have you had anything stolen from you recently?"

"Not that I know of."

"Has anyone spoken of desiring something you have?"

"What kind of stupid question is that? Look Lady Viece, even if someone did steal something from me, I lost far more in the explosion, ergo there's no way of knowing. Asking me foolish questions can hardly help you. I thought maybe whoever did this knew about the fulmin—" Brass winced.

"What?"

Brass hesitated.

"Professor Brass," Isabelle huffed impatiently. "We are investigating a series of similar cases. By not answering our questions as thoroughly and accurately as possible, you are obstructing justice, which is punishable by law." Except she wasn't legally acting on behalf of the constabulary, but that wasn't important right now.

Brass eyed her sidelong. "I've been making fulminates," he began slowly. "Powders, implements, and the like for . . . an anonymous benefactor for a few years now. I don't know who he is, mind you. That's what anonymous means. Only that he pays me well for everything I make so I don't ask questions. The fulminates are state of the art, original and flawless, so I started selling to other parties as well. Putting them to other uses, like gunpowder, and selling them at a premium. Working on the patent for a real special one as we speak, as it were. That's when all this started happening." He gestured toward his smoldering home and then to the paper Corbin had tucked under his arm.

Isabelle cocked her head.

"Don't think it's a coincidence that no sooner do I start selling my wares to other parties that suddenly all this headache starts up. Know what I think? I think my original benefactor wants me out of the game, so he can patent my fulminates for himself." He nodded and crossed his arms, resolute.

Isabelle's eyes widened, and she smiled. A trail was forming that did not bode well for her quarry, but would surely launch her several steps closer to reaching the Puppet Master. She'd have to play it carefully, however, lest Brass catch on to her machinations. "Can you arrange for us to meet with this benefactor?"

Brass blinked. "Suppose I could. Why?"

"He is the main suspect in this case, especially if you have cause to believe he would steal from you."

"And try to off me."

"Then it's settled. What is the earliest time you can arrange the meeting?"

"Er . . . well, it doesn't work that way. Was supposed to meet with him tonight, though, to sell him that new fulminate I'm patenting." Brass said with a frown. "Strange location though. Some construction site at the edge of the city."

Isabelle glanced at Corbin sharply.

"What?" asked Brass.

"You are now working as a constable, Professor Brass. You are going to have that meeting tonight, and we are going to find out who this buyer is."

"But—"

"I'll go over the details of the plan with you in a moment. But first, I would like to peruse your estate."

"The one what's on fire?"

Isabelle grimaced. "As soon as the fire is put out, of course. You'll need to retrieve your fulminate for the exchange."

Hours later, after the fire brigade left, Isabelle lay on her stomach on the wooden floors of Professor Brass's workshop. It smelled strongly of char and there was that massive hole in the corner that let in the mist. But otherwise, it seemed safe enough. She carefully brushed some dust into a vial.

Brass busied himself with salvaging as much from the room as possible. He had already located the briefcase he kept the fulminate in. He did not like the plan Isabelle had laid out for him, and she could hardly blame him. Using him as bait was risky, but necessary.

"Found some metal bits splayed around the room," Corbin said as he wandered over to Isabelle. "I think that's how the fire was started.

Some kind of canister filled with a flammable substance, light up a single match and boom!"

"Hmm," Isabelle heard him, but frankly didn't care. The method of destruction was hardly as important as the motive at the moment.

"Lady Viece," Corbin said quietly. He bent down on one knee next to Isabelle, fiddling with that pocket watch of his again. "Something don't make sense."

"You mean how these construction workers could break into your tenement yesterday with traces of dust on their boots from a location they only visited this morning?"

Corbin blinked. "Well . . . yes. Yes exactly. This explosion *just* happened. So if they had traces of that metal on their boots, then that would mean they've been here *before* they robbed me."

Isabelle cocked her head. "Professor Brass?"

The eccentric inventor poked his disheveled hair (authors are required by law to describe inventor characters as eccentric and having disheveled hair) out from behind a closet door, followed by his head. He held a multitude of scorched draft tubes in his arms.

"You said nothing of yours was missing before the explosion, correct?"

"Not that I know of. And I think I would've noticed. I keep a pretty fastidious inventory."

Which was apparently a closet stuffed haphazardly with draft tubes. She locked eyes with Corbin. "So your assailants were here before they robbed you, but they didn't take anything. Perhaps they didn't find what they sought."

"So they came back a few days later? To steal the wrong fulminate?"

"Hmm. I fear we're missing a vital piece of information here. You're right. Something is amiss. Perhaps the men responsible for this event are not actually your construction workers, but rather another group that is *aware* of your construction workers? What if they visited the construction site and then came here, and that's why both your assailants and whoever stole from Professor Brass tracked in the same white dust with traces of fulminate?"

Corbin didn't look convinced. After a moment of consternation, he shook his head. "No. Look at the door. Ripped off its hinges and laying in the same place mine was. And that table. Cleaved in two. This room was not destroyed just by the explosion."

"The explosion was a cover up for the theft," Isabelle said, nodding. "And that table cleaved in two . . . a mallet perchance?"

"Looks familiar, don't it? Judging by the distance of the boot prints from the table, and the distance between the two halves, what with the force a fellow must apply to cause that split, and taking gravity into account, mathematically, it must've been destroyed by a man roughly six feet, four and three-quarter inches tall with a thick beard, and curly bodily hair all over him. Same as the fellow what bashed in my desk."

Isabelle blinked. "You can configure the math in your head?"

"Well, not exact numbers. But just eyeballing it . . . er . . . yes."

"That's incredible."

Corbin blushed. "Ain't nothing. Usually all I can do is tell you how long it'll take to walk to the bakery, judging by your shoe size, leg length, and if you stay at a steady pace all the way and don't get mugged by street urchins on Baker Street. Not generally very useful."

"Well in this case, it was extremely useful." Isabelle smiled at him as she sat back on her knees, revising her earlier opinion that she should've left him behind. "All right then. What do we know? We know the men who robbed you are, in fact, the same ones who robbed Professor Brass. We know they are construction workers, and they're connected to the construction site where Brass is to meet with his buyer tonight. We know the buyer did not want anyone else purchasing the fulminate and that he likely wants to patent it himself."

"And we know those construction fellows were not here before the explosion."

"Precisely. So how did they have fulminate on their boots?"

"They must've gotten it from somewhere else."

"Or, only one of the construction workers, our mathematically hairy brute, was part of both the theft of your mousetrap, and this explosion."

Corbin cocked his head.

"Bear with me a moment. The theft at your tenement was sloppy. Perhaps the first mistake our Puppet Master has made."

"Puppet Master?"

"The mastermind behind all this," Isabelle said, waving a dismissive hand. "They made a mistake, and now this explosion. After several years of flawless execution, a sudden burst of sloppiness could imply a shift in authority. What if there's been an internal struggle? Imagine the construction workers want more of the cut? Could they be going rogue? Trying to make it look as though the Crimsons are the ones suddenly growing sloppy?"

"To what? Prove they can do a better job?"

"Perhaps. But I digress. Either way, this meeting tonight will take us to someone who works directly for this businessman Brass has been selling to and, I venture to say, works directly for the Puppet Master."

Corbin nodded, following Isabelle's reasoning, his eyes glittering with triumph. "This could be a double-cross. You know, like the buyer thinks these construction workers work for him but really they're betraying him."

"Or working for someone else . . . such as the Crimsons. It's not uncommon for the cronies executing the more laborious aspects of a job to think themselves above the master and mutiny. Who better to lead said mutiny than the most notorious criminals in the country?" She shook her head, getting to her feet.

"We're getting ahead of ourselves. This is all speculation at this point, and I dare not traverse that territory too deeply without sufficient evidence. Much will be revealed at tonight's meeting."

"Right." Corbin's genuine smile stabbed Isabelle with guilt. Lost in the thrill of the case, it was easy to forget she was manipulating him. Squeamish coward though he may be, he was a sweet and gentle fellow. Not to mention he had already proven quite valuable.

"Well done today," she said. "Chief Brighton would be proud." Beaming, Constable Corbin took his leave and went to help Brass with his draft tubes, leaving Isabelle to swallow her guilt. *It's for the greater good*, she told herself firmly.

Chapter 7

VIECE FINANCES, STATUS FALTERS AMID HALF-BAKED TREASON ACCUSATIONS

DESPITE LACK OF EVIDENCE, TREASON ACCUSATIONS AGAINST LORD ISAIAH VIECE BOIL OVER, PUTTING VIECE HOUSE IN HOT SEAT AS HOUSE SOLICITORS SCRAMBLE TO SIMMER DOWN POT OF RUMORS.

It's for the greater good, Isabelle told herself as she laid out her plan to Constable Corbin.

It's for the greater good, she told herself as they picked up the apprehensive Professor Brass from his charred estates.

It's for the greater good, she practically yelled at herself as she sat in Brass's coach—she'd traded hers for Brass's when they picked him up to maintain the pretense.

Isabelle sat primly in her modest black dress. She endeavored to cover as much of her skin as possible, hoping to hide in the shadows during Brass's meeting. Long black gloves, a wide black hat, black lace petticoats . . . she dared say she was a fearsome sight to behold.

The situation with Brass was precarious and one should never go into any situation unprepared. Extolling the virtues of improvisation was just a euphemistic attempt to cover one's negligence. In fact, her satchel was practically bursting with everything she may need, including a pistol she'd never used.

An obnoxious snore from across the carriage snatched Isabelle's attention. Brass was out cold, threatening to drop his head onto Constable Corbin's shoulder. Constable Corbin politely leaned out of the way. He clutched a large satchel on his lap. Scooting over to sit against the door, there was no escape for Constable Corbin. The more space he gave Brass, the more space Brass consumed. Isabelle smiled despite herself.

"You can sit beside me, if you like," she offered.

"Oh I could n–n–never, Lady Viece. That would be most improper."

"As would arriving to a clandestine operation with an old man's drool soaking your coat."

Corbin blushed. "I'm alright. D–d–don't you worry about me."

Isabelle shrugged indifferently and reverted back to her thoughts. It wasn't long before Corbin began fidgeting with that pocket watch of his again. "That watch," Isabelle said. "Does it carry some sort of sentimental value?"

Constable Corbin blinked. "Er . . . well yes actually. I–I'm sorry if I'm bothering you with it. I'll put her away."

"It's not bothering me. I'm merely curious. You fidget with it so often, I can only assume it represents a deeper value to you."

"I . . . well . . . it's just kind of a reminder. You know?"

Isabelle raised her eyebrows, politely prodding him to continue.

"Well it doesn't work, you see. But it used to. First thing I ever made what actually worked. Only for about a minute but . . . I was trying to make a watch what could count time instead of tell it. But it *did* work! I swear it did. Never could get it to work again though. I guess I just keep it to, I don't know, keep me motivated."

"Motivated to do what?"

"Keep trying. Remind me that everyone's got a purpose. Even pathetic, good-for-nothing Alexander Reginald Corbin. I just gotta keep trying. My day will come, you know?"

My day will come? Isabelle stifled a snort. If she'd waited any longer for her day to come, her family would've had her saddled in a profitable marriage by now. Sometimes one had to seize their day, seize their purpose. Still, she understood his sentiments, and hardly faulted him for it. His optimism was admirable.

"Were you born into poverty?" she asked, then winced at her lack of tact. "Forgive me. That was poorly stated." *Poorly? Honestly Isabelle, are you so ill-mannered?* "What I mean to ask, is under what conditions were you brought up?" Better.

"Well my father was a tanner. Did okay for himself. And for us. We were fed. Happy. Not really wanting for much. I'm the youngest, see. Five older brothers, all big and beefy. Not very bright. So I would use my smarts to keep them pitted against one another, you know, so they'd leave me alone."

Isabelle smiled.

"They all became tanners too. I never wanted that. The very first clock I ever saw, I knew I wanted to make things. Invent some new, fantastic thing that would change the world. Then we'd see who was the little Lexi Mouse. Problem is, I'm . . . well I'm actually not very good at it."

"You want to be an inventor but you can't invent?"

"Well I have all these great ideas, see. But they never quite work, you know?"

"Like your better mousetrap."

"No! See that one actually worked. S'why I have to get it back. Th–th–that was my ticket on the train to success. That was my ticket," he repeated softly, looking away out the window, though it was too dark to see anything.

A part of Isabelle found his story silly. Why would you pursue an occupation you were inept at? But the other part of her sympathized with his plight. The world loved to tell people what they could and could not do. She was trying against all odds to prove the world wrong, so why should Constable Corbin not have his chance to do the same? And on the very eve of a breakthrough, his dream was stolen?

Leaning forward, Isabelle held his eyes. "I promise you Constable Corbin. I will see your invention returned to you. You have my word."

Constable Corbin with his earnest eyes, smiled sheepishly and nodded. "Thank you."

Isabelle nodded back, her mind set and her resolve to crack this case as firm as a rock embedded in a mountainside.

It had been dark for hours by the time they finally pulled to a stop in the undeveloped, forgotten, and otherwise neglected side of Liverpool. Just about everything in this sector of the city was under construction. Half-completed buildings, damaged roads, scaffolding on every other corner, and virtually no one in sight. Garnet Industries had purchased this plot of land intending to redevelop it into a center for manufactories. No homes, no schools, no churches, no taverns. He had been very proud the day he announced his grand Industrial Quarter idea several years back.

It was progressing nicely by the looks of it. It was pitch black outside, with the cloudy sky hindering the moon's light and only a handful of lit gas lamps in the near vicinity. It—

It was nighttime at a construction site. Why would there be gas lamps lit when no one was present? And so few? And only over *there*?

With a frown, Isabelle gestured for Constable Corbin to wake Professor Brass. Looking out the coach window, Isabelle scanned the surroundings for anything suspicious. Aside from the lit gas lamps, nothing else was out of the ordinary. The coachman opened the door a second later.

"Don't like this one bit," he grumbled.

"All will be well, coachman," Isabelle replied with what she hoped was a reassuring smile. She spared a glance for Constable Corbin. The gentle constable poked and shook the professor in much the same way one might stroke a kitten that was too tiny to hold. Rolling her eyes, Isabelle leaned forward and slapped the professor across the face. The leathery old man jolted awake, slurping up the drool that had been pooling onto Constable Corbin's shoulder. Lovely.

"We've arrived, Professor."

"Where?"

"The so-called Industrial Quarter. Now, where precisely were you to meet your contacts?"

"I don't know."

Isabelle blinked. "You don't know?"

"I was told I'd know when I arrived."

"You mean w–w–we rode all the way into a dark, empty, dangerous p–p–part of the city, where we could get offed in–in–in a—" He snapped his fingers. "Like that, and we don't even know where we're going?" Constable Corbin exclaimed.

"Relax, both of you," Isabelle said calmly. Much calmer than she felt. Gracious, her hands were sweating in their gloved confines despite the chill. "Those lamps didn't light themselves and they certainly aren't here to light the streets for the rats. Press onward."

Professor Brass loosened his dark green cravat. "Of course."

"All will be well. Trust me."

She scooted over to the left side of the coach, motioning to Constable Corbin to watch out the window to her right. As she peeked out the coach window to scan the darkness for evil, it took every ounce of self-control she had not to let her excitement burst through her mask of decorum.

Over the last few years that she'd seriously begun field investigations, she'd attempted to apprehend the Crimson siblings, personally helped put a number of thieves and murderers behind bars, investigated bank note forgeries and suspected embezzlement, and had even been in a chase, though it ended poorly. This however, was new territory. On her own, confronting a potentially massive scandal, sneaking about in a dangerous part of the city, her only backup a squeamish constable afraid of his own shadow. Not terribly wise, she granted, but exhilarating nonetheless.

But most importantly, she had her quarry on the ropes. One more solid piece of evidence, and she'd have that, the mousetrap, two witnesses, and possibly a verbal confession to secure arrests. The first intellectual property scandal in history, busted by Lady Isabelle Viece.

The coach pulled to a stop in front of a half-complete building, surrounded by scaffolding, and all manner of construction equipment laying precariously at its base. Isabelle nodded to Constable Corbin, and the two slipped out the left door of the coach without a sound. As soon as they stepped onto the street and closed the door, Professor Brass opened his door and stepped out on the right side of the coach, facing the building under construction. They couldn't hear anything more as they waited.

"Lady Viece," Constable Corbin whispered, still clutching his satchel. Isabelle's was secured with two straps: one crossing her chest, and the other wrapped around her waist like a belt. "Your p–p–pardon, but isn't this a bit . . . f–foolhardy? Shouldn't we have called for backup?"

Yes, they absolutely should have. Except that backup wouldn't have allowed her to be present in the first place. "It's an exchange. Our purpose is to find out who is behind this and determine for certain that he is, indeed, patenting stolen inventions. That means stealth and caution, both of which are beyond the capabilities of the constabulary." There was also the legal side of the matter to consider. Her only justification for being present was that Brass technically invited her along. So her presence was narrowly legal.

Ignoring Corbin's further objections, Isabelle crouched down and peeked around the side of the coach.

Spotlighted on the top of the wide steps before the building, a couple of gruff looking fellows welcomed Professor Brass inside, but Isabelle couldn't see anything more.

She motioned Corbin into action. He would keep watch at a vantage close to the building face while she tried to enter and eavesdrop. Narrowly legal indeed. Crouching, she rounded the coach, headed around to the side of the building, feeling her way along the rough stone wall in the darkness, until she came to the back of the building. From there, the frames that would eventually contain doors were no more than rectangular openings, so slipping inside was as easy as . . . well slipping inside (Isabelle is not very good with metaphors; it's definitely *not* that the author of this book isn't good at metaphors).

The first thing she noticed was the dusty smells of construction. With the darkness very nearly complete, her eyes drew right to a single source of light across the way from her, a soft glow, like an oil lamp. One step in that direction revealed acoustics that put the royal music chamber to shame. Only once it had faded completely did she dare breath. Doing her best to swallow the indignity, she reached down and slipped off her boots, stuffed them in her satchel—they sort of fit—and crept the rest of the way through the dark room in her stockings. Fortunately she didn't trip on anything as she carefully ducked behind a wall beside yet another doorframe.

". . . on his way," a raspy male voice said.

"Well tell him to hurry," said Brass. "I'm an old man. It's way past my bedtime. Your boss is being mighty inconsiderate to keep me waiting like this."

"Yeah, yeah, shut up," replied the raspy man. There was a pause in the conversation, so Isabelle risked a peek into the room. It was still far from finished, with the wooden floors missing boards, exposing concrete beneath, construction equipment lining walls that were mostly still rafters, and all manner of metal implements lying about from hammers and nails, to pliers and spikes. In fact there was just generally a lot of metal. And were those fire pits? Construction wasn't precisely Isabelle's forte but it appeared Matt Monty's assessment was correct. They were welders.

At the very center of the room was a simple wooden table circled with equally simple chairs. Professor Brass occupied one, the others were empty. Four men in dirty trousers, suspenders, and various colored linen shirts with the sleeves rolled up or torn off stood menacingly around the room. They were on edge. A rhythmic tap of one man's boot, a sharp pop of another's knuckles . . . .

A frown was about all Isabelle had time for before a tall, burly, curly-haired fellow filled the room with his presence. He dropped into the chair directly across from Professor Brass and scowled. "You," he declared with a pointed finger. "How are you not dead?"

"Sorry?"

"That explosion should've killed—"

"Oh that! Of course. Rumor spreads faster than mold these days. Well I'm fine, as you can plainly see."

"You don't say." The man gritted his teeth. He must be the one fond of cleaving tables. Tall and heavily muscled, and as Constable Corbin had somehow mathematically determined, had curly dark arm hair and some more peeking out of his shirt from the neck. These were the men Isabelle had been chasing, the ones who stole Corbin's mousetrap. The one's who tried to cover their tracks at the Brass estate with an explosion. This was it! If—

Unease clearly beheld on the expressions and body language of every man in the room.

Late to his own meeting.

You should be dead.

A sudden wave of nausea tightened up Isabelle's throat as realization crashed over her like a stormy wave upon the rocks. These men hadn't tried to cover up their theft. They had tried to cover up a murder.

"It's no matter now. I have the fulminate."

Gears clicked into place in Isabelle's head faster than she could keep up. These men already had what they wanted from Brass. This meeting wasn't supposed to take place any more. This fellow was late to his own meeting because he hadn't expected Brass to show up. He didn't know the attempted murder had failed.

"You don't have what my employer agreed to." He reached into his tattered coat and pulled out a vial of fulminate. "I do."

Brass stared at the vial calmly. "Sooooo. You are the bastards who broke into my mansion this morning and set my home afire."

Brass opened his briefcase on the table. "You stole the wrong fulminate I'm afraid. This is what our mutual friend wants. He won't be best pleased to get that vial of dirt you're holding. What was your plan? Steal the fulminate, kill me, and tell your employer I blew myself up? For what, I wonder? Rather sounds like you're attempting a double-cross."

The other men had been on edge while waiting for their leader to come because they were responsible for setting up the murder. This implied a strong system of hierarchy, significant funds to afford such an expensive murder weapon, and the intelligence to set up and execute an elaborate plan.

The lead welder, surprisingly, smiled. "Following orders, actually."

Brass seemed startled for the first time that night.

"Did you think we wouldn't find out who else you've been selling to? No one breaks a deal with our boss, mate."

"So he sent you to kill me? After everything I've made for him, he's simply going to kill me?"

More than that. If the Puppet Master himself had ordered Brass's death, then he likely was the one responsible for slandering the professor's good name. This had been brewing for some time. The Puppet Master needed Brass to complete the invention, but not quite finalize the patent. Perhaps just have the blueprints. Once his reputation had been tarnished, he could get rid of the professor cleanly, without suspected foul play. Brass would die in a seemingly accidental explosion and no one would ever guess he had been robbed first. It was all orchestrated just like the others: discredit the inventor, steal the invention, secure the patent, walk away cleanly.

The burly fellow motioned one of his buddies toward the entrance of the building. The slender welder nodded and headed for the entryway. "My employer won't be pleased about this, but as he always says, wrap it up, and lock it up, to shut it up."

Brass chuckled. "You don't want to do that, friend. I'm not here alone."

Isabelle's heart stopped. Brass hadn't spoken at all to these men with the same tone or swagger he used back at his estate. What was going on?

"Your coachman?" The welder asked wryly, reaching behind him and pulling out a wicked metal mallet.

Brass licked his lips and swallowed. "Constables as it were. Ah—detectives. They know. They're onto us. They—"

The burly fellow swung the heavy mallet right into Brass's face.

Alex jumped at the sound of a feminine yelp.

Lady Viece! He watched diligently from behind a pile of cinder blocks. A slender man exited the building and moved up to the coach. He looked up at the coachman, and pulled a pistol out of his trousers.

Panicked, Alex pulled out his own pistol, but he was too far.

The slender man fired.

The coachman fell to the ground.

Horrified, Alex remained frozen as the slender fellow casually tucked his pistol back in his trousers. He strolled back into the building.

Thoughts came slowly, trying to claw their way through the thick veil of fear that threatened to consume Alex. *Thoughts. Think. Must think. Lady Viece. She's in trouble. Professor Brass.* They might already be dead.

What to do?

What do I do?

Somehow mustering up courage he swore he didn't have, Alex dragged himself out of hiding and forced himself to move toward the building entrance. He holstered his pistol—he didn't know how many people he was up against; best not to announce he was armed—and removed his coat and hat. He untucked his shirt, pulling it over his hip holster to hide his weapons.

Swallowing the lump in his throat, he let out what he hoped was some semblance of a feminine yelp.

Isabelle pulled out of sight, but more importantly pulled her own sight away from poor Professor Brass's gruesome corpse. She threw a hand over her mouth to stifle her scream, though a yelp had already slipped through. She'd never seen anyone die before.

"Well . . . that was . . . um . . . efficient," said a nasally voice.

They were going to find her.

"Good job, Cleaver," said a different welder with a deep, crisp voice. "You're certainly living up to your name."

That mallet would be aiming for Isabelle next.

"Well I think this cleaving business is a bit much," said the nasally-voiced welder. "I got some concerns to bring up in the next staff—I mean team. Sorry mates. *Team* meeting."

Get a grip, Isabelle!

"Happy to hear your complaints, Cog," replied Cleaver. "For now, did anyone else hear that scream?"

You can do this!

"I did," replied Cog. "Someone else *is* here. Brass was telling the truth."

Calm.

"Relax, Cog. You and Strangler search the place. It sounded like it came from back there. Smithy, clean up the body."

Deep breaths.

"Can I burn him up?"

. . . Burn him?

Cleaver paused.

What sort of sick question was that?

"I don't like all this burning people's flesh off stuff neither," said Cog. "Makes me uncomfortable."

Who are these people?

"Next meeting, Cog. We'll let you speak first, all right? Smithy, you may burn the body, but do it in the back away from the rest of the crew until we've had the chance to discuss it proper."

A distant gunshot echoed in the chamber around Isabelle. *Constable Corbin! Oh no!*

Determination clawed its way through her crippling fear. She needed to get out of here. Get to Constable Corbin. Get them out of there! Oh Professor Brass . . . .

Think Isabelle, she yelled at herself. *What are your options? All right, you need a distraction. Get them searching for you in another direction, slip out the back and . . .* a feminine yelp resounded from outside the building.

"I heard it again!" declared Cleaver. "Came from there this time. Go check the streets, boys."

Isabelle listened carefully, trying to hear over the sound of her own heart thumping out of her ears. The sound of footsteps trailed away, so she risked a peek into the room. The men faced the building entrance, their backs to her.

Another feminine yelp. She hoped they wouldn't kill the poor girl. Taking advantage of the distraction, she slowly backed away.

"Sounds like some drunken broad," said Cleaver. "What time is the train tomorrow, Gauge?"

"Nine in the morn," replied Gauge, who had a fatherly way of speaking. "Mr. Boss Man ain't going to appreciate this mess. Might come back to haunt us, two dead men on our welding site."

Despite everything that just happened, Isabelle hesitated about halfway into the room, listening to the conversation.

"Don't worry about that right now. We did what we had to. Besides, we ain't the ones who gotta tell him. We're meeting the fence clowns tomorrow. They'll have to break the news to the boss, not us."

"But—"

"We got *two* inventions in *two* days. He can't ask for better work than that."

"Should we tell him what Brass said? About detectives being on to us?"

Cleaver hesitated. "Yeah. Just in case. Let him decide if Brass was lying."

Finally, Isabelle ducked out of the building and traced her steps back to the front. She froze. The welders were outside, confronting someone.

"What the bloody hell are you doing?" The short, stocky fellow, who spoke with the nasally voice had his hands on his hips, genuinely confused.

But it wasn't the welder who held Isabelle's attention. It was the fool who stood before him. Alex Corbin.

Constable Corbin swallowed, staring wide-eyed at the welder, looking around himself nervously. Then he yelped again, a high-pitched squeal that could've maybe been an approximation of Isabelle's throaty exclamation. Watching a full-grown man stand there with such terror, clearly unsure what to do, but nevertheless crying out in a girlish squeal might've been an occasion for comment under other circumstances. But Isabelle silently blessed the man for his efforts.

The welders exchanged confused glances, then rolled their eyes. "Oh for the love of God, go be an idiot somewhere else, mate." The short welder shoved Constable Corbin, then the two welders turned and stalked back into the building.

Corbin darted to snatch up his discarded coat and pistols as Isabelle reached him, grabbed him by the arm and hauled him behind the coach. She hastily pulled the door open and shoved him in. She reached out to give the horse a slap, but froze at the sight of the dead coachman on the ground. With a shiver, and a quick prayer for the poor man, Isabelle slapped the horse into motion, climbed into the moving coach, and hoped the horse would simply go straight.

After several minutes of subdued silence, Isabelle was sure no one was following them. It was such a small victory, but she would take it.

"Professor Brass?" Constable Corbin asked suddenly, wringing his hands.

Isabelle's eyes must've answered the question because Constable Corbin simply nodded. "God give him peace."

Isabelle didn't respond. Her mind whirled with mixed information. Brass had implied, right at the end, that he had deliberately brought her and Constable Corbin to the meeting in order to stop them from cracking the scandal. It was a clever last bid for his life, but something about it still nagged at Isabelle. He had been so calm, so collected. It was a far cry from the crazy old geezer back at the mansion.

Isabelle's heart was another matter entirely. She couldn't do anything about that burly murderer right now, and for the sake of the larger case, she'd just have to let him get away with his atrocity for the time being, much as it galled her.

"I . . . suppose I can . . ." Constable Corbin swallowed hard, his eyes still stunned wide open. "I should get in the front and . . . I'll steer us home, Lady Viece."

Isabelle nodded curtly.

Constable Corbin climbed out of the coach, leaving a shaken Isabelle to ponder her next move. This was proof of sabotage. Proof that the Puppet Master she hunted was indeed actively orchestrating the discrediting and/or "removal" of the inventors he stole from.

His cronies were traveling by train at nine in the morning to bring him his prizes. *Two inventions in two days.* Constable Corbin's mousetrap, and Professor Brass's fulminate. Reaching down to slip her boots back on, Isabelle opened the coach door and called to Constable Corbin. "Take us to the railway station."

"The station? I suppose that would be faster, but I can't afford a ticket."

"I shall compensate you. Consider it a gift of good faith after your rather unorthodox inebriation act."

"Uh . . . thank you. Lady Viece."

"Thank you as well. Truly." She took a deep breath. "Thank you."

Swinging back into the coach, Isabelle allowed herself a moment of unladylike posture and simply lounged on the cushioned bench. She could be ladylike tomorrow. And tomorrow, she would catch the welders. Tomorrow, poor Professor Brass and his unfortunate coachman would be avenged. Tomorrow, justice would be served.

Chapter 8

CITIZENS, ALLIES RALLY BEHIND VIECE FAMILY, DECLARING ACCUSATIONS "LOAD OF CODSWALLOP"

DESPITE ACCUSATIONS OF TREASON, LADY ISADORA VIECE'S CONNECTIONS TO SPAIN, AND WINSOME HEIR GALLIVANTING ON MISGUIDED ADVENTURES, PUBLIC SUPPORT OF BELOVED VIECE FAMILY REMAINS STRONG, WHILE HOUSE SOLICITORS FISH FOR SOURCE OF RUMORS, CONVINCED FAMILY IS "NOT OFF THE HOOK YET."

"All right," Cleaver declared from his seat at the Round Table (no, not like King Arthur). "I hereby call this meeting to order."

Sitting in various positions around the table was Cleaver's team. "Now before we begin, I have a few things to say." Cleaver pulled out a wrinkled notebook, and read his own atrocious handwriting. "Item one, I know we're all new to this criminal business, and I just have to say I think you boys are doing a fantastic job. Couldn't be prouder of you."

The men beamed, clapping each other on the shoulder.

"So far, the boss has honored all of our requests, he's treated us like the right handsome men we are." He earned a round of whoops for

110

that comment. "And he's paid us fairly. That's what we deserve lads. Don't ever settle for nothing less."

His men pounded the table and cheered.

"Now, with that said, second item." Cleaver read through item two before looking back up and addressing his men. "I know that some of you still have some concerns about this new life, and about each other, about the boss, about me. Well here at the Round Table . . . ." He gestured for the men to finish.

"Everyone is seen," his men filled in.

"Here at the Round Table . . ."

"Everyone is heard."

"Here at the Round Table . . ."

"Everyone is worthy."

Cleaver nodded, leaning forward and resting his elbows on his knees, notebook held out in front of him. He looked at each of his men in turn, acknowledging their presence. Men he'd worked with, drank with, and busted his butt with for years on various construction projects across Liverpool. His boys were the best welders. He was proud of every one of them. Yet every project brought with it another asinine boss who worked his boys into the ground, paid them a pittance, cared nothing for their safety, and frankly didn't care about a job well done either.

Well hell if Cleaver was going to put up with such injustice any longer. Without his boys, half the city wouldn't even be here. They deserved a fair wage. They deserved fair treatment. And they definitely deserved to be heard.

That's what started these Round Table discussions. He always liked the story of King Arthur's "all men are equal" statement declared with the simple shape of a table (okay maybe this is a little like King Arthur). So he decided to run his team exactly like King Arthur (okay fine; yes exactly like King Arthur).

"Good lads," he said, nodding his approval. "Now, as promised, we're gonna start with Cog today. So Cog, you have the Table. Anything you want to talk about?"

"Yeah," Cog stood up, taking off his cap and wringing it in his hands. "I um . . . has some concerns."

The other men nodded at Cog encouragingly, murmuring words of encouragement, until he was so encouraged that he could have broken into song. "So, well first, we agreed in the original plan that Brass was going to explode in his mansion. But when he showed up here alive, I just think we should've discussed it first before you whacked the old coot in the face."

"Well the job was to kill Brass, Cog," Cleaver replied gently, careful not to make Cog feel that he couldn't speak his mind. "You knew joining up with the criminal business meant we'd have to get our hands dirty. You having trouble with the whole murdering people thing still? I'm sure Gauge would be more than happy to counsel you through it again."

"Oh no it's not that. It's just . . . well maybe Strangler wanted to practice his strangling. Or maybe I . . . well I wanted to see if all my practice throwing blades is paying off."

Cleaver nodded. "I see. You think I've been overstepping a bit since I got experience? Like I'm not giving you lads the chance to hone your own criminal skills?"

The men at the Table began slowly nodding and muttering their agreement.

"Yeah, I think what Cog is trying to say is we'd appreciate it if you gave us a chance to do the heavy lifting," added Strangler. "I mean you let Smithy burn the body."

"Yeah about that," Cog jumped back in, still standing. "It's a right fearsome gimmick to be known by, make no mistake. I want to be supportive of all our calling cards, you know I do lads. But I honestly just can't get behind this whole burning people's flesh thing. I'm sorry Smithy, but it has me concerned about you. And I think it's time we talk about it."

"I've been a bit concerned myself," added Steve, the only other person among them besides Cleaver who had committed crimes prior to their current employment. "Seems an unsustainable way to murder someone. Eventually one of these pretend peelers is going to connect the burn murders to you."

"I haven't killed anyone," protested Smithy. "I just disposed of a body. And it's a perfectly clean way of doing that."

"You call that clean?" Cog asked. "Burning flesh stinks to high heaven!"

"It does make me a bit uncomfortable, Smithy," Gauge chimed in.

"Well I think we ought to leave the man alone," said Strangler. "We're all getting used to this new line of work, and we can't really fault Smithy for just being the quickest to adapt. He's doing a right good job, better than any of us, and I think you're just jealous 'cause Smithy's taken such a quick shining to the criminal world."

Cog looked offended, and Cleaver took that as his cue to settle things down. "All right, lads. I think the two opposing viewpoints here have been presented very well. I want you—"

"Excuse me," Cog butted in. "I wasn't finished."

"You've said your peace, Cog. Sit down."

"But I. Wasn't. Finished."

"You've already done all the talking, Cog," said Strangler. "Let someone else have the Table. Sit down and shut up."

"Hey now! That's a violation of the fourth statute of our organization, code 66.3985 and a half."

"We only have three statutes, idiot."

"I can't work like this, Seth," Cog exclaimed, throwing up his hands. "I mean Cleaver. Sorry, Cleaver. I am an equally contributing member of this team, and I ain't going to just accept being called names."

"And we don't expect you to, Cog. Strangler, I think we can all agree that name-calling is not acceptable behavior at the Table. Cog has every right to bring up his concerns, and right now, he's concerned that Smithy's hobby is a bit much. You provided a counter argument in favor of Smithy, so thank you for your valuable contribution. Now I say let's all go sleep on it and we'll resolve this one at the next Round Table.

"Cog, as for your first concern, I understand how my actions could have been taken as devaluing your abilities. I'll do better to give all you men more chances to practice being bad guys."

Cog nodded and sat down.

"All right then. Next order of business. Steve, have you selected a bad guy name yet?"

Isabelle stepped out of the washroom looking somewhat less than pristine, but it would do. She had changed her gothic vigilante outfit for a more utilitarian coffee-colored skirt with a long-sleeved white blouse, and corset with brass buckles, spraying herself with her favorite lavender perfume, and controlling her curls in a braided updo. It was the next morning after the disaster at the construction site and Isabelle did not want to dwell on how miserable her night had been.

Despite the early hour, the Liverpool Railway station was already bustling with activity. It was a modern marvel, funded by her own family. No matter how many times Isabelle visited the gigantic, glass-enclosed station, she still had to check herself to keep from gawking.

Checkered with curved metal bars, the domed glass ceiling was so high, it may have been an alternate sky, especially considering the cloudy sky clearly visible beyond the panes. Elegant iron spiral staircases led up to two geometric-patterned bridges that arched over the train tracks, connecting one side of the station to the other.

Isabelle stood near the loading platforms, lined with benches and gas lamps, each a precise distance apart, all the way down the long cracked tiled walkway. Massive metal columns jutted from the cracked tiles all the way up to support the glass ceiling. Signs hung from metal poles sticking out from the side of the columns, denoting the names of each platform: PLATFORM 1, THE NEXT PLATFORM, A PLATFORM NAMED DESIRE, THIS IS NOT YOUR PLATFORM . . . .

Isabelle wasn't looking for her platform though. A thick mist coalesced around the embroidered hem of Isabelle's skirts, and she hugged herself against the chilly morning air while she scoped the station for Constable Corbin.

"Lady Viece! Lady Viece!" Constable Corbin shouted in a loud, childishly excited voice. Isabelle finally spotted him, running toward her from the food vendors. He carried an awkward bundle in his arms, looking likely to drop it at any moment as the other passengers knocked him around while he scurried toward Isabelle.

Isabelle contained her embarrassment. *Yes, that fool is with me*, she thought. She waved him over with as much dignity as she could muster, but did not help him with his burden. If he wanted to be so foolish as to transport more than he could carry, then she'd leave him to it.

"I brought breakfast, Lady Viece," he said, beaming as he opened his package and revealed fresh bread and jam.

Well . . . this would hardly be the first time she was glad she hadn't spoken her mind. "I—how very thoughtful of you," she said instead, heat rising in her cheeks. "Thank you, Constable."

She had only eaten two rolls when the ticket booth opened, and so, dusting the flour off her hands, she glided over to the booth and very pointedly cut to the front, earning a slew of angry exclamations. Rather than respond to them, she pulled out her detective badge and showed the Ticket Sales Guy behind the counter (that is his actual job title).

"Where is the nine o'clock train headed?"

The gangly, pimply fellow blinked slowly, eyeing the badge, but otherwise didn't react. "It's headed for . . . hmm." The next few minutes were agony as Isabelle witnessed the very first human being to have managed moving slower than a snail. He slowly pulled out a paper with a list of dates and times, carefully looked over each and every number, sluggishly scratched his head, and leisurely set the paper down.

"A pity these steam engines can't accelerate the capacity of the human brain," she said flatly. "I could perhaps look into one for you, if you like."

He looked at her, blinked, "The ninnnne o'clock trainnnn," he drawled. "It's leeeeeaving at ninnne o'clock . . . Sharp."

"Yes, where? Where is it headed?"

"It'sssss headed . . . um . . ."

"Just give me a station!"

"Wagon. Wagon Station. It should arriiiiiive at . . . one o'clockkkk. In the afternoonnnnn."

"Thank you. I certainly hope that will be the most difficult thing you ever have to do in your life. Two tickets please."

Apparently selling someone tickets was the hardest thing the man had ever had to do in his life, as it took twice as long. Sufficiently annoyed, Isabelle then made her way to the communications office. She had two messages to send before the train arrived, one to The Crow, her contact at *The Times*, and one to Chief Brighton at the constabulary. She only hoped it would be enough time.

"AAAAAAAAALLLLLLL ABOOOOOOARD!!!!!!!!!"

"I think it's time to go." Constable Corbin stuck a finger in his ear and shimmied it.

Isabelle chuckled. "That gentleman could've been a foghorn in another life."

Constable Corbin grinned back at her.

The train was a marvel in its own right and yet it baffled Isabelle how quickly it was becoming just another convenient mode of transportation. Walking beside the massive locomotive, Isabelle was one of the first people to arrive at THE PLATFORM NAMED DESIRE. The woman in front of her held a child's hand and complained to the Ticket Collector Guy that she'd lost her ticket.

"I had them just a moment ago," she exclaimed. "You just ask the Ticket Sales Guy. I've been robbed I tell you!"

An admirable attempt at free passage, thought Isabelle impatiently, *but honestly, the rest of us paid our dues. Might I suggest doing likewise?*

"No one gets on board without a ticket miss. NEXT!"

The woman grumbled at the fellow's tone but she did take her child and shuffle away. Isabelle shook her head as she handed their tickets to the Ticket Collector Guy.

"Poor lady," Constable Corbin said as they stepped up onto the train. He tucked the bag with the remaining rolls into his satchel.

"You actually believed her sob story?"

"She had a child."

Isabelle sniffed. "Leeches will use anything they have to get the better of you. If she was sincere, then I dare express my sympathies.

But more than likely, she's just another bottom-feeder preying on the compassion of the surface dwellers."

"Well what if she *was* robbed? Plenty of people who would steal train tickets these days."

"Anything short of a Crimson run won't sway my opinion."

Though Isabelle was accustomed to first class, she chose third class on the assumption that's where the welders would be. Two rows of benches that could comfortably fit two people—though passengers were managing three and sometimes even four quite *un*comfortably— extended on either side of her. They weren't even upholstered. Come to think of it, Isabelle had never been back here. It was stuffy, dirty, and decidedly awkward. *Much like my companion*, thought Isabelle dryly as Constable Corbin shuffled into a seat on the right, cheeks bulging with his breakfast. He smiled at her despite his mouthful, and Isabelle couldn't help a small smile back. Silly as he was, there was an endearing charm to one who didn't spend his life putting up a pretense to impress others.

Isabelle slid onto the bench next to him and glared daggers at everyone who attempted to scoot her over and fit three on her bench. They sat four rows from the back, hoping to keep an eye out for the welders.

"Do you see them?" she asked Constable Corbin.

"There," he said after scanning the car. He pointed toward the front, and sure enough, they took up three benches just by themselves.

"I count six. That's one more than were in the building yesterday."

"Could the extra guy be the employer?"

"Traveling with his cronies in third class? Awfully polite of him. I dare say *I'd* contentedly work for the man." She took in the scene, wondering where the inventions were hidden.

Constable Corbin swallowed, wringing his hands on his lap while he stared at the welders. "So . . . what's the plan? We just follow them back to wherever they're going?"

"Hardly. I notified the constabulary. They'll meet us at Wagon Station and we'll have them arrested."

"Arrested? You told the chief we have evidence?"

"We do. They're carrying both your mousetrap and Professor Brass's fulminate. We are eyewitnesses to the professor's murder and can take the constables right to the murder location. Furthermore, I heard from their leader's own mouth that the explosion at Brass Manor was their doing and it was an attempt to cover up murder, not theft."

Constable Corbin's mouth fell further agape as she explained. "Oh God," Corbin whispered when she finished her tale.

"Now that we know this," Isabelle continued with a great deal more poise than she felt, "I'm certain we'll look back through Brass's scorched manor and find even more incriminating evidence. We have the puppets on their strings. And potentially these, and I quote, *fence clowns* whom they are supposed to meet at the station. It is my guess this will be the Crimsons. Now we just need to convince any one of these men to implicate the Puppet Master. It shouldn't be difficult. These men have more to lose than their employer. We offer to give them their lives if they give us what we want. They'll betray their own mothers. Rest assured."

Constable Corbin didn't look like he was resting and he certainly didn't look assured, fidgeting with his pocket watch rather more aggressively than usual.

"Is everything well?"

"Poor Professor Brass. They just . . . hacked him to death?"

"It seemed he passed quickly," Isabelle said stiffly, recalling a gory memory she wished to forget. In fact, her mind was determined to push the memory away. She hadn't given it as much attention as it deserved. If she did, she wouldn't be able to think straight about the case and so, logically, she had to reject the memory. Every book she'd read about proper investigation techniques supported mourning for the dead later. Focus on justice now.

"We will serve justice," she declared firmly. "That's how we beat them. That's how we honor Professor Brass's memory."

"But we're the ones who sent him in there in the first place. He died because of us."

She . . . hadn't considered that. She *refused* to consider that. "We had no way of knowing what would happen," she insisted. To herself more than to Corbin.

"W–w–what did you *think* was going to happen?" Constable Corbin's voice acquired some heat, his eyes sparkling with passion. Or tears.

Isabelle placed a hand over her heart, startled.

"We sent him in there and we had a hunch it might be the same fellows what stole his fulminate. We sent him in there s–s–s–so that they'd . . . so they'd think he was there for, you know, the meeting. But they already tried to kill him. W–what did we expect? That they'd just, you know, apologize and leave him be? We sent him into a viper pit without p–p–protection. Without backup. That poor old man is dead because of us."

The train whistle blew and they lurched as the train set in motion, giving Isabelle a moment to process the blow. "How can you suggest such a thing?" Isabelle demanded. "We listened to him, offered him aid, and we acted upon it. The result was unfortunate."

"Unfort—he's dead. Two people died last night because of us. You call that *unfortunate*? I call that a right terrible tragedy."

"It is. It *is* a tragedy. But to blame ourselves for something unforeseeable? Something we endeavored to prevent?"

"We didn't even talk about the possibility of a life-threatening situation. W–w–we didn't . . . we didn't even try to prevent nothing. We just . . . didn't think it through. You and me, we're better than this. We should've thought of this. We should've protected him."

Isabelle crossed her arms firmly. "We did our job."

"We failed."

Isabelle bristled with indignation. "Failed? Have you given up already then? I didn't think a respectable member of the constabulary would be so easily defeated. What did you think this job would entail? Did you expect no loss? No sacrifices? No difficult decisions? I hazard to say you are unfit for this duty if you thought it would be a lovely walk in the park. We're this close"—she gestured with her thumb and index finger—"to solving the case of the century. The first case of such grand scale in the new industrial regime, and you would call that a failure? We crack this case, we win. Do not submit to failure. I won't have it. We *will* beat them. We *will* serve justice. And you will stop wallowing in self-pity and scorn, and do your job. *Constable.*"

She stood up.

"What are you doing?" Corbin asked not looking up from the pocket watch in his lap.

"My job."

"I mean—w–where are you *going?*"

To get away from your scathing words that ring too close to the truth, a small voice said in the back of her head. "To gather information," she declared confidently.

She entered the aisle and casually slipped into a seat a couple rows behind the welders.

". . . bothering with a stupid name," one of the welders was saying.

"They ain't stupid names Steve. They're codenames. You know, to strike fear into everyone what crosses us."

"And you think Cog is a scary name? *Ahh help run! Cog is coming!* Oh yeah, very frightening."

"If they know my name, they'll know what I'm good at, and they'll be afraid."

"Oh that's right. You throw rubbish at people and they get scared. *Look out, he's throwing a banana peel! Oh God, he's tossing out fish bones and moldy old chips! Run for your lives!*"

"There's no call for that, Steve," replied Cleaver. "Cog's just trying to do his job."

"By throwing rubbish at folks?"

"I don't throw rubbish! I throw metal stuff. That hurts when it smacks you in the face."

"And folks won't be afraid of you if you just go with Harry? You have to call yourself Cog?"

"What's your problem, Steve?" said the fellow to the far left, by the window. "We're The Welders. It's our mob name. All the greats have one. So we should have bad guy names to go with it. We're a fearsome lot, but we don't want no one thinking we're sissies just 'cause we're alone, now do we?"

"Well you could at least pick something original. Strangler? Honestly David? That's the one you're going with?

Strangler fumed. "I. Strangles. My. Prey."

"No. You. Don't. You're just trying to learn how to strangle folks so you can call yourself *the Strangler*. But you remember the last poor git you tried to strangle? You got tired of holding the rope before the fellow's air ran out. Why not try to pick a name what actually suits you . . . Like Twig."

David or Strangler or whatever he called himself, stood up, ready to fight.

"Sit down Dav—I mean Strangler," Cleaver intervened. "Everyone has a right to be heard. Now Steve, that's really not fair of you. Strangler's doing his best, and when he's got this strangling business down, he'll be quite fearsome. No villain became notorious overnight."

"Yeah and at least Strangler came up with something for himself," another chimed in. "The name Steve don't frighten a pigeon."

"Neither does Smithy."

Smithy bristled, but Steve jumped in before the man could say anything.

"Now, look mate. I'll be fair," Steve said amenably. "At least your bad guy name makes sense. You've always liked to burn stuff, and you've got that portable, fire-blowing contraption thing you carry around. Ain't nothing wrong with liking a bit of fire. I intend to vote in favor of letting you keep doing your thing in the next Round Table."

Smithy nodded his head sharply, fondly patting a bundle at his feet. Cog however, glowered at the statement.

"Even you Cleaver," Steve continued. "Hell, even Gauge's name at least sort of fits him." Steve nodded at the last man in the row who hadn't spoken yet. Gauge seemed to be the calmest, most calculated of the lot. "You all want to call yourselves by some damn fool gimmick, be my guest. I ain't got no problem. But Steve is the name my mother gave me, and it's always been good enough for me."

"Steve," Gauge said tenderly. "We're all very fond of your dear mum, you know that. But I think she'd be proud to read about her boy in the papers with the name Jawbreaker. Or Bone Cruncher. Eh? What say you to those names? You're a strong lad, good at breaking things. How about it?"

"No."

"What about having a name that's just added to yours?" Strangler offered. "You know, like Steve the Stalker. Or Steve the Striker. Double names always strike fear and terror into folks. What say you to that?"

"I say fear and terror are the same thing."

"No they're not. Fear is like 'ah!', whereas terror is more like 'AAAAAHHHHHHH!!!!!!!', you understand?"

"No."

"Damn it Steve, now you're just being unreasonable!" yelled Cog.

"How about Steve the Stupid, eh?" added Strangler. "What say you to that?"

Evidently, Steve had nothing to say to that. He stood up and prepared his fist for a solid, jawbreaking punch. The other welders interfered, some taking Cog and Strangler's side, others holding Steve back, and the whole thing turned into an argument that Isabelle . . . frankly didn't have time for.

Well, that was fruitless, she thought as she stood up and sidled into the aisle. Someone bumped her rather forcefully from behind.

"Excuse me," Isabelle said irritably as she headed back to the aisle where Constable Corbin sat. She opened her mouth to deliver instructions to him, but promptly clicked her teeth shut and whirled around. That man who had bumped her . . . He walked down the aisle between the benches, his back to her. A long black coat, a wide-brimmed hat sitting at an angle atop dark, wavy hair, jingling with metal accessories of all sorts, that sauntering gait, his head tilted down and his hat shading his face . . . Jasper Crimson?

She was vaguely aware of Constable Corbin saying something to her as she moved to follow the mysterious man. He stopped two rows shy of the welders and waited a moment, casually looking at the rolling countryside through the window.

Blast! Why did he have to show up now? Isabelle was not ready to confront him, hoping instead to have handled the lower tier criminals first. But on the other hand, if she could deliver both the welders and the Crimsons to the authorities . . . .

The train suddenly lurched and Isabelle had to grab hold of the bench backs on either side of her to keep from falling. The lurch conveniently allowed Crimson to fall right next to the lunchbox at Cleaver's legs.

It seemed that they exchanged some words as Crimson went on his way, but Isabelle couldn't make it out. With the welders on the left, Crimson had snatched the lunchbox and held it close to his person. He left the car, shaking Isabelle out of her confused stupor.

The drop point was not at the station. It was here. On this train. And the Crimsons were indeed the fences. The evidence must be inside the lunchbox. The momentary excitement welling up in Isabelle faded with another, more pragmatic realization: Jasper Crimson, the notorious criminal featured in every Saturday paper like some sort of legendary larcenist, had her evidence. No one had ever recovered anything that made its way into the Crimsons' possession.

Isabelle charged down the aisle after him. Out the car door, over the treacherous bridge connecting it to the next car, and into the dining car. Crimson was already on the other side. He tipped his hat to a pretty young girl, who foolishly blushed at his attentions, then went out the door again.

Isabelle followed. Out the dining car door and into the first class car. It was much quieter here, as she was more accustomed to. This car was more spacious, with an aisle running along the right side, lined with windows, and sliding doors to private cabins on the left. Crimson entered one at the end of the car.

Isabelle considered for a moment, then dug into her satchel. She pulled out her pistol, her only weapon, something she could barely use, and crept forward. The sliding door before her was the only thing separating her from the most notorious criminal in England, a man who had bested her on more than one occasion, had humiliated her on a few more. But this time, she hadn't chased him. He didn't know she was there. Being on a moving train, he had nowhere to run. No edifices to climb. No rooftops to bound.

With a deep breath, her pistol poised to level at Crimson's haughty face, Isabelle reached for the sliding door handle AND . . . .

The door suddenly slid open, revealing Crimson's imposing figure standing not two feet in front of her, his head bowed so that his wide-brimmed hat obscured his face.

Before she could react, he snatched the pistol out of her hand, grabbed her arm, and pulled her into the cabin.

Chapter 9

Useless, Alex thought for the tenth time. He didn't follow Lady Viece as she trailed that fellow with the black coat out of the car, because he would just be useless anyway. He'd get in her way, ruin her life and give her an ulcer. That was all he was good for.

Amid the onslaught of self-disparaging thoughts, a passing curiosity snuck its way in. Alex remembered that fellow with the long black coat from the lounge where they met that Monty chap. Must be an acquaintance of Lady Viece.

Alex wasn't sure what she heard the welders discussing, but he increasingly doubted his own role in all of this, and therefore kept his opinion to himself. Lady Viece claimed they were to work undercover as detectives. *She* certainly encompassed the role, but he was beginning to wonder if his invitation was merely to placate him. Keep him out of the way of the "real" constables. Chief Brighton thought him the most incompetent fool in the constabulary. Surely he wouldn't have suddenly assigned him clandestinely to a high profile case like this.

What was he missing here? There was something off about—

Movement out the window cut off his musings. He could've sworn he saw a boot flash across the top of the window pane. He pressed his cheek against the window, straining to see the roof of the train. *Don't be a fool Alex*, he told himself. No one was *outside* the train.

Settling back in his seat and trying not to think of the troubling events of last night he . . . why did Lady Viece follow that fellow in the black coat? It took him a moment to put his thoughts together but eventually it hit him. The woman and her child inexplicably missing their tickets, Lady Viece diverting from her mission to follow a strange fellow with an unsavory look, someone who had robbed every person in Monty's lounge, someone climbing outside on top of the train . . . oh no.

Leaping out of his seat he . . . promptly tripped over his own feet and fell flat on his face in the aisle. AND THEN LEAPING TO HIS FEET . . . Alex began what was the most humiliating rescue attempt on record. He supposed he should at least be proud to say he made it to the first class car with all of his clothes on.

The car was quiet. Odd. It had only been a minute or so since Lady Viece left. He had expected to find her at a standoff or something with Jasper Crimson. Instead, the aisle was empty.

Creeping forward, Alex pulled out his two pretentious pistols. Though he was trained to use them, his hands shook as he listened intently for any sounds out of the ordinary. Despite his vigilance, it still caught him unawares when Crimson himself stepped out of the cabin just in front of him. The thief slid the door closed, and turned to head away from Alex.

"Freeze!" Alex's voice cracked. Embarrassment number two for the day. He leveled both pretentious pistols at Crimson's head.

The thief turned around, completely unconcerned, as though an old friend had just amiably called his name.

"What . . . w–w–what have you d–d–done with Lady V–V–Viece?"

Crimson raised an eyebrow, but that was all. Something thumped behind Alex, and he whirled around to come face to face with Scarlet Crimson. The window beside her was open. Hah! He *had* seen a boot out the window!

Realizing he was surrounded, Alex hastily leveled his pretentious pistols at the girl, elbows straight. Then he turned around and pointed them at the brother. Then he pointed one pretentious pistol at the brother and the other at the sister, both arms straight out to his sides.

He looked at the brother wide-eyed, his hands trembling. The sister reached a hand into his pocket and stole his pocket watch. He turned back to look at the sister, but then the brother reached into his pants pocket and stole his pocket book. He looked back at the brother and pointedly shook his pistol in the man's face, to remind him there was indeed a deadly weapon in his face. You know, in case he hadn't noticed. Wasn't that supposed to make people feel uncomfortable or something?

Of course, as soon as he took his eyes off the sister, she snatched at his belt and undid the buckle. The brother then swiped the belt right off his trousers and slung it over his shoulder. The sister opened the sliding door behind Alex while the brother snatched one of the pistols out of Alex's hand and moved in front of him, putting Alex between Crimson and the open cabin door behind him. The sister apparently knelt down behind Alex and the brother shoved Alex over.

It all happened so quickly. He fell backwards, tripping over the hunched sister and landing hard on his back inside the cabin . . . right beside Lady Viece.

The brother closed the door and Alex could hear the two of them burst into laughter down the aisle as they left the car.

As soon as Isabelle saw Constable Corbin fall into the cabin beside her, she could've screamed. She *would've* screamed. Except Jasper Crimson had gagged her with a crocheted scarf.

"Oh dear! You all right, Lady Viece?" Alex exclaimed as he removed the gag.

"No," she grumbled irritably. "Untie my wrists, if you please."

Constable Corbin obliged, though he spared a confused look for her state. "He tied you up with your own coat?"

Isabelle didn't say anything, her full lips pinched together in a thin line. As soon as Constable Corbin undid the knots that bound her wrists together, she reached down and undid her bootlaces.

"He tied your ankles together with your own bootlaces?"

"No. I did this myself. I thought perhaps it would be a rather ironic joke to have you come rescue me from my self-inflicted captivity."

Constable Corbin blushed. "Well what happened then?"

"Nothing!" she exclaimed as she climbed to her feet. "He pulled me in, spun me around, pulled my coat off most of the way, and then somehow used it to bind my arms." She carefully slid the door open, except the door wouldn't budge. Of course they were locked in. Perfect. Just perfect!

"Then he pushed me face down on the floor," she continued with a grunt as she wrestled with the door. "And tied my feet together. When I tried to scream for help, he shoved that scarf in my mouth. Then he left. Is that enough detail for you?" She looked back at him, then suddenly blushed and turned away, irritation piling on. "What happened to your trousers?"

Constable Corbin yelped. His pants were nearly down to his knees. "I've . . . ah,"—Corbin grunted, wrestling his trousers back into place—"been robbed."

"They stole your belt?"

Corbin nodded, his eyes downcast. "And my pocket book. And pocket watch. And one pistol."

Isabelle rolled her eyes. "We don't have time for this." She reached a hand toward her satchel to retrieve her own pistol and . . . (wait, Jasper stole that). She reached toward the pistol Constable Corbin still held in his hand. "Give me your weapon."

"What? Why?"

"So I can shoot the lock off the door."

"What? You can't do that. You'll start a mass panic."

"And the Crimsons are getting away."

"Wha—a—g–getting away where?! They don't got nowhere to run. We're on a *train*!"

He had her there. "It doesn't matter. We must catch them."

"Why? Why not just leave them be? Don't we have bigger problems?"

"They have your invention."

"They . . . so they *are* the fences? Of course! But I thought they'd be meeting at the station? The drop point was on the train? What sense does that make? It—"

"We don't have time for speculation, Corbin! For the love of God, hand me that gun!"

"No. Everyone will panic."

"We don't have time to argue!"

"We got plenty of time to argue. We. Are. On. A. *Train*!"

"DO NOT GET SMART WITH ME CONSTABLE! GIVE ME THE GUN!"

"WHY DO YOU ALWAYS GOT TO—"

A loud crash from the aisle outside cut off their argument. After sharing a perplexed glance with Corbin, Isabelle pressed her cheek against the door and listened.

"It's the welders!" she hissed, listening to them tromp down the car, yelling obscenities. At Jasper Crimson, by the sound of it, which was . . . peculiar.

Constable Corbin added his own curse to the mix but it was rather pathetic, especially after the impressive vulgar eloquence of the welders. "Now what are we s'posed to do?"

Isabelle only spared a few seconds to think before coming up with something brilliant and completely original. "Out the window," she announced, following her own orders.

"The . . . w–window?" Constable Corbin scratched his head. "But that's not proper. You're wearing a dress."

Isabelle ignored the comment as she removed her satchel and coat. She lifted the window open. A rush of cool air blew the few free strands of black curls off her forehead. Perhaps this was going to be more difficult than she had assumed. Nevertheless, she stuck her upper half out the window and climbed out. She managed to get her footing on the window casement and hoisted herself up to peek over the rim of the roof . . . and yelped.

A body slid toward her, feet first. She barely managed to get out of the way, one foot supporting her on the casement, while the other foot flailed uselessly, as Gauge fell down beside her, dangling by a chain wrapped around his waist, and holding on awkwardly for dear life. Isabelle now had her back against the warm metal of the train wall, her left hand snatching at air as she tried to find something to grab onto.

Steve dropped to the other side of her and she grabbed his shirt. He held on to a chain wrapped around one arm, and Isabelle found herself falling toward him, losing her last footing on the window casement. She screamed as she clung to Steve's waist, her legs kicking freely. Steve screamed even louder.

Ignoring Steve's grunts and curses, Isabelle scrambled up the length of him in what was likely a sight to behold, her white bodice ripping at the seams. Once she had her legs up on the man's shoulders, her thick brown skirts suffocating the poor fellow, she snatched the chain he hung from and hoisted herself up. With half her body on the roof, and her lower half still dangling along the side of the car, she caught her first glimpse of what was going on.

Pandemonium.

Alex helplessly watched Lady Viece cling desperately to the welder. What could he do?

What should he do?

What to do!

Suddenly, the door to the cabin unlocked and slid open. The Crimson girl stepped in. Her tattered cream- and tan-colored dress with lots of lace was too short for her. With at least four brass-buckled belts wrapped around her waist, moth-eaten lace gloves, rather boyish boots, and a corset that had seen better days, *The Crimson Run* column didn't do the girl any justice. She had more knives sheathed haphazardly on her person than a butcher's shop, and she moved with the lithe grace of a dancer. But what really caught him was how young she was.

Feeling an absolute evil git, he leveled his gun at a young girl. For the second time in one day. It was just as effective the second time. She ignored him and climbed out the window. Not a second behind her, the tall welder who liked to cleave stuff—Alex knew he had curly arm hair!—stepped into the cabin. So Alex leveled his gun at him instead.

"Don't move!" he cried.

Cleaver decked him in the face.

Three of the five welders on the roof were already hopelessly entangled in chains. They weren't trying to escape the chains. They maneuvered carefully so as *not* to untangle themselves. Odd that. How they got entangled in the first place quickly became evident as Isabelle caught sight of Jasper Crimson dancing around the two free welders' punches.

He ducked, spun, and wrapped the chain around Cog's shoulders. He ducked, leaned sideways, and continued to wrap the same chain around Strangler's arm. Within seconds, the thief had both men comically tied together in an absurdly long length of rusty chain links. In fact, all the welders were incapacitated using the same chain.

Crimson kicked Smithy sideways and the poor man fell off the train opposite Isabelle. The chain she gripped suddenly yanked forward after him and she screamed as it dragged her across the steel roof. The chain stopped abruptly, and Isabelle's momentum pulled her onward. She gripped the chain in white knuckles, barely stopping herself from going over the side. Her feet swung in an arc over the edge of the roof. She screamed, but held tight.

Her respite was short as Jasper Crimson kicked Strangler off the train, which yanked Isabelle down the length of the roof again, toward the back of the car.

Well that explained why the welders were in no rush to untangle themselves.

The chain stopped again, and again Isabelle's momentum flipped her head over heels. She landed with a grunt as the Crimsons—when had the sister made it up here?—pushed Cog over the side. Taut chains extended in every direction across the roof. Five men now hung from either side of the train, all alive, all soundly humiliated, and all hopelessly incapacitated.

Isabelle tried to stand, but only managed to get up to a crouch. Grateful to finally have her footing, she didn't dare let go of the chain. Squinting against the wind, she could see Cleaver holding a gun to the sister's forehead. Isabelle wasn't sure how he had managed to get her in that position, and spared him a moment of respect for the accomplishment.

"Give me the lunchbox, or she dies!" he bellowed over the mechanical rumbles of the locomotive.

Isabelle rescinded her respect a moment later, as Scarlet stepped backward into Cleaver, forcing him to take a step back. His foot caught in the length of chain, throwing him off balance. He dropped his gun.

Jasper Crimson darted forward and quickly secured Cleaver's foot in the chains.

Isabelle scrambled for the fallen firearm, using the chain to pull herself forward.

Crimson shoved Cleaver over the side of the train.

Isabelle reached for the gun.

So did Crimson.

By less than a second, Isabelle lost the race. She still crouched over it, hand extended to snatch it up, when Crimson picked it up first, cocked it, and leveled it at Isabelle's face. He was so fast! But her marvel evaporated instantly as she stared wide-eyed into the barrel of that gun. She froze.

Crimson held the gun steady in one hand. He held her eyes for a moment, neither of them moving. All this time she had been chasing him, this was as close as she'd ever seen him. He had always managed to obscure his face somehow but not this time. Younger than she originally assumed, Jasper Crimson was clean-shaven, with dark wavy hair, and, she was mildly startled to realize, quite handsome features.

The sister stood behind her brother, even less hindered by the train movements than he was, though her smaller size might've helped. In fact she was almost too tiny. Too young.

The sister didn't move, or react in any way. She just stood there, head slightly tilted. While the sister's eyes contained no hint of what she was thinking, Crimson's eyes were intense and expressive. And . . . these were the things Isabelle noticed when her life was in danger.

Yet those eyes . . . As she looked into Crimson's dark, mischievous eyes, she knew.

He wasn't going to shoot her.

The siblings hadn't killed any of the welders. There was no concrete evidence to convict them of any of the murders they were accused of. Could it be the column had inflated their crimes? Could it be they had a falling-out with the Puppet Master and planned to sabotage the operation by stealing the lunchbox for themselves?

Wait. Neither of them carried the lunchbox. In fact, Crimson hadn't had the lunchbox when he pulled her into the cabin and tied her up. He must've left it in the cabin.

Crimson motioned with the pistol for her to sit down.

Isabelle obliged. She sat down carefully, never taking her eyes off of the thief. The pistol remained trained on her face as he bent down on one knee and reached for the hem of her skirt.

Isabelle's eyes went wide as saucers, panic constricting her throat. His hand reaching for her skirts frightened her more than death. *He wouldn't, would he? Here? Now? On top of a train? With his sister watching?*

Rather than lift her skirts, he grabbed her ankle, wrapped her foot in the chain, and grinned.

Before Isabelle could react, the sister yanked on one of the chains, thrusting Isabelle sideways, and over the side of the train to dangle beside Cleaver. Isabelle's skirts fell over her head and obstructed her view. Her relief at being alive and pure quickly dwindled in favor of humiliation.

Unfortunately, the worst was yet to come.

Chapter 10

THE CRIMSON RUN: ARTICLE 66
THE TRAIN HEIST HANGING

THE LATEST CRIMSON RUN SEWS CHAOS THROUGH LIVERPOOL'S
NEW, VIECE-SPONSORED, STATE-OF-THE-ART RAILWAY STATION.
THE NOTORIOUS SIBLINGS LEAVE THE CONTROVERSIAL LADY
ISABELLE VIECE, A SUSPICIOUS GROUP OF WILY WELDERS, AND THE
STRUGGLING CONSTABULARY HANGING.

An hour after the train finally coasted into Wagon Station, the platform was still in chaos. Chief Brighton had done an admirable job at calming the situation but with six criminals held in custody in the station office, the train turned into a crime scene, and every train on the schedule that day officially cancelled, chaos and malcontent were unavoidable.

Isabelle sat on a bench with her arms tightly crossed—the first aid minders finally satisfied with her condition—glaring as the constables escorted the last of the civilians away. The press was present, including the Crimson Articles author, The Crow.

While The Crow interviewed many of the travelers who witnessed the latest Crimson run, the constables combed through the cars for evidence. When Brighton himself had helped Isabelle down from her

138

entanglement, he only said he'd deal with her later and relegated her to the triage area.

Normally, she would not have allowed him to speak to her that way—indeed he would not normally have overstepped himself so—but her exhaustion and humiliation were more effective incentives. Not to mention the scrapes and bruises from the chain and her tussle with Jasper Crimson that needed attention. For once, she didn't argue with her position, though she did insist that Brighton thoroughly search the cabin Crimson had locked her in.

Finally, Chief Brighton came stomping out of the train and over to her bench. He handed her satchel and coat to her, and Isabelle immediately checked her satchel to ensure nothing was missing. She frowned at the sight of her pistol, and glanced up at Brighton, who simply shrugged. He wasn't supposed to know she had that, but she supposed that was a conversation for another day. "Thank you," she said, clearing her throat. "Did you find anything?"

"Yes," he replied through gritted teeth. "But it's not a lunchbox. Made to look like one. But it's not one. It's got the design of a briefcase. Not so easily opened as a lunchbox."

"Where is it?"

"With all the evidence we found. Not a bit of it enough to arrest your welder whelps there." He nodded to where a group of constables roughly ushered the welder gang into a barred coach. "We could've arrested the Crimsons though, if that makes a difference to you."

"Trust me Chief Brighton. Open the lunchbox and you'll have your evidence. And there's more. Last night Constable Corbin and I witnessed the murder of Professor Thomas Brass at the hands of the tall, curly haired one. He calls himself Cleaver. At a construction site in the Industrial Quarter. They've likely cleaned up the body but—"

Chief Brighton abruptly grabbed Isabelle's arm, hauled her to her feet and yanked her into the station office. The tiny room contained a telegraph, writing implements on a birchwood desk, and a short-range communicator that was still quite an annoying experiment. That contraption took up an entire wall and gave the room a particularly industrious feel.

Chief Brighton shoved her toward the desk, where she barely kept herself from falling to the ground.

Something in her snapped at the treatment. With everything she'd been through since last night, this was her reward for apprehending criminals? "How dare you?" she exclaimed indignantly. "Have you no—"

"Do you have any idea what you've just done?" Brighton roared, his face beet red, contrasting intimidatingly with his stark white mustache. "A load of crappy evidence. Six random welders in custody I now have to convince the magistrate are guilty of *something*. The Crimsons at large, leaving a right big mess in their wake, and you right in the middle of it, exactly where I told you NOT to be. And now you're telling me you went to the Industrial Quarter, in the middle of the night, and witnessed a *murder*?"

"I was invited. Professor Brass had a business meeting there and he invited Constable Corbin and me. We were present legally and—"

"*Legally?*" Brighton yanked at his hair with both hands, looking around him dramatically for an answer to the question written all over his face. "That's what you're concerned about? Not the fact that you went into a shady situation in a shady part of the city to meet shady people with no weapons, no backup, and no training?" He grabbed her shoulders and shook her rather forcefully. "You could've been killed! You could've died! What were you thinking?"

"Professor Brass is dead!" she exclaimed tremulously, dodging the question. "They killed him. I brought them to justice."

"You did nothing but put all of us in a sticky spot, that's what you did. The Industrial Quarter belongs to Garnet Industries. That slimy bastard owns the whole quarter. Any crime committed on his turf is a potential business nightmare, it is. It'll ruin his business. You want to try bringing this before the courts? You're not just trying to put those welder louts away. You'll have to face Lord Garnet himself and he *will* win. You got lots of money, but so does he. And more ambition to boot. *And* more to lose!" Brighton growled, a frightening sound Isabelle had never heard from the man.

Despite her conviction, Isabelle recoiled slightly.

"If this gets out," Brighton continued, "he'll come after the constabulary. If we can't prove these welders are guilty of . . . well anything, the constabulary will be the laughing stock of the city and there ain't no amount of money you can throw at it to save us."

"They are guilty of theft, conspiracy, and *murder!*" Isabelle insisted. "Near as I can tell, the Crimsons were attempting a double-cross against them, and the welders tried to kill them for it. They held the sister at gunpoint. I *can* prove all of it. You continue to think me incompetent. I did everything within the law, nothing without having proper evidence to proceed, and—"

"And you stole a detective's badge! You did everything *legally* after stealing the badge that let you do it *legally*. That makes it all *illegal!* Now put that nonsense to rest, woman! This ain't about legality."

"I just solved the biggest scandal case of our time. That's what this is about. I acquired the proper evidence, and apprehended most of the men responsible. All we need now is to interrogate them in order to catch the Crimsons and finally the Puppet Master!"

"The . . . Puppet Master?"

Isabelle blushed. "The one behind all this. He's within our grasp. If we can catch him, we can—"

"We. Now, *now* you say we. All this time it's been 'I did this' and 'I did that.' And now that it's falling apart on you, you try to rope me into it? Hang me by it? Is that it?"

"No, I—"

"Are you listening to anything that's coming out of my bloody mouth right now? You are in deep trouble. How should I explain to the magistrate—or to your father, for that matter—that you stole a detective badge, manipulated an officer into helping you, and broke every law in the book while foolishly thinking you were abiding *by* the law? How? How did you think this would end? You come from a good family with a good reputation that's under fire right now, and *now* you're threatening to put it in its grave for good with your foolishness.

"And for what? Your own pride? I ain't standing by it. No I ain't. I sent for your coach and you *are* going to get in it, go home, and stay there. No more of this. Your . . . I don't know . . . *assistance* with the constabulary of Liverpool ain't no longer needed."

Startled, Isabelle found herself spluttering. "But–I–what–you hardly have the authority to do that. My patronage—"

"Your patronage be damned! We don't need it. Pull your funding and go home. Might just save your fool life." Finally, he released her shoulders and went to the door, leaving Isabelle to rub where his thumbs had clenched her upper arms. Chief Brighton stopped at the door with a sigh. "You know why I came? When I got your telegram?"

Isabelle swallowed a lump in her throat.

"I came because I believed in you. Bloody hell, I still believe in you. If any of those blowhards at the governor's office had half your kindness, a smidgeon of your passion for justice, and doing what's right, Liverpool would be a glowing city, you know? Pretty as Christmas. This city needs you, Lady Viece. Just maybe not in the way you think. Or want."

This city needs me? Isabelle thought as Chief Brighton left. *Just not in the way I think or want? Just in the way you want.* Isabelle smoldered with anger as the full weight of Chief Brighton's words sank in. After everything she had done for the constabulary? He was simply going to dismiss her? She charged out of the station office and onto the wooden platform outside. She searched out Chief Brighton, blinded to anything else.

"Lady Viece are you even l–l–listening to me?!"

Isabelle finally registered Constable Corbin was speaking to her. She turned around and started. The slight man stood not a couple feet away. She hadn't seen him. "Where is Chief Brighton?" she demanded.

Constable Corbin gaped at her. "You . . . you really don't care, do you?"

"About what?"

"I see. I'm just another low-class glock what's not good for nothing except, you know, getting you where you want to go."

As her fierce anger faded, Isabelle began to register what Constable Corbin had been saying. "I . . . what? Why would you say that?"

He flashed a shiny metal pendant in her face. Her detective badge. "Felt a right fool talking to Chief Brighton about our 'secret mission'. Hah! It all makes sense now. You lied to me. You stole this. Gave me some poppy cock story about a secret mission and I fell for it." He threw the badge on the ground.

"Constable, I—"

"I even know exactly why I believed you," he said softly, eyes growing distant. "I just got excited. You know, that someone actually believed in me for once." He dragged his feet in utter defeat down the platform away from Isabelle.

With each step he took, the last embers of Isabelle's anger faded. Anger had been an effective tool to avoid acknowledging her guilt and embarrassment. Frankly, everything Brighton said was spot on, but she just . . . couldn't concede. She *wouldn't* concede. All she wanted was justice. All she had done was pursue justice and she'd very nearly succeeded. Hadn't she?

Unbidden tears welled up in Isabelles eyes. She gracefully sat down on a bench, and waited for her coach to arrive and bare her home.

Chapter 11

VIECE HOLDINGS UNDER WATER AS GARNET INDUSTRIES PREPARES FOR DEFENSE EXPO

IN MIDST OF UNFOLDING SCANDAL INVOLVING VIECE FAMILY, LORD MORGAN GARNET MOVES FORWARD WITH AGGRANDIZED PLAN FOR DEFENSE EXPOSITION, PROMISING WAVE OF NEW TECHNOLOGY TO SHIFT POWER TIDES IN EUROPE.

"Now," declared Cleaver, "I think we can all agree that this has been a valuable learning experience for us all."

His crew nodded glumly. They were all crammed into the same holding cell. With their knees up against their chests, sitting shoulder to shoulder, the Round Table had become a place for sharing thoughts and ideas, as well as stench, personal space, and breathable air. They'd attracted an audience in the other prisoners, who piled up to the ceiling in the surrounding cells, their limbs sticking out between the bars.

"Learning experience?" exclaimed Steve. "We're in prison! We've been caught! They got our faces, our our real names, our home addresses—"

"We're done for!" wailed Cog. "We ain't never gonna get to be proper criminals now."

"Hey, now, we did our best and that's what matters," offered Strangler.

No one responded.

Strangler looked around for support. "Right?"

"Strangler is right lads," Gauge chimed in. "I know your first time in prison can be unsettling, but trust me. This is just part of the growing pains. You just gotta keep your chins up, and as Cleaver said, think of it as a learning experience. Now, who would like to say what they learned first?"

Cog's hand shot right up into the air, punching one of the prisoners in the nose behind him on its way up.

Cleaver nodded encouragingly to Cog.

"I learned you can't trust Steve."

Steve blinked. "Me? What did I do?"

"Well we was all talking about our bad guy names, and you had to be disagreeable. That distracted us. So when that Crimson idiot showed up, we didn't react fast enough. Didn't even notice he took nothing from us. We gotta be more diligent men!"

"Hey now, that's right unfair. I'm the one what got to them first. On top of the train, mind you. While it was moving!"

"We was all on top of the train, Steve! You was the first to get his rump roasted, chewed up, and spat back out by that bloody Crimson pretty boy."

"I had him on the hook! He got lucky, that's all."

"Actually, it's more like *he* had *you* on the *chains*." Smithy's attempted joke brought out nothing more than forced chuckles.

Cleaver watched the dynamic unfold in consternation. There was something different about his men after the events on the train. A tension that wasn't there before. Gauge was right. He and Cleaver were the only one's in the crew who had done time in prison before, and your first was certainly unsettling. But still, there was something more here that Cleaver couldn't put his finger on.

"All right, let's be fair men," Smithy announced, breaking the escalating argument. "I think we can all agree that we are all a little responsible for what happened. We're a team, right? So we all gotta take responsibility together."

"Responsibility ain't the problem, Smithy," said Strangler.

Cleaver perked up at that comment. "Then what is?"

"Well." Strangler dropped his eyes and wrung his hands in his shirt. "If no one else'll say it, then I damn well will. I . . . the truth is that, well I feel embarrassed. And humiliated. And I don't think that sort of emotion is really appropriate for a bad guy to feel."

That was it then. The somber expressions, and dropped eyes from the rest of the crew revealed the truth.

"That's very brave of you, Strangler," Gauge said, putting a hand on the man's shoulder. "Way to be the first to speak up."

"I'd like to second Strangler's notion," Smithy jumped in. "I'm embarrassed too. I ain't felt this emasculated since my wife left me for Nathaniel."

"The barber?" asked Cog.

Smithy nodded, earning a collective, deflated "aw" from the prisoners.

"Didn't think I'd ever feel as bad as I did that day. But now this. All I ever wanted was to be a successful criminal. I had potential, what with what I did to that hair-cutting louse. Didn't get arrested for that, no. And that was a proper, evil crime, mind you. No, instead, I get arrested for a failed crime what ended in humiliation. Successful criminals don't get put in jail fellas. So what does that make us? Failures, that's what."

"Aw, Smithy," said Cog. "You ain't a failure. All the greats had to start somewhere."

"Doubt they started from prison on their first big job, Cog."

"Always the nay sayer, ain't you Steve."

"Cog, that's enough," Gauge put his hands up to Cog and Steve. "Now Steve, do you want to share how you feel about today's debacle?"

Steve looked like he was chewing glass and ready to spit it at anyone who dared say hi to him. "Me? I'm angry," he declared. Despite the grief Steve had been giving Cleaver lately, Cleaver admired the man's unabashed disposition. He was who and what he was, and he wouldn't let anything or anyone dissuade him. Perhaps that was always part of Cleaver's problem with the man.

"I'm angry," Steve continued, "that we failed so miserably when every man here is worth his salt as a hardened criminal."

That earned a round of cheers.

"What do the likes of the Crimsons got that we don't? We're just as smart and crafty and diabolical as they are. They have no right humiliating us honest men like that."

Even the fellow prisoners joined in on the cheers. They had likely had less-than-flattering encounters with the Crimsons themselves.

"The fact is," Cleaver announced, spreading his hands. "The Crimsons have been at this game far longer than most of us, and I think our lack of experience showed. We shouldn't be humiliated by that. We should learn from it. Just because we call ourselves criminals now does not mean we automatically have the respect of our peers. We have to prove ourselves."

"But how do we prove ourselves to the likes of those buggers?" asked Cog. "I think we should blame them. They're the ones what ruined our plan."

"They're not here to defend themselves, so that's against the rules of the Round Table." Cleaver said firmly. "Now we've had ourselves a bit of a setback, that's all. Being in jail is problematic, yes, and the fact that the Crimsons have the boss's weapon might get us in a lot of trouble. But I think we can all agree this is the last time those Crimsons or any other git will get the better of us!"

The welders cheered their agreement, throwing out some encouraging punches (poor fellows have no idea what's coming up in the next chapter).

The Constabulary Headquarters/Station/Not-So-Secret Hideout/House of A Thousand Coppers—they hadn't been able to agree on what to call the place yet—had originally been built with the intention of providing a base of operations for the new system of local law enforcement. After only a few days of opening, they had hastily added a few holding cells to keep arrested criminals until they could be moved to the district prison.

Just weeks after that, the cell block had expanded to triple its size, with twelve cells, situated just off the west wing of the building and only accessible by going through the main room, down the hallway, turn right, go all the way down past the offices, make a left, follow the blue tape on the ground until you get to a corridor, go right, enter the haphazard door that looks like the entrance to an evil science lab, go up the precarious wooden staircase and most likely you probably arrived at the mini prison.

Maybe.

Sixty percent chance.

Fortunately, Chief Brighton had made the trek enough times he did indeed arrive at the mini prison. Each cell could comfortably fit half a dozen criminals. Each cell could *un*comfortably fit a dozen criminals. Each cell could absolutely *not* fit two dozen criminals, and yet that was how many crammed into each barred cell.

Inmates sat on one another's shoulders, some smashed up against the ceiling, while limbs stuck out between just about every gap in the cell bars. It was horrendously loud, obnoxiously stuffy, and unethically odiferous within this cramped infernal holding block. But what could Brighton do? Most of these fellows would be released with warnings soon. But until then, arms and legs would just have to continue jutting out of the bars.

The first cell, among its other occupants, contained the Wily Welders, or so *The Times* had taken to calling them. Right idiotic name, if you asked Brighton (*The Times* lacked the creativity to come up with a better name; NOT the author). They were an unexpected lot that did seem to have a cohesiveness that spoke of a higher caste of criminal. *Or knitting circle*, Brighton thought with a chuckle as he noted the strange and distinctly circular pattern they currently sat in.

"Constable Terry," Brighton barked.

The constable who had accompanied Brighton stood at attention beside him. "Chief!"

"Bring me that one." He pointed at one of the welders, and then simply left. Across from the cells was an interrogation room. The dim lighting illuminated two chairs and a rickety table in an eerily empty space.

Brighton sat down and stifled a sigh. It increasingly felt too good to sit down. He hated getting old.

A few minutes later, Constable Terry brought in one of the welders, an entirely unremarkable fellow. Just an ordinary git. Constable Terry shoved the handcuffed welder into the unoccupied chair and left without another word.

Brighton eyed the man, who stared right back.

"What's your name?"

"Steve."

"Steve what?"

"Just Steve."

"No surname to go with that? You ain't got a surname?"

"No."

Brighton raised an eyebrow but let it drop. It didn't really matter anyway. "All right then, Mr. Steve. Care to tell me what happened on the train?"

"No."

"Well I can make you."

"I know."

Brighton sat for a moment, gathering his thoughts, and applying a quick assessment of his charge. As ordinary as his appearance apparently appeared, this man was not your run-of-the-mill criminal. He was too calm. Resolved. And there was something odd behind his eyes.

"All right then. Let's try this another way. Do you know why you're here?"

"No."

"You're being accused of conspiracy to murder. A certain Professor Brass. Know the name?"

"No."

"Then why would you be accused of conspiring to murder the fellow?"

"I don't know."

"Well if you don't know who he is, and you don't know why you're being accused of anything, then I'm afraid there's little I can do to get you out of here. Listen." He leaned forward on one elbow. "Steve, was it? You tell me what really happened, and I'll get you off a bit easier than your Wily Welder friends back in the jail cells. You don't really want to be stuck in prison for killing a man you've never even heard of, now do you?"

"No."

"Good. Then let me help you."

"Stop."

"Stop?"

"Just stop. Stop pretending like you want to help me. You want a confession so's my friends'll get clapped for a crime they didn't do so's you can get more money and a promotion and some fancy cufflinks to smarten up that centuries-old suit. You look like an ambitious fellow. Trying for a spot in parliament too? I ain't done nothing wrong, and ain't about to get you no promotion just 'cause you asked me nicely."

Brighton leaned back again, sighing. So this Steve was one of those constable-haters. Great. "If you did nothing wrong, then you have nothing to fear."

"Except a hanging. Or life in prison."

"No one said anything about hanging you."

Steve stood up. "Stop pretending like you care about me! The constables ain't never cared about anyone but themselves. So don't insult me with all this nice talk."

Brighton shrugged indifferently. "All right. Sit down before I knock your block so hard you can't even think about standing."

"There it is. That's what you really wanted to say to me from the get go."

"Actually I would much prefer to have had a cordial conversation, but if you insist . . . ."

"Oh yeah, go ahead. Turn this into a 'hostile criminal' situation so you can have an excuse to mistreat me. Pulling every foul trick in the book, are you?"

"Sit. Down."

Steve sat down, never breaking Brighton's gaze. Brighton had dealt with this man's kind before. Criminals who hated being caught and therefore hated those who caught them. Unfortunately, that meant he probably wasn't going to get anything out of Steve. "Soon as you're done complaining about the law and everyone who upholds it, we'll get back to business."

"I wasn't complaining about the law. We need the law. Otherwise we got nothing but chaos. The law ain't the problem."

"Is that so? Then what is?"

"Let me ask you something, Chiefy. You arrested little ole me because someone accused me of conspiring to murder. Yet there have been accusations thrown about against the Viece family for years, and not a single arrest. Why is that?"

Brighton raised an eyebrow. "You asking me why rich people get off easy and poor people can't get away with nothing?"

"I'm asking you what the point of having laws is if you ain't going to keep it for everyone. Take *your* position for example. You're the chiefy. You point your boys toward the criminals and make them patrol the streets and whatnot. Because it's your job. Your job ain't to serve justice. It's to *look* like you're serving justice. It's not to make people safe. It's to make people *feel* safe. Your job ain't about arresting criminals. It's about making the aristocrats *look* like *they're* doing something about criminals so that the common folk will like them and then they can get away with whatever else they want. You, Chiefy, are nothing but a paid actor."

"And what does that make you, Steve? Whose play have you been cast in?"

"One I actually auditioned for. And unlike your playwright, mine actually told me the ending. It's gonna be quite the showstopper." He grinned.

"And who is your playwright?"

"The Lord Almighty," Steve said sarcastically, with a wink. "Be sure to say your prayers tonight, Chiefy." The man snickered.

Brighton called for Constable Terry to remove the prisoner, but even minutes after they left, Brighton remained seated in the interrogation room. He changed his mind. He had *not* seen the likes of this Steve before. As average as they come, but clearly he was dedicated to whatever he was involved in. Whether that proved to be Lady Viece's theory or something else. Perhaps it was Lady Viece's voice in the back of his mind, making this criminal's words get to him.

Or perhaps it was simply that the man's words rang all too true in Brighton's aged, haggard ears.

Chapter 12

CONSTABULARY ENDURES HEAT AFTER VIECE HEIR TRAIN FIASCO

AFTER FINALLY STEPPING OUT OF THE FRYER, CONSTABULARY JUMPS INTO FRYING PAN, SUFFERING BACKLASH FROM LATEST VIECE HEIR CONTROVERSY INVOLVING CRIMSONS, IRATE LIVERPOOL RAILWAY COMPANY, AND BOILING-OVER LOCAL JAILS.

Bubbles. Lots of bubbles. Bubbles dribbled over the side of Isabelle's copper tub, making a sudsy mess on the tiles. Bubbles foamed into the air every time Isabelle shifted in the tub. Something about the way they engulfed her body, built up around her face as she submersed herself up to her chin in steaming hot water had always made her feel safe. As a child she would fantasize about being a naval officer hunting pirates, but now it was simply a place to ponder. A place she could forget about her goals, dreams and pains for a time, and honestly attempt to understand her world, herself, others. The more bubbles in her tub, the better she could ponder.

And there was an absurd amount of bubbles in her lavish bathing chamber.

That was partially because she was having an exceedingly difficult time keeping her mind off the case. *The case is solved, isn't it? Just interrogate the welders and they'd find out who the Puppet Master was.*

Or off Chief Brighton. *That ungrateful fossil! After everything I've done for him and the constables, after delivering six guilty criminals into his custody, he presumes to excommunicate me?* The fact that it was the Crimsons who technically "delivered" the welder gang was of minor note.

Or off Constable Corbin. *How could he not see what I was trying to do? I extended a trusting hand to him with my invitation to join the case. He should be grateful to me for giving him far more purpose than he had in the constabulary.*

And yet no matter how many times she justified her actions in her own eyes, she couldn't shake that familiar, unmistakable beast gnawing insistently at her heart.

Guilt.

But why should she feel guilty?

Professor Brass's death was not her fault. She had the case very nearly in her pocket. They had recovered the inventions. Between that, the explosion at Professor Brass's manor, the white-gray dust, her witness to the murder, the blueprints from Count Downey's briefcase, the countless number of defamed inventors and doctors, and *The Times's* placement of the Crimsons at nearly every crime scene, surely they had sufficient evidence to move in for the kill. They just needed a name.

In fact, if she could just convince Brighton to find *that*, all of these inconveniences and humiliations would be settled. But how?

Part of her had to acknowledge the truth in Chief Brighton's concerns about Garnet's inevitable hindrance of the case. Especially considering Garnet owned that particular quarter. He had so many industrious projects these days, she frankly didn't care to keep track. But still, two murders on his turf would not bode well for him with the press. She needed to avoid his involvement.

"I need more bubbles," she declared.

Akane attended Isabelle's needs from where she sat reading in a corner. The woman had such a graceful way of moving, she hardly made a sound as she rose from her chair to pour more of the translucent violet liquid into Isabelle's bath. The entire chamber smelled overwhelmingly of lavender.

"Just pour the rest of it," Isabelle said.

Akane obliged.

"Thank you. There's honestly no need for you to bore yourself to tears sitting here watching me think. Take the rest of the evening for yourself."

"It is not trouble, Lady Viece," Akane said sheepishly in her thick Japanese accent. "I will stay and attend."

Isabelle smiled. "Thank you, Akane. But I'd like to be left alone."

"Your mother—"

"Akane, please."

Akane grimaced, but complied and left the bathing chamber.

Isabelle swished the fluid around in her bath to generate more bubbles, vaguely amused at a concept that occurred to her. Pour this liquid into water and it created pleasant scented bubbles and soap by which to clean. Drink it, and you die. She'd solved a murder case once several years ago where a woman had killed her husband by poisoning him with bubble bath. Not the most difficult case to solve, but it had taught Isabelle a valuable lesson. Guns and knives were not the only tools that killed.

She frowned. Most murder cases she'd read about did not involve actual weapons. The perpetrator often used a kitchen knife, a shovel, or some other common item. A lamp might appear to only light a room, but throw it at someone and it could suddenly become lethal.

An inventor renowned for his work on the steam engine, another working on inventing light, a couple heavily involved in the arms industry, doctors, scientists, chemists . . . all specifically selected from the masses. All experimenting with harnessing or creating substances.

Constable Corbin's mousetrap was the only actual completed invention the Puppet Master wanted. But then there was the impressive weapon in Count Downey's blueprints. The Puppet Master was building an arsenal, patenting ideas and inventions before they were turned into weapons. The patents were just a small part of his plan, a cover for his true motives. If everyone focused on the inventors and the patents themselves, he could get away with building an empire in the arms industry.

Isabelle hurriedly wrapped herself in a white robe and ran out of her suds-infested bathing chamber.

"Notes!" she exclaimed to herself. "Where are my notes?"

With one hand still sloppily tying her robe closed, she snatched her pen and jotted down all of her thoughts in her leather-bound journal.

The construction site: owned by Garnet Industries.

The construction site welders: employed by Garnet Industries.

Professor Thomas Brass: former chemical engineer for Garnet Industries until he started his own company.

The current industry leader in metal fabrication: Garnet Industries.

Yes. It made sense. It was the only consistent thread.

"All right, Isabelle," she said. "Let's piece this all together." She cleared her throat and started to pace, still clutching her journal in one arm and gesturing with her pen in her right hand to match every thought she spoke aloud. "Garnet hired the Crimsons to steal the items he needed. He patented those items, discredited or murdered the actual inventor, and no one would be any the wiser because the story would leave out missing items that no one knew were missing. Further, readers would be distracted by the fact it was a Crimson run, and therefore wouldn't suspect anything more."

She whirled around, waving the feather of her steel point pen like a wand, and continued pacing. "Now, the Crimsons must've wanted a bigger piece of the pie, and so Garnet promoted them, and then the welders . . . ." Isabelle stopped pacing and frowned, looking back at her wall of notes and tapping the one that had THE WELDERS written upon it with her pen.

The welders. They were expecting a drop at the station, not on the train. And they were fighting the Crimsons. Which meant the Crimsons were likely acting outside the will of the Puppet Master. Unless . . . .

Isabelle took a deliberate step back from her wall of notes, nibbled her bottom lip, and looked at all of it together. Years of accumulated information.

And then she saw it. "Idiot," she breathed. "The Crimsons were never involved to begin with."

In each legitimate Crimson run, the Crimsons were blunt, clearly seen and identifiable by the public. Except the ones she had investigated in connection with this case. The evidence pointed to them. But few if any eyewitnesses placed them at the scene.

The run on the circus had left evidence. The run on Corbin's tenement had been staged to look like a Crimson run.

"Garnet is using the welders to stage Crimson runs to hide the truth of what happened at these scenes," she declared. "The Crimsons just happened to be at the circus the same day as Count Downey. And had just happened to be on the train where they ironically stole the lunchbox of evidence."

Isabelle laughed mirthlessly as everything came together. Hastily scribbling a quick note on a blank sheet, she tore it out of the journal, then hurried to the four-post canopy enveloping her bed and yanked on a cord dangling beside the drapes. A bell sounded, calling her maid. A moment later, Akane came sliding back in with her white apron and bonneted head. "Lady Viece?"

"Akane, take this note to the courier. I need him to deliver this to the magistrate's office. And then return to me. I'll be going out again."

Akane nodded with a knowing smile and ran off. Good woman. No questions asked. Isabelle had always liked Akane. The Japanese-born maid had always found Isabelle's hobby fascinating and had covered for Isabelle on more than one occasion.

Fortunately, Isabelle's parents weren't home at present—or ever as it seemed anymore—so she gathered her essentials in her black leather satchel, and then began braiding her wet black curls. Armed with this new knowledge, perhaps Chief Brighton would finally listen to her and request an arrest warrant from the magistrate for the Puppet Master: Lord Morgan Garnet.

She had everything else in place. All the evidence she needed to convict Garnet in the courtroom, except a confession from the welders. Thankfully, the Crimsons had failed to steal her hard evidence, leaving the lunchbox behind at the crime scene.

She frowned. No one knew the Crimson files better than Isabelle. And she had never heard of a single item being recovered from them. Why abandon the inventions in the train car when they had such a field day with the welders?

The answer was obvious.

Isabelle stalked across the room and, throwing open her wardrobe, she searched for something black, utilitarian, and intimidating.

"I don't feel any better," Alex grumbled to the bartender.

"S'cause you gotta drink it."

Alex stared at the shot glass in his hand. He'd never had a sip of alcohol in his life. But despite his upbringing, he found himself sitting on a rickety stool in a crumbling brick-walled tavern, doing what everyone else did when they were at the depths of despair.

He sighed, then downed the shot . . . and promptly choked and coughed up a lung. "I still don't feel better," Alex wheezed. "All I got now is a nasty taste in my mouth and a sore throat."

The bartender raised an eyebrow. "You gotta drink more than one, boy."

"More? How many exactly?"

"As many as you can hold."

"And that's supposed to make me feel better?"

"You really don't know how this works?"

"I think y–y–you're just, you know, preying on the depressed and unfortunate to to to sell more drinks. You got this vile concoction from the crapper, didn't you? And then you sell it at a premium and and and convince people to buy so many they eventually just, you know, pass out and that's called feeling better."

"So you *have* done this before." He grinned. "Look, you want actual help with your problems, go see a doctor." The thick-armed bartender moved on to help another customer who'd already had four shots.

Alex just held his empty one, unmoving, staring at the splintery counter top before him. This would hardly be the first time someone had used him, but most people were gracious enough to inform him and threaten his life if he didn't cooperate. At least then, he could hold on to the dignity of knowing there wasn't anything he could've done differently.

But with Lady Viece . . . . For once he had actually thought he was good for something. Someone believed his invention worth stealing. Someone found him a valuable person. But no. He was nothing more than a pawn. Again.

A riotous round of laughter sounded from behind him. That lot had been going at it for the better part of an hour. Alex didn't look, though he longed to be part of it. Part of a team. The truth was, he'd enjoyed working with Lady Viece. He had contributed, hadn't he? Even if she was playing him for a fool the entire time, he'd proven his worth. It was his deduction that led them to the construction site, his quick thinking that helped Lady Viece escape with her life. For once, he had felt needed.

But apparently, he wasn't nearly as good at it as he had thought. He wasn't good at anything. He couldn't invent. He couldn't keep the law. He couldn't keep the peace. He couldn't play poker. He was useless. How could God create a man with absolutely nothing to offer the world? Where did people like him go?

The group behind him let out another round of laughter. Finally, he did turn around, and started. The entire group of big, burly, beefy men stood in a circle around a table, though Alex couldn't see what held their attention. Each man wore an outlandish clown costume, muscles bursting through polka-dotted stretch pants and pompom covered arms. The outfits were silly, but with those muscles, and intimidating postures, it had a more disturbing cast than comedic.

Where did men like him go?

He sighed, then stood up and shuffled bashfully over to the circus performers. Once he got close, thinking of what he was going to say, he froze. Between the ridiculous costumes, through the cloud of testosterone, Alex saw *him*. Sitting at the table in the middle of the circus performers, commanding their attention, was Jasper Crimson.

And he had Alex's mousetrap.

Darkness descended upon Liverpool (that's how all the fancy pants writers say "it's night") by the time Isabelle's coach arrived at the constabulary precinct. She had planned out exactly what she would say, and even accounted for Chief Brighton's reactions.

First things first. The best way to get to the chief after their falling-out would be to simply barge in before anyone could stop her.

So she barged out of her coach and up the steps into the precinct. She barged through the double iron doors of the precinct, purpose and determination driving her forward despite numerous protests. She barged right into Chief Brighton's office and—

"Lady Viece," Chief Brighton said, startled, but it was not the white-haired chief who held Isabelle's attention. Standing before him in an austere, fashionable suit, green cravat, shiny silver cuff links, and a silver-handled cane, Lord Morgan Garnet himself eyed Isabelle coolly.

"Why Lady Viece," Garnet said, turning toward her, his chief administrator at his side. "Such a delightful surprise to see you. Still insisting on fraternizing with the city's vermin, are we?"

Chief Brighton's eyes flashed with anger at the insult but he said nothing.

"Lord Garnet," Isabelle replied, matching his cool voice, trying to adjust her ruined plan to accommodate Garnet's presence. She had only ever met him at parties and the like, and only in passing. Her father endured a more propitious relationship with him, as Lord Garnet often needed Viece investments and bank authority for his ambitions. Other than commenting on Isabelle's beauty, she couldn't recall any notable conversations with the steel tycoon. "To what do we owe the honor of your presence in this vermin-infested establishment? Surely you do not seek the protection of said vermin from the misfortunes encountered at your construction site."

Chief Brighton groaned, and Lord Garnet looked utterly floored at the comment. "What?"

"I'm certain Chief Brighton would be honored to offer you and your welders protection."

Lord Garnet blinked, but to his credit let nothing slip in his reaction. Isabelle glanced at his administrator for a reaction just in case, but the sinuous, dark-skinned man was completely impassive. "It is good to see you too, Lady Viece. May I ask after your health?"

"Of course, forgive me, Lord Garnet. Where are my manners? Good day to you. I am doing quite well, thank you. And you? How is business these days? You must be splendidly proud of your innumerable new patents. Surely you hold more than anyone in all of England now."

Garnet raised an eyebrow. "Business is excellent, as it were. My company's patents are growing steadily and our profits increase each quarter from the innovations of my scientists. Quite kind of you to notice."

Isabelle gave him a sassy smile. "There was precious little to notice. I must commend you for that." Garnet opened his mouth but Isabelle plowed on. "If you are not here to seek protection, what business brings you to the constabulary? Surely no lowly constable possesses anything of interest to you."

"Of course not. I am not here on personal business. Good Chief Brighton requested my presence."

As he turned back to face Brighton, Isabelle could only raise a questioning brow at the chief.

"Lord Garnet has kindly agreed to keep custody of the suspected criminals we apprehended at the train station. If you recall." Brighton said stiffly.

"And what is wrong with the prisons? Are there not cells reserved for suspects?"

"There's no more room. We ran out of room ages ago. Been letting minor offense criminals go early just to make space for the real sick ones. The ones what ain't right in the head."

"As it should be," Lord Garnet said. "Suspected criminals like these so-called *Wily* Welders should not be allowed to roam around, especially if they are truly guilty."

"And even more convenient if they are held in custody by their own employer."

"Lady Viece," Chief Brighton's eyes offered far more warning than his words or his tone, but Isabelle wasn't having any of it. She could not allow Garnet to effectively nullify her best chance at implicating him.

"Where do you plan on keeping your welders, Lord Garnet?"

Garnet still looked genuinely confused at Isabelle's comments. "I am sponsoring the local circus, as I'm certain you know. Many of the cages there, while somewhat undignified, can be repurposed as temporary confinement for our suspects."

Our? Cleverly spliced in word to suggest a mutual goal. Isabelle could've spat. Garnet was . . . wait. The circus? That's right. Sponsored by Garnet Industries. That was where Count Downey had dropped his briefcase, though for who, she still did not know, now that she had exonerated the Crimsons. "And who will be watching them? The clowns?"

"Heavens no!" Garnet chuckled. "Chief Brighton has already assigned a contingent of constables to guard the cages. I am merely providing the place and the means."

Isabelle shared a look with Chief Brighton who nodded, eyes begging her to stop. "I see. Will they be held in the same cages that held the Platypus of the Americas? Or the Beardless Man? Or perhaps the one hiding the Stolen Patents of Vainglory?"

"Lady Viece that is enough!" Chief Brighton suddenly stood.

"I can see you are determined to accuse me of something only you seem to be aware of," Garnet cut in calmly. "I tried being gracious with you, as I know your father has often been apologetic of your unseemly pursuits, but frankly you are grinding my goat. I would not seek to offend your father, and so I shall ignore your cavalier slights. You are young yet, I am certain you will mature out of these childish misconducts. Chief Brighton, I shall await the arrival of your men and the suspects at the circus's back entrance. Good day to you both." With that, Lord Garnet shoved past Isabelle, tipping his top hat to her on his way, his chief administrator following on his heels.

Blasted man was too good at this game. Discrediting Isabelle's character belittled her arguments against him and, however illogical, would most certainly favor him with high and low society alike.

"Chief Brighton, you cannot honestly be considering releasing our most poignant evidence into the custody of the man responsible for the entire scandal!"

Chief Brighton didn't respond. He sat back down, suddenly looking every bit his age. Rubbing his temples in one hand, he closed his eyes.

"Chief Brighton? Are you well? I have discovered new information that will surely close this case. It—"

"Are you done?" he whispered.

"I have not even begun. Garnet Industries is facilitating the entire—"

"I don't care. I don't BLOODY CARE! They can be thieving, pillaging, warmongering . . . . I. Don't. Care!"

"How can you say that?"

"Let's say you're right. Let's say Garnet is behind your whole patent scandal. You just blurted out right in his face that you're on to him. Told him everything you know. You," he pointed a pointed finger in her face. Pointedly. "You just made yourself a bloody target! Stupid woman. Bloody stupid woman!"

"Do not take that tone with me, Brighton. You would dare insult my intelligence when you are ignoring every piece of evidence implicating Garnet and his company?"

"You are on the right train to getting yourself killed, Lady Viece. That's the part *you're* ignoring!"

"Garnet won't harm me. I'm a Viece."

"Is that what you think? You think a man as ambitious as Garnet won't find a way to hurt you? That's assuming you're right and he is behind everything."

"You don't believe me?"

"It don't matter. It don't make no difference what I think. I told you, the fact is a murder happened on Garnet soil and that means hell for his business regardless of his involvement in your patent scandal theory. I'm telling you, Lady Viece. Please listen to me. Leave this one alone. You're getting in over your head now, and I ain't keen on losing you. Or my job for that matter. You ever consider that? Maybe Garnet can't touch you, but he sure as hell can ruin me. And my lads. Ruin us right good. I don't like none of this. Best we can do for now is get these welders in prison for theft."

"You can't."

"Oh now you're the naysayer?"

"Without the inventions they stole as proof, you can't imprison them."

"We have the inventions."

"You have the lunchbox. It's empty."

"How would you know that? We haven't been able to get the bloody thing open."

"The Crimsons had a very obvious and disparate advantage from the very beginning of the entire affair. And they didn't have the lunchbox through most of it. Why would they abandon the lunchbox so quickly after stealing it? A simple matter of misdirection. The lunchbox is empty, mark my words. The Crimsons have the inventions."

Chief Brighton frowned. "That lunchbox is locked with a lock I ain't never seen. There ain't no way to open it without destroying the whole thing. The Crimsons don't have nothing."

"Believe what you will. I won't try to convince you otherwise. Just heed my words on this one point: do not release the welders into Garnet's custody. You will lose our only chance at implicating Garnet."

"Good. At least then Garnet will rest easy and he won't decide to take it out on us."

Isabelle gaped. "You coward," she whispered.

Brighton leaped to his feet, fuming. "You get out, Lady Viece. And you don't come back here. And you don't accuse no one else of nothing until I've decided what to do with you. I don't care if you are a lady. I don't care if you got more money than the Queen. I don't care if you're a Viece. I will keep you safe and keep my lads employed if it kills me. I ain't letting you ruin nobody's life, not even your own!"

"You're doing that yourself!" she yelled right back. "You were supposed to be a keeper of the law."

"We are keepers of the *peace*! We weren't ever supposed to get involved with the likes of Garnet. We ain't trained or equipped for it."

"I am."

Brighton burst into laughter. "No you are not! Quit fooling yourself, child! You got no more power than poor Constable Corbin. Now get out and I better not find you anywhere near Garnet, or this precinct, or my ugly old mug!"

Silence.

Isabelle glared fire at the chief. "One day you'll wish you had done what was right instead of what served you best." As she left the precinct, part of her knew her words were not entirely fair. He was a good man, but he was also far too careful. He looked after his own, and stayed in his lane, never willing to branch out of his comfort zone to do something truly great. Fortunately, Isabelle was not so reserved.

Chapter 13

MOUNTING TREASON ACCUSATIONS AGAINST VIECE FAMILY SECURE FIRST COURT HEARING

WITH RUMORS OF TREASON PILING HIGH, LIVERPOOL JUDGE SENDS
CASE TO HIGHER COURT DESPITE CURRENT LACK OF EVIDENCE.
UNCONCERNED VIECE FAMILY ACCEPTS CALL TO EXONERATE NAME.

Alex was not easily angered. In fact he really couldn't remember a time when he *was* angry. Distressed, upset, hurt, constipated? Yes. But not angry. Seeing Jasper Crimson so casually tossing his mousetrap from one hand to the next, doing magic tricks with it as though it were nothing more than a toy, unlocked something feral within him.

If nothing else came of this embarrassing experience, he would at least recover his invention. Stepping forward, he punched Jasper in the face, knocked the haughty thief out of his seat, reclaimed his invention and glared daringly at the troupe of big, burly, beefy, buff, benign bears as they licked their chops, tasting gamey Corbin flesh as they used echolocation to communicate who got first dibs on his rump . . . .

169

Ok so he *didn't* punch Jasper in the face. He did however notice one of the circus performers, a shorter man dressed as a clown, had already had too much to drink. He stumbled away from the masses, presumably seeking the privy.

Still seething with anger, and not entirely sure what he was doing, he followed the inebriated clown out of the tavern to where the privy reeked. Taking a deep breath, Alex followed the clown into the privy AND . . . this was a horrible idea. Now stuffed in a privy barely large enough for one, Alex stood face to face with a drunk clown who started at the sight of him, looking Alex up and down, utterly perplexed.

Now what?

The clown frowned deeply.

. . . um . . .

The clown looked around him, searching for an explanation. Alex did too. *Now what?!*

The clown opened his mouth to speak, but then closed it again, shaking his head as though answering his own unspoken question.

Pistol! Alex hastily reached into his satchel and searched for his pistol. Fortunately, at that moment, the clown passed out. *Un*fortunately . . . at that moment, the clown passed out. He fell forward, right onto Alex.

Gentle, misty rain settled atop Isabelle's hooded cape, tiny droplets sparkling on the wool. The sun never offered much light in England anyway, but as it set, it cast the circus into a dreary, elongated shadow, creepy enough to inspire an Edgar Allen Poe poem. The circus tents before her, encircled by a high fence, looked worse than last time, though maybe it was her new vantage point, as well as the bleak weather (or because this scene looks really dark and gothic in my head, which might be inconsistent with the original description of the circus from chapter 1 . . . oh well).

She sat at a small table with benches, just outside a tavern with a view of the circus back wall. The makeshift roadway used to haul the circus equipment and attractions into place was now a muddy thoroughfare, forcing coaches and pedestrians alike to find an alternate route as the circus closed up for the night. In fact, the streets were growing quieter by the second, the gas lamps illuminating the way for the last few stragglers.

Presumably, the coach holding the Welders would reveal itself after the circus closed. Sure enough, it came trundling down the road only seconds after the last of the circus goers disappeared. The coach pulled up to the back gate, immediately hampered from entering by the muddy grounds.

Rather than dig the wheels out of the mud, constables filed out of the coach, prodding the cuffed welders forward. They were too far and it was growing too dark for Isabelle to make out much more than that. The back gate creaked opened, and admitted the group of constables and criminals, then closed silently, ominously behind them.

After a few minutes, Isabelle darted over, straight through the mud, kicking it up onto the lacy hem of her fine black dress, until she slopped up to the gate and tried to wedge it open.

Of course it's locked you fool, she chided herself. She might be able to climb over, but her wet dress was beginning to weigh her down, and her boots would hardly allow her enough traction. It was too cold and muddy to remove anything that hindered her. Fortunately, she'd already accounted for this in her plans.

Following the gate all the way over to its hinges, Isabelle reached up and pulled the bolt from the barrel of the hinge and . . . she pulled the bolt from the barrel of the . . . she pulled the bolt as hard as she could. It didn't budge.

Staggering her legs and putting her back into it, she grabbed the head of the bolt and heaved as best she could, but without having a firm grip in this weather, it was hopeless.

She huffed, and began to consider other options. Fortunately her conundrum was short-lived. The gate opened suddenly as Garnet himself stepped out of the circus, cursing about mud and how it ruined his new shoes. Isabelle stifled a snort, and darted forward to squeeze through the gate before it closed.

"Oi!" said the young man guarding the gate, closing it all the way. "Who are you?"

As quick-witted as she was when it came to insults, thinking up a *plan* quickly was not her forte.

So she threw out an insult. "And what business is that of yours, you blemish infestation? I've already had to trek through mud and rain to get here, my shoes are ruined, my dress is atrocious, and I'm cold as an ice box. I won't have you and your twenty noses standing in my way as I'm half tempted to decapitate the next fool who asks me a silly question!" She hurried forward, and counted herself lucky the boy didn't pursue her further, though she harbored some guilt for insulting an innocent lad just doing his job.

Once she was out of the boy's sight, she hurriedly ducked between a couple large cages and leaned against one, collecting herself for the next part of her plan. Find the welders. So far, this was going quite well.

This was not going well. The clown outfit was too big and Alex had never felt so ridiculous in his life—which was saying a lot—but it would have to do.

This ain't going to work, he thought as he wandered up to the circus troupe, doing his best to look like he belonged. *I'm a right miserable actor, I'm freezing my goods off in this thin costume, and I'm not nearly as thick in the arms and waist as that fellow.* Whom he had left unconscious in the privy. *This ain't going to work!*

But no one challenged him as he laughed along with the performers watching Jasper flaunt Alex's mousetrap. *If you break it,* Alex thought. *I'll . . . I'll . . .* honestly he'd probably just hang his head and slink off into oblivion.

Something looked different about it though. A few extra parts. Those welders must've added stuff to it.

"Oi Jasper," one of the circus performers called. "What does it do?"

Jasper's wide-brimmed hat shaded half his face, making that naughty grin even more unsettling.

The smell of rancid oil from the rusty old gas lamps illuminating the circus "back stage" stubbornly permeated the air despite the rain's best efforts to settle it. The lamps dimly illuminated box after box, crate after crate, car after car, and cage after cage, but none held the welders.

Clicking her tongue, Isabelle sloshed down yet another meandering row of cages, twice as tall as she was, each one sitting on a large wagon and raised a couple feet off the ground. The back and smaller sides were covered by wooden planks, but the fronts were only vertical, smooth steel bars.

A lion sleeping in one.

A bear practicing his right hook on a punching bag hanging in the middle of his cage in another.

The Loch Ness Monster stuffed into one with a bathtub full of water. That poor creature needed a larger cage.

But no sign of the welders. She . . . had been down this row before. The entire circus beyond the public area with the tents was a horribly unorganized labyrinth. That it was illuminated at all, however poorly, was a miracle. She huffed, quickening her step all the way down the row, when she heard voices.

Finally!

Peeking around the corner of an over-sized crate, she found them, all six of them, tied up and gagged in the same cage. The six constables supposed to be guarding them were all sitting in a circle a little distance away on precarious stools, a tent hitched up to protect them from the rain, though it was open on the side facing the cage. She couldn't make out much in the dim lighting and gentle rain, but she could tell quite clearly what they were doing: playing cards.

Idiots. They were on duty, entrusted with guarding these most dangerous criminals, and this is what they did? Well, she could castigate them for their negligence later. For the moment, this worked in her favor. She needed to keep them distracted, per her plan, so she could interrogate the welders without their interference. Fortunately, she didn't have to do anything. Something alerted them from the north side of the grounds. Setting down their cards and picking up weapons, they left to investigate.

Smiling, Isabelle walked freely up to the cage. The rain fell harder now, making it even more difficult to see clearly. She placed one hand delicately on the bar. Foreseen problem number one: she had never interrogated anyone before. Though she'd studied interrogation techniques, the advanced course hadn't seemed viable. Regardless, reading about it and putting it into practice were two completely different concepts.

Foreseen problem number two: she had a strict time limit.

Foreseen problem number three: she had nothing to threaten them with.

*Un*foreseen problem number one: they were gagged.

Well, that one at least was a quick fix. As she reached into the cage, one of the men shuffled toward her, hope brimming in his eyes. Odd that. The others caught on and tried to scoot toward her too. They exclaimed through their gags, moaning and cooing indiscernibly. Isabelle recoiled. *What is this?*

And then she saw it. Looking into that man's eyes, the one with the hope, who had seen her first. Despite the darkness, she knew those eyes.

"Hey!"

Whirling around, Isabelle came face to face with the constables, who tromped toward her through the mud, weapons poised for use.

Unforeseen problem number two: these men weren't constables. That one at the center, the tall leader with curly hair, caught her attention immediately. Cleaver.

Unforeseen problem number three: Isabelle was in serious trouble.

Chapter 14

GARNET STEPS UP AS FIRST WITNESS IN VIECE TREASON CASE

AS FIRST TO LEVEL TREASON ALLEGATIONS AGAINST VIECE HOUSE, LORD MORGAN GARNET ANSWERS PROSECUTION CALL TO BE FIRST WITNESS, DECLARING, "THEY'VE DECEIVED THE PUBLIC, THE GOVERNMENT, AND HER MAJESTY LONG ENOUGH!"

Isabelle's mind stopped working. Every panicked instinct in her body said run. But of course she didn't get far before the constables—well, the welders dressed as constables—converged on her. Two sets of burly arms forced her to the muddy ground at Cleaver's feet, pulling her head back roughly in the process. Panting, Isabelle fought to gain control back over her frantic mind.

"Trying to free our prisoners?" sneered Cleaver.

"Your prisoners?" she snapped with more fire than she felt. "You mean the rightful owners of those uniforms you're soiling with your metallic stench."

Cleaver froze.

"She knows," said Smithy. He wore a strange contraption on his back, with all manner of coils, and a large copper cylinder container.

"Quiet," Cleaver barked.

"Of course I know. I . . . ." She trailed off. Looking into Cleaver's eyes, Professor Brass's face reflected back at her, his terrified expression the moment before this monster bashed his face in with his wicked mallet.

She licked her lips, tasting the rainwater as it pelted her face. It was coming down harder by the minute.

"I know everything," she found herself saying, a fragment of a plan trying to wiggle its way through her fear. She forced her voice to remain steady. "Did you think you'd get away with it? Honestly, that explosion at the Brass estate . . . terribly sloppy."

The welders shifted, glancing at one another.

"How do you know about that?" the man to her right—Steve, if she wasn't mistaken—demanded.

"I said quiet," Cleaver barked again.

"Is that why you murdered Professor Brass? To keep him quiet? For a man so fond of silence, you certainly do favor loud methods of murder."

"Oh, I told you, you shouldn't've offed Brass," exclaimed Cog.

"Indeed you shouldn't have," agreed Isabelle, as Cleaver sucked in a supremely annoyed breath.

"How long do you think you can keep this up?" Isabelle plowed on. "Stealing inventions from the hapless, murdering the inconvenient, plotting against the powerful. Lord Garnet will no doubt pay his way out of conviction, but what about you? How do *you* intend to escape the noose?"

The welders blubbered over each other. "We ain't really going to the gallows for this are we?"

"You're the one what offed Witss, Cleaver. Why do the rest of us gotta pay fer it?"

"I ain't dying for Garnet. No I ain't."

"He promised us protection."

"I SAID SHUT UP!" yelled Cleaver. His constable uniform was too small for him, pulling tightly across his powerful chest. Brains *and* brawn. Wonderful.

Isabelle opened her mouth to lay on some more accusations as these morons were poised to confess their ancestors' sins, but someone leveling a gun at your face had a way of ending conversation.

"Now Cleaver, you sure you want to do that?" Gauge asked, but Cleaver held the firearm steady.

Last time Isabelle stared into the eyes of a man who held her at gunpoint, she was certain he wouldn't kill her. This time, she saw callous apathy. This man would shoot her without a second thought. "The constabulary already knows," she said quickly, trying to keep him talking. "I spoke to Chief Brighton before I arrived here. He'll have you arrested and—"

Cleaver pulled the trigger.

Chief Brighton rubbed his temples (yes, this cut scene is for dramatic tension) as he rocked in his office chair. The lunchbox sat open before him.

It was empty.

He thought the most cliché old guy thought that any old guy ever thought: *I'm getting too old for this.* It had taken them all afternoon to pick that infernal lock. The box had actually been pressure-sealed somehow, steam seeping out beneath the lid as they removed it. He doubted he'd ever figure out how those bloody Crimsons got it open, resealed it, and made off with its contents, let alone as quickly and cleanly as they had. But that wasn't exactly what occupied his mind at the moment.

"Could Lady Viece be right about the patent scandal?" asked Constable Terry, standing with crossed arms across from Brighton's desk.

"She could," Brighton replied.

Terry nodded. "All those suspicious thefts, suicides, ruined reputations . . . ."

"All related."

Terry paused, taking in the implications. "And Lady Viece?"

"Is hellbent on getting herself dead, and we gotta prevent that from happening." Brighton stood up and walked to the window, watching the heavy rain. "You young folk think justice can be served for everyone, but an old man knows better. When you get to be my age, you realize everything you do is meaningless. A bloody waste of time. All you can do is care for yourself and your family. You give up on fool notions of changing the world and accept it for the rubbish pile it is."

Headstrong and naïve though Lady Viece was, she didn't have the decency to be wrong every once in a while. She really did have an inspector's head on her. Unfortunately, she often ruined it with her impulsive, presumptuous inclinations. As soon as she outgrew that, there'd be no one in all of England who could stand in her way. But Lady Viece was still young, altruistic, and untouched by the realities that had so cruelly zapped his own zeal as a young man.

"You can't blame Lady Viece for trying," Terry said softly.

Brighton glanced over at the younger man. Terry was another altruistic fool with loads of potential. "Why do you think I continue working with her?" he smiled paternally.

"Are you? I thought you cut her off."

"Bah! Idle threat in the hopes she'll see reason."

Terry rolled his eyes. "Oh come on. Would you have seen reason as a young man? If you were in her position?"

Brighton smiled broader. "No, I suppose I wouldn't have." He chuckled, shaking his head. "In my younger years, I was a pistol. I'd plow right into the fray, alone if I had to, guns a'blazing . . . ." The smile slid right off his face. *Ugh, damn it.* Brighton snatched up his raincoat and barked orders for Terry to rally the remaining constables in the precinct.

The gun clicked, but did not fire. Of course it didn't fire. It was pouring rain. But that hadn't stopped Isabelle's heart from leaping into her throat, nor the pitiful yelp that escaped her lips.

Cleaver grimaced. "Get out your blades boys," he said as he replaced his gun with that wicked mallet, the edge glinting with malice in the lamp light. "I call her Cleavage," he said proudly.

Swallowing and shaking on her knees, Isabelle recalled what the crassly-named mallet had done to Professor Brass, and wasn't keen on meeting her personally. "I haven't introduced myself have I," she said quickly. "Lady Isabelle Viece, heir to the Viece fortune."

"Are you now?" Cleaver said, raising Cleavage above his head.

"Cleaver, wait," said Gauge, but Cleaver wasn't listening. He held Cleavage in a firm, practiced grip and was a split second away from letting her fall.

At that moment, the circus performers, an entire group of muscled clowns, ripped acrobats, tough beast-tamers, buff jugglers, brawny comedians, and the Beardless Man, came slopping through the mud just across the way. The troupe stopped and stared in quiet confusion at the welders—who were dressed as constables.

The welders stared back at the troupe, motionless.

Standing at the head of the group was none other than Jasper Crimson himself, his sister standing beside him, drenched, holding a moth-eaten and perforated parasol open over her shoulder.

The welders blinked at the Crimsons.

The Crimsons shared a glance between them.

"Lady Viece!" a lone voice yelled from the back of the troupe. The entire troupe turned toward him, and Isabelle could barely make out a scrawny clown standing amongst all the meat. "That's Lady Isabelle Viece," he said uncomfortably. "We have to help her!"

"Say, ain't that one fellow Jasper Crimson?" Gauge asked. "The maggot what stole our lunchbox?"

"Alex!" Isabelle shrieked back, banishing propriety for the sake of time. All her thoughts came out in a jumbled heap. "The constables are the welders the real constables are in the cage get the constables attack the constables!"

Moment of silence.

"GET EM LADS!" yelled the ringmaster . . . and then all hell broke loose.

The Crimsons were the first to act, making a run for it. As soon as they took off, the welders launched their pursuit, but not before the troupe intercepted them—there were at least ten of them—and a chaotic brawl ensued. Clowns delivered roundhouse punches to constables who were not really constables, who tried to subdue the Crimsons, who quickly wound up at the bottom of a dog pile of flailing limbs.

Isabelle scrambled away from the mess as Constable Corbin hurried over to her.

"Lady Viece," he cried. "Are you alright? W–w–what in God's good name is going on here?"

"I'll explain later. We need to get the constables out." A clown, punched in the face by a welder stumbled into her, knocking her over.

Another clown shoved a welder in Constable Corbin's direction, and that welder threw a punch that landed Corbin on the ground right next to her.

A clown suddenly flew right over their heads and crashed into the cage holding the real constables captive. The wooden panels on the side split. The clown was out cold, but the constables began squirming in their bindings out of the hole he created. One by one, they plopped on the muddy ground. Isabelle crawled over to them, removing the gag on a familiar face.

No sooner was his gag removed than Brooks let out a curse so impressive it has been censored from this book as Isabelle untied his wrists and ankles.

"Free the others. They—" She shrieked as someone grabbed her leg and dragged her through the mud. Not toward the fight though. She struggled as the man grabbed a fist full of her hair and yanked her to her feet. A second welder was there an instant later and next thing she knew, she was hauled away like a sack of grain, her legs kicking rifts in the mud, her screams drowned out by the brawlers' yells and the pattering rain.

Brooks tried to rush to her aid, but was quickly yanked into the scuffle. Corbin was next to try to run after her, but he too was swallowed up into the fight.

The welders—Strangler and Smithy—dragged her a short distance away until a crisp voice broke the pandemonium.

"Everyone freeze!"

Strangler and Smithy stopped, giving Isabelle a chance to awkwardly look over her shoulder and see a new force of constables, led by Chief Brighton, approaching with truncheons.

A wave of relief washed over her. But the fray did not stop.

"I said freeze, you glocks! By the authority of the Queen!"

At mention of royalty, everyone suddenly stopped what they were doing, still clutching fists full of hair or shirt, frozen in mid body slam, paused in chokeholds. All went silent and Chief Brighton didn't seem to know how to proceed.

"More imposters!" someone yelled.

Oh no.

Chapter 15

The circus troupe drew the new group of constables into the fight. Unfortunately, Chief Brighton's men didn't know about the uniform switch. They fought off the troupe's onslaught while also trying to arrest the real constables.

Before Isabelle could determine anything more, her captors resumed dragging her away. For once, she didn't need to swallow any pride to scream for help. "Chief Brighton!" she shrieked at the top of her lungs. The seasoned soldier turned but did not catch sight of her before a burly juggler came at him with a pair of club-like objects he juggled with.

No! She thought as she continued struggling in her captors' relentless grip. But Brighton held his own against the juggler, knocking him to the ground. Seeing that he was clearly faring better than she, Isabelle turned her attention back to her situation.

Suddenly, one of them released her and dropped to the ground. With an arm now free, she instinctively turned and slapped the other across the face. Someone else tackled him from behind.

Constable Corbin, hitting him over the head repeatedly with another one of those juggling batons. "Run Lady Viece!" he said as he clonked away. "Get out of here! I'll keep them busy!"

A quick assessment of the fight was all she needed. A brawl was definitely not her arena. That meant run. Feeling like a complete coward, she ran for all she was worth.

Alex screamed as Strangler stomped on his leg, breaking bone. Pain seared through his shin like a lightning bolt. He gasped, eyes bulging in fear as Strangler pulled out a leather cord from his pocket and moved to wrap it around Alex's neck.

"Leave him!" yelled Smithy. "After the girl!" Smithy took off running after Lady Viece, somewhat hindered by that strange metal contraption on his back. With a curse, Strangler left Alex where he was and bolted after his companion. Hopefully Alex had bought Lady Viece enough time to get away.

As they chased after her in that soaked, mud-laden dress, he knew immediately they'd catch her. He needed to get her some help. But the pain in his leg was almost unbearable.

Courage Alex! He screamed at himself, tears mixing with rain down his cheeks. Teeth gritted against the pain, he began dragging himself back to the fray, where he hoped to find a friendly face he could send after Lady Viece.

Chief Brighton could only shake his head as the largest arms he'd ever seen cracked knuckles in front of him. *Bloody hell!* Wasn't he done with this sort of crap? Why get promoted to an old man position if you still had to get your hands dirty? Still, it had been a long time since he'd been in a good scuffle. The behemoth lunged forward, thankfully. That allowed the more experienced Brighton to simply step aside and smack the acrobat across the face with his truncheon. The fool actually laughed and complimented Brighton on a good swing "for an old man." Idiot. Brighton laid his knee into the fellow's gut, then clonked him over the head. He dropped.

Turning to smack another clown, he stumbled as he noticed a soaking wet child in a tattered skirt, covered in mud, standing atop one of the cage wagons. She waved her arms and several circus performers grabbed constables and tossed them into the cage. The girl closed the cage door and secured the latch, locking it tight.

What the . . . .

Chief Brighton fought his way out of another clown's hold from behind only to see a couple more of his men tossed into wagon cages and locked up. An acrobat shoved another constable into a crate, somehow stuffing the man into its cramped confines, then sitting on its lid with his arms crossed.

With his force dwindling, Brighton gritted his teeth. What a god-awful mess this was going to be to explain to the magistrate. Something drastic was in order.

"Constable Terry!" he barked, catching sight of the young man who was proving his merit in the fight. The constable whacked his assailant in the face with his truncheon laid into the man's gut with his knee, then clonked him over the head. Out cold. It was the same move Brighton had just used. Good man.

"Nicely done! Send word to Lord Garnet. We need reinforcements."

Constable Terry nodded and ran off just as yet another clown came gunning for Brighton. Brighton laid a fist into the clown's face, smashing his red ball nose. With that, he hurried away from the brawl and tried to round one of the cage wagons where three of his men were trapped. Undoing the latch, he barked orders at them to follow him in formation. It was almost a good formation. He was proud of them.

Around the cage wagon and toward the one he had seen the little girl standing on, he led his small force into a flanking ambush. The girl leapt onto another wagon and beckoned the clowns to throw some more constables in.

Scarlet Crimson, Brighton thought. Which meant the brother was here too. Great. He nodded to his men to flank the cage wagon. Sneaking up beside the cage, Brighton reached up and quickly grabbed the girl's foot. She yelped as Brighton yanked her off the wagon and she plopped into the mud like a caught fish. His three-man force was there a second later to subdue her.

Well, at least to *try* to subdue her. No one had ever come close to catching one of the Crimsons and Brighton now understood firsthand why. The girl didn't struggle the way every other apprehended criminal would. Instead, while lying on her back, she threw mud in one of the constable's faces, kicked the legs out from underneath the second, rolled backwards and onto her feet quicker than humanly possible, and then slid one leg toward Brighton, doing the splits.

Scarlet's split put one leg between Brighton's and the other behind her as the last constable stepped forward to grab her. The girl twisted expertly on the ground, swiping the legs of both Brighton and his last constable, using the slippery muddy terrain to her advantage.

Clever, Brighton thought as he lost his balance, the other constable falling to his hands and knees right behind him. Scarlet placed her tiny hands on Brighton's chest and pushed. She had nothing close to physical strength, so this shouldn't have worked, but she had positioned Brighton and his fellow constable rather perfectly. Her push was just enough to send the already unstable Brighton careening over the back of the tripped constable behind him. And just like that, four men, bested by a child.

Scarlet didn't seem hindered by the mud at all as she bolted away no differently than if the ground were rock. The first two men she'd discombobulated were already after her, though they slipped multiple times along the way, and Brighton and his third constable were off seconds later.

"Don't let her get away boys," Brighton yelled. "And don't tell anyone about this," he added softly.

The two constables in the front, Brooks and Rivers, didn't get far before a brick wall of a man barreled into them from the side. They both splatted into the mud. The fellow who had tackled them wore a constable's uniform.

"What the hell?" Brighton breathed as he and his last man, Constable Heller, picked up their pace to help their fallen comrades.

Out of the corner of his eye, Brighton caught sight of something shiny hurdling toward him. He dove to the ground, and the knife soared right past where his chest was moments before. As he climbed back to his feet, another constable was upon him.

" 'ello Chiefy," the fellow said as he swung his baton right into Brighton's face. The flash of pain and momentary blindness forced

Brighton to stumble back, but he'd been hit in the face enough times not to lament the loss of beauty. He turned the momentum to his favor, spinning with the force of the hit, and raising his own truncheon for a counterstrike, which landed on the other man's upper arm. He cried out even as he swung at Brighton's face again. This time, Brighton ducked the blow. But not the unexpected knee to his gut. Brighton dropped to one knee, gasping.

"Proud of yourself, Chiefy?" He kicked Brighton across the nose, sending him sprawling in the mud.

Chiefy. Steve the Welder then. How had the man acquired a constable uniform?

"Came to help that Viece woman, yeah? Cause she pays your salary and whatnot. I understand. You got mouths to feed." Steve whacked him again with the baton.

Brighton took the blow as best he could, and swiped at Steve's legs. Steve landed on his bum and Brighton staggered to his feet, holding nose and stomach. He'd dropped his truncheon. If he had been ten years younger, he would've gotten a rush out of fighting this idiot by himself. But he'd learned a long time ago not to waste energy on such prideful pursuits. Instead, he made a run for the pavilion, where his reinforcements had just chased the Crimson girl.

Isabelle ran for her life, swearing this would be the last time she wore a dress. The welders were on her heels. Not knowing, or caring, where she was going, she had somehow managed to wind up in the circus proper. The main pavilion dominated the darkness just before her.

To her left, another group of constables chased a man in a long black coat. Isabelle could only assume that was the silhouette of Jasper Crimson. He deftly threw himself to the ground, sliding feet first the rest of the distance toward the pavilion, and slipping in under the bottom of the tent. The constables arrived seconds later, but had trouble getting inside, so they headed for the main entrance.

The first excuse for something that could possibly pass as some semblance of a "plan" since Isabelle's original one failed blossomed in her frantic mind. She couldn't fight the welders. But the Crimsons could. With the welders currently masquerading as constables, that made the Crimsons temporary allies. She hoped.

Isabelle ducked into the pavilion's front entrance, momentarily confused. It looked completely different. The center stage looked ready for a magic show, with all manner of strange contraptions and bright colors. Wooden benches lined three quarters of the vaulted tent, while a bright red curtain hung just behind the stage, hiding that section of the pavilion from public eye. Another opaque wine-colored sheet draped directly over the center benches, like the ceiling of a gypsy camp.

The constables gathered on the other side, near the stage, truncheons at the ready. A second, smaller group of constables stood on the opposite side of the stage. Panting at the entrance, Isabelle glanced from one group of constables to the other, trying to decipher the situation.

Moments later, Brighton came stumbling in beside the smaller group of constables. He looked somewhat worse for wear, darting his eyes around in confusion too. Despite the multitude gathered, an eerie quiet pervaded the dimly lit pavilion, broken only by the heavy rain pelting the tent outside. Right in the middle of the room, just in front of the stage, Crimson skidded to a halt, looking about him, realizing he was surrounded.

Suddenly, a spotlight highlighted the center of the stage drawing everyone's attention. Throughout the pavilion, a creepy, girlish giggle haunted them from all directions. All the constables and welders shuffled, glancing around, subconsciously huddling together.

Jasper Crimson smiled.

Oh no.

Chapter 16

COURT PLOWS FORWARD WITH PAPER-THIN CASE AGAINST VIECE FAMILY

DESPITE INCREASINGLY CONSPICUOUS LACK OF EVIDENCE AND IMPRESSIVE DEFENSE, LORD AND LADY VIECE ARE CALLED TO TRIAL IN LONDON, SEEDING SPECULATION OF DEEPER MACHINATIONS, AND BLOSSOMING INTO A GROVE OF CONSPIRACY THEORIES.

Jasper Crimson's sly smile was all anyone needed to get moving.

Isabelle bolted toward him just as Smithy and Strangler barged into the tent behind her.

The constables that had chased Crimson into the pavilion lunged at him, reaching him before Isabelle made it across the tent. Crimson leapt toward the nearest pillar holding up the tent and within seconds had scaled it all the way to the top. Isabelle passed the pillar, craning her neck to see what Crimson was up to, but Smithy and Strangler were upon her.

Crimson's shadow appeared up on a ledge attached to one of the poles keeping the tent up. He cut the fabric draped over the benches, grabbed a fist full of it, and swung down toward the constables.

Strangler and Smithy reached for Isabelle.

A split-second decision saw Isabelle dive in the way of the fabric just as Crimson careened past. Part of the fabric was still attached to another pole, so Crimson managed to pull the fabric over Isabelle and the group of constables like a blanket, encompassing them. Isabelle let the momentum take her as it willed, sweeping her into the fabric's fold and depositing her on the stage. Crimson released the corner as he soared over the stage, flailing wildly with a yelp. He landed on the stage on his feet and immediately ducked into a roll to absorb the impact.

Wide-eyed and disoriented, Isabelle scrambled to her feet, looking for Smithy and Strangler in the heap of constables, who struggled to unravel themselves from the fabric. The welders weren't there. She darted a look over to Crimson, who blew sparkly dust off his hand into the face of the single constable who had escaped the fabric. The dust enveloped the entirety of the poor fellow and when it cleared, he was gone. Simply gone.

Of all the emotions galvanizing Isabelle in that moment, envy surprised her. He was so capable, easily besting everyone who approached him, and there Isabelle was cowardly hiding in his shadow.

Someone pounced on her from behind. With a yelp, she struggled in the broad, powerful arms. Desperate, Isabelle chomped her teeth into her assailant's arm. He cried out and fortunately let go, dropping Isabelle like a rag doll onto the hardwood stage. She tried to scramble away, toward Crimson, but Strangler grabbed a fistful of her hair and yanked her backward. She hit the stage again with a grunt. Wearing a wicked sneer, Strangler dramatically pulled out a thin cord from his pocket.

Brighton rolled his eyes as that Crimson git somehow launched one of his officers into the air, leaving the man bouncing up and down like a yoyo from an unseen cord.

Great. A funhouse. The perfect playground for the Crimsons. This was not going to end well.

With a resigned sigh, he rallied his men. "Brooks, Rivers, with me."

"The Crimson girl went behind the stage sir," said Brooks.

"We'll get her later. Steve is—" As if on call, Steve burst into the tent, knife in hand. He sneered at Brighton, but a quick glance to his right diverted his attention. Brighton looked too. Another welder dressed as one of his constables. Only, he looked just like Steve. He *was* Steve. Or at least, a porcelain doll version of him. It was a mirror image, with blacked out eyes and porcelain skin.

Brighton, Brooks, Rivers, and Steve stood gaping at the mirror image, blood drained from their faces. Scarlet Crimson appeared beside the mirror image a moment later, a porcelain doll herself, though the real her was no where to be found. It was as if she lived inside this strange mirror. Her face cracked, one eye socket empty, half her hair pulled free, exposing a ceramic skull. She quirked her head and giggled, pulling out a knife and stabbing Steve's porcelain doppelgänger. He . . . shattered.

Steve—the real Steve—shrieked in horror, and got the heck out of the cursed pavilion. Brighton had half a mind to follow.

Where the mirror had been, the real Scarlet Crimson now stood. She giggled, then darted up onto the stage.

Brighton shook himself. "After her!"

He and his two remaining constables, still shaken by the mirror illusion, chased Scarlet Crimson up onto the stage, where she dropped to her knees, and slid right under the fabric. Rivers arrived first and plowed head first into the fabric, which had somehow become hard as a stone wall. Dropping to the ground, Rivers was out for the count.

"Sir!" cried Brooks, pointing. Brighton turned to see Jasper Crimson himself, wreaking havoc among Brighton's constables.

"But I haven't gotten to strangle anyone yet, it's my turn!" Strangler had the cord wrapped around Isabelle's throat, but Smithy had started barking orders at him to hold her in place instead of strangling her. Apparently, he wanted to burn the flesh off her bones first.

"I know, and I'll let you have your turn. I just want to give my old girl a breather." He tapped that wicked contraption on his back. Isabelle threw her head backward, right into Strangler's mouth. Even as he dropped her to the ground, she could hear Smithy chastise him for sloppiness.

Hoping their argument would last, Isabelle tried to scramble away. She could get out of this. She just needed a plan. Crimson leveraged everything in his general vicinity, smoothly using his environment to his advantage. Perhaps Isabelle could too.

"Here, let me show you," Smithy said. Then kicked Isabelle in the stomach. She'd never been hit in the stomach before. The awful feeling caught her unaware, and she gasped as much out of shock as from having the wind knocked out of her. She had to do something. This man would kill her. *Do something!*

Her satchel! She had—

Smithy grabbed a fistful of her hair and jerked her head up, hauling her upright. "See if you hold up her head like this, it opens the throat up and you get a nice clear view of the vocal cords where you're going to strangle her."

"I know how to strangle people! Stop telling me how to do my job!" Strangler tried to take over where Smithy's hand held Isabelle's hair. Unable to breath, she wasn't sure how she pushed out a scream. She frantically looked around for options.

Smithy threw her to the ground. She landed on her hands and knees, coughing, gasping for breath.

"Look I'm just trying to help," Smithy said to the chagrined Strangler. He stepped his boot on Isabelle's back, pressing her in place. "If you want to be a proper criminal, you gotta learn to take advice. Real criminals take advice!"

Use . . . your . . . surroundings!

"I am already a proper criminal!"

"You've never even strangled a goat!"

There!

"Why the hell would I strangle a goat?"

Right in front of her was a lever.

"All right, you know what? Fine. Here, take the wench and practice your strangling. I won't say nothing. You wanna look like a bloody fool? Be my guest."

Subtle, easy to miss if you weren't looking for it, but it looked robust enough to at the very least do something that might cause a distraction.

Smithy lifted his boot, allowing Strangler to step in, but not before she took that split second of freedom to yank the lever.

Jasper Crimson flicked a card into the face of one of Brighton's men. And another. And another. The rapid succession of cards was an impressive sight to behold by itself. But it didn't stop there. Each card stuck to the unfortunate constable, one after the other until he was completely covered, unable to see. The constable flailed his arms in a panic as the cards molded together and somehow started to flatten.

Brighton gaped as the constable stopped moving, and became simply an image on a man-sized card.

How in damnation?!

Jasper danced around a truncheon swing from another constable, using his momentum to push the constable into the red curtain hanging behind. Helplessly tangled up, the constable tried to regain his balance. Brighton rushed to help, but Scarlet reached her arms under the fabric and yanked at the constable's ankles. Before Brighton could get there, the constable fell to his knees, and Jasper kicked him into the fabric again. This time, he *sank* into the fabric as if it were liquid and vanished.

All right, that's enough. With a scowl, Brighton motioned for Brooks to back him up in a rush maneuver. Brighton would hold Jasper's attention, while Brooks took him down.

Jasper, of course, had other plans. Instead of facing Brighton, the thief ran to the center of the stage and leapt up onto a box. Well, *into* the box. He laid down inside, closed the lid, and the box collapsed flat as soon as Brighton arrived. Confused, Brighton stepped on the flat plank, sharing a look with Brooks. Suddenly, Brooks sank into the stage like quick sand, until he was waist deep in wood. He twisted and struggled but could not move. "Oh for the love of God!" Brighton howled.

Someone tapped his shoulder. He turned around, and looked down.

Scarlet Crimson grinned as she blew some kind of powder into Brighton's face. Brighton stumbled back, blinded and sneezing, right into an upright box. Scarlet closed the door and all went dark. Except for a hole at the top. Brighton lurched forward as the box crashed down. Now lying on his back, he groaned. Too old for this indeed.

Struggling toward the hole at the top of the box, Brighton managed to poke his head out and look around. Scarlet stood there looking at him, her head tilted to the side mischievously, making her appear even more childlike. Brighton's eyes widened in horror as this crazy little girl lifted a saw over her shoulder and giggled.

The lever released something from the ceiling. A flat piece of midnight fabric pulled tight in a vertical rectangle frame swung down, right toward Isabelle. She dropped flat to the ground, watching the fabric swing above her and whack Smithy head on. Only it didn't *smack* as expected. It *enveloped* him, and in a split second it had passed.

Confused, Smithy glanced at Strangler, who had grown pale, running his wide eyes across the length of his friend. Smithy looked down and screamed. He was covered in little black spiders. He flailed about wildly and took off running, diving right into the side of the tent, tearing his own outline in the fabric as he ran out into the rain.

Isabelle took the opportunity to run away, but Strangler was on her in an instant, yanking her dress and wrestling her to the ground again. She lay on her stomach, Strangler breathing right next to her ear.

"You're clever, I'll give you that," he sneered. "Lucky for you Smithy's terrified of spiders." He sat on her back, but left her arms free. "Now maybe I can actually practice my strangling in peace."

Rather than futilely struggle against Strangler, Isabelle pounded at the planks, hoping to land on a button or something that would trigger another ridiculous magic trick.

Strangler wrapped his cord around her neck from behind.

"How long do you think it'll take before you pass out?" He began to pull it tight. Isabelle's eyes began to bulge as her air cut off, but just before it did, she caught sight of an X mark in the plank next to her.

Desperate, Isabelle slapped the ground near the X. Then again, closer. Then finally managed to slap the X itself, which pressed into the floor like a button. She slapped it again, harder, making it press into the floor completely, just as her vision began to go dark.

The floor gave way beneath her, dropping her and Strangler into a pit of darkness.

Cleaver stared in disbelief as the Constable Chief was sawed in half by the Crimson brat. He just got here, and was already pissed. It was absolute madness! He still wasn't entirely sure why they were all fighting each other, but frankly he didn't care. He spotted Jasper Crimson up on stage and beelined for him, forgetting about Viece, hoping his men could handle themselves in this mess, and determined to secure his budding reputation.

Jasper had the lunchbox. And today, Jasper would meet his match.

Courage, you useless coward! Alex yelled to himself, as he crawled toward a cage wagon. He leaned against the wheel, gasping for breath. The pain in his leg was nearly blinding, and it wasn't useable. Despite the pain, the cold, his misery, and his fear, he continued to lug himself through the mud. Inch by inch, he crawled, drawing closer to the sounds of men acting like baboons. So close. Just a little further.

C–c–courage. Please, God, give me courage.

Suddenly, someone grabbed him from behind and hauled him to his feet. He shrieked. His assailant thrust him forward and he came face to face with Lord Morgan Garnet himself. A fellow standing just beside him moved toward Alex. He held a bat in his hand.

Alex panicked. "AH! NO! LORD GARNET SIR! I'M A CONSTABLE SIR! PLEASE DON'T HURT ME!"

Lord Garnet motioned for the thug to lower his bat. "A constable? Last I checked, your uniforms were far more professional, though I dare say the clown outfit is more fitting."

His thugs chuckled.

"Really. I am, sir. Please believe me!"

"Then tell me, constable. What on earth is going on here?"

It all came out in a hysterical jumble. "The welders are the constables and the constables are the welders and Lady Viece was taken by the welders who was dressed as constables but they're really welders and I fought these two welders dressed as constables what tried to off Lady Viece and one of them broke my leg and now they're after Lady Viece again and–and–and–and they're going to kill her and you have to help her!"

Lord Garnet blinked. "I'm fairly certain that was English."

His men chuckled again.

"She's really in danger! You gotta help her Lord Garnet sir! Please! They're going to kill her!"

"Slow down, you fool! Who is going to kill who?"

"The welders, dressed as constables, are going to kill Lady Viece."

Garnet looked . . . confused. Alex would've expected alarm. Instead, Garnet suddenly rolled his eyes and sucked in an annoyed breath. "Where is she?"

"They went toward the circus proper. The pavilion I think."

Garnet began barking orders at his men. The man who held him upright suddenly let go, crumpling Alex to the muddy ground like the worthless sack of moldy potatoes he was.

Wincing, Alex glared at the man through teary eyes and . . . recognized him. Gauge? Panicked, Alex screamed for help. Garnet turned back toward him with an irritated glare.

"What is it now?"

Alex said . . . Alex said . . . he said. Nothing. Because on second thought he didn't want to die here, and Gauge didn't know Alex was on to him. Better if he revealed this to Lord Garnet at a time when Gauge was not standing right next to him.

"Nothing, sir," Alex said instead.

Lord Garnet rolled his eyes. "Stay put and out of the way, constable." With that, he rushed off, followed by his entourage, Gauge included, leaving Alex right where he was, dismissing his entire existence. Typical.

Isabelle luckily dropped onto a cushion. Strangler bounced off to the side, giving her the chance to scramble to her feet, gasping for air and rubbing at her neck where the cord choked her moments before. She was in some sort of underground staging area with a variety of wooden supports and beams, presumably for the various circus acts and magic tricks.

A short distance away, Strangler stood up as well.

In the dim lighting, Isabelle wasn't sure how to get out, but she staggered away anyway. She didn't get far before Strangler seized her from behind, ramming her into a steel support column with crisscrossing bars forming an X pattern all the way up to the ceiling. She struggled and screamed, trying to escape him, but she was so tired. And clearly outmatched in multiple ways.

But still, she continued to fight on, refusing to concede defeat. That is until Strangler wrapped a rough chain around her neck.

Eyes bulging, she slowly lifted off the ground, barely scraping the floor with the tips of her toes. Isabelle's panic reached another level as she quickly ran out of air, but this time, her vision began to blur immediately.

So this is what it was like to be hanged.

Cleaver rushed up the stairs to the stage and faced Jasper, who took out the only other man standing in the pavilion. A constable, so Cleaver didn't care.

"Jasper Crimson," Cleaver called, holding up Cleavage threateningly. He braced himself for a fight as Jasper turned around and darted directly toward Cleaver. A direct fight. Just the way Cleaver liked it, though he hadn't expected it from the otherwise elusive thief.

Still, Cleaver raised his mallet to swing it at the thief, except why was Jasper coming at him so fast? Without a weapon. He was only about fifteen feet away, and yet was closing the distance at a sprint. What the—

As soon as Jasper was within fighting distance of Cleaver, the man jumped into the air, feet before him, grabbed a lever in the stage about waist-high, and let his momentum pull it.

The stage floor gave way beneath Cleaver's muddy boots right as Jasper landed on his side. The two men fell into darkness below.

Isabelle clawed at the chain around her neck. Then at the X patterned support beam in front of her. She managed to grab hold of a beam, and pulled herself toward it, trying to use it to climb out of her makeshift noose.

But Strangler had other ideas. He kicked at her legs, knocking her foothold free after she managed barely one gasp of air. Dangling again, swinging back and forth, her vision began to darken. A crash pulled her attention briefly to the side, where Cleaver landed in a heap on the black padding, followed immediately by Jasper Crimson. She wasn't sure why, but reached a desperate hand toward him.

Cleaver lost his mallet when he hit some sort of padding at the bottom of the hole. Jasper landed right next to him with a grunt, but scrambled to his feet much quicker, immediately adapting to the surroundings. Or rather not seeming to care about his surroundings. With a flustered growl, Cleaver reached for Jasper's legs, but Jasper flipped over his outstretched arm, snatched the edge of the top sheet of the padding, and rolled Cleaver's arm in it, pinning the arm in place with his knee. It was all one, fluid motion for Jasper, as though he'd rehearsed it a million times.

With his free arm, Cleaver reached for his mallet a few feet away. But Jasper angled himself to dodge the incoming swing, moving so quickly, Cleaver was sluggish by comparison. Jasper caught Cleaver's arm mid swing in the other side of the padding, then wrapped the mallet and Cleaver's arm in yet another all-too-smooth motion.

Before Cleaver could even grow angry, Jasper laid the embarrassing onslaught on even thicker, by twisting the padding, forcing Cleaver to roll onto his back so as not to break his arms. But that was what Jasper intended.

Next thing he knew, Jasper had him completely rolled up like a swaddled baby. Struggling and writhing and otherwise throwing a big hissy fit, Cleaver howled in frustration. "Fight me like a man, you thieving glock!"

But Jasper had already moved his attention elsewhere. He pulled out the strange mousetrap invention that looked like an unusually fat-barreled pistol, without a proper hand grip. The weapon. Cleaver's weapon. He pointed it directly at Strangler.

Isabelle's mind started counting the seconds to her own death. She figured she had five seconds left before she passed out.

Four seconds.

Her eyelids began to flutter closed, and her outstretched hand futilely reaching for Crimson fell limp at her side.

Three seconds.

With a foot up on Cleaver's stomach, Crimson pointed some sort of contraption that vaguely resembled a pistol at Strangler's face. Strangler's eyes went wide.

Two.

Crimson pulled the trigger.

One.

The last thing Isabelle remembered before blacking out was a blinding flash, deafening explosion, a startled yelp from Jasper Crimson, and a scream of horror from Cleaver.

Chapter 17

THE CRIMSON RUN: ARTICLE 67
A HEIST OF SMOKE AND MIRRORS

IN A MAGIC TWIST OF FATE, THE CRIMSONS DEAL YET ANOTHER
HEAVY BLOW TO THE FLOUNDERING CONSTABULARY WITH CUNNING,
CHARM, AND A CHEEKY ALAKAZAM!

Oh but they were hardly done yet, today's Crimson Run article read. Isabelle wasn't sure why she was subjecting herself to this torture, but she read on anyway.

No, on the contrary, the fun had only just begun for our dastardly pair. It was to be their finest show yet. They would stage a magic show like nothing the world has ever seen.

"And now, a volunteer from the audience to aid me in performing my next daring and incredible act," declared the winsome Jasper.

"Come my dear friends. There is no need to be bashful. Surely you are not so shy as to decline the opportunity to shine in the spotlight! I would be remiss not to provide my audience

with a spectacle extraordinaire, and you my friend, you are the star!"

Angered by his goading words, the constables brashly accosted Jasper Crimson, falling right into his ingenious trap. Jasper stood center stage, a spotlight illuminating his imposing, handsome figure, even as the constables approached, and with a sharp snap of his deft larcenist fingers, disappeared in a swirling cloud of luminescent smoke.

Luminescent smoke? Hah! The Crow really didn't need to embellish. The actuality had been quite thoroughly embarrassing enough. But such was the way of the Crimson articles. Adjusting the pillows supporting her back, she reached for the cord dangling beside her luxurious bed to request breakfast, and winced.

Her whole body felt like she'd been trampled beneath a horse and coach. She reached again for the cord, yanked it quickly, then dropped back down, huffing.

Even as Jasper Crimson mysteriously disappeared, the intrepid Scarlet Crimson had not concluded her mischievous act. Swinging from the trapeze overhead in a graceful arc, she held a harness in her arms and frowned in sorrow. "Would that I only had one so brave as to perform this high-flying act with me."

Isabelle chuckled mirthlessly. Scarlet had barely been visible through the entire event, let alone was swinging from overhead.

Spotting a lady in the audience, Scarlet smiled in delight, swinging down from her perch and latching the harness onto her newfound performance partner. The lady rose high with Scarlet but she was unhappy, for the lady screamed and thrashed in terror. No, this would not do for a performance partner. The lady, as it were, was none other than Isabelle Viece.

. . . What?

Lady Isabelle Viece endeavored to catch the siblings yet again, and yet again to no avail. Scarlet Crimson could not very well continue to use Lady Viece as her trapeze partner and so, with a heavy heart, Scarlet descended to the stage floor, leaving Lady Viece dangling precariously from the—

Crumpling the newspaper into a wad, Isabelle threw it across the room at her double doors just as Akane entered with her breakfast. With a yelp, the poor maid staggered out of the way, dropping her tray of breakfast and splattering its contents all over the carpet.

"Oh, I am very sorry, Lady Viece," Akane exclaimed. "Oh do forgive me. I—"

"No, it's quite all right, Akane," Isabelle said hoarsely, struggling to get the words out. "The fault is mine. Please forgive me." As Akane set herself to cleaning up the broken china, eggs, muffin, and tea, Isabelle fumed. Akane left saying something about retrieving more but Isabelle heard none of it.

She sat back in her bed, comfortable in her night gown, and sighed, running her hands over her face, then wincing as she touched her wounds. She had woken up in her bed, bandages covering wounds she did not remember suffering. With every movement, she discovered a new bruise, scrape or sore spot. The bandage she'd discovered around her neck had frightened her most. That memory was branded into her skull for life. She couldn't speak very well, and breathing was difficult, but she had not yet seen the extent of the damage.

Shivering, she forced her thoughts away from that rusty, cold noose as Akane brought in her second round of breakfast. It wasn't long after that her father came in to check on her. He didn't say anything. Just sat on her bedside and stared at nothing. He looked stressed, worn out. Understandable, given Isabelle's close brush with death.

"Father . . . ."

"How are you feeling?"

Isabelle swallowed. She'd never seen her father like this before, so distant, eerily calm. "It's not what it appears, Father."

"Isn't it?"

Once again taken aback by the strangeness in Father's voice, Isabelle narrowed her eyes. "I am well, Father. It's merely a few scratches."

"And your neck? Is that merely a scratch?"

Silence would have been prudent. "You mustn't make of it more than it is, Father. It—"

"I mustn't make more of my daughter nearly being hanged? I mustn't fret over my daughter nearly being taken from me?" He looked at her then, fire in his eyes, and also something deeper Isabelle couldn't put her finger on. Something dangerous that frankly frightened Isabelle to her core.

"You have taken this much too far, Isabelle. This," he gestured toward her neck, "could. Have. Been. Your. Death. I forbid you from ever involving yourself in another case. You will obey, and you will assume your rightful place in my household. And you will thank Lord Garnet for his selflessness."

"I—Lord Garnet?" Isabelle asked hoarsely.

"Yes. He saved your life and brought you home safely last night. In this frightful state, to my everlasting horror. You will make your gratitude known to him at your earliest convenience." He stood up.

"Lord Garnet did not rescue me," Isabelle whispered.

"Oh? You rescued yourself then? It was you who carried your unconscious form home in the dead of night?"

"Jasper Crimson saved me." Even as she said it, she could hardly believe it, but that was her final memory before blacking out. Whatever manner of weapon Crimson had shot Strangler with had knocked Isabelle unconscious, and so the welder must be dead. There was no other explanation: Jasper Crimson had saved her life.

But Father was clearly not convinced as he barked a mirthless laugh. "Is that all you have to say? Crimson, the unsavory miscreant, who cares nothing for anyone save himself, *rescued* you? You'd rather believe *that* than Lord Garnet, corroborated by the papers this very morning, found you and brought you home as a responsible gentleman would? Wake up to reality, girl!

"The constables are completely incapacitated, and may indeed never recover from your reckless idiocy. Chief Brighton was sawed in half, God only knows when he'll be back at his post, the circus has closed down permanently after being deemed unsafe to proceed, which means dozens of good men are now out of work. And you humiliated Lord Garnet, casted unfounded aspersions at his reputation, and brought further humiliation upon your own household.

"Don't even try to assuage your guilt by laying blame on the Crimsons. Again. Clearly you suffered a terrible hit to your head, and are feeling remarkably unwell. Now rest and recover from your traumas. Unfortunately, you will be required to attend a university opening ceremony and banquet tomorrow evening. Your mother and I must journey to London, so you will be the soul Viece representative. I *expect* you to do your duty well. You may express your gratitude to Lord Garnet then."

"But—"

"I demand it!" Father roared, rising to his feet and looming over her with all the authority of his station, and all the intimidation of a father. "Until then, you are not to move from that bed or so help me—" He fumed for a moment, licking his lips—"I'll kill you myself." He let his words hang in the air a moment, breathing heavily.

Isabelle swallowed, unable to avert from eyes from her father's livid face.

"Am I clear?" he asked quietly.

Isabelle nodded immediately.

"Good. I'm pleased you're safe." With that, he composed himself, strode to the door and left without looking back at his daughter.

A part of Isabelle was shaken at her father's unusual outburst. He was under a lot of pressure right now, managing these ridiculous accusations against their house, but still. She had survived, and her injuries were perfectly healable. Her father's worry was understandable but . . . but . . . . She sighed. They were perfectly legitimate. Father was right, and she knew it.

A hoarse scream escaped her ruined throat and she threw a pillow across the room. Not satisfying. She snatched her glass of water and hurled that, shattering it on the far wall. Much better. "Is there anything else," Isabelle yelled hoarsely into the air, "that could possibly make this quagmire worse? Come on then. Let's have it already!"

She still had no evidence to move her case forward, she was now officially in the thick of something she could not—would not—back out of, her backup and support in the constables vaporized, relegated to bed rest, and a decidedly irate father. If thanking Lord Garnet for his "chivalry" was the worst of her punishment, she could certainly endure it, but she would not give in to that man's games. She had two days of bed rest ahead of her. Plenty of time to figure out how to put him behind bars.

The problem was that she was now alone.

Unbidden, she found herself gently touching her neck. She thought back to Cleaver's eyes as he held his pistol poised in her face, and pulled the trigger. She remembered Strangler and Smithy arguing over how to kill her.

She remembered Constable Alexander Corbin, dressed in that silly clown outfit, distracting her assailants and begging her to run. She remembered Chief Brighton showing up suddenly and without invitation. She could only assume he had guessed where she would be.

And Jasper Crimson. She remembered the notorious thief bothering to rescue a girl in over her head.

The massive weight of what she had done, the people she'd endangered, the failure she suffered, and just how close she'd come to death suddenly crashed down upon her.

Tears silently rolled down her bruised cheeks.

The dark interior of carriages was just about all Morgan ever saw anymore. That and Mr. Barrington, who sat beside him, rifling through papers. Morgan always thought once a man reached a certain level of influence, he could send others to do his bidding. But his experience had been quite the opposite.

He found it refreshing though. He enjoyed his carriage rides, having a personal hand in his machinations rather than trusting his henchman to execute them. Last night's mess at the circus for instance would not have yielded the important information he had needed (it's much too important to list here) had he not gone to the site himself. That Spanish vermin who had his claws in everything Morgan considered holy had originally respected his preference to be personally present, a trait they shared. But he had no idea just how involved Morgan liked to get. Morgan never went into business with anyone without having the upper hand on information.

Until now.

The carriage continued trundling along as the door opened abruptly and a shadowy figure stepped in, out of the rain. The robust figure sat across from Morgan, lowering the high collar of his fine coat to reveal a rugged face—one of those I-punch-people-for-a-living-so-don't-mess-with-me kind of faces. Morgan learned a long time ago not to sniff or snort or show any kind of disrespect to this man, regardless of how distasteful his appearance. He'd never been able to learn the man's true identity. He only knew him by his underground title: the Informant.

"Punctual as they come," the man chuckled in a thick Irish accent (he actually does chuckle in an Irish accent).

"I have a schedule to keep. Now, first order of business—"

"First order? Am I to understand you have another job for me?"

"Possibly. First I've an inquiry."

"An inquiry you say?" The Irish reprobate rubbed his chin thoughtfully. Those crystal blue eyes of his were so piercing, so knowing. Morgan had also learned long ago to never assume this man didn't know what you didn't want him to know. Accept that you had nothing on him, he had everything on you, and proceed with as much caution as one would when approaching a wolf with bared teeth.

"Do you intend to charge me extra?" Morgan asked flatly.

"Perhaps. Depends on the nature of the inquiry."

"You've no doubt heard of the disaster at the circus last night?"

"The one that put those poor fellows out of business? Shame that. Never did get the chance to go myself. Was so looking forward to seeing that magic show." Something about the way he said "magic show," the ever so slight curve of his lips, was all Morgan needed to determine this man knew exactly what happened at the circus, what Morgan's part in it was, and he even knew enough to mock him. Bastard.

"The Crimsons are friends of yours, I take it?"

Curiously, the Informant went silent for a moment. "I know them."

Morgan waited for more, but it didn't come. Curious indeed. "Their recent thefts have been . . . peculiar," he said carefully. "Wouldn't you say?"

"I might be persuaded to say that."

Morgan stifled the urge to roll his eyes. "My inquiry is this. I have heard a theory that the Crimson runs are all connected. That they are actually conducting the bidding of a higher authority. What is the word in the underground about this theory?"

The Informant snorted. "I imagine Jasper would find that theory quite amusing."

"What is the popular opinion on the streets?"

The ever-calculating Informant leaned back casually and considered. Morgan had found this man's tendency to take his time, heedless of how it would be perceived, to be quite effective.

"There are always theories floating about, attempting to explain why the Crimsons do what they do. Some have made a hobby out of unraveling that mystery. It's become a sort of conspiracy theory, you might say. But most consider it just that. A conspiracy theory. Although, there are a few of us who know better . . . ."

Something about the way he said—

Aw hell. The man knew. Of course he knew. He knew everything. "All right, Informant. I have a second job for you after tonight." He motioned to Mr. Barrington, who promptly handed a leather folder to the Informant. "The Crimsons stole something of mine. I want you to recover it. Everything you need to know is in there."

"What could they possibly have taken from you that you actually want back?" The Informant chuckled as he perused the folder. "A shoelace? Some lint they swiped off your bum? Perhaps it had more meaning to you than you wanted anyone to know? A sort of sentimental value?"

"A weapon."

"A . . . weapon?"

Ok, perhaps he didn't know everything? Blast! It was so hard to know with this man. "Did you not wonder how the only casualty of last night's affair happened to be a complete, gruesome decapitation? One with seemingly no explanation? It was done with a weapon stolen by the Crimsons. I want it back." There. Best to be direct with this sort.

"Are you trying to tell me the Crimsons are murderers?" he asked skeptically.

"According to my sources."

Mr. Avery had explained the entire horrific event, though Morgan suspected he was leaving a few things out, likely to protect his own pride. The entire fiasco had been quite an embarrassment.

The Informant sat silently for a moment. Finally, he shook his head, handing the folder back. "Not interested. I'll stick with the current job, thank you very much."

Morgan's jaw nearly dropped. "Not interes—how do you mean? I haven't even offered you a price yet."

"Not interested. Now, about tonight's job."

"You can't be serious. You will be handsomely rewarded, as always. Have I ever failed to fulfill my end of our arrangements?"

"It can't be done."

"Can't be . . . ."

"You don't recover *anything* from the Crimsons. You can't even *find* the bloody Crimsons."

"You said they were friends of yours."

"I said nothing of the sort. Besides, it doesn't matter. It. Can't. Be. Done."

"You've the most infamous reputation among the criminal underground along the entire West Coast. Nothing happens on these streets or below them without you knowing about it and likely having a profit in it. Are you not the Informant I've worked with for the last seven years?"

"Aye, that I am. The Informant. A man who knows all that passes through these ports. So if I say it can't be done . . . ."

Morgan looked the man over. Good God, he was serious.

"We're out of time. About tonight's job?"

"Yes. Of course." Morgan nodded to Mr. Barrington, who took the folder from the Informant, and then picked up a briefcase, handing over their settlement. "I don't like your plan," he found himself saying, because that was what he had wanted to say before learning his ace-in-the-hole would not even attempt to recover his weapon.

"Have I ever failed you? You just keep the girl occupied, ruffle her up a bit at the party, bring her home, and I'll do the rest."

"And at what point in this plan do you plan on actually acquiring the evidence I require?"

"I'll get it. Trust me."

"I don't. You find what I want before we return from the party."

"Isaiah is too clever for that. Else he would've been executed a long time ago. I'm telling you, my boys can rip that estate to shreds and not find what you want. You hired me to get evidence. Now let me get your evidence. It's a sort of compromise you might say. Do we still have a deal?"

Morgan hesitated a moment, sharing a furtive glance with Barrington. He didn't respond. He rarely did. With an exasperated huff, Morgan nodded curtly. The Informant was the best there was. Even as the man silently slipped out of the carriage with his settlement, Morgan was still unnerved by him.

"That man is dangerous," said Barrington.

"Really. I hadn't noticed," Morgan replied dryly.

"Sir, I don't recommend we continue our relationship with the Informant. He's likely collecting just as much information against us, as he is doing our bidding. He is *too* good at what he does, and he knows it."

"And yet he refuses to go up against the Crimsons."

Curious indeed.

"Now I think we can all agree," declared Cleaver. "That last night was—"

"A clear sign we should retire," yelled Cog, supported by a round of agreement from the other welders. What was left of them anyway. Cleaver tried not to let that discourage him. His failure weighed heavy on his shoulders, even more so than the sheer humiliation of being so soundly beaten by the Crimsons a second time.

"Let's face it boys," Cog continued, leaning forward in his rickety chair. "We ain't cut out for this crap. Those Crimsons showed us exactly what it takes to be a successful criminal these days, and we ain't even close. They made a mockery of us. A mockery, I tell you! Twice!"

The others grunted their agreement. They were a subdued lot today. Cleaver was hardly in the mood for the Round Table today either. But he was their leader. A leader didn't have the luxury of "not feeling like leading today."

Cleaver's briefing of the circus fiasco to the boss had not gone well, to say the least. Fortunately, the boss wasn't an unreasonable man. He allowed his welders to "rest" for this next portion of his plan, but Cleaver knew what that really meant. They'd been sidelined for the time being, an order Cleaver had every intention of keeping. A good criminal couldn't go off doing his own thing. That was the surest way to get yourself killed.

The welders held their Round Table session back in their headquarters at the construction site. Home. Cleaver had hoped regrouping here would give his men a sense of comfort. Now it was time to back that up by allowing them to dump their feelings.

Cleaver cleared his throat. "Now boys, we took a big hit. And I know you're all hurting. It's ok to hurt. Sometimes, things just don't feel good. Living itself don't feel good. Smithy, I know it didn't feel good to have them spiders running all over you."

Smithy looked away. "No."

"How did it make you feel?"

"I don't want to talk about it."

"I understand, Smithy," Gauge said. The older man leaned toward Smithy from across the circle of chairs. "It's hard to talk about the things that shame us."

"Ain't that the truth," Cleaver agreed. "Ain't no shame in being afraid."

"I ain't ashamed," muttered Smithy. "Did you see the size of those spiders?"

"How about you, Steve?" asked Cleaver. "You had quite the scare with that Crimson girl. How did you feel, when you turned into a porcelain doll?"

"I felt scared. And humiliated. And I questioned. I questioned my value. As a human being . . . ." Steve, normally so unshakeable, broke down in tears. Cog put a comforting arm around him, patting his back.

"Being afraid of spiders is a manly fear," Smithy sniffled. "Being afraid of your grandmother's creepy dolls ain't befitting of a criminal."

"That's not true. We're all afraid of things," Cleaver interjected. "There's no such thing as a fear unbefitting a criminal."

"Clowns," said Cog, who had spent most of the fight at the circus cowering under a cage wagon.

Cleaver scratched his head. "Ok maybe there are some fears unbefitting a criminal but hey, the point is we face them. And we face them together." That's something a good leader would say, right? "We gotta pick ourselves up and carry on."

"For what?" Steve challenged. "We've been sidelined for the information run on Viece manor already"—Cleaver winced; he'd hoped his men wouldn't figure that out—"How we supposed to conquer our fears if we're not even allowed on the ground anymore?"

"I say we go anyway," said Smithy. Cleaver was concerned about him. He was growing pretty dark and not channeling it in a proper "bad guy" fashion to improve his notoriety. He was just behaving like a maniac.

"You would, Smithy," Cog mumbled.

"What's that supposed to mean?"

"It means you are looking for any opportunity to burn people these days to the point I'm wondering if my rump is safe when it's your turn to cook."

"Now, now, Cog," Cleaver intervened. "Sounds like you got something to say, but we don't put anyone down at the Round Table. Do you have beef with Smithy?"

Cog took a breath. "Yeah, I do. Smithy, I don't like how—"

"Uh–uh," Cleaver intervened again. "Remember the proper way."

"Right, sorry. Smithy, I think you're a right good bad guy, and you're doing a great job and all."

Cleaver nodded his approval, encouraging Cog to go on.

"But, I just think we gotta address this burning people thing."

"It's my criminal calling card," Smithy said, offended. "Just cause I'm further along than you lot . . . bloody hell, that's not even why I'm saying we should go."

"Isn't it?" Steve challenged, wiping his nose on his dirty sleeve. "You didn't get to burn anyone at the circus, and you want another chance at it. It's sick, Smithy. You're sick."

"Now Steve, what did we say about insults at the Round Table?" He said it evenly, but Cleaver's patience with Steve was wearing thin.

It didn't matter anyway, as Smithy simply plowed right over Cleaver's chastisement.

"This ain't about me, Steve. Or have you completely forgotten that we lost a friend at that infernal circus?"

Everyone quieted at that, subconsciously glancing at the empty seat in the circle. They hadn't wanted to confront that.

"The last thing I said to Strangler was that he wasn't good at strangling."

The others gasped, slapping hands over their mouths.

"Those Crimsons hit us hard, and this is all that Viece woman's fault. And I for one intend to do something about it."

Smithy stood up and strapped his blowtorch contraption to his back.

"Wait," Cleaver stood up. "Where do you think you're going?"

"The boss can't sideline me. Not now I've lost a friend."

"Our orders were to rest, Smithy."

"I don't need no rest! I need to make this right."

"And you think disobeying our orders is going to make it right?"

"I think burning the flesh off that Viece whore will make it right."

Smithy turned to go, but Cleaver caught his arm in a firm grip. "You stay where you are, welder."

"Let go," he said dangerously.

"Killing Viece won't bring Strangler back. Ain't nothing good ever come out of revenge."

"Why are you protecting her?"

"I'm protecting *you*!"

"FROM WHAT?"

"YOURSELF, YOU DAMN FOOL!"

Smithy shook off Cleaver's grip and pulled out his blowtorch in a threatening stance.

"Let him go, Cleaver!"

Cleaver turned toward Gauge, still sitting calmly in his seat. "Just let him go."

Cleaver turned back to Smithy, but the stocky man was already out the door. Cleaver controlled his fury as he turned back to Gauge. "Round Table's over."

After exchanging a few uncomfortable glances, the others slowly retreated from the room, their forlorn footsteps echoing softly in the empty chamber.

"Why did you do that?" asked Cleaver calmly. He busied himself with replacing the chairs to their rightful place. Being busy always helped him keep his anger under control.

Gauge stood up to help. "For your sake lad. And for Smithy. He needs to go. See this through."

"And get himself in big trouble with the boss. We don't even know what the boss is planning right now. If Smithy goes and messes it up—"

"That's on him. I know you want to care for these lads, Seth, but they're their own men. They have to find their way."

Gauge only addressed Cleaver by his actual name when playing the father card. When he was particularly concerned. "I don't like this, Gauge."

"I don't neither. But we lost a friend last night. Everyone grieves in their own way. If this is what Smithy needs. Revenge. Let him seek it. Who knows. Maybe he'll actually find what he's looking for."

Cleaver picked up Cleavage from where she rested against the far wall. He held her up, admiring her craftsmanship. His choice of weapon was simple, straightforward, and honest. It got the job done. Smithy's choice of weapon was elegant, innovative, and downright sadistic. "That's exactly what I'm afraid of."

Chapter 18

"Oh Lady Viece," Akane exclaimed as Isabelle gracefully descended the grand staircase that led down to the main floor of the estate. "You look very beautiful!"

Isabelle smiled. "Thank you, Akane." Though she felt far from beautiful. The high neckline of her navy blue evening gown hid the bruises from where the chain had dug into her flesh—her physician suspected she'd have a permanent scar from it. Beads and white jewels dangled from the hem, matching the sparkling jewelry she wore around her wrist and the fan she held in black lace gloved hands. With her hair done up in a loosely braided coil, she likely should've felt beautiful. Instead, she felt rung-out.

The nerve-grating doorbell did nothing to help. "I suppose I shall be about it then."

Lord Morgan Garnet, dressed in a smart gentleman's suit, with white gloves, a perfectly tied green cravat, and diamond cufflinks. He expertly swung a cane as he swaggered in. "Why Lady Viece! You look most resplendent this evening. You seem to have recovered well from your fright earlier this week?"

"I've been informed I owe my healthy condition to you." She practically gritted her teeth the entire time, but she managed to get it out. "I owe you my most sincere gratitude for your act of chivalry."

"Oh, it was nothing, Lady Viece." He held out his arm to her, and she took it without breaking his gaze. "After this evening there should be no more need for hostilities against me, my dear."

"Is that so."

"Yes. After this evening, I believe your family and mine shall enter into a most profitable arrangement."

Isabelle doubted that. But she had at least fulfilled the first part of her family obligations. Now all she had to do was accompany this louse to a party and she'd be free of further family obligations.

The Viece estate was imposing enough in the daylight, but its majesty against the sunset backdrop left a feeling of inadequacy in the pit of Alex's stomach. So what else was new? He struggled on two crutches, still nursing his broken leg from the circus fiasco.

"You all right boy?" asked Chief Brighton beside him. The chief walked gingerly himself, still recovering from being sawed in half.

"Yeah. Right as rain, I am." The chief held a careful hand to Alex's back as the two hiked up the steps to the front doors of Viece Manor.

They had tried visiting Lady Viece sooner, but she hadn't been taking visitors yet. With the constabulary all but incapacitated after the circus disaster, Chief Brighton, Alex, and a handful of others were all that was left to serve their district, as well as several surrounding ones Brighton had called upon for backup. They worked extra hours, and a late evening visit was about the only time they had to do anything. Chief Brighton hadn't expected Alex to insist on accompanying him, but Alex had some things to get off his chest.

Brighton knocked on the grand entry doors. The austere butler (because being stern and austere is in the butler job description) opened the door and nodded his greeting to Alex and Brighton. "I assume you are here to visit Lady Viece?"

"Yes, we are," said Brighton. "Is she receiving visitors?"

"I'm afraid you just missed her. She left for a family obligation less than an hour ago. She will not be returning until late tonight."

"Oh." Alex deflated.

"You are welcome to take some tea in the sitting room to recover from your trip before returning home. If it pleases you."

"Thank you, good man," declared Chief Brighton politely.

"Ok," Alex mumbled, head down as he hobbled into the manor's atrium. The butler led them to the sitting room, where he left to fetch tea. Alex took his seat on the formal couch right next to the fire, wincing at the pain in his leg. He set his crutches against the wall next to the fireplace. They clattered to the tile floor of course. Because Alex couldn't even do that right. But that was why he was here, wasn't it? To do something right?

"I'm glad you were there."

Alex glanced up to see the chief standing tall before the fireplace, hands behind his back. He looked . . . worn. In that way a man earns. Scarred, weathered, and callused, the chief was a man who got where he got by sheer virtue of work ethic. The man would never know how much Alex admired him.

The butler came in and delivered his chamomile tea in the most beautiful china Alex would ever see in his life.

"G—glad I was where?"

"At the circus," the chief said, as he sipped his cup. Odd sight, that. The fancy china was too dainty for the likes of Brighton. "You pull a lot of stupid stunts, Alex. But you got a good heart and a keen mind. You just might amount to something some day."

The chief probably meant that as a compliment, but Alex just wilted further. Some day, he'd amount to something. He'd been telling himself that for years. "I didn't do nothing, Chief. Got myself into a right mess I couldn't get out of. Was stupid, is what that was."

"Yes. Yes it was. But I'll take your stupid acts of selflessness any day over the intelligent acts of evil men. My whole damn department is . . . *was* full of brutes with muscle and no brains. Or balls for that matter. You may not have the muscle, but you got it where it counts."

"I ain't got nothing, and when you got nothing, it counts for nothing."

"Oh quit bathing in self-pity, Alex. You know what your problem is? You know what's wrong with you? You got all these talents and you're trying to do everything that doesn't include them. You ain't got a damn muscle on your body, but you want to be a constable. You ain't got delicate, practical, careful hands, or good ideas, but you want to be an inventor. You ever considered trying to do something what actually suits you?"

"Like what?"

"Bah! Do I have to solve all your problems? It's your life, you figure it out. Think long and hard. When you got something, let me know. I'll see what I can do."

He downed his tea in one gulp. That suited him a little better. "Shall we be on our way?"

"You go, Chief. I need to rest my leg a bit longer. I'll find my own way home."

"Suit yourself."

The chief left without another word.

Alex took a moment to ponder the chief's words, before making a decision. He had been thinking long and hard about the brief exchange he had with Lord Garnet at the circus, and how the gentleman had been irritated, not shocked at the events ensuing. Why was the man there in the first place? Something was off about him, and Alex suspected he must be in on the patent scandal on some level. Whatever Lady Viece had done to Alex, she was right about this. He just knew it. And so did Chief Brighton. They couldn't just keep waiting for her to be ready for visitors.

Glancing around the room, he found a desk at the back with paper and a pen. Composing the letter in his mind as he struggled his way over to the desk, he became more and more convinced of what he had to do. Lady Viece was on to something big, and she was the only one with the incentive, initiative, resources, and care to serve justice. That was why Alex forgave her, even if she wasn't sorry. It was the right thing to do.

Once his thoughts were on paper, he folded up the letter and stepped out into the hallway. He called for the butler, but the fellow was nowhere to be found. Well, he supposed he could leave the letter in Lady Viece's chambers.

The chief had said he had no good ideas. Going up the stairs with a broken leg certainly proved that. Step after step, he grunted and groaned his way up, huffing and puffing, but forcing his body to move all the same. UNTIL FINALLY . . .

He made it up one stair.

Alex wasn't entirely sure how long it actually took him, but he was quite pleased with himself upon finally arriving at the top. He took a moment to curse the man who invented stairs—and then immediately felt bad because the man was likely just doing his job—before proceeding to—and then felt bad again because what if the inventor of stairs was a woman—before proceeding to Lady Viece's chambers—and felt bad again for invading a lady's privacy. What was he thinking? Going straight to Lady Viece's quarters like this. Idiot! And how did he know these were her quarters anyway? (I don't have an answer to that question, so just don't worry about it, okay?)

He glanced down at the letter in his hand, then up at the grand doors to Lady Viece's chambers. With a deep breath, he opened the door and hobbled in.

He only intended to leave the letter on her bed, then leave quickly so as not to invade a lady's privacy longer than an idiot had to, but once he placed it gently on her pillow, he couldn't help but glance over at the massive wall on the far side of the room. Frowning, he hobbled over and took it all in.

He took it *all* in. With each passing moment, his jaw dropped further and further.

This was amazing! Lady Viece had figured it out. From details on the specific people she suspected were victims of the patent scandal, to why she suspected Lord Garnet himself was who she called the Puppet Master, it was all here. The deduction was sound. The evidence was . . . well, not. She had solved a case but didn't have enough evidence to move forward in court.

If she had his mousetrap, it would've been a start, but a confession from Lord Garnet—which clearly would never happen—or the welders would've been better. She had actually exonerated the Crimsons from blame, which he had long since suspected was true. But their confession would mean as much as a clump of dirt in court.

How about . . . the blueprints! Her notes suggested they were possibly held at the circus, where she'd apparently recovered one from a certain Count Downey. Alex had become good friends with the circus performers. Did they know about this? Did they have the blueprints?

A loud crash from downstairs startled Alex off his feet. He hit the ground hard. What on earth? Crawling to the window, Alex peered down into the courtyard outside. Ruffians gathered in front of the manor, breaking in through the doors and windows they shattered. Alex huddled back down against the wall beneath the window casement. *They're here for the evidence,* he thought immediately. All of Lady Viece's hard work. He couldn't let them have it. With the racket downstairs unfolding, and despite the growing pit of fright threatening to freeze him up, Alex got to work.

Gliding through the stone walkways in the courtyard of the new university, arm in arm with Lord Garnet, Isabelle passed groups of acclaimed professors, scientists, historians, and the like, who chatted amiably with various other people of note. All dressed in their best, holding glasses of the finest wines provided by sharply dressed servants.

"Do excuse me a moment, Lady Viece," Garnet said, releasing her arm. His shapely, rotund wife held to his other. "We should like to make our rounds, and I'm certain you have friends who'd like to ask after your health. Save a dance for me, will you my dear?" He kissed her hand and strode off with his wife by his side.

Isabelle glared after him, heedless of who might see. With her sour mood, frustration, and exhaustion, putting on a face tonight would be difficult. But despite her griping, she could—and would—serve her house well.

She gingerly made her way around the university grounds, speaking amiably with various professors, then moving on to certain family allies. Doing her due diligence as the Viece heir. She didn't mind really. It was the extravagance that bothered her, not the duty itself. If all the politicking and machinating could be done without the overt opulence, pandering, and cheating, she might've thrived better in this world. She wasn't one of those fools who craved the life of the commoner. No, she loved living comfortably, and had seen enough of the underbelly of society to be grateful to her father for providing such comforts. She was just . . . so bored.

"Isabelle!" Lady Sarah trundled over to her.

Isabelle smiled half-heartedly at her friend. "Sarah, dear." She nodded cordially as the young woman arrived.

"I heard of your terrible theatrical ordeal at the circus," she said. "I was so frightened for you. Do tell me you've quite recovered?"

Isabelle grimaced. "Well enough. Thank you."

Sarah smiled. "Well you certainly look as radiant as ever. You've caught many eyes this night. Despite your prudence." A very calculated, and nearly-but-not-quite insult to her fashion.

"Curious that I would attract so many eyes with my prudence the rest of you couldn't attract if you were naked." Not her best retort. Much too direct. But she was out of sorts tonight. There was a reason Isabelle did honestly consider Sarah a friend however.

She just laughed. "Well said, dear. But honestly, don't bother with your apathetic pretense. You delight in the attention. Admit it. Every eligible young man here wants a dance with you."

Despite the lies she often told herself, her throat constricted at her friend's statement. It was a compliment, but an untrue one. Any eligible man here would only associate with her by want of connection with the Viece family. Her mixed heritage hardly put her in the position of desirable.

"I'm afraid I'm still recovering from my, how did you put it, *theatrical* ordeal? I regret that I must decline all physical exertions for the evening."

"Lady Viece?"

Isabelle turned around. Lord Mayberry stood with his hands behind his back, looking smart in his gentleman's suit. For once, it didn't look unusual on him. Perhaps he was finally growing used to his new societal role. "Why Lord Mayberry, a pleasure to see you again. Your family is well I hope?"

"Isabelle was just telling me how much she'd love to dance, but no one has yet asked her." Sarah shook her head solemnly.

Isabelle glared at her, realizing the interaction was staged. Obviously. *That scheming little—*

"Well I would certainly be honored to have a dance with you, Lady Viece," Lord Mayberry said smoothly. Oh yes. Contrived indeed. "If it would please you?" He held out his arm in askance.

Doing her best to hide her annoyance, she took his arm and smiled graciously. "The honor would be mine."

The young man beamed as he led her toward the dance floor. Glaring behind her at Sarah, who simply grinned innocently, Isabelle resolved herself to the impending toe-stomping. The music was a fast-paced waltz, allowing her to get her blood pumping, and despite her apprehension, Lord Mayberry turned out to be quite an admirable dancer.

But a dance was NOT precisely what she needed right now after all. It was NOT helping her rest her mind amid the millions of moving pieces currently occupying it. And she most certainly was enjoying herself.

Was NOT enjoying herself! She was NOT. And that's that.

"You dance beautifully."

"You're too kind, Lord Mayberry."

"Jonathan. Please. Never did like Mayberry much."

"Why ever not? Your family name carries considerable prestige in its wake. Surely you should be proud of it."

"I was proud of it before. That name belonged to honest farmers. Why can't that have been enough?"

"Was it enough? Your father worked hard to bring your family into status. I dare say it sounds as though you lament your old life."

"I don't lament starving. Or smelling like a pigsty. But I do miss the freedom." He paused. "You look beautiful, Lady Viece. Truly stunning. But don't you ever get tired of always having to put on a face for society? Don't you ever wish you could just . . . be?"

"All the time," she said softly.

"Well then you're the first new acquaintance I have in upper society who feels that way. Everyone else looks at me like I've grown a pig's snout." He forced a chuckle.

Isabelle smirked. "Try using a working class expletive in their presence. You'll witness first-hand how the steam engine was invented."

Mayberry chewed on the statement for a moment, before understanding dawned on him and he graced her with a genuine laugh.

The waltz ended, and they bowed to one another as the next one picked up. Instead of picking up the rhythm, however, Lord Mayberry stepped closer to Isabelle and took her hand. "Lady Viece," he said cautiously. "I'm not certain how to bring this up and I . . . hope you won't be offended at my . . . forward . . . ness. But—"

"May I cut in?"

Isabelle very nearly groaned. As uncomfortable as Lord Mayberry's attempts were, they were far preferable to a dance with Lord Garnet. The man's severe expression was likely what so often got him what he wanted. Add the way he so thoroughly owned his gentleman's suit and molded into his melodramatic persona, and he likely would've risen to power without his shrewd intellect.

Mayberry, to his credit, managed to maintain his composure—and dignity—as he murmured "of course" and took his leave. Isabelle reluctantly bowed to her new partner and they took up the dance. She spared a glance for poor Lord Mayberry, but to her surprise, the expression on his face was one of concern. He raised his eyebrows at her, as though to ask "is everything all right?".

"How has your evening been so far? You've been properly regaled I hope?"

Isabelle turned her attention back to her current dance partner. "I am well," she swallowed, forcing out the words she'd prepared.

"Only well? It would seem young Mayberry thinks you are more. Such a beautiful young gem you are, despite your mixed heritage."

Isabelle stiffened at the slight to her family.

"What any young man would covet, to be sure. I can certainly understand young Mayberry's infatuation."

"That is hardly appropriate of you, Lord Garnet."

"Ah but of course. Forgive me. Many assert that age means wisdom. But for me, age means cultivating an apathy toward things that once seemed so desperately important. I shall endeavor to correct my erroneous discourse and draw the conversation to something you might find more amenable. How about this? Young Mayberry is finally fitting into his new role in society, wouldn't you say?"

"He is learning the dance well," she said carefully, as they moved across the dance floor, flowing between the other couples. This dance was a six eight, a mild pace, played by a string quartet set up upon a dais to the side of the dance floor.

"Hopefully quicker than his father. There's hope for the boy. But he still doesn't understand that wealth does not mean one can venture anywhere he pleases. One still has limitations. A place. I hope you are not encouraging his advances?"

"I beg your pardon, Lord Garnet, but that is of no concern to you."

"I am merely looking out for the interests of your family's future. You will need to marry well to recover."

Isabelle raised an eyebrow. "Recover? From what, pray tell?"

Lord Garnet smiled tenderly, like a wizened father lecturing a child. "Why the matter of your family's unfortunate plight, of course. Or didn't your father tell you?"

The pace of the music picked up, moving into a brisk dance, every measure ending in a staccato. Like Isabelle's heart beat. "I am being civil with you this evening upon my father's request. You may have him convinced of your innocence, but I will not acquiesce. Your veiled threats will not intimidate—"

Lord Garnet pulled Isabelle closer into a firm, and borderline scandalous grip, barely still considered a dance position. She could smell the wine on his breath. "I don't waste time threatening, Lady Viece," he said. "I take action to ensure that no one is able to stand in my way even if they so desired."

The music picked up to something frenetic. "What have you done?" Isabelle whispered. The music clipped with a dramatic pause, signaling the ending of the piece.

He smiled. "You read the newspapers regularly, I presume? Tomorrow's headlines promise to be exceptionally sensational."

He pulled away and smiled. "Enjoy the rest of your evening. I shall see you back to your estates after the ceremonial speeches have concluded. A woman in your condition ought not to be out too late."

The rest of the evening was a blur. Isabelle retreated to a table and practically snapped at anyone who approached—including the unfortunate Lord Mayberry, who was kind enough to only focus on ensuring her well-being rather than continuing his advance from earlier.

She remained seated during the speeches, motionless as everyone else applauded, and hardly even remembered tea and cakes served. Lord Garnet and his wife came by to escort her from the party and she said nothing as they departed.

She said nothing the entire ride back to her manor, enduring the smug, slight smiles generously doled out by Garnet and his lady wife.

She said nothing as she stepped out of the carriage, eager to get this night over with. With one slippered foot on the ground, and the other still in the coach, Isabelle froze.

Her home had been ransacked.

Chapter 19

Isabelle leapt out of the carriage, hiked her dress up to her knees, and bolted up the steps to the broken doors, ignoring Lord Garnet's cries behind her, as well as her own protesting body.

Where were the servants? The maids? Akane!

Inside, despite the darkness, a scene of chaos unfolded before Isabelle. The furniture, china, paintings, busts and other artwork, all destroyed. The once pristine marble floors were covered in fragments of wood, shattered glass, and ceramics, dimly lit only by moonlight and a few oil lamps on the walls. Isabelle needed but one scan of the atrium to discern whoever had been here had been thoroughly, and hurriedly searching for something.

"Well I can hardly say this is unexpected," Garnet said in the eerie quiet. "Has the look of another Crimson run. Unless, someone decided not to wait for a search warrant."

Completely aghast, Isabelle turned slowly, searching Garnet's eyes.

He gave her an icy smile. "Its curious how one would spend so much time digging up the muck surrounding others but conveniently blind oneself to their own family's unsavory dealings."

A frightening, feral anger possessed her. The dark, soft, dangerous voice that escaped her mouth didn't sound like her own. "You did this."

Garnet gave her a smug look. "I did this? Lady Viece, I know this must be terribly upsetting, but I was with you all evening. How could I possibly—"

Isabelle snapped. With a disembodied screech, she lunged at Lord Garnet, slicing at his face like a cat clawing at a vicious dog. Garnet endured it in shock for a moment before finally slapping Isabelle across the face. Vision swimming, Isabelle plopped to the ground, suddenly exhausted.

Garnet straightened his coat and composed himself. "You are completely out of line, you miserable whore. I was going to offer that you stay with my family for a time until this mess could be sorted, but I've thought better of it. Rot here in this hellhole for all I care. It serves you and your traitorous family right. I hope whoever was here found what they were looking for."

He stormed out of the manor, leaving Isabelle in the dark, on the floor, rubbing her cheek.

"Miss Isabelle?" a timid voice called.

Isabelle let out a breath of relief. "It's all right, Akane. It's me."

"Oh Miss Isabelle!" Akane scrambled over, helping Isabelle to her feet. "It was awful."

"Are you all right?" She held the woman's arms in her own, scanning her for injuries.

"I'm ok, Lady Viece. I'm ok. These men came in and threatened us. We told them to take what they wanted and leave, but they just kept breaking things."

"Where are the others? Is everyone else well?"

"They are all right. Everyone is all right. Just very scared. We can get this cleaned up miss. Please do not worry."

"No. Everyone leave. It's not safe for you to be here. Do not return until you are fetched. You'll still be paid your wages, I'll make sure of it."

"But Miss Isabelle—"

Isabelle locked Akane in a death gaze, causing the poor woman to stumble back in alarm. "Go."

With a swallow, Akane nodded and curtsied. "Yes, Miss Isabelle."

It's curious how one would spend so much time digging up the muck surrounding others but conveniently blind oneself to their own family's unsavory dealings.

Standing alone in the middle of the ruined main room, beneath a broken crystal chandelier swaying precariously overhead, moonlight casting a pale glow upon half of her body, Isabelle clenched her teeth, fists tightening at her sides. She had been so focused on her patent scandal, she'd simply dismissed the accusations against her house as the common prattling of gossip. Nothing to be concerned about. Her father would deal with it. But this, this was an intrusion. Why would someone go this far looking for evidence against her family unless they had ample reason to believe it existed? In fact, too many people had come forward with the same accusation.

A part of her, the detective part, had always wondered about her father's affairs, but dismissed them out of hand as silly. But she had never asked. Never investigated.

She glanced up the grand staircase, at the double doors leading to Father's study. She had never been allowed in there as a child. That was where her father conducted his affairs. If there was anything to hide, she might find it there.

Step by step, she carefully, gracefully climbed the staircase, never taking her eyes off the doors to the study. Pushing those doors open still made her feel like a child about to be scolded.

She stepped inside, revealing the same mess that had befallen the rest of the manor. The room had always been cold, even when the hearth was alight. Isabelle had once referred to this room as the dungeon, having always felt small and insignificant inside. She now simply found the study austere and pragmatic. A little too pragmatic. Her father was fastidious to say the least, his business dealings well documented. A mahogany desk dominated the room. Isabelle set her jaw, lit the hearth, and got to work.

The shattered grandfather clock in the hallway outside chimed twice. Two o'clock in the morning. Isabelle leaned back in the desk chair again, wrung out, eyes practically dry from staring so hard at the documents in her hands.

Incriminating documents.

Documents that would be enough to see her father hanged for treason. Only worse. They implicated her mother too. Somehow, her parents were involved with a Spanish mogul, conducting both political and financial business illegally, though she couldn't deduce what. At face value, these letters strongly implied a war conspiracy. And her parents were complicit.

Isabelle could see her entire life, her family, her good name, crumble before her eyes. Her patent scandal seemed trivial now, laid beside treason. But it was her family. How could she have missed her own family's involvement in such a diabolical affair?

She would no doubt be asked to testify in court at some point, but how could she, knowing the truth? All her aspirations, her dreams, her ethics dangled on the edge of a cliff. If she testified truthfully, provided this evidence, and implicated her family—as would've been right by the law, as she honestly would've coldly done for any other aristocrat caught red-handed in treason—her parents would hang. Her house name would be forever subjected to ridicule. But if she protected her family, she'd become the very thing she had fought so ruthlessly against.

She'd lose everything.

Swiping the desk's contents onto the floor, Isabelle leaned forward and gripped the edge of the wood in white knuckles. Her lovely hair had long since come undone, her dress wrinkled, her gloves haphazardly discarded.

Rubbing at the wound on her neck, she wasn't sure how long she sat there before throwing her arms up in the air and screaming. This could not be. It simply could not be! This had to be a set up. Garnet more than implied involvement. He must've planted the evidence. That's why he looked so smug. He had created these masterfully forged documents, hired someone to ransack her home so that it appeared someone had been there looking for it, when really they were planting it.

The question was who did the planting?

She collected the pile of documents she'd found implicating her parents, shuffled them neatly into a perfect stack, and stood. Straightening her wrinkled gown, she calmly glided over to the crackling hearth and tossed the entire stack into the fire.

Most men, Morgan mused, would likely abhor sitting in a dark carriage, a reasonable distance away from Viece manor, in the dark, unable to make a sound, unable to see a thing, and bored silly. Most men would likely prefer to spend the evening after a grand party with a bottle of wine, in the company of a lovely woman with a . . . disinterest in modesty.

Not Morgan. He was happily married, and preferred to spend his time plotting his eventual acquisition of England's arms industry. Yes, the entire industry. He wanted it.

But nevertheless, when the Informant boorishly hopped into his carriage a couple hours after he'd left Lady Viece to her ransacked home, he did have to admit a level of relief, especially considering he was alone tonight.

It was about time.

"She burned the evidence."

Morgan blinked. "She . . . what?!" He just about leapt out of the carriage himself to stop her.

"Relax. It's handled. My associate will bring what you require in a moment."

"And if Lady Viece catches your associate?"

"My associate will bring what you require."

Morgan stewed for a moment. The Viece heir was on to him, and much as it irritated him to admit, she was more of a threat to his plans than he thought possible. This situation might actually present a different opportunity. "Wait. Have your associate kidnap her."

The Informant hesitated. "Sorry?"

"I'll pay you double if you kidnap her. Take her to the underground, somewhere she's been known to go gallivanting on one of her so-called investigations. Take her there and kill her. Decapitation. Mimic the death of the casualty from the circus fiasco the other night. And then start spreading some rumors about the Crimsons, if you take my meaning."

That ought to solve several problems all at once. He could no longer use the Crimson runs as a scapegoat, but that part of his plan had wrapped up anyway. If citizens thought the Viece heir had been murdered by the Crimsons, it may flush those two out. In the meantime, he'd flood the underground with his own eyes and ears. He would destroy Lady Viece, and recover his weapon at the same time.

"Lady Viece?"

Isabelle whirled around to see Akane standing in the doorway. "I thought I told you to leave hours ago."

"I could not leave you, Miss Isabelle. What is that?" She pointed to the fire.

"Forged documents implicating my parents' involvement in a treasonous affair."

Akane gasped and ran for the tongs. "You burning evidence?! You cannot burn evidence. You be hanged."

"Didn't you hear me Akane? Forged. It was planted."

"Then judge will decide." Akane reached into the fire with the tongs, but Isabelle put a hand on her arm.

"No one will believe it's fake. We have to be rid of it. We don't—" Isabelle hesitated a moment. "I've been in here for hours. You only just now come to inform me that you're still here?"

"I did not want to disturb you."

"You're my maid. It's your job to disturb me. You said they scuffled with you when they broke in. But your dress looks perfectly pressed."

"I—"

"And I never heard anyone else leave when you said the other house attendants were still here. You dismissed them long before I arrived."

The two women locked eyes. "Oh Akane," Isabelle whispered, her face contorting with betrayal.

In a sudden display of unexpected athleticism, Akane twisted the arm that Isabelle still gripped hers with, spun Isabelle around and shoved her to the floor.

Isabelle scrambled back to her feet, struggling against the lack of flexibility in her dress, eyes wide as she regarded Akane. The maid deftly removed the pages from the fire with the tongs, and set them on the tile hearth, stomping out the flames. Isabelle lunged for it but quick as a flash, Akane skillfully used the tongs as a baton, twirling them in hand and whacking Isabelle in the upper arm. As Isabelle cried out, Akane spun and kicked Isabelle away. Isabelle grunted, crashing into the bookcase behind her.

In her moment of disorientation, Akane slipped out the double doors with the half-burned documents. The woman didn't make a sound on the carpet as she fled, and moved with a grace Isabelle thought impossible in that bulky white maid's dress.

Isabelle forced herself to her feet and scrambled after Akane, slamming her shoulder into the door in her haste. No. Not the door. A broad, robust, brick wall that disguised itself as a man.

Towering over her with a wicked smile was Smithy. The welder. And he had that strange portable welding contraption strapped to his back.

Isabelle scrambled backward. She backed right into her father's desk. Smithy moved forward. Slowly. Illuminated only by the light of the fire. Isabelle's breathing trembled as he approached.

"You ain't got no where to go now, missy," he drawled. "Ain't got no train. Ain't got no bloody fence clowns. Ain't got them damn Crimsons. You're all alone. Just you and me now."

Isabelle bolted for the other side of the desk, where one of those drawers held a pistol, but Smithy grabbed her hair and yanked, throwing her across the room. Scrambling back to her feet, Isabelle turned to see Smithy calmly approaching her again. He casually held the thin, long nozzle of his welding contraption before him, tapping the trigger gently twice, then stopping. Tapping it twice, then stopping. Those inches long flames, with a bluish-green tint, reflected in Isabelle's terrified eyes as she backed away from Smithy.

"Do you like my baby girl? She's called a blowtorch. Can sear straight through solid metal, she can."

Isabelle wasn't exactly sure what he was going to do, but she had no intention of finding out. Her eyes darted frantically around the room for a way out, but it was too small. There was no way around him. He'd grab her if she tried to run.

He took another step closer.

Isabelle mentally rummaged through the files in her mind for something to help her understand how her more sadistic suspects regard their victims. Did that make her a victim now?

This is about power, Isabelle, she forced her herself to think, recalling her notes.

Let him think he's won.

She allowed him to take another step closer. She didn't move. But she glanced at everything within reach that would be remotely useful.

He'll want to get close, personal, look you in the eye so that you know you are beaten. He wants to possess you. That was so much easier to read about and speculate than to be on the receiving end. Is this how the victims of her cases felt? Weak? Helpless?

The next step brought Smithy within reach.

Isabelle inched just a tad closer to the hearth, subtly grasping at the air by her side. There would be a poker for the fireplace nearby. If she could just grab it without Smithy noticing.

Fortunately, Smithy apparently liked to savor the moment.

Smithy pointed the blowtorch nozzle toward her face, and tapped the trigger again. She could feel the heat on her cheeks. An inch closer, and it would burn her skin.

Let him think he's won. Let him think you're weak, and beaten.

She started weeping, looking away in fear of the blowtorch—she didn't need to fake that—which gave her an innocuous reason to glance down to her side to see where the poker was.

Smithy grinned a salacious, sinister grin.

Now!

With a screech, Isabelle snatched the poker handle and didn't even wait for it to pull free from its base. She picked the whole thing up and swung as hard as she could at Smithy's face.

Heavy metal scraped across his nose.

She swung again, and lacerated the side of his neck.

With that swing, she lost the metal stand, but still held to the poker. Smithy came at her with the blowtorch, but it was a cumbersome thing and she was faster. Isabelle swung her makeshift weapon again, and this time she caught his eye with the hook. The welder screamed, scrambling backward, and dropped his blowtorch.

With a feral snarl she didn't know she had in her, Isabelle lunged for the blowtorch, which was still connected by a long, thick tube to Smithy's back. She pointed it at Smithy's face, and pulled the trigger. All the way.

A burst of bluish-green fire exploded from the nozzle, alighting the entire room, and engulfing Smithy's face in flame.

Another shrill scream tore from the man's lips as he leapt to his feet, clutching his face, eyes squeezed shut. He turned around, still shrieking until he ran himself into the bookshelf on the far wall. The abrupt silence that followed was nearly as haunting as the scream that still echoed through the study.

She dropped to her knees, trembling. *Did I . . . did I just do that? Did I just kill someone?* This wasn't just bringing down a criminal. This was revenge. Once she had whacked him, she could've gotten away. Instead, she had attacked again. She had wanted to hurt him, cripple him. Kill him . . .

She hugged herself tight, still sobbing like a child for all she had told herself in her notes to *feign weeping.*

"Come on, Isabelle," she whimpered. "Pull yourself together."

Ok, she thought. Gracious, even her thoughts were trembling. *What do you have to work with? What do you know?*

One, she didn't have much time. Someone would no doubt eventually come to check on Smithy. She'd give herself one minute to decide on a course of action.

Two, Akane had taken the planted evidence against her family. She had to find her before she could get the evidence to Garnet. Which meant she couldn't stay in this house. She needed to be mobile.

Three, Garnet had apparently sent Smithy to kill her. Garnet wanted her dead. Could she perhaps, simply oblige him?

Now that some semblance of a plan was taking shape, Isabelle struggle to her feet, renewed purpose distracting her from what just happened.

Ok, dilemma number one: how do you fake your own death? She kept a wary eye on the unconscious, lacerated, horrendously burned—possibly dead—man lying by the bookshelf as she thought through her plan as quickly as she could.

"What do you have to work with, Isabelle?" she asked herself hoarsely, sniffling. She looked around. Books, the discarded poker, some valuable artifacts on the shelves, the desk, the chair, the dead brute, the welding contraption . . . gas tank strapped to his back. Remembering the unfortunate incident at Professor Brass's manor, Constable Corbin had found evidence of those canisters on the scene. That was how the welders had exploded Brass Manor.

Isabelle hurried over to the possibly dead brute, but once she got near him, she reached down slowly, checking for a pulse. Alive. Regardless, he was definitely out for the count, so she carefully unstrapped the gas tank from his back and carried—well, dragged it with great difficulty—to the double doors of the study. Once she twisted off the cap, the gas would leak out and hopefully wouldn't reach the fireplace until she had managed to slip out the back.

Right? . . . Right.

Isabelle scurried back to the gas tank and set her hand on the cap.

She had no idea if this was going to work (honestly *I* have no idea if this is going to work, so here goes nothing), but . . . well here goes nothing. She twisted off the cap, closed the doors to the study, then ran for all she was worth.

Down the stairs, through the atrium, into the kitchen, out the back door, into the gardens and . . .

KAAAAAAAABBBBBBBBOOOOOOOOMMMM!!!!!!!!

Chapter 20

LORD VIECE SPILLS THE BEANS

IN DISTURBING TURN OF EVENTS, LORD ISAIAH VIECE REVEALS ALL TO PRESS, LEADING AUTHOR TO USE THIS CHAPTER AS "SPILL THE BEANS" CHAPTER, LAYING OUT VILLAIN'S EVIL PLOT IN DESPERATE ATTEMPT AT FORESHADOWING.

". . . cares what I has to say." Alex sniffled, dangling his feet off of the crate where he sat. His crutches rested beside him, and he clutched a large satchel, taken from the Viece estate, to his chest. It was stuffed beyond capacity.

"Aye, that's tough," said Cedric, the circus ringmaster. One of the others patted Alex's shoulder consolingly as Cedric continued. "Ain't that just typical of those prickly fickly important types? Never a care for the common man."

The circus troupe tipped their ale mugs to that. When these clowns had discovered Alex knocked out one of their own and stole his costume, the lot of them had simply laughed up a storm. The entire fiasco actually secured his acceptance as part of the troupe. He had never felt so appreciated in his life. They were the ones who had helped him in the hours immediately after the circus incident.

They had spent the last few days trying to catch all of their animals and clean up the mess at the fair grounds. With all their . . . circus stuff . . . (Entertainment implements? Laughter-inducing equipment? Tomfoolery paraphernalia?) With all their tomfoolery paraphernalia largely unsalvageable, they left most of the mess on the fair grounds, and had to hire a ship due to the complete annihilation of their cage wagons.

Getting all those animals to the docks without proper cages had been a nightmare. Alex was somewhat certain a few of them were still on the loose, and he was *most* certain the large tuna they'd stuffed into the Loch Ness Monster cage was . . . well, *not* the Loch Ness Monster.

After the incident at the Viece estate, Alex had gone to find his new friends, though it turned out to be for naught. They didn't know anything about any blueprints, though they had believed every word Alex told them about Lord Garnet without question. Alex had spent the last few hours recounting his story to them. They thought it was the grandest tale of adventure and tragedy they'd ever heard.

Alex reclined on a crate amongst a bunch of unused or broken ones piled on the docks, sharing a few pints with his new friends— now dressed in not-so-traditional Scottish attire (I'm picturing them in awesome steampunk kilts). The night wore on and the gloom clung to the air like a nursing babe, but Alex couldn't stop venting. With each word he uttered, his spirits lifted.

"I just thought Lady Viece was d–d–different, you know? I thought she believed in me. Turns out I was just another tool in her satchel. Nothing more. Nothing less."

"Women," the shortest clown said, shaking his head. "You can't live with 'em." *Hiccup.* "You can't live without 'em." Another round of agreement and clinking mugs.

"But I helped her out, I did. She wouldn't have d–d–discovered those welders without me. She wouldn't have been able to, you know, even get on the case if not for my invention getting stolen. She p–p– practically owes me her life."

"By Joe," said another Scotsman. "Ain't nobody ever appreciates what's right in front of their eyes until it up and dies." Another round of agreement and swigs followed.

"But I couldn't rescue her none, either. In the end, I failed her. I'm just, just a coward. Plain as the nose on my face. My d—dad always said I wasn't good for nothing. He was right. I always get in the way or mess things up."

"Hear, hear!" The short Scotsman raised his mug but was greeted with silent stares. "I mean . . . if at first you don't succeed, try, try again." The others sounded off their agreement and took another round of swigs.

"Angus is right lad," Cedric declared. "You can't let no prissy sissy lassy tell you how to be a man. Chin up! Flex your muscle and keep on a'fixin' tah fight for what you believe in."

The Scots cheered.

"Don't throw in yar sponge and wallow in yar own grave just a'waitin' for the good Lord tah put yah there!"

Cheers all around.

"You go and show those fundy dundy welders what it means to be Scottish!"

A crescendo of cheers.

"But . . . I'm English."

Silence.

"Oh, right. Well I'm afraid ya're doomed then."

Alex dropped his face into his hands. "I knew it! I knew I d—d—didn't stand a chance. I may as well just d—d—die now and get it over with."

"Ya're not dead, till ya're dead, lad. Chin up, remember? Yah can still put up a good fight."

"Not without a mug of ale in your hand and lass on your leg!"

The other Scots cheered again.

"I say we go a'pub hoppin' boys!" shouted the short Scotsman. "First round is on me!"

Alex tried to protest, but somehow, he was simply swept up in the Scottish wave and quickly found himself on his way to hop over pubs . . . whatever *that* meant.

No sooner did Isabelle groggily wake than her mind began asking a million questions all at once. *Where am I? What's going on? Why can't I move? What happened?*

"Wakey, wakey," someone said in an Irish accent.

With considerable effort, Isabelle wrestled her mind under control. She fought that welder fiend; no, she *killed* him. No, he was unconscious. Then she blew him up. So, yes he was most certainly dead now. That's right, she created an explosion to fake her own death. That's what happened. She made it to the garden and . . . then what?

She sat up cautiously, groaning, and squinted at the Irishman who had spoken. He was of African decent, dressed in what looked like once fine clothing, and a bowler hat. He stood with his arms crossed, leaning against the far wall, perfectly at ease, with a smug tilt to his lips. This man was not putting up a false front. This was a man of intention, controlled . . . Like Matthias Monaghan.

Glancing about her, Isabelle began to take in as many details as possible. She lay on a cot, still wearing her fine evening gown, complete with jewelry and slippers. Though she had a considerable amount of ash and dirt on the garment. It was also shredded in multiple places. She was alive, free to move around, and otherwise unharmed.

"Did you have a nice sleep?"

Instead of answering, Isabelle looked around. She was in a small, all wooden room. It was empty except for the cot she lay on, and a chair beside a simple table next to the Irishman.

She listened. Several masculine voices chatted amiably just beyond the room. At least three distinctly different accents. And was that a tugboat horn? Foghorn? Bells for sure.

"Ears still ringing? Don't worry. The headache'll clear up on its own."

She sniffed the air. Sea salt, body odor, glue, fresh wood, fresh paint . . . .

"Bet you're wondering where you are."

"The shipyards off Uptew Lane. This is the incomplete hull of a ship under construction, and we are in a smaller room that will eventually become sleeping quarters. It's the middle of the night, which means I've been unconscious for several hours at most. You are a shipwright, if I'm not mistaken, but given that you're here at this hour, and wearing attire that might've been considered fashionable roughly five years ago, you have a second life dealing in the underground. Which means you work for Matthias Monaghan."

The Irishman blinked, but before he could respond, clapping just behind the doorway announced . . . . "Deductive as always, Lady Viece." Matt Monty himself strode into the room with his characteristic controlled air, and Isabelle relaxed for the first time in ages.

Between his bowler hat, short coat worn over a dark, dirty linen vest with missing brass buttons, and his plain boots and trousers, one would never guess this man ran an underground criminal syndicate.

Isabelle suspected he ran smuggling operations in most of the ports off the West Coast. Otherwise unremarkable, the only notable thing about Monty was his bearing. He carried himself with such authority. Like a boulder in the wind, he would not be moved. That made him dangerous. And alluring.

Monty took the empty chair, placed it in front of Isabelle and sat on it the wrong way, resting his arms over the ladder-back, and lacing his fingerless-gloved hands together. "How are you feeling?"

"I'm tired, but otherwise well. Thank you. It's good to see you."

"And you, Lady Viece. Blimey, that was an incredible explosion! I'm still not sure how you survived."

"You were there?" Isabelle asked cautiously.

Monty shrugged. "Found you out in your garden, unconscious after that impressive explosion. Garnet wants you dead, so I brought you here. A sort of heroic gesture, you might say." He winked at her.

Isabelle frowned. "You saved my life?"

"You might say that." He cocked his head with a smile.

Isabelle's frown deepened. "My manor, is it—"

"Gone? Completely. That whole bleedin' building is in hell now."

What?! She had thought that explosion would blow up the room at best, not her entire home. Her home . . . . "Why were you at my home?"

Monty stood up with a grin. "That is an excellent question. What do you say we have a little chat over a drink, eh?"

Hopping over pubs turned out to be a euphemism for "let's give God absolutely no reason to even consider letting us in to heaven". From one disreputable, vermin-infested stink hole to another, the Scots dragged Alex along to sample different kinds of vile sewer fluids called liquor. The Scots cheered and bellowed, and pounded Alex on the back, and he felt so welcome that he found he didn't mind the experience. He held Lady Viece's satchel tightly as he placed his order at the bar.

The Scots held up their mugs, toasted to Alex himself, and took deep swigs of their ale. With a shrug, Alex drank. He drank deeply. He downed the hell out of that mug of water like there was no tomorrow. And there probably wasn't.

". . . tavern for sailors of every sort," Monty was saying as he led Isabelle into a seaside inn and tavern called the Hull's Haul. "You go on and have a seat while I track down a drink or two for us." He nodded to a table on the far side of the bustling tavern. It had to be near dawn, yet this tavern was brimming with inebriated sailors of apparently every ethnicity.

Isabelle sat down less gracefully than she would've liked, exhaustion finally catching up to her galvanized mind, though she refused to succumb to it. As pleased as she was to be in the company of a friend, she was more interested in what Monty represented: information. Garnet had been two steps ahead of her the entire way, and she was tired of losing. Tired of failure. Tired of . . . she was so tired.

Monty sat down, placing a cup of wine before Isabelle. He had a mug of ale in his own hand.

"What do you know of it?" Isabelle asked.

"Sorry?"

"What do you know about my family's case?"

"What makes you think I know anything?"

"Oh don't be tiresome, Monty."

Monty raised his eyebrows at her sudden vehemence.

"I'm here, in your custody, in the middle of the night, drained in every way a woman can be, with a headache like a hammer. Lord Garnet has been up to all manner of machinations, has been scrutinizing my family's every move, sent the worst kind of maggot to kill me but only after he'd *had his fun.*" She shuddered as she recalled that blowtorch next to her face.

"I blew up my own home to fake my death, that I might have a moment of peace from that wretched man, who is now in possession of forged evidence, which could see my family escorted promptly to the noose! Humor me. I know you have an extensive network of informants, as your most timely presence at my mansion clearly indicates. Tell me everything you know about the allegations cast upon my house!"

Monty eyed her for a moment, slightly stunned at her outburst, then chuckled. "You've had a time of it, haven't you?" He took a swig of his ale. "Word on the street is Lord Viece has been arrested for high treason. Something about secretly sending funds and resources to an estate in Spain. No one really knows exactly who or what for."

"But you do."

"Naturally. It's a private operation," he said with a smirk as he lit up a cigar, puffing it smoothly. "Government's not involved. Your father never told you about his dealings?"

"Of course he did. These accusations are based on lies, forged evidence, as I believe I mentioned. How could he speak to me of hands he never dealt?"

"You're so convinced your family's hands are clean? I tell you, there's not a noble in all of the world who has clean hands. Everyone's involved in one sort of treason or another."

"Not my family."

"Well then you should have little to fear. Your family is disgustingly rich and influential and, you seem certain, is quite innocent. Surely they won't have a problem getting out of the noose. Doubt you need to be concerned."

"I need not be concerned about Lord Garnet planting false evidence to convict my father of treason? His house is just as prominent as mine and would be a formidable adversary in our attempt to acquit my father of the accusations laid against him."

"So Garnet has the upper hand. He outmaneuvered you. That's how these blood feuds work. It's your move now. He thinks you're dead. He got some dirt on your family, sure. Now you get some on his, and act accordingly."

"Well if you recall the patent scandal I approached you about recently, I know Garnet views that as a threat to his empire. In fact I wonder if that's why he has taken to such a blatant attack strategy on my family lately. I am clearly more of a threat than he dares admit, especially if he wants me dead. Which means I'm right."

Monty took another casual puff, eyeing Isabelle coolly. "This patent scandal. If Garnet is threatened by it, does that mean you have enough evidence to put him away? A sort of ace-in-the-hole to topple his empire?"

"Not enough. I really needed the weapon."

"Weapon?"

"The Crimsons stole a weapon that was on its way to Garnet. I nearly had it, but as soon as the Crimsons acquired it, my momentum in the case stumbled to a halt. I originally thought the Crimsons were working with Garnet, but alas I was mistaken. Garnet has played this one well. If I could just recover that weapon, I may have what I need to put him away." She grimaced as a thought struck her. The blueprints were the other piece of evidence she secured. They were in her room, which had been destroyed in the explosion.

"Or something you could use as leverage to save your family." He leaned forward, resting his elbows on the table. "What does this weapon have to do with the patent scandal anyway?"

"It's proof of what he's doing with the patents he's stealing. I can prove each of the aspects that make up the workings of the weapon were stolen from inventors who—"

Isabelle paused, her tired mind trying to piece . . . something together. It was too convenient. Monty, a friend and ally, finding her unconscious and taking her back to his lair? How had he known she was there? And what of the timing? Right as she'd found—and then had stolen from her—planted evidence against her family?

It was still night, and she was still in her same clothes, which meant it was the same night. Monty would've had to have found her immediately after the explosion, before the fire brigade arrived, else she would've been in a hospital.

Monty had built his smuggling empire on the power of information. He was even called the Informant by those who weren't in his circle. And now he had her gabbing on about everything she knew regarding Lord Garnet's nefarious intentions.

Gear number one fell into place: she had not been rescued from her exploded home. She had been kidnapped.

Isabelle remembered Monty's club with its boisterous laughter from the bar. She had already noted this particular tavern was too busy for this time of night. Not because this lot of reprobates needed to sleep, but because by now, they would all be too drunk to stand. And yet everyone was still functional.

Gear number two clicked: no one was drinking as much as they pretended. This place was another one of Monty's hubs. The consistent noise level was planned, a distraction to cover for the clandestine meetings at the booths in the back, which were very similar to the ones at his club.

In fact, the air in his club always reeked of alcohol, sweat, and oil. Dim lighting. Rustic tables and chairs, that conspicuous machine that took up half the back wall, the barmaids and their plunging necklines, ogled by every man who walked in. The Hull's Haul had a similar set up, if a different theme.

Gear number three: this was a sophisticated criminal operation, beyond any scope Isabelle could have conceived. She'd physically visited two now. How many were there?

Akane had taken the planted evidence. She was the only other person who knew Isabelle's life had been in danger. The only other person present. Akane must've saved her life, and brought her here.

Gear number four: Akane didn't work for Garnet. She worked for Monty.

Isabelle glanced about the tavern, and looked at each sailor, some of them shipwrights dressed similarly to the Irish fellow who had been there when she first woke. These men built ships with their secret cargo *in* the ship structures themselves.

Chilled, Isabelle winced at her own naivety. How could she have ever considered herself clever for coming up with the idea to "befriend" a well-connected crime lord who would be of use to her investigations? *There's not a noble in all the world that has clean hands.*

Gear number five clicked in her head . . .

"You're playing me."

Monty raised an eyebrow.

"You're in Garnet's employ. I'm your prisoner here. You own this tavern. Everyone in here would stop me from leaving. You knew I'd be comfortable enough with you that all you had to do was keep me placated, and you could tease out some valuable information, perhaps a way for you to get the better of Garnet."

The men nearest to her table, close enough to hear her, suddenly stopped cajoling, and eyed Monty warily. Monty himself didn't respond. He sat motionless, unblinking, idly caressing his mug of ale with his thumb.

He took a long drag on his cigar, then finally, he smiled. "Deductive as ever, Lady Viece."

Chapter 21

LORD VIECE'S COMPELLING CONFESSION NOT ENOUGH TO SWAY TRIAL AFTER EVIDENCE FINALLY ARRIVES

LORD VIECE'S STARTLING ADMISSION TO CONVERSATIONS WITH SPAIN TO OPEN INTERNATIONAL BUSINESS DEALS CREATES FRENZY IN CORPORATE WORLD AS OTHER COMPANIES SCRAMBLE TO IMITATE INGENIOUS MOVE; FAILS TO PERSUADE COURT TO DROP TREASON CHARGES IN THE WAKE OF FIRST PIECE OF EVIDENCE.

The next pub in line for Alex's very first pub hopping experience was the Hull's Haul, which turned out to be a popular seaside inn and tavern for foreign sailors. Well, for any sailors, but there were an unusual number of accents and languages here. Most were Spanish, Italian, French, and occasionally North African. But then there was that one woman in the back. She was dressed in black, nimble clothing of oriental origin. She eyed the room with distinct tilted eyes, her straight, jet black hair pulled up in a utilitarian ponytail. Her people were rare in these parts.

She stood inconspicuously in the background, but those discerning eyes, the way she leaned against the wall . . . she was waiting for someone.

Not a lover, as she was hardly eager about it. But someone important nonetheless. She had business to be about tonight, which meant . . . nothing to Alex.

So Alex turned to the bar and shared his first round with his new Scottish friends, who were a mixed breed of misfits themselves, though to a man they all insisted they were Scottish. They perfectly fit in with this lot. Must be nice, to fit in somewhere.

Alex reached into his pocket to fiddle with his pocket watch. Oh yeah, the Crimsons had stolen that. The one thing he thought he had done right in life, but nope. He couldn't even have that. With a sigh, he graciously accepted a full mug from the bartender and drank. He drank deeply. He downed the hell out of that mug of water like there was no tomorrow. And there probably wasn't. Not for Alex and his pathetic deductive abilities. He—

Was that . . . Lady Viece?

"You planted the incriminating evidence against my family." Words cascaded out of Isabelle's mouth as her horrified mind connected piece after piece of a puzzle she hadn't even known was there. "Garnet asked you to spy on us until you could find something condemning that he could use against us. To destroy us."

Monty leaned forward, looking into his mug of ale without an inkling of concern on his face. "First of all, Garnet didn't *ask* me to do anything. He paid me for it."

Casual shuffling caught Isabelle's attention to the side. Were the shipwrights moving closer?

"And I didn't plant anything. Garnet *hired* me to *find* incriminating evidence against your family." He puffed casually on his cigar.

Isabelle's stomach lurched as though she'd been punched. "You . . . You didn't plant it?"

The shipwrights slowly, nonchalantly surrounded Monty and Isabelle. The others in the room poignantly ignored the situation unfolding. If Isabelle needed any more confirmation Monty owned this tavern, that was it.

"Of course not," he said calmly. "If I wanted to plant evidence, it would've been much easier for others to find. I practically had to murder and maim to get the dirt on your father. That man is cunning. Covered his tracks well, he did."

"My home was only just ransacked hours ago. The evidence was still there. That can only mean it was planted. It . . ." Isabelle trailed off as Monty actually gave her a sympathetic look.

"I'm sorry love, but if you must know, your father did such a remarkable job covering his tracks, I figured the best person to find any real evidence would be you."

Isabelle stiffened.

"You do have a knack for finding the dirt others take painstaking precautions to hide. A sort of *specialized* housemaid. Wouldn't you say?"

"I burnt it," she whispered.

"I know."

Of course he did. Akane had taken the evidence from the fire. The room was suddenly stifling. Isabelle took a moment to swallow, blink hard, and shift more gears into place. "When?" she whispered stiffly. "When did Garnet approach you about this?"

"Psh. Years ago. Long before I ever met you. I didn't think he was ever going to use the information. He just liked to have something to sit on, you know? A sort of leverage, you might say. Seems it did come in handy after all."

"So you've known about my family's . . . affairs for years. But only just now found the evidence needed to convict us?"

The shipwrights stood ominously around Monty and Isabelle, coldness in their eyes.

"Why didn't you tell me?" she whispered, betrayed, feeling like an utter fool.

"Tell you what? Every bleedin' rich bastard that walks into my club hires me to find them information on every other bleedin' rich bastard? Hell if I can keep any of it straight. Well, actually I can, but honestly I'd forgotten all about that bit with Garnet until your father was called to London for questioning."

"Which is when Garnet approached you about ransacking my home. That act alone is illegal. You could testify in court," she added hastily, desperately. "Explain how Garnet hired you. It may nullify any evidence illegally obtained to convict my family."

Monty just frowned at her. "To put it plainly, I have no desire to surrender my lucrative business on account of your family. And I did mention that every wealthy bastard under the sun has approached me to—"

"Others have asked after my father's affairs?"

"Sure. And about yours too. They didn't offer me anything worth my time though. Garnet was the only one who truly knew the value of what he was asking me for. So don't worry. He's the only one who knows the truth of your family's treason."

This entire situation threw her right back to the incident at the circus. In over her head, a lone stupid woman facing an entire band of looming gorillas.

Her mind raced for a way out, her eyes darted all around, searching for something useful against said looming gorillas.

"You've never asked me for payment," she said quickly. Keep him talking. Monty liked to talk. And gloat.

"Of course not. You've been helping me stay on top of the food chain. Putting all those would-be crime lords away for me. Busting big time heists that, if the fellows succeeded, could've shifted power down here."

Though Monty said it so casually, as though he and Isabelle had worked together on this, Isabelle took it as a slap to the face.

Monty cocked an eyebrow again. "You really didn't know what you were doing? You never once thought to ask after payment? I assumed it was your plan. I help you solve crimes and maintain authority in your society, and you put all my competition behind bars, helping me maintain *my* position in *my* society. A sort of mutually beneficial arrangement, you might say."

Isabelle sucked in a breath. Keep talking. Find something he wants. Then wrestle control of this world-shattering conversation away from him.

"Garnet," Isabelle insisted. "What evidence did you give him against my father?"

"See now, this sort of thing does *not* serve my interests."

Fuming, Isabelle had simply had enough. She huffed and stared Monty in the eyes with more intensity than the midday sun. "You are the fool who never asked me for more than insurance against losing your most coveted position as leader of the rat infestation," she snapped.

Monty didn't react. His men however exchanged confused looks.

"If you wish to haggle over payment now, very well. My family is, oh how did you put it, disgustingly rich? And influential? And owns half of England? And likely pays your miserable salaries?"

"You—"

"And then of course there's my personal influence in the constabulary to consider." Yes, interrupt him. Men of power did not like to be interrupted. "After all, you have done a marvelous job at helping me *maintain authority in my society*. Even if you did plant a few spies within it. I can't reasonably be upset by that, given how many I've placed in yours."

Apprehensive murmurs spread through the shipwrights. Monty eyed his men coolly. He likely suspected her bluff, but since he didn't react with amusement, she could conclude there were some people in this room whose loyalties he could not confirm. So he played her game. Perfect.

"No," she continued blithely. "I suspect we can come to an agreeable solution . . . a sort of *understanding* you might say."

That last gibe actually got under his skin. A subtle twitch of the eye. The shipwrights stood stiffly, waiting for Monty to speak. But he merely eyed her with that intense gaze that could turn rocks into diamonds.

"Shipments," he said finally. "Your father covered his tracks well but the shipping ledgers have to be thorough. If you look closely at the shipping companies your family owns, at each of the ship ledgers for the past three or four years. Not just months. But overall. You'll see the pattern. Something less than business savvy about shipping goods to another country without completely filling the hull. Begs the question: what *is* filling the hull? Not really a matter of what *is* there, but more of, what is *not* there that rather should be."

"That's all? You based your entire theory of my father's guilt on a couple alleged flaws in the shipping records? Found over the course of multiple years, mind you. My, my Mr. Monaghan. You must've had to look deeply indeed. And still came out with a tenuous, paper-thin *guess*? To maintain your position on Garnet's payroll, I presume?"

The two of them entered into an unspoken staring match. No one moved. No one breathed. No one swatted that fly that threatened to ruin the intensity of the moment. Isabelle stared daggers into Monty's eyes, daring him to speak. If his eyes could turn rock into diamond, then hers could skewer a boar and roast it on a spit.

They stared.

And stared.

AND . . . stared.

AND THEN FINALLY!!!! Monty blinked. The shipwrights exclaimed their disappointment, throwing hands and insults into the air, and passing lost bet money back and forth.

The irritation on Monty's face was not an expression she'd ever seen on him before. He began to clap slowly, silencing the shipwrights. "A detective's badge doesn't suit you, Lady Viece. I think you missed your calling as a solicitor."

"Have I."

"Indeed. In fact, you've been so laudably persistent, I'll confess to everything." He spread his hands grandly. This was not a defeated man by any measure. He had likely been gauging her reactions with each tidbit of information he revealed.

All right, Isabelle stifled a sigh. *Let the real gloating begin.*

"Garnet hired me years ago to uncover some dirt on your family. All I could find were the discrepancies in the shipping ledgers. Those discrepancies led to a theory that your family was involved in a sort of war conspiracy originating in Spain. The theory is solid, and likely true, but Garnet couldn't use it unless he had hard evidence to convict your family. He hired me again to slowly leak information over the past few years, start some inconvenient rumors, convince your family to use some of my ships to smuggle their seemingly pointless scraps of metal, so I could keep an eye on them and uncover more information.

"Finally, when the case against them officially moved forward, and they would be out of the house, leaving you to mind the family's affairs, that was my chance to strike. Garnet occupied you, while I had my boys ransack your home as though looking for something they didn't find. The idea was that you'd come home and find it for them. Which you obligingly did. And then subsequently burned, which I couldn't have planned better myself. We retrieved the evidence, handed it over to Garnet, who is now on his way to London to provide the last piece of evidence to finalize the conviction in your family's trial. So now, thanks to you, Garnet has legitimate evidence that looks as though your family was trying to hide it, and I—" Monty sat back smugly, puffing the last bit of his cigar—"am richer than the Queen."

"I think they be a'courtin'," the large Scotsman said. "That rugged fellow's a smooth talkin' his way toward something."

"Fairly certain we know what that something is," another Scot chimed in with a wink.

"So you don't think she needs me?" asked Alex. He'd been debating with himself on whether to approach them. Something was off. Lady Viece didn't look well, with her dress in shambles, dirty, slumped. He wasn't sure what had happened at her manor after he left, but given Lady Viece's state, it couldn't have been good.

Suddenly, Lady Viece stiffened. There was a noticeable lull in their conversation. Something was not right. Alex had to go over there and make sure. It was his duty. But . . . what if he was right? What could he possibly do? Go confront Monty and that brute squad making a show of standing around the table? They'd eat him for breakfast. He turned back to face the bar, holding his mug of water in a trembling hand.

And then he drank. He drank deeply. He downed the hell out of that mug of water like there was no tomorrow. And there probably wasn't. Because he couldn't do anything. He was useless. Again. He was so tired of being useless. Tired of being scared. Tired of . . . he was so tired.

Isabelle couldn't breathe. It was like being stabbed in the gut. The evidence was real. Her family was guilty. And she . . . she had just sealed their fate. "What have I done?" she whispered, losing the ground she had recovered.

"Lost. Happens to the best of us."

"No," Isabelle whispered. "It doesn't happen to you. It doesn't happen to the Crimsons. In fact, it doesn't seem to happen to anyone who doesn't play by the rules."

"You've a point there. All you high-borns seem to think you've got the game rigged. But fellows like me . . . we know it's all bluster. A sort of sham, you might say."

"*You* might say. *I* would say it's more of an act. A play you might see at theater. So why not put on a different show?"

Monty cocked an eyebrow. "What did you have in mind?"

Summoning whatever meager courage she had left, Isabelle leaned forward. "How much did Garnet offer you for my death?"

"A lot."

"I'll offer you all of it."

Monty blinked. "Come again?"

"You want to be richer than the Queen? How about richer than God? Help me bring down Garnet. He's running an illegal operation. He wouldn't dare keep his *illegal* profits in the same location as his *legal* profits. If we expose the scandal, and suggest his illegal banking operations have been compromised, the first thing he'll do is move those illegal profits to a more secure location. But given the scandal, no bank is likely to take any deal Garnet offers. He knows this. So he likely won't even bother with the banks. He'll go to someone who has experience dealing with the transportation of illegal funds . . . ." She raised her eyebrows in askance.

A slow, mischievous smile spread across Monty's lips. "Oh *that*," he declared, "is clever. He won't have any ground to demand the money if he's set to rot in prison for his crimes. The money remains undeclared and therefore can't be traced. No one will ever know I have it. Haha! I like it. Brilliant!"

"We have an agreement then?"

A long silence ensued as Monty musingly milked the monumental moment mmm . . . momentously. Anyway, he clearly already made up his mind, and yet he insisted on the pretense of consideration.

Finally, Monty nodded. "Aye. That we do."

An immediate internal breath released inside of Isabelle. "Excellent." She stood up abruptly, hoping to ensure this verbal wrestling match ended here. "Now if you would kindly take me back to your ship. I'd very like to get some rest before we begin planning Garnet's downfall."

"Oh? You mean your *informants* planted in my tavern don't have a safe house to whisk you off to?"

Isabelle blinked. One last power grab. She needed to show him she would not be cowed. Somehow, some way, it was at that moment she caught sight of Constable Corbin, sitting at the bar, watching her, exchanging whispers urgently with . . . the circus troupe? Who happened to be a rather intimidating lot. Isabelle smiled at Monty, then waved for Constable Corbin and the circus troupe to attend her. *Please come,* she thought desperately to herself.

After a few more urgent whispers, Constable Corbin led the unit hobbling on crutches, an entire group of burly men cracking knuckles and tromping over to her side.

The dark glare on Monty's face represented the most chagrined she'd ever seen him. She smiled again, and allowed her improvised entourage to escort her out of the tavern.

Chapter 22

VIECE ESTATE BLOWN TO BITS; HEIR MISSING

DISASTER ABOUNDS FOR VIECE HOUSE AS AUTHORITIES INVESTIGATE CAUSE OF VIECE ESTATE EXPLOSION IN WAKE OF CONDEMNING EVIDENCE ARRIVING IN COURT. LADY ISABELLE VIECE, HOUSE HEIR, PRESUMED TO HAVE PERISHED IN BLAZE.

Sleep did very little for Isabelle's exhaustion, but it did further cinch her resolve. As it turned out, Constable Corbin's new band of friends were indeed the unfortunate circus troupe put out of business thanks to Isabelle's mess. The ship they had loaded their cargo onto—or what was left of their cargo—now served as her hideout. The captain of the *Transparency*, a merchant with mixed African and Western European origins like Isabelle herself, named Fallou Seydi, happened to be an amiable fellow, and as coincidence would have it, had been hired by her father on several occasions to ship wares up and down the West Coast, all the way down to the African ports, where he often collected exotic wares. He had graciously given his quarters to Isabelle for the duration of her stay.

But she didn't intend to stay long. Sitting at the tiny built-in vanity beside her bed, she looked at herself in the mirror. Bags under her eyes, hair a mess of slovenly black curls, her normally warm skin now bordering on pallid. She was dead, as far as the world was concerned.

And she had to keep the world believing that a little while longer.

Reaching across the vanity, Isabelle gently picked up a knife, courtesy of Captain Seydi. Hand shaking, she pulled her long, thick hair around her shoulder, and began the process of sawing it off, piece by piece. When she finished, her hair barely brushed the top of her shoulders. A silly thing to bring a woman to tears, but it felt as though Isabelle were cutting away a piece of herself. A piece that would never return to her.

With a deep breath of resolve, Isabelle continued her transformation. She grabbed a jar of dark powder she had requested from Captain Seydi and dumped it on her hair. When she had asked the captain for dye, he had laughed and said her black hair would never take it. He offered the grey powder as an alternative to make her hair look dirty and ashen. Indeed, once she saw the effect, she agreed that nullifying the shiny black was enough to give her a completely different look.

A simple, utilitarian dress followed, along with a simple scarf to hide the wound on her neck. The woman who stared back at Isabelle in the mirror was not a Viece. She wasn't sure who that woman was. But she knew what that woman was going to do: save her house.

With another resolved sigh, Isabelle tossed all sense of decorum, fashion, beauty, and modesty out the window to make space for her plans. A few sheets of paper, a jar of ink, and a single quill were all the weapons she had left. Blinking away her exhaustion (which absolutely works; it's a medical fact), she began to sketch out her plan, relying on her memory to piece together all the information she'd collected—and then exploded—over the years. A knock at the door interrupted her before she touched pen to paper.

"Come," she barked with barely-stifled chagrin.

"Good morning, Lady Viece," said Constable Corbin sheepishly, as he lumbered through the narrow doorway, awkward on his crutches. A brief sorrowful expression crossed his face as he took in her new look.

Isabelle ignored his sympathies and plowed on. "Did you get a message through?"

"Yes," Corbin replied, locking eyes with her. "He'll come. I'm sure of it."

"I hope you're right," Isabelle said turning back to her vanity. She wasn't able to put too much in the way of apology into the message she had Corbin covertly deliver to Chief Brighton, but she hoped it was enough to garner his help.

She glanced back at Constable Corbin, and swallowed, unsure how to proceed. "Thank you again for your assistance last night."

"Of course. No . . . um . . . it was no trouble."

Isabelle took a deep breath, then opened her mouth to speak the apology she should've said long ago. But Corbin spoke up first.

"I know things been sh–shaky between us . . . um . . . Lady Viece, but . . . well here."

Alex held out a worn leather satchel. *Her* satchel. She gently took it and peeked inside, hoping against hope. "My notes!" she whispered, tears glistening in her eyes. She riffled through the satchel with increasing amazement. These were the notes from her bedchamber wall. At the bottom of the satchel was her pistol. The one she barely knew how to use.

She looked up at Constable Corbin. He smiled. After everything she had done to him, used him, made a fool of him . . . "Oh Constable Corbin. I'm so, terribly sorry. I've been absolutely awful to you, haven't I?"

Corbin looked down at his feet, blushing. "S'all right, Lady Viece. I already forgave you. You're trying to do something the likes of's never been done before. And with your family and all . . . s'all right."

"No. No it's not. Nothing justifies my abhorrent behavior. You've been the only support I've had in this investigation and . . . I'm just so sorry."

Corbin smiled even broader at her. "It's all right. Really."

"Thank you, Constable. Truly. I couldn't be more grateful to have you on my side."

Corbin stood up a bit straighter, and beamed. For Isabelle, it was a weight off her shoulders she'd been denying was there.

"So," Corbin said finally. "I was thinking. About this whole mess with Garnet. And with that message you sent to Chief Brighton. And . . . well I thought you could use some extra help."

Isabelle arrived in the same shipyard she had woken up in just the other night, the half-completed ship itself dominating the massive brick-walled structure, facing toward a large metal and wood sliding door hiding the sea on the other side. She wasn't sure what she had expected. But most certainly not this.

Constable Corbin stood on his crutches by her side, beaming. But all she could do was gape, unbidden tears welling in her eyes once more.

Standing next to an area designated for work tables, with all manner of strange metal implements, was Chief Brighton, a small group of weary, ragtag constables, the circus troupe of burly performers now dressed in normal work clothing, and Matthias Monaghan, accompanied by Akane, and a small group of shipwrights.

"Lady Viece," said Chief Brighton with a grin. "Can't tell you how happy I am to see you alive. I'm so relieved you ain't dead. Now, I know we ain't much, and there ain't much of us, but here we are. At your service."

"After what happened at the circus," Corbin said. "We ain't strictly speaking supposed to be constabularing right now. Not until the court hearing, but . . . well someone's gotta serve justice, you know?"

"Is that what we're a'doin' here?" asked one of the shorter circus performers. "Servin' justice? I thought we were a'gunta beat up some rich dandy?"

"That's part of it, McShorty," said Constable Corbin. "But we gotta bring him down first."

"Oh? He's that tall, eh?" mused another circus performer. He nudged McShorty. "Let's get ya a ladder then." The joke earned a round of hearty laughs from the circus troupe, McShorty included.

"Shut it! The lot a ya!" yelled the ringmaster, Cedric, a tall, particularly muscled Scotsman who could give Cleaver a run for his biceps. He had an impressive red beard, a receding hairline, and blue eyes far too intense for the current climate. "We're a gettin' into some serious business right now. And if ya keep a'crackin' wise, I'll pass ya off to them shipwrights to hide your roasted rump in the ship walls, where you'll never be able to crack a right stupid joke ever again."

Well that effectively silenced everyone.

Cedric nodded in satisfaction. "Now, let the lass speak."

Wiping away a tear, Isabelle simply laughed. It wasn't the professional, organized and disciplined crew she had been working to mold the constables into, but this was far more help than she could've hoped for.

She laughed some more as she moved to stand among her team of misfits, exchanging gracious pleasantries, finally properly meeting the circus troupe, and nodding politely—well, there may have been a pinch of tension, and a dash of scorn—to Mr. Monaghan. He kept to the back and merely observed everyone, though she noted him eyeing her up and down, taking in her new look. Isabelle subconsciously adjusted the scarf around her neck to ensure her wound was hidden.

"So," Chief Brighton said, crossing his arms. "Now that we're all here, we can address the problem at hand. I'd start barking orders if I thought for a moment you didn't already have a plan concocted in that pretty head of yours. So I'll button my lip and stop talking. What do you got for us, Lady Viece?"

Isabelle chewed her bottom lip. Then she glided over to the work table where a large sheet of paper with the blueprints of the ship under construction lay, a pencil on top. She flipped the paper over and wrote four words, Brighton and Corbin hovering over her shoulder curiously.

"Here's my plan," she said. "Undermine. Negate. Isolate. Publicize. If we can accomplish these things, in this order, Garnet is as good as hanged."

The circus troupe collectively cheered their support, ready to jump right into action.

Everyone else stared at Isabelle with blank faces. Except Mr. Monaghan, who looked thoughtful. He likely already suspected where she was going with this, thinking ten steps ahead. Isabelle would have to be careful about how much she revealed, lest he attempt to sabotage her efforts. Hopefully, their deal would keep him in line.

"Ok," Brighton said slowly. "Undermine, negate, isolate, and publicize what?"

The circus mob deflated at that, murmuring to each other, realizing that was a good point.

"Undermine his reputation," Isabelle explained. "Bring his right to authority into question. Negate his assets and resources. Isolate him within his own ambition. Give him nowhere to go, and ensure the public turns against him. And lastly, publicize his crimes. I want to catch him in the act to not only secure his arrest, but ensure there's plenty to convict him with in court. Everyone will know of his treachery."

The circus troupe renewed their cheering.

"Lofty goals there, Lady Viece," said Constable Rivers, staring in confusion at the overtly excited circus troupe. "It'll take some time, by my reckoning."

"I intend to bring him down by his expo. *At* his expo, to be precise."

"In one month," Brighton said flatly. "Not sure that's possible. You know bringing down wealthy bastards can take decades."

"Legally," Mr. Monaghan chimed in with a smirk.

Brighton glared at him, but turned his attention to Isabelle. "Now Lady Viece, we're all honest men here. I—"

"I'll not require anything ethically questionable. I intend to . . . *skirt* past the law. Not disobey it."

"How?" asked Cedric.

"By turning this mission into a story the public won't be able to resist. A hidden villain who deceived the people. An average man who becomes the lone hero standing for justice. A charismatic pair of thieves whose allegiance remains elusive, keeping everyone guessing at every turn."

While everyone else in the group was confused, Corbin perked up. "The Crimson Run column? That's your play?"

"Everyone reads that infernal column, and follows it closer than a youth follows his first fancy. Now, leave dissemination up to me. The rest of you will be responsible for making the story true. The villain of the story is of course Garnet himself, and as you guessed, the thieves are the Crimsons."

"And the hero?" asked Brighton.

Isabelle smiled and settled her gaze on a single man standing beside her. "Why our very own Constable Corbin."

All eyes darted to Corbin. The blood instantly drained from his face. "Me?"

"Him?" asked Brighton.

"That?" sneered Monaghan.

"Ahahahaha!" Cedric clapped Corbin on the back, knocking him to the ground. "Good on ya, lad! Hah! I'm gunta love watching this!"

"Calm yourselves. All of you. There are of course a plethora of details I must work out for each of your roles in my plan. I'll discuss them with you individually as they become relevant. In the meantime, go about your normal business, and speak of this to no one. And thank you. All of you. When this is over, we'll have done the impossible. And we'll all be lauded as true heroes."

. . . the devious villain of our story has done, Lady Viece's letter read.

Despite his heinous schemes, he maintains a reputation as pristine as sparkling wine. The people view him as a man after their own hearts. They practically worship him, completely oblivious to his true nature. That is until some most unfortunate information spreads among the people that plant a quickly growing seed of doubt in their minds. This is the first step. To undermine our villain's reputation. To bring his right to authority into question. I leave this part of the plan in your capable hands, Mr. Monaghan.

Looking up from the letter, which arrived that very night after she laid out her plan to bring down Garnet, Monty smirked at the constable who had delivered it. They stood at the bar of his club, Monty leaning casually against the once fine varnished wood with a cigar in one hand and the letter in the other.

"Lady Viece said you'd know what to do?"

Monty eyed the constable. The man wasn't winning any weightlifting competitions, but he was doing a remarkable job keeping his discomfort off his bearing. Monty only saw it because the man was just a bit too still. Not stiff, but he didn't lean or lounge the way a man at ease would.

Monty smirked. "Aye. I do."

"Excellent," the constable exclaimed. "And the second request?"

This constable had potential, but still a lot to learn about masking his emotions. Take Monty himself for example. By leaning casually against the bar, puffing periodically on his cigar, but more importantly just holding something that gave the appearance of ease, and by taking his time to carefully read the letter, he masterfully and completely hid his seething indignation.

The Crimsons will unfortunately be vital to my plans, the letter continued.

We must recover Constable Corbin's mousetrap, as it represents the only original invention stolen that we can prove was indeed stolen with additionally nefarious intentions for it. My plan is simple in theory: the Crimsons are impossible to predict, and so we shall lure them to us. While they've been known to appear in the most unexpected places, I believe they can be relied upon to appear wherever there is excitement. I

*understand you and the Crimsons are essentially colleagues
of an unusual sort, which is why I request your assistance in
creating said excitement to lure them.*

It wasn't the instruction that irritated Monty. It was that he hadn't thought of it himself. It was positively brilliant. A stroke of genius one might say. And it *wasn't* his idea.

Swallowing his pride in the face of the constable messenger, Monty crafted the physical and verbal response that bespoke only what he wanted the man to infer: confidence, mystery, intelligence, and danger. And so he plastered a carefully crafted sly grin on his face, tilted his head just so, and slowly looked up at the constable. He then eyed the man once from head to toe, which instantly made the youthful constable shuffle uncomfortably. Years of honing this skill had helped Monty achieve his reputation of possessing exclusive knowledge. Which he did. But in his experience, having a reputation was more effective than having a skill.

Fortunately, Monty had both.

"Sir?" The constable asked again. "The second request?"

There was, perhaps, a way he could sway this entire distasteful situation to his advantage. "I have a few ideas."

Construction always, inevitably, was delayed. Construction crews would find a way to delay the opening date if it killed them. In fact Morgan was fairly certain it amused them to see their employers sweat, curse, kick, and scream to no avail. Construction crews would finish when they felt like it. That was part of the reason Morgan had opted to have his laboratories operate in a construction zone. He was actually building a new industrial district for Liverpool, but on the assumption delays would set opening day back two to four years, it was the perfect place to temporarily house his illegal fulminate lab, where all of his acquired patents were being turned into actual weapons.

It was brilliant, except for one thing. Construction was moving *faster* than anticipated, not a single delay occurred, and they were actually set to finish two to four years *early*. Morgan about blew a gasket. The poor engineer who owned the firm had bent backwards, worked his butt off, and skipped sleep, meals, and the birth of his firstborn so that he might stand proudly before Lord Morgan Garnet and announce the great news. He was hoping Morgan would hire him for future projects. Frankly Morgan was inclined to do so. If he weren't so utterly irate!

Morgan had to delay the project himself with all manner of obscene requests the poor engineer continued to knock out of the park (Morgan loved American baseball, so he was familiar with baseball metaphors; even the ones that didn't exist yet). But nevertheless, the project was successfully delayed.

With his faithful administrator, Mr. Barrington, at his side, Morgan stepped into a lift hidden within one of the new high-rise buildings about a year away from completion. Two well-dressed body guards accompanied them, lowering them down into the bowels of the building. The loud scraping of metal on metal as the infernal contraption grated its way down made Morgan grit his teeth, but it was the violent sounds of machinery at his destination that really threatened to explode his brain. Add the metallic smell and lingering fumes, and Morgan wasn't sure how the construction crews could bear to be down here.

Once the lift crashed at the bottom floor, the operator opened the gate, and Morgan stepped out. There was an art to a grand, authoritative entrance, and Morgan couldn't very well execute it with his brain rattling in his skull from the rough landing.

But his intentions were for naught, as standing right in front of the open lift gate was Morgan's crew leader. The burly fellow cast quite a shadow in these new, but rare electric lights. Standing atop metal grates that formed the raised walkway surrounding the entire lab, Mr. Avery extended his hand to greet Morgan. A hand easily twice the size of his. Morgan mentally counted his money as he stepped onto the catwalk, his body guards looming behind him.

"What do you have for me, Mr. Avery?"

"Cleaver, sir."

Morgan rolled his eyes. "Very well, *Cleaver*." These nicknames his crew insisted on using were positively silly in Morgan's estimation, but he obliged them. Whatever kept his minions in line. That was how you bought the loyalty of lesser men: you made them feel special. Even if those lesser men were twice your size and could eat you for breakfast . . . Morgan mentally counted his money again. "What do you have for me?"

"Everything you asked."

Morgan almost missed a step as he and Cleaver reached the railing, leaning over to see the entire laboratory laid out before them. The lab bustled with workers of all sorts, and assaulted Morgan with the loudest metallic cacophony ever to deafen a man. Beakers and Bunsen burners, copper coils attached to large wooden boxes covered with gauges and knobs of all sorts . . . Morgan assumed those all did something important. To the average fool, this place appeared to be an evil scientist laboratory from the stories, and Morgan actually didn't mind the moniker. "Everything?" he shouted. "Everything is done?"

"Yes, sir. Well . . . everything we could."

"And what, pray tell, does that mean?"

Cleaver grimaced as he handed a clipboard to Morgan with the details of all the new arms they were building here. A solid three-quarters of the original list were complete. The last quarter . . . . "I take it these can't be completed without the mousetrap?"

"It wasn't the mousetrap per se, sir. It was the fulminate we really needed."

"Do we at least have the blueprints?"

Cleaver grimaced again. "All destroyed in the circus fiasco. Those clown idiots completely packed up, disposed of almost everything, and moved on."

Morgan swallowed his chagrin at that. Those would've needed to be destroyed eventually anyway, but he had hoped to keep them a little longer.

He glanced at his lead henchman. The man had not been himself since the events at the circus. "Have your men recovered from that fiasco yet?"

Cleaver was freely doling out grimaces today. "We're holding up. Strangler had his head blown off and I haven't heard from him since. Figured I'd just give him some time off."

"I see." He tried to remember who that was, but shrugged instead. He really didn't care. "Next time clear that with me before granting my employees extended leave."

"Then what about Smithy?"

"What of him?"

"He exploded in the Viece mansion. I figured I'd give him some time off too."

Morgan scowled. "I ordered your men to sit the Viece Manor events out. What was Smithy doing there?"

"Don't matter now."

"I will not tolerate insubordination, Cleaver. Your orders were clear."

"Yes, sir."

There was something dark in the man's voice and expression that made Morgan hesitate before scolding him further. "You run a good crew, Cleaver," he said instead. "But recent events are beginning to sew uncertainty in my mind as to the competency of your crew. You have until the end of my expo to earn your way back into my good graces. And to further demonstrate my exceeding benevolence, I'll even divulge precisely what I desire of you to ensure your success.

"Bring me the mousetrap. Take the Crimsons out. Accomplish this however you will, but those are my orders. Remember, a bird in the hand is worth two in the bush."

Cleaver frowned.

"You know what I mean." Honestly, no one appreciated a good expression.

"Understood."

"I should hope you do." Morgan hesitated a moment at the sight of his clearly disgruntled henchman. "Have you more to say?"

"Yes I do, sir. Two of my top men are out for the count. Count Downey was found out and fled. Mayberry pulled out. The Crimsons stole our most valuable asset. And Lady Viece figured out our whole scheme . . . before getting herself blown to bits, that is."

"I'm sorry, was that a question?"

"Well yeah. You still sure you know what you're doing?"

Morgan bristled. "Do you trust me, or don't you, Cleaver?"

"I don't."

Well . . . all right then. "You don't have to. Do as you're told, collect your payment, and be silent." There was really no call to be annoyed with

Cleaver. Morgan had been careful to keep his actual overarching end goal between him and his wife. He couldn't rightfully be upset with his henchman for judging his competence with only half the facts. But still, the nerve! "And bring me my mousetrap!"

Chapter 23

GARNET DEFENSE EXPO EXPECTED TO DAZZLE

INDUSTRY LEADERS FROM AROUND COUNTRY HAVE SIGHTS SET ON GARNET INDUSTRIES' MUCH ANTICIPATED DEFENSE EXPOSITION. DATE, LOCATION, AND TIMES FOR INDIVIDUAL SHOWCASES REVEALED.

Despite their recent fallout, Isabelle couldn't help but once again be impressed by Monty's—*no! Mr. Monaghan; do not allow yourself to be pulled in again*—Mr. Monaghan's plan to lure the Crimsons. He had chosen his shipyard as the location, which Isabelle agreed with. Plenty of interesting things to steal here.

His newest ship was just about ready for her maiden voyage, so Mr. Monaghan simply declared she was ready, and announced a grand public viewing party for any and all to come see her majesty before she set sail.

He ensured the shipyard was filled with more people than likely would've attended something like this. Clever. Make it look like something interesting was happening, and perhaps it would entice the Crimsons to come.

He had his men cavalierly drop invitations in the streets, and send ostentatious invitations to key wealthy members in the merchant and trading circles. It was highly unlikely the Crimsons *wouldn't* hear of it.

Lastly, Monaghan strategically placed his own men throughout the shipyard. Akane positioned herself at the top of the rafters to keep an overhead lookout in case the Crimsons started climbing.

Isabelle had insisted on being present to ensure Mr. Monaghan didn't try to seize the mousetrap himself. She dressed herself in shipwright clothing, complete with the hat, her hair pulled back in a low tail, and a matching scarf around her neck.

She settled herself on one of the catwalks that rounded three sides of the shipyard, giving her enough distance from the ground to obscure her face, but keeping her close enough to identify the Crimsons below. She shook her head to Mr. Monaghan as he glanced up at her. He shook his head as well, but was quickly distracted by a wealthy merchant couple admiring the majestic new ship.

Isabelle searched the expansive shipyard for Chief Brighton. He and a few constables attended on the pretense of crowd control. She spotted him, and waited for him to make eye contact. He shook his head. No sign of the Crimsons.

A gigantic banner hung across the ship, just above a gangplank, announcing the ship's name: THE KNOTLESS. A sign off to the side invited guests to take a tour, an activity that drew most of the excitement.

No sign of the Crimsons.

The only potential caveat in this plan was the lack of guarantee that the Crimsons would have the mousetrap on their person, but

Isabelle suspected they carried everything they owned on their person. This should work.

Except that it's the Crimsons.

Hours stretched on, and the excitement waned. No sign of the Crimsons.

Evening arrived. The crowd had begun to dissipate.

No sign of the Crimsons.

A jolt on the catwalk startled Isabelle, but when she spun to see what had caused it, Akane came striding over to her. The Asian woman wore all black, fitted clothing that made no sound when she moved (yes Akane is essentially a ninja because ninjas are cool and I want a ninja in my story). Isabelle hadn't spoken to the woman since her manor explosion and found herself glaring at her former maid as she approached.

Akane rested a hand on the railing beside Isabelle and looked down at the waning crowd below. "They're not coming."

Isabelle started. There wasn't a hint of accent in her voice. With a groan, Isabelle confronted her former maid. "You played your part well. Were you spying on me from the beginning, or did Mr. Monaghan hire you after your confirmed employment by my family?"

"I have always worked for Matt Monty. And I was hired to spy on your father. Not you."

That made sense.

"I always liked you, Lady Viece. You were so kind to me. To everyone who worked for your family. Other wealthy families I have spied on treat their servants like dirt. Or they take them for granted. Not you."

"Is that supposed to flatter me? Given your ulterior motives?"

"No. You were no more difficult to fool than any of the others, despite the attention you gave me. You made the same mistake in assuming my place in the world was beneath yours, even if you never treated me so. You are doing a good thing here, Lady Viece. I don't wish to see you harmed because of your own arrogance. You—"

Isabelle stopped listening, her eyes going wide as she locked eyes with a burly, curly haired brute standing in the middle of the shipyard below.

"Lady Viece?" asked Akane, frowning.

Isabelle hurried down the catwalk.

"Lady Viece," Akane said as she followed. "What do you see?"

"I thought I saw . . . ." Isabelle scanned the crowd for . . . there! She bolted down the catwalk and pushed through the crowd until she reached Chief Brighton.

"You," he declared. "Are supposed to be lying low. Staying out of sight. Being—"

"The welders are here."

"I . . . what? Why?" But then realization struck him, and he slapped his forehead. "This is just all boiling down to who can get to those bloody Crimsons first, isn't it?"

"I'm afraid so. It would seem my plan was not as unique as I presumed."

"I'll go get rid of them."

"Wait. This must be handled delicately. Cleaver may have recognized me. And if you're here . . . ."

Brighton nodded slowly. "I have an idea."

"As the people begin to lose faith in the villain of our story," Lady Viece had said, *"they cry out for truth. They chatter among themselves, debating if these accusations, these flagrant obscenities could possibly be attributed to a man they once adored. Thus steps in the hero of our story, who does not yet*

know his own strength. An average constable, with nothing particularly heroic about him. But he is honest and true. And he has stumbled upon evidence implying the most devious scandal of our generation. One that involves the new patent system, steam technologies, and legal order. If our hero is correct, it could be disastrous for England's industry boom, and stop our forward progression in its tracks. He has the evidence, but our villain is much too powerful.

Thus we come upon step two of my plan. Negate. Resources cannot be an escape for him but he is simply too powerful, and we have too little time, to deplete his resources. Therefore, we need to take them out of the equation. Fortunately, our hero knows precisely how to accomplish this."

Alex had no idea how to accomplish this. Fortunately, the first step was already laid out. He and Lady Viece had worked out the details of how to start Alex's heroic reputation, which had to happen first before he could start negating Lord Garnet's resources.

As one of the few remaining constables left, no one really questioned Alex wherever he wanted to go. Even as he stood before the remains of Brass Manor—he'd traded his crutches for a cane—he had made it known where he was going and why. That part had been important, and was also why he had an entourage.

Brooks and Rivers completed the constables present at the scene, while the circus ringmaster's sons—a set of triplets, all dressed in black-and white-striped shirts, wearing dark eyeliner of all things, who referred to themselves as the Flavin Trio—brought the grand total up to six. They had been at Brass Manor all night, setting the stage for the show.

For what Lady Viece had in mind to begin establishing Alex's reputation, the circus troupe was a most fortunate resource, though the Flavin Trio was missing at the moment.

And so the show's advertisements began. Lady Viece needed the press to catch wind he was on to something big and was on his way to confirm it. Brooks and Rivers made a big show of the "constables being about important business," announcing it bluntly to every fool who passed by as they had made their way to the ruined estate.

Now that they had arrived at their destination, however, Brooks and Rivers started to ask questions. "What do we honestly think we're going to find in this rubbish dump?" asked Rivers, kicking charred planking out of his way. No one had arrived just yet. Alex estimated they had maybe an hour before press, private investigators, and curious bystanders began to trickle in.

"There's nothing here," agreed Brooks. "The place is completely devastated."

"Be lucky to find a half-intact sofa."

"Why would we want to find a sofa?"

"We don't. Just saying. We ain't finding anything of value here, mark my words."

"We ain't here to find nothing of value, Rivers. We're looking for evidence."

"That's what I meant."

"No it ain't."

"Why you bothering me, Brooks?"

"It amuses me."

"Well bother Corbin. *That* amuses me."

"Can't. Corbin's *the hero*. Gotta make it look believable. Ain't never been a hero whose guards don't respect him."

"I should've been the hero. I'm taller."

"Frankly anyone would've been a better choice than Corbin."

"Even that dead rat."

Alex perked up a moment, ignoring the rest of Brooks and Rivers insulting conversation. Dead rat? Alex found what Brooks was referring to (it might've been Rivers; I lost track of who was saying what) and went to inspect it. There wouldn't be any dead rats from the explosion on the outskirts of the mansion. They'd be buried in the rubble if there were any. What was this rat doing here? It looked freshly dead, no sign of char. What an odd place for a rat to die. Poison perhaps? He could use this.

Just like that, ideas began forming in his mind. He had always had a knack for deductive reasoning. If he reversed that reasoning, he could instead set up the evidence to lead to a certain deduction. The truth. Evidence to support what had actually happened at Brass Manor. And all the staged Crimson run scenes. And all of Garnet's apparent holdings. Throw all the resources he might, it wouldn't stop the flow of information constantly bombarding the public about Garnet's dealings. Resources negated.

". . . fool with a cat fetish," Rivers was saying.

"All brilliant, insane scientists have a cat fetish. It's required."

"Brass was another kind of—"

"Beggin' your pardon," Alex interrupted tentatively. "But are you two done? Because, we, you know, we have work to do."

Brooks and Rivers exchanged looks. "Work what? There's nothing here. Or weren't you listening to anything we just said?"

"The plan was never to find anything here. The plan was to make it look like there's something here to find."

At that moment, the Flavin Trio just kind of appeared beside Brooks and Rivers. Brooks jumped, but the Flavin Trio was completely unresponsive.

"There you are, Flavins," Alex said, slightly unnerved. "Is everything in place?"

The one in the middle calmly puffed on a cigar. A smooth nod was all the response he gave.

"All right." Alex drew a breath, resting both hands atop his cane before him. "The stage is set. Now we just need to give ourselves something to find."

With that, he put his team to work. To his surprise, they actually listened.

Cleaver was beginning to think his strategy to catch the Crimsons was misguided. This was the third event he attended since his resolute chat with the boss, and the third time the infamous duo didn't show. In fact, there hadn't been a new installment of the Crimson Run column since the circus fiasco.

His chances of catching the Crimsons were slim, but he had hoped if he kept attending exciting events, that maybe the Crimsons would show up to one of them. Unfortunately, he only had Steve supporting him today. Cog attended another event that had "Crimson run" written all over it, while he sent Gauge back to the Brass estate ruins. Brass kept his blueprints in fireproof tubes, and so Cleaver hoped they might be able to salvage a few from the wreckage before it was completely cleaned up.

With just himself and Steve, he kept watch at the *Knotless's* maiden voyage party, hoping the Crimsons would show up. Until he just happened to glance up at the rafters, catching sight of something he didn't expect. The woman had turned to walk down the catwalk, her back to him, but for a moment he could've sworn she was that Viece woman. The hair wasn't right though. And she was dead, of course but . . . no. Focus on the task at hand.

"Anything?"

Cleaver whirled around, ready to punch whoever had snuck up on him.

"Blimey! Relax, Cleaver. It's only me."

Cleaver lowered his fist. "Sorry, Steve. I just—"

"See something? Are they here?"

"No. I thought I saw . . . well Lady Isabelle Viece."

"The one what's dead?"

"Yeah that one."

"Well she's dead."

"What if she ain't? She knew the whole plan. What if she survived somehow? I swear that woman looked just like her!"

"If she was alive, why would she be here?"

"Same reason we are."

Steve hesitated at that. He opened his mouth to say something, but then groaned as he glanced over Cleaver's shoulder.

"Well, well, well," said a familiar gruff voice. "If it ain't my old friend Steve the welder. Fancy seeing you here."

"What? A man can't admire a new ship at a public event without getting harassed by the so-called peace keepers?"

"When that man admiring a new ship at a public event happens to be a man what tried to kill me, then yeah. He's going to get harassed."

"Shove off, peeler," said Cleaver. "We ain't done nothing wrong. We're allowed to be here."

"First of all, I ain't no peeler. Them's from London, and this ain't London. Second, you ain't allowed to be here if I says you ain't allowed to be here. And I says you ain't allowed to be here."

"What, you gonna arrest us?" Steve folded his arms and raised his chin.

"I'm thinking about it."

"On what charges?"

"Well let's see. Let me think. Trespassing in my personal space, attempted murder with that foul breath, stealing space in my vision . . . take your pick."

A quick glance around the room and Cleaver knew they were in trouble. They were drawing attention now, as Steve's voice grew louder.

"You think you can just get away with that? Arresting me for no damn good reason? What happens when word gets out about it? Constables arresting honest men what are just enjoying a public event?"

A second glance around planted a frown on Cleaver's face. He wasn't actually there to look at the ship, but a good amount of the people were casually standing around, eyeing the room with practiced nonchalance. It wasn't so much what they *were* doing as what they *weren't* doing that caught Cleaver's attention. Something was off.

"You really want to throw that *honest man* nonsense out there? Now that we all know you're in bed with Garnet Industries, ready to sell your soul to the devil himself?"

Steve opened his mouth, ready to vomit what Cleaver could only imagine would be an impressive wave of anti-constabulary rhetoric, but Cleaver shouldered his friend out of the way, and stood eye to eye with the constable chief.

"Apologies. You mistake us. We've lots of friends what worked on that ship there, and just thought maybe they had need of welders for the next job. Don't know where you got this notion about us working for Garnet, but it ain't true. We don't want no trouble."

Steve glared at Cleaver, but fortunately didn't say anything. He trusted Cleaver. All his men did.

"I'll tell you what," said the chief, tapping the side of his cheek. "You and your idiot sidekick there get the hell out of this yard, and I'll forget you was ever here."

"No way!" yelled Steve. "We have a right to be here!"

Cleaver gave him his best *shut up* stare, even as the chief barked back. "You push me and I'll arrest you."

"Oh right, for *stealing space in your visio*n."

"For whatever I damn well please!"

"You can't hold us!"

"You're right. I can't. But I can arrest you, toss you in prison, and by the time the paperwork and the so-called *peace keepers* decide it was a false charge, you'll have been rotting in there for at least a few days. That would brighten my gloomy day, make no mistake. So go ahead. Push me one more time. See what happens!"

"I—"

Cleaver punched Steve in the face, knocking the man to the ground.

The chief stood there, blinking, then snorted in amusement.

"We'll take your offer and leave, Chief. Thank you."

With that, he roughly pulled his idiot friend out of the shipyard.

By the time they were outside, Steve had mostly recovered from the punch, though he'd have a bruise and swelling to deal with. "What the bloody hell was that about?" he roared.

"*That*,"—Cleaver threw a finger in Steve's face—"was me salvaging our future. You think we can afford to spend a few days in prison right now? We are on thin ice with the boss as it is! And now you want to get personal with the chief of the constabulary? You don't think, Steve! You're one of my best men, sharp, capable, and reliable. Stop letting your personal vendetta with the constables get in the way of doing your bloody job!"

Steve maintained his challenging glare, but he didn't reply. So Cleaver let out a long, frustrated breath, as he plopped down on a crate, listening to the squawking sea birds, and inhaling the salty air.

"Right," Steve finally said, crouching next to Cleaver. "Look, the Crimsons didn't show, it was a bust anyway. Why you all bothered?"

"You're not? Do you pay attention, Steve? Do you see anything that's not right in front of you? That chief said everyone knows who we work for. But I thought everyone was excited about Garnet Industries. Why'd he make it sound like they're in trouble?"

"I don't know. Probably a propaganda push. Just like *The Times* maggots to push a propaganda story, something juicy to sell papers and mislead the general public on a—"

"Oh for the love of God, Steve, shut up for a moment about your conspiracy theories! Something's not right here."

"All right, fine. I'm listening. What?"

Cleaver thought for a moment. "What street is this?"

"Nogoud Lane I think. Why?"

Cleaver leaned forward, resting his chin on his hand. "These shipyards are managed by the Informant. Any event held in these parts is bound to have some measure of criminal activity attached to it."

"All right. So that explains why the chief was here."

"Except he'd be here to shut it down and arrest a few poor fools."

"And?"

"And so why didn't he?"

Steve nodded slowly. "He could've arrested us. His constables, the ones at the circus sent to guard us, they would've sold us out by now. Chiefy knows we're up to something and he could've arrested us for our part at the circus."

Cleaver nodded. "Something ain't right here. The chief's on to us, but he let us go?"

"He *wouldn't* have let us go," Steve said thoughtfully. "He would've arrested us, if it was up to him."

That was a very good point. Cleaver leapt to his feet. "He's got orders. He couldn't have known we would be here today. We messed something up." Cleaver snapped his fingers. "The Chief's after Garnet. He's trying to get the mousetrap from the Crimsons. That Viece wench must've told him everything she learned, and now he's trying to bring down the boss."

"Not if we bring him down first," Steve said with a wicked grin.

"We might have more than the chief to worry about." Cleaver couldn't be sure just yet, but something about today made him think the Informant might be up to some double-crossing here. The boss hired him for evidence against Isaiah Viece. But if the chief was here today, could they be working together? Were Cleaver and his gang ready to go up against a criminal mastermind like the Informant, take on the constabulary, and do what no one had ever managed before: catch the Crimsons?

Honestly, no. Not by a long shot. But Cleaver was determined to prove himself wrong.

That evening, the show began, and Alex was anything but a showman. Limping on his cane, he rummaged through the charred wood, broken china, slashed paintings, shattered porcelain, and ruined blankets and upholstery, doing his best to look smart and determined. Like he was actually looking for something. He hoped it looked more authentic than he felt.

Brooks and Rivers didn't seem to be having any trouble pulling off their part.

"Stay back, the lot of you!" shrieked Rivers at the encroaching crowd. "This here's a crime scene! Can't have you ruining the evidence with your lumbering stompers now!"

Brooks swung his truncheon threateningly. "Oi! You! There's important business going on here. Don't think I ain't watching you."

"What are you investigating constables?" asked a reporter from the small crowd.

"All manner of heinous crimes are afoot." Rivers answered. "You needn't be concerned. We constables are making sure you and your families stay safe."

"Why wouldn't we be safe?"

Alex almost smiled. Stroke of brilliance to drop that line. By saying we'll ensure your safety, it implied there was a reason to believe the public had something to fear.

"This crime scene is weeks old," said someone from the back of the crowd. "There ain't nothing going on here."

"By Joe!" yelled another from the back of the crowd. "If they're still investigating here, there must be something big and terrible happening!" It was of course Byjoe, one of the circus troupe members.

"I think you're right!" yelled another fellow, louder than needed. "Constable, are we going to be robbed? Are we safe?"

That would be the one they called McShorty, both planted in the crowd to stir up emotions.

"Is it the Crimsons?" another reporter asked.

Brooks glared at the reporter. "Does this look like a bloody Crimson run to you?"

The crowd began to stir, and murmur their thoughts.

"Forget it!" Brooks yelled, likely realizing that that's exactly what this looked like. In fact the original crime was reported as a Crimson run. "Just because there's chaos and disaster doesn't mean it's a bloody Crimson run! We're looking into some real serious criminal activity here. So everyone just stay calm, keep your distance, and Constable Alex Corbin,"—Alex froze—"will give you a briefing shortly."

Alex cleared his throat. Well, here goes nothing.

Hiding a wince as he struggled to climb atop a pile of wood that the Flavin Trio had artfully arranged to look like a stage, Alex cleared his throat again and looked over the crowd. A hush fell over the estate grounds. Alex rested his broken leg up on one of the wooden beams, also carefully placed there so Alex could strike this particular dramatic pose. The Flavins had even placed a few controlled fires throughout the ruins, causing smoke to dramatically curl in the air around Alex. Hopefully no one would think to ask why there was still fire weeks after the incident.

The stage was set. The hero was in place. All Alex had to do was address his people, ease their fears, let them know now that he was here, they had a chance to win.

There was just one problem.

Alex was terrified of public speaking.

He opened his mouth. Nothing came out.

Heart pounding, vision lurching, Alex panicked. *I'm going to blow it! Crap, I already blew it! I ain't no hero. I'm the biggest coward what ever walked the earth. I'm an insult to the Cowards Club.*

"Constable Alex Corbin, thank the Almighty you're here!"

Alex blinked and scanned the crowd. His eyes fell on McShorty. This was the fellow whose costume Alex had stolen in the privy.

"You'll keep us safe, won't you?"

Alex swallowed, eyes as wide as they could go. "Y–y–yes. Yes it is my c–c–c–commitment to you. T–t–to all of you. As a constable of the law, I–I–I–I PROMISE . . . to keep you safe. Yes."

"What are we in danger from?" Byjoe called out.

Bless them. "We are . . . um . . . we are investigating a possible . . . ah . . . patent scandal. We b–b–believe Professor Thomas Brass was a victim of . . . of . . . of . . . this terrible crime."

"Oh no!" McShorty wailed. He grabbed the random person next to him by the shoulders and shook him. "Whatever shall we do?"

"We're all going to die!" cried Byjoe. The crowd murmured their concern, chattering among themselves at this revelation.

"Now, now!" Alex continued, drawing strength from his friends. "I, Constable Alex Corbin, am here for you to make sure that doesn't happen. We at the c–c–c–constabulary are committed to your safety and, well, and . . . . I'll be damned if I let a single one of you suffer any more at the hands of these criminals." Lady Viece wrote that line. She said to make sure he stated his name, and mentioned the constables.

"Who?" McShorty demanded. "Who is responsible for this?"

The crowd exclaimed their mutual demand for an answer.

"We don't know yet, though we have a suspect. Until we have concrete proof, there won't be a stone we won't look under, no wooden slab we don't overturn, no piece of furniture we won't dismantle, or even piece of *garnet* jewelry we haven't scrutinized in this pile of rubble before this is over."

Well it wasn't the most graceful way to drop a subliminal message to the crowd, but there were not a lot of ways to casually use the word garnet in a sentence. Fortunately, Alex had his circus friends to clean up the sloppy mess.

McShorty, Byjoe, the Flavin Trio, Brooks, and Rivers let out such an infectious cheer, that it got the entire crowd cheering their assent. Alex could only assume McShorty was the one who started the Corbin chant. Next thing he knew, he stood on his contrived dais of charred wood, smoke dramatically curling behind him, basking in a crowd cheering his name.

A shy, unbidden smile slipped onto his lips as Alex glanced through the crowd. They were cheering for him. They were ALL cheering for him.

Except that guy.

But everyone else was—

Alex yanked his gaze back to the one fellow in the crowd who wasn't cheering. He was frowning in fact, scrutinizing Alex, weighing him. But that wasn't the problem. Alex recognized him. Gauge. The welder.

Chapter 24

GARNET DEFENSE EXPO MOMENTUM HITS WALL, QUESTIONS RAISED

AFTER RECENT, SCATHING CRIMSON RUN INSTALLMENT DETAILS ELABORATE PATENT SCANDAL, SCRUTINY BEFALLS ARMS TYCOON MERE WEEKS BEFORE MUCH-ANTICIPATED EXPO. EXCLUSIVE INTERVIEW WITH REAL LIFE HERO FROM THE COLUMN: CONSTABLE ALEXANDER CORBIN.

Isabelle waited impatiently under the dilapidated old bridge in the oldest part of Liverpool, inhabited by the occasional old vagabond strolling over the bridge. Not a pleasant place for a clandestine meeting, but most certainly an *ideal* place for one. Darkness had already wrapped its cold arms around the city, and an eerie mist formed around Isabelle's boots where she stood with her arms folded tightly. Tonight, she wore a

300

long black woolen coat with the hood up, exuding secrecy with her very breath and hoping no one noticed.

Isabelle waited.

And waited.

AND . . . waited.

AND THEN FINALLY! Her contact at *The Times* came sneaking over. First he snuck behind that lamppost there. Then he snuck over to the pile of old grocery crates over there. Then he snuck his way through the open cobblestone street, diving and rolling on the ground as if that might actually help him avoid being seen. Isabelle raised an eyebrow at the display as The Crow scuttled the rest of the way to the bridge, only to flatten himself against the wall just in front of Isabelle, face and stomach firmly planted against the wet stones.

Isabelle rolled her eyes. "Are you quite finished?"

"Sshh! It's not safe to speak yet."

"Oh for heaven's sake . . . ."

"Sshh!" He kept his ear against the stone, listening.

"Is it safe yet?" she asked flatly.

"Ssshh!" He paused, then slowly pushed himself away from the wall, and moved in close to Isabelle, looking around him to make sure no one was watching them (no one was, just so you know). "You uh . . ." He looked around again. "You got some *information* for me?" He quickly swung his head in either direction, as though he had revealed a secret juicier than a royal affair.

"I have it on good authority the Crimsons stole a weapon that was to be showcased at the Garnet Industries Defense Exposition next month." She began to dig in her satchel, but The Crow hastily grabbed her hands, holding them there while he frantically looked around again.

"Okay," he whispered. "The coast is clear."

Isabelle shrugged him off rather abruptly. Paranoid fool. She pulled out the notebook, *her* notebook, the one she'd been working on for the past two years, with all of her research and investigations regarding her patent scandal theory. She clutched it in black gloved hands, running one hand gently over the leather cover. With clenched teeth, and unshakeable resolve, Isabelle firmly handed the journal to The Crow. He snatched it quickly, and slid it into his oversized coat, scanning the vacant area once more.

"It's ah . . ." The Crow's eyes darted to either side of him. "It's all here? Everything about the ah . . . you know." He looked at her then and winked.

"Yes, it's all there," Isabelle snapped. "Read it thoroughly before you begin writing the story. This must be written carefully, and adhere to every detail."

"Don't worry Clara," The Crow tapped his nose. "Leave the story-tellin' to me." He winked.

Clara? Well he was nothing if not careful.

Abruptly, The Crow leaned forward and gave Isabelle a hug. "I'm glad you're all right."

Isabelle relaxed slightly, but was otherwise not sure how to respond. He released her and took a deep breath.

"Right. Now." He looked around him again. "You held your end of the bargain. Time for me to make good on mine." He leaned in close to Isabelle. "I looked into your hunch. With the patents. At the circus. You were right. The specs for the circus grounds and layout? The permits? It was all a front. They're using the circus to move something around the country without anyone batting an eye. Couldn't quite confirm what exactly was being moved though."

With a sigh of relief, Isabelle beamed. *I knew it!* "You have proof?"

"I don't. No. A respectable reporter follows a strict code of conduct. But the circus troupe has all the proof you need. From what I could tell, they weren't in on any of it."

That was another relief, considering how close they'd become with Constable Corbin, and their invaluable help over the past couple weeks with Isabelle's master plan. She recalled the welders referring to them as "the fence clowns", so they must not have been aware of what they were fencing. She'd have to confront them about that. "Thank you, Mr. Crow."

"*The* Crow, Lady Viece. *The* is capitalized." He smiled, tipped his hat, and then proceeded to vacate the premise with the same silly stealth maneuvers he'd arrived with.

Isabelle shook her head and strolled away like she owned these streets.

"I think we can all agree," declared Cleaver. "That this approach isn't working."

"Isn't working?" exclaimed Cog. "It's been an absolute tragic waste of everyone's bloody time!" The Round Table was held at a dockside tavern today. The Hull's Haul was one of those places the good sort of folks steered clear of. Hence why Cleaver chose this place to hold the Round Table session. He hoped it might lift his men's spirits to share drinks among their peers, late at night when mischief was made. Maybe it would help them feel like they belonged.

"Let's face it, Cleaver," Gauge said calmly, resting a reassuring hand on Cog's tense arm, and offering a reassuring nod. It was surely quite reassuring, to be sure. "The Crimsons have been at this far longer than we have. The boss gave us an impossible task, and it is beyond our skill and experience."

"I was not saying we should give up, Gauge." Cleaver leaned forward. "This plan isn't working. No one has seen hide nor hair of the Crimsons since the circus . . . events."

"Disaster," Cog exclaimed.

"Failure," said Steve.

"Misstep," added Gauge.

Cleaver reigned in his annoyance. "Yes. That. Have those two ever disappeared for this long? The Crimsons must be lying low. They know we're after them."

"You think they're hiding from us?" Cog asked skeptically.

No. "Yes. We've proven more of a problem to them than they ever could've thought." *We are way out of our depth.* "They've never faced anything like the welders before." *If they think we're pathetic, I'd be grateful. At least they noticed our existence.* "Our plan was a good one." *What the hell were we thinking?* "And I couldn't be prouder of how well you all conducted yourselves." Except Steve and his hotheaded vendetta against the constabulary. And Cog who seemed determined to give up at every hiccup. And Strangler for getting himself decapitated. Let's not forget Smithy who took the whole criminal calling card WAY too far. Gauge was the only one deserving of praise at the moment, but Cleaver just couldn't chastise them. The two empty chairs at their Round Table were too much to bear.

"You've been saying that Cleaver, and right good chap for it," said Cog. "But honestly, it just ain't true. If we can't compete with the likes of the Crimsons, or the Informant, then why should we even bother continuing this whole criminal business?"

"Spoken like a true coward," Steve muttered into his ale.

"What did you say?"

Steve swallowed a swig of ale. "Oh I said *coward*. You know, that word what means you're a *coward*. You may have heard it used to describe people who are *cowards!*"

Cog's eyes flared red hot coals. "You been insulting me ever since we started this job, and I ain't taking it no more!"

"Now lads," Cleaver said quickly. "Remember the rules of the Round Table."

"To hell with the Round Table!" yelled Steve, loud enough the other patrons paused their conversations. "I'm sick of this. Cleaver, you're the heart and soul of this crew. Gauge, you got the smarts. I got the passion. What do you bring to the Round Table, Cog?"

"Steve, that's enough."

But Steve brushed Cleaver's warning off like a speck of dust on his collar. "We're s'posed to speak our minds at the Round Table. S'posed to be safe to be honest. Well I'm being honest. You don't belong here, Cog. Me, Cleaver, Gauge . . . we can handle this. We'll deliver that damn mousetrap to the boss, and we'll—"

Cleaver punched Steve dead in the face, apparently the only effective way to deal with the man these days. The force was so strong, it knocked Steve to the ground, his eyes rolling around, trying to focus. He struggled to stand back up, but Cleaver pushed him back down, and crouched by his side. "You just revealed a whole lot of information to every seasoned criminal in this tavern." His voice was low, as dark as he had ever sounded.

The pressure from the boss, his dreams of becoming a world-class criminal in his own right, his failure to even remotely inconvenience the Crimsons, and his inability to properly lead his own crew all bore down on him like a printing press. He had been squished between the plates for too long. He had tried to be optimistic, encouraging and supportive, the way a leader should be. The way he had always wished his own bosses were back when he worked in construction. It wasn't working.

Nothing was working!

"Here's how this is going to go, Steve. You're going to sit back down at this table and you're never going to insult another member of our crew again or I'll pummel your head right into your stomach. Get it?"

Eyes wide and still woozy, Steve held his face where Cleaver's fist connected. The two men locked eyes. For once, Steve simply nodded.

"Good. Now get back in your bloody chair, shut your bloody mouth, and do as you're bloody told."

Steve did just that.

"Sir?"

Before Cleaver sat back in his own char, he whirled around to address the idiot who thought now would be a good time to introduce himself. "What the hell do you want?"

Towering a good foot taller than the fellow before him—a shipwright by the looks of that hat—Cleaver fully expected his foul mood to cover any last lingering thoughts this fellow had about where he stood. He was only mildly put off by the man's complete lack of response.

The shipwright looked up at Cleaver lazily. "Glad to see you got your man under control, but I'm required to tell you we routinely toss oafs out of this tavern for infractions."

"Infractions?"

"We have a reputation to maintain," the man said, not bothering to hide his boredom. "You mess with the up-to-no-good air, you're tossed out on your rump. Plain and simple."

"How about you get the bloody hell out of my face? Plain and simple."

That actually got the bored shipwright to quirk an eyebrow. "You threatening me?" He looked around at the other patrons. "I think he's threatening me." A low chuckle erupted, but quick as it started, everyone went right back to what they were doing without another remark.

That settled Cleaver right down. He eyed the bored shipwright suspiciously.

"Do you know whose club this is?"

Club? Cleaver looked around. Took in the place's reputation, it's "air" as the shipwright mentioned. A shipwright. *Do you know whose club this is?* Cleaver almost grinned. Instead he simply nodded. "Don't worry, friend. I'll keep me and mine in line."

The shipwright nodded and let them be.

Cleaver took his seat and was about to launch his men, such as they were, on their next criminal activity, when Gauge beat him to it.

"Cleaver," Gauge said in that low voice of his when he was about to say something nobody wanted to hear. "I think your frustration is warranted. And God knows Steve more than deserved that. But I think we can all agree that wasn't very sporting of you. Remember the Round Table is—"

"Forget the Round Table for a moment," Cleaver said, eyes alight with renewed vigor. "We know the Informant is working with the constabulary to stop the boss. The Crimsons have a vital piece of goods the boss needs, but it also represents the only piece of hard evidence that could connect all of us to this crime. We focused on Lady Viece, we're now focusing on the Crimsons. But who is the one with connections to all of these people?"

"You actually want to go after the Informant?"

Cleaver shushed him, and leaned forward. "You said this constable, what's his name, has been spreading rumors about the boss?"

Gauge shook his head. "Investigating the truth. He's spouting the same things as Lady Viece before she died."

"So he's onto us?"

"No, he's figured us out. I wager he just can't prove it. Been hearing a lot about him lately too. But here's the problem. I remember him from the circus . . . misstep."

"Disaster!" exclaimed Cog.

"He was at Brass Manor the other day. Giving some fine speech."

"And why do we care?" asked Steve, still rubbing his face.

"Because everything he said was exactly what's going on. Lady Viece figured it out. Corbin was with her before she died. On the train, at the circus . . . . He knows, Cleaver. He knows everything, and he has the legal jurisdiction to do something about it."

Cleaver cursed at his own oversight. He pinched his lips together and inhaled. "In the spirit of the Round Table, thank you for your insight, Gauge. By my reckoning, we have our next play. Here's how I see it. We're never going to catch the Crimsons. But we *can* get a meeting with the Informant, who knows everything that happens in this city. He's bound to know where we can find the Crimsons. And we *can* take down this lone constable. Cog, Gauge, find a way to incapacitate him. Don't kill him. We don't want anyone thinking he's right about the stuff he's been saying. Making a martyr of him would be counter-productive."

"Understood, Cleaver," Cog clapped his hands once and got to his feet. "Let's get to planning the take down, Gauge."

Gauge threw a warning look at Cleaver before nodding and following Cog out the door.

"Sorry," said Steve.

Cleaver looked his friend over. "I ain't."

"Here now, that's not—"

Cleaver threw his hand in the air and Steve flinched, clicking his teeth shut. But all Cleaver did was lift his thumb and forefinger to indicate a small amount. "This is how close you came to ruining everything we've been working for. You wanted this life, Steve. You wanted out of the *legal* criminal world that is out there,"—he extended his arm and pointed out the door—"and into the *illegal* criminal world that always treated you better. Where you could get justice off the constables what wronged you. Where you could get back at this god-forsaken city for abandoning you and then having the gall to blame you for it. Is that still the Steve I know?"

Steve glared at the table, but refused to meet Cleaver's eyes. "Can I? Can I get back at this god-forsaken city? Because the more we try, the more it seems we're chewed up and spat back out. You wouldn't even let me have at that constable chief."

"What good would that have done, Steve? You gotta think bigger than that."

"I don't wanna!" he snapped. "The world is too big for me. I don't give a damn about the world. Or this country, or this city!"

"Since when? What is your problem, Steve? What is with you and this personal vendetta of yours?" But even as the words flowed out of his mouth, he knew. His face softened. "It was a constable, wasn't it?"

Steve took a long drag of his ale, finishing it off. "Yeah."

"Why didn't you tell me?"

"It's my vendetta. Didn't want to get you chaps pulled into it."

"Why not? That's why we formed The Welders. That's what the Round Table is for."

"And you all accepted me. My parentage makes no difference to you. I wasn't about to betray that. My reasons for working for the boss are different than yours, Cleaver."

Cleaver dropped his gaze. That was probably the truth of it for all of them. They were all committed, but their reasons were too different for them to ever be an effective team. Steve wanted revenge, Cog wanted notoriety, Gauge wanted a challenge, Strangler wanted to prove himself, Smithy was insane, and Cleaver . . . well he had his sights on change. Revolution. He was a dreamer. He was an idiot.

Despite his earlier excitement at the prospect of a new approach to their goal, Cleaver knew he had a much bigger issue to solve. But later. For now, he resolved to complete the task at hand. Steve sensed his resolve and sat up straight, clearing his throat. "So. How exactly do you propose we get a meeting with the Informant?"

"We're not."

Steve raised an eyebrow, but Cleaver just smiled. "Do you know whose club this is?"

"HEAR YE! HEAR YE!"

"Well he's up early," Ruth, Morgan's wife, declared as she gracefully stepped out of the coach at the wet, dank, miserable docks ahead of him.

Morgan grimaced. "The magistrate ought to hang those blasted gossipmongers daring to call themselves professional reporters." There had been a few stories lately that had him on edge. Half truths and implied accusations that drew too close to the truth. He wasn't concerned about it—what could they honestly do even if they'd figured out his scheme? But still, it was annoying.

Ruth nodded sharply. Morgan extended his arm and led his wife toward the docks. This area was unusually busy today as Morgan's men prepared the warehouse for the expo. Tall warehouse buildings where fish were processed lined the docks in the distance, but where he and his wife ventured was more industrious, with smoke stacks pluming into the air from just about every brick building in the near vicinity. The dirty streets were covered in wet litter of all sorts. Unsavory characters hid in the shadows and in the narrow streets, making Morgan's skin crawl, and don't even get him started on the smell.

But that would all be cleaned up by the time his expo began. He wanted everything on this street, where his guests would arrive, to be immaculate. Not to mention he had already bought this entire area, courtesy of his wife's careful research, which would be turned into Garnet Shipping Co., a subsidiary of Garnet Industries.

Setting aside his increasing irritation with the press, Morgan was determined to enjoy this day. The final shipment of supplies for the expo had arrived. This expo was the culmination of years of planning, plotting, scheming, and cheating. It was finally coming together.

"THE CRIMSON SIBLINGS DONE IT AGAIN!"

What else was new? Morgan pointedly ignored the crier, a skinny youth standing up on a monument, yelling his news in a cracked voice while he tried to sell papers.

"IN THE MIDST OF THE GREATEST SCANDAL OF OUR AGE, THE CRIMSONS PULL OFF THE GREATEST HEIST!"

Quite a few muscled helpers bustled up and down the loading ramps, carrying various boxes of various sizes to various wagons taking the various boxes to the expo warehouse. Variously. The expo was coming together beautifully.

"HUNDREDS OF PATENTS STOLEN FROM UNDER THE NOSES OF THE PEOPLE!"

Morgan scanned the area for Mr. Avery—or Cleaver; whatever the man insisted he be called. Those welder fools had been drinking late into the night again. Morgan would've chastised them for that, except Cleaver was always on his game, drinks or not, leaving Morgan with no justifiable reason to scold him.

"INJUSTICE AND DEVASTATION AROUND EVERY CORNER!"

Striding toward him from the gangplank, Cleaver had a couple of his men in tow this morning. They . . . were most definitely not striding. In fact, the three practically barreled toward Morgan.

Something was wrong.

"GARNET INDUSTRIES AT THE HEART OF IT ALL!"

Morgan froze. *What?*

"WHO WILL STOP THE STEEL TYCOON FROM STEALING YOUR INTELLECTUAL PROPERTY?"

"Morgan," Ruth said urgently beside him.

"WHO WILL STOP THE EVIL GARNET FROM STEALING YOUR MINDS?"

Morgan ignored his wife. The men were sprinting toward him now, shoving the eager listeners out of their way.

"Lord Garnet!" Cleaver said urgently as he accosted Morgan. "You need to get out of here."

"A THIEF I TELL YOU!" The crowd gathered around the crier cheered. "TAKES A THIEF TO BRING DOWN AN EVEN BIGGER THIEF! A CORPORATE THIEF! THE REAL MISCREANTS OF ENGLAND!"

This was not possible. Surely he had misheard. Normally he didn't care about the nonsense written in the Crimson Run column. It was all merely entertainment born out of a modicum of truth.

Cleaver shoved a newspaper in Morgan's hand. "This is bad, sir."

"It's all in there. In detail!" exclaimed Gauge. "I've never read an article what was so spot on."

"READ ALL ABOUT IT IN THIS WEEK'S EPIC AND UNBELIEVABLE INSTALLMENT OF THE CRIMSON RUN!"

Morgan scanned through the article . . . and blinked. He scanned through it again.

. . . stolen from Professor Thomas Brass . . .

. . . killed inventor to . . .

. . . turning stolen, patented items into weapons . . .

. . . Crimsons stole crucial piece . . .

It was all here. Everything from the specific inventors he had removed after stealing their patents, to the construction site where he ran his laboratory, to his intention to sell the stolen inventions at the expo. It even mentioned the Viece family's awareness of it, which was why Garnet had them accused and arrested. It. Was. ALL. HERE!

"Morgan," Ruth said again.

Morgan looked up from the paper clutched in white knuckled fists. The crowd around the crier was growing larger, and angrier. Papers were selling like hotcakes.

An entire crew of reporters holding notebooks in their hands came running toward him, papers flying in the wind behind them as they raced to accost Morgan first.

"Lord Garnet!"

"What do you have to say about—"

"Can you explain—"

"Who—"

"What—"

"When—"

"Where—"

"Hi—"

In mere moments, Morgan was surrounded. His guards and the welders forced the reporters back, one ushering him and his wife away from the crowd.

"This is decidedly untimely," his wife declared beside him as they rushed across the cobblestoned street back to their coach. "The expo is in two weeks. And no one suspected a thing before. Now this. I dare say, this sounds very like a deliberate and calculated maneuver. The question is by whom?"

Morgan grunted his agreement. The public read that infernal column religiously. They'd believe anything written in it.

And the Crimsons themselves . . . they stole his mousetrap. They stole his blueprints. How had he ever thought they were merely a couple of harmless, simpleton thieves? He had been staging Crimson runs to cover for his thefts and support his larger machinations. Had they caught on? Could the notorious duo be responsible for this masterful play to undermine his plans?

As he was ushered rather roughly back into his coach, Morgan grabbed Cleaver's collar in a white-knuckled fist and yanked the man close. "The Crimsons," he said darkly, almost a whisper. "Find them. Kill them. At any cost, kill them!"

Chapter 25

CRIMSON RUN: ARTICLE 83
WHAT'S LEFT AFTER THE RUN

AS THE LAST CONSTABLE STANDING, ALONE, FACING UNPRECEDENTED ODDS, CONSTABLE ALEXANDER CORBIN RETURNS TO THE SCENE OF A FAMILIAR CRIME. A PLACE THE CRIMSONS HAD HIT NOT A FEW WEEKS AGO. WHAT DID THEY LEAVE BEHIND? WHAT DID CONSTABLE CORBIN FIND THAT LEFT HIM SO UTTERLY STUNNED, HE TOOK IT DIRECTLY TO THE MAGISTRATE? FIND OUT IN THE NEXT INSTALLMENT OF THE CRIMSON RUN . . . AFTER THESE MESSAGES FROM OUR SPONSORS.

Monty's club was closed for the night. Isabelle didn't know it ever did that. Only a couple bartenders remained, cleaning mugs and wiping down dark-stained tables. Monty himself sat at the only occupied table, sipping a mug of ale with a pensive expression Isabelle had never seen from the man. She glided toward the table and slid into the rickety chair across from him.

"Any news about my family?"

Monty shook his head. "Waiting for a final decision. It doesn't look good though." He eyed Isabelle carefully. "My sources anticipate a public execution."

Isabelle gasped, throwing a hand over her mouth. "When?" She cleared her throat. "When do they expect the final verdict to be divulged to the public?"

"Never can know with these things."

Sitting back in her chair, Isabelle stared at the table. She still had time. If she could discredit Garnet before the final verdict, she could stop the execution on the grounds of a mistrial. She still had a week left. If the courts could just hold off that long. "What gossip permeates Liverpool's underground?" she asked, trying her best to stay focused, to appear strong and resolved in Mr. Monaghan's presence.

"It all went as planned, if that's what you're asking. Word is spreading quickly, though a few gossip hubs on the other side of the city needed a sort of nudge, you might say. It's all taken care of. The seed of distrust has been planted in all the right circles." He took a swig of his ale. "Stroke of genius that. Putting the information in the Crimson run instead of the headlines. Guarantees everyone would read it."

"This whole infernal city regards those reprobate siblings as anti-heroes. And because the column is based on their actual heists, albeit extremely inflated, I hoped the general public would buy into it. It appears I was correct."

"Haha! Brilliant. You realize you painted a bullseye on the Crimsons' backs though, right? And Corbin's."

"I'm aware. I care not what happens to the Crimsons, but is there a way you can help protect Constable Corbin?"

"Already have a few safeguards in place. Never thought I'd think a man fortunate for being so unremarkable. He can float through any sea of fools without being noticed. A sort of ghost, you might say."

"He's the perfect everyman hero for our story."

"Mmm." Mr. Monaghan shrugged, sipping his ale again. Isabelle's eyes narrowed. He was probably aware of Corbin's unique skillset. Hence why he hadn't offered any dissent regarding Isabelle's decision on the matter. She'd worry about the possible implications of that later.

"Do you think all this will be enough to turn buyers against Garnet at the expo?" she asked.

Monty shook his head. "We need a way to turn this into an actual legal issue buyers won't want to involve themselves in. Right now, it's still just gossip and entertainment. The only way this will backfire on him the way we want is if legal action is taken."

Isabelle noted the use of the word "we" instead of referring to the plan as hers. A subtle change, but yet another power grab. He'd soon shift such phrases to declare the plan as his own. There was a time that would've bothered her, but she was surprised to realize all she wanted now was for the plan to succeed. Regardless of how or whose plan it was. "Which means someone must officially accuse him of theft."

"And now enters the hero of our story," Monty declared grandly, spreading his hands out to the side, ale still in hand and a smug smile upon his lips.

Isabelle smiled. She opened her mouth to continue the story but cut off as a loud crack, followed by a crash, jolted her out of her seat.

Four welders came barging into the club, decked out in their welding aprons, gloves, and masks. Though she couldn't see their faces, it could only be *the* welders. The largest of them had broken down the locked front door, holding a battered and bleeding bouncer by the scruff of his neck. Isabelle dove beneath the table just as they barreled in, barely noticing the momentary confusion on Monty's face before the darkness of the tablecloth enveloped her.

The welders approached Monty from behind. Had they seen her? She didn't think so, but why would they—

"You," the familiar voice said. It was definitely Cleaver. "You're Matt Monty?"

"Depends on who's looking for him," Monty said coolly, as if this sort of thing happened all the time.

"I am, you idiot."

"Pleasure to meet you, You Idiot. What can I do for you?"

Cleaver grunt. "You can tell me where I can find the Crimsons."

"Well if you'll kindly lend me a knife, I can certainly show you where you'll find some crimson."

"Are you threatening me, Irishman?"

"Actually I was threatening you. Not your Irishman. What's his name by the way? Might be a cousin of mine."

"Wha—I—"

"Of course no cousin of mine would be caught dead in the company of a mindless goat like yourself."

"Shut up, you glock. You ain't funny, and I ain't got time. The Crimsons. Where are they?"

"What makes you think I know?"

"You aren't best chums or nothing?"

"With Jasper Crimson? Hah! He comes here sometimes, though we usually don't know it until after the fact, but chums? Not quite."

"I don't bloody care. Just tell me where he is."

"Have you checked the crapper?"

"Yes. He ain't there."

"Well did you check *after* you took a shite?"

Though Isabelle could only see legs and hear voices, something about the feel of the situation grew more intense. Had someone pulled out a weapon?

"You want to play games, *Mr. Informant*? Fine. Let's play a game, you and me. Tell me, what has one eye, one leg, one arm, and one testicle?"

"Oh, you'll find plenty who fit that description in the tunnel outside. You think you're the only idiot who thought he could threaten a man in his own pub?"

Isabelle heard a click. Yes, someone had pulled out a gun. Her arms tightened around her knees and she held her breath, eyes locked on the gang's boots.

The club went completely silent. Something happened in the room that Isabelle couldn't make out, but whatever it was, Monty reacted by surreptitiously pulling out a gun from beneath the table. Isabelle hadn't even noticed it there, strapped to the under side of the wood. He rested it gently on his lap.

Everything went still. Like a wound-up top, waiting to be released. Finally, Cleaver sighed. "Right. If that's the way you want to play it." The other welder—Steve if Isabelle remembered correctly—stomped toward Monty, who rather than trying to shoot off his gun, dropped it for Isabelle.

The sudden violent flurry of movement masked Isabelle's involuntary yelp as the table shifted, threatening to expose her. But she managed to frantically move with it, shoved up close to Monty's legs. She held her breath again and squeezed her eyes shut.

"All right, mate," said Cleaver. "Start talking."

"Well see I was born in Dublin, to a whore, actually. But my father—" He grunted and his legs twitched.

"I'm going to ask one more time. Where are the Crimsons?"

"You think it's that easy? Look, there's not a man in England who knows where to find Jasper Crimson. That one may as well be invisible. A sort of phantom, you might say. No telling where he'll appear next. Besides, why would anyone want to find that one?"

"He's got something of ours. We want it back."

Monty laughed. "What? Your toenail clippings? What could he possibly have taken from you that you actually want *back*?"

Monty grunted, and Isabelle guessed one of the welders must've smacked him.

"None of your damn business, smuggler," said Cleaver. "Now I ain't going to ask you again."

"What, you mean you're leaving already? Shame, that. I thought we were becoming friends." And that's when Monty's screams began.

The welders dragged Monty, still sitting in his chair, back away from the table, and though Isabelle couldn't see most of what was going on, she could see boots beneath the edge of the tablecloth, and blood spraying onto the ground. Isabelle threw a gloved hand, soaked in her own sweat, over her mouth, eyes squeezed shut as she listened with horror to Monty's agonizing grunts, and the various crashing and breaking sounds she could only assume were chairs being broken *on* him.

What could she do? She couldn't just sit there, cowering under a table while they beat Monty senseless, tortured, and even maimed him. She had to do something.

Monty shrieked.

Push the table into the welders. But how would she get the leverage on it from underneath?

Monty's scream cut off and abruptly became a gurgle.

She could push the table backwards, cause a distraction, and perhaps give Monty the chance to—

Gasping for breath, Monty whispered an obscenity to Cleaver. A thud followed by a grunt suggested what Cleaver thought of it.

The shotgun! Monty had dropped it for her. Where? Off to her right, a bit of metal glistened and Isabelle snatched it up. Where to shoot? Who to shoot first? Could she even shoot someone?

No. That wouldn't do anyone any good. She'd maybe take one down, but the rest would converge on her. She needed her first shot to count.

The welders dragged Monty toward the mass of machinery at the back of the club. She couldn't even stomach the thought of what they intended to do with him there. But it gave her an opening as they moved away from her.

With a deep breath, Isabelle crawled out the back of the table and used it for cover, peaking over the top. The men had their backs to her, while two of them carried a bleeding and nearly unconscious Monty toward a collection of overlapping gears. They forced his face toward it. Isabelle couldn't make out what they were saying, but Monty must not have obliged, as they moved his face closer to the gears.

Isabelle frantically searched out something clever to shoot that would stop the machinery. A large brass tank caught her attention, looming straight ahead of her. She had no idea what was in it, but all the piping stemmed from it. And she had long since run out of time. Resting the shotgun on the table, Isabelle aimed it in unpracticed hands and blasted the tank.

The recoil jolted her back as her shot ripped through the tank like a spray. Bits of metal exploded out of the tank along with a flood of water and steam. A water tank then.

And the water was boiling.

It showered the welders. Their gear protected them, but it still had the desired effect. The two holding Monty dropped him abruptly. The two closest to the tank scratched at themselves, screaming. Isabelle's eyes widened, and she gasped. Their masks were melting, and their heavy aprons steaming. Maybe it wasn't water after all.

The entire machine made a shrill sound that echoed off the walls of the club as bolts sprang free. The welders ushered each other out, scrambling their way to the exit. A primal part of Isabelle screamed at her to leave too, but she darted for Monty instead. Throwing herself at his side, she shook his shoulders.

"Monty. Monty!"

"Top of the morning, sunshine," Monty looked a fright but he still managed a conceited smile.

"Come on!" Isabelle grunted as she tried to pull him up.

"Not to the front," Monty whispered hoarsely. "Behind the bar."

With Monty's arm over her shoulder, she managed to get him to the bar, where she found a latch in the wood floor. She slid down the hatch and into a tunnel. Monty grunted at the bottom, but was still moving, somehow. "Close it!" he yelled.

Isabelle yanked the hidden door closed just as the pub exploded. She hit the ground, more out of shock than from any force caused from the blast. In fact, the blast wasn't nearly as bad as she'd expected.

"It's just the pipes bursting," Monty said, leaning against the grimy brick wall just beside Isabelle. "Nothing to fret over."

"So we're safe here?"

Monty nodded, wincing. "This tunnel leads out into the streets."

Isabelle nodded, panting. "Are you . . . all right?"

Monty's left eye was swollen shut, he cradled his arm, blood dripped down his face, soaking his shirt collar, he could barely move and his breathing came in raspy gasps. "Why wouldn't I be?" He grinned, then coughed. "Ugh. That was a right good beating. Those lads are no pansies, I'll give them that."

Isabelle fumed. "They tried to kill you! How can you be so nonchalant about this?"

Monty raised an eyebrow. "Did you notice none of my lads came to my rescue? Odd, don't you think?"

Isabelle frowned for a moment, then nodded slowly. "A rather extreme way to get information, *don't you think?*"

"Nah, idiots talk a lot more when they think they have the upper hand. Don't you worry, love. If things got hairy my boys would've been on them in seconds."

Isabelle fumed, though part of her wasn't sure why. She found herself at a loss for words, bottom lip trembling, and eyes wide. "You know them, don't you," she found herself saying.

Monty groaned as he tried to move. "Those welder morons? I've seen them around. They're new players in the underground circles, but no. I don't know them."

"Not them. The Crimsons. You know them."

"No one really *knows* the Crimsons."

"You do."

"What makes you say that?"

"You admitted they come into your pub. And yet you refused to even give the welders a lead? You keep tabs on everyone who comes into your domain. You know them. You're protecting them."

"Viece—"

"They have the only piece of hard evidence to convict Garnet with! Why are you protecting them? We could—"

"I don't know where they are, Viece!" Monty winced, gasping, throwing a hand over his side. "I don't know where they are," he repeated more calmly.

Poised to argue further, Isabelle hesitated as she looked at his face. "No. You don't, do you? But you *do* know them. Or at least have crossed paths with them. And they got the better of you. Possibly more than once. They're a stain on your perfect record. That's why you won't speak of them."

Monty didn't respond. But there was a . . . smolder behind his eyes.

And then she realized what she was looking at. Hatred. Monty *hated* the Crimsons.

It was an element of vulnerability, of humanity she rarely witnessed in Monty. But she could hardly mull that over under the current circumstances. There was always a way to catch thieves. They always had weaknesses. Even Monty himself, the crime lord of the Western Coast, had his limits. And yet these Crimsons, these silly, aimless thieves had even the brightest minds guessing at what they would attempt next. "I need that prototype, Mr. Monaghan. If you don't know where they are, how do you intend to obtain my evidence?"

"I can't. Plain and simple. Might I suggest,"—Monty groaned again as he tried to stand—"a plan B."

Isabelle went to his side and helped him up as best she could. "You assured me you could."

"Did I now?"

Isabelle's eyes darkened. "If we don't succeed, my family hangs and you don't get your fortune. Why in God's name would you imply you can catch the Crimsons when you are obviously unfit for the task?"

"Why would you hang the success of your entire plan to save your family on finding the only two people in the world who have never been found? Your plan is otherwise working just fine. It'll succeed without recovering the invention."

"How? I need that evidence!"

"Yes, yes." Monty got to his feet, leaning against the wall for support. "To continue this pretense that you abide by the law."

"Pretense? You think I'm playing pretend when my family's lives are—"

"Oh please. That's all you've ever done. Ever since the first day you walked into my club, dressed in that carefully crafted costume to make it look like you belong, but are yet a little above everyone else."

Isabelle froze.

"You play dress up for your family with your over-the-top color choices that make you stand out to your peers, but not enough to be scandalous."

Isabelle blushed.

"You stole a detective badge, did you not? Playing pretend detective now too, are we?"

Isabelle turned away.

"Look, it's quite clever. You know how to present the persona you want everyone to think of you as. But that's all it is. A persona. A costume. At some point, you gotta be able to back up who you pretend to be with who you really are."

Isabelle shoved the injured crime lord out of her way and stormed down the tunnel, tears glistening in her eyes that she didn't want Monty to see.

Cleaver coughed up a lung as he dragged Gauge out of the Informant's burning pub. Steve and Cog were just in front of him, leaning on one another as the four of them escaped the blaze. Poor Gauge was the oldest of their crew, and certainly not in any condition to have been torturing information out of anyone tonight, but Cleaver was out of options. His crew was so thin these days, and he'd needed every one of his men to confront such an infamous criminal in his own club.

"Hang in there, mate," he said as they stumbled a safe distance away from the fire. Cleaver ripped Gauge's mask off and slapped his friend's back as Gauge coughed up four lungs and a kidney.

"You all right?" Cog asked Gauge, taking his own mask off. Bloody hell, their masks were actually melted! What on earth had been in that tank?

"I'm fine," Gauge wheezed.

"No you're not, mate." Cleaver took a look at the older man's face. Whatever that infernal liquid had been, it left Gauge's face bright red despite the mask. Wearing their welding gear had been intended as an intimidation ploy—and admittedly a play for unique notoriety. Tonight, it had saved their lives.

"I'm fine, lad!" Gauge yelled, though his subsequent wince demeaned the tough front a bit. "But damn I thought we had him."

"That would've been something." Cleaver decided not to tell his men that once again, they'd been out of their depth. After the initial banter, Cleaver had been convinced the Informant never would've talked. And Cleaver had the deflating suspicion Matt Monty had actually been toying with them to get information himself.

Sighing, Cleaver helped Gauge sit on the curb, under a lamppost. He sat next to the older man, joined a moment later by the beleaguered Cog and Steve. As they watched the building burn, they held their welding masks like one would hold his hat at a funeral.

He had been really hopeful about this little excursion. To no avail. They still didn't have the slightest clue where to find the Crimsons and Garnet was out of patience. More than that, Cleaver hated leaving a job unfinished. Especially when he had no other recourse.

This was a complete failure, adding to the increasing pile of failures in Cleaver's ledger.

"Cleaver, did you happen to smell lavender while we were interrogating the Informant?"

Cleaver glanced sidelong at Gauge. "Not that I remember. Why?"

"I only ever smelled that lavender smell once. On that Viece woman."

"At the circus?"

Gauge shook his head. "On the train."

Cleaver frowned. "Viece is dead."

"I know."

Cleaver narrowed his eyes, exchanging glances with Cog and Steve. "All right, I'm listening. What are you thinking?"

"I'm thinking Garnet is right. There are too many moving parts right now that all seem to be working against him. Stinks of sabotage. Who is the only person who ever had us completely figured out? Who is the only person with reason to care enough to do anything about it? We thought we took care of our opponent, but frankly, everything has gone worse for us ever since. I ain't buying it's the Crimsons. Those two don't care about nothing but themselves. So logically, our opponent likely remains the same opponent we've always had."

"What about that Corbin fellow you talked about last night?" asked Cog. "You said he was with Lady Viece and probably knew all the same stuff."

"Oh he's definitely still involved, but think about how the boss got as far as he has? By getting others to do his bidding. He pulls the strings in the background. That's the way of it. Corbin might be the public face, but someone else is pulling the strings. Besides, he definitely doesn't wear lavender. Combine that with you saying you thought you saw Lady Viece at the shipyard, and the fact that a body was never recovered, nor any remains for that matter . . . ." Gauge spread his hands, and raised his eyebrows.

Cleaver considered for a moment. He really could've sword that woman at the shipyard was Viece. "Let's say you're right, and Viece is alive. And she's *still* a thorn in my big toe. We haven't caught wind of that broad until tonight." Cleaver rubbed his chin. "You still planning to bring down Corbin at the next public announcement?"

Gauge nodded.

"Keep to that plan. You handle Corbin. Steve, your aim is to give the constable chief hell. Cog, I still think we have a chance of catching the Crimsons at some sort of exciting event. Keep your eyes open for them. You and me, recovering the mousetrap and offing the Crimsons is still our primary goal. If Lady Viece did somehow manage to cheat death, she'll still be after the Crimsons too."

Cleaver sighed deeply, and leaned back on his palms. They were running out of time, but maybe, if they were lucky, all of their problems would be solved during a single event.

Chapter 26

THE CRIMSON RUN: ARTICLE 84
THE PUNGENT CAPER

EVEN AS GARNET UNDERHANDEDLY VIES TO SEIZE OWNERSHIP OF THE NEW STEAM TECHNOLOGIES FROM THE PUBLIC, OUR DEAR CONSTABLE ALEXANDER CORBIN CLOSES IN ON THE PERFIDIOUS TYCOON, REFUSING TO LET GREED AND WEALTH DEFEAT TRUTH, JUSTICE AND HONOR. A FOUL STENCH IN THE AIR ODORIFEROUSLY ANNOUNCING THE CRIMSON SIBLINGS NEXT LARCENY SPREE MAY JUST GIVE HIM WHAT HE NEEDS TO CLOSE THE CASE.

Morgan threw *The Times* out the coach window, but with paper lightly flopping in the wind, it just wasn't satisfying. So he grabbed Mr. Barrington, who was sitting next to him leafing through the agenda for today, and chucked the poor man out the window too. Much more satisfying.

After reading the latest installment of the Crimson Run, Morgan was convinced someone was setting him up. And they were doing a superb job of it. In the last week alone, he had four reporters at his doorstep asking for his thoughts on whether the accusations cast upon his name in the recent Crimson Run installments would impact the success of his Expo. Not a single question about the expo itself.

While the Crimsons had always been popular figures of dissent among the plebeian masses, this Constable Corbin was a new breed. He was actually visible. The Crimsons never took any credit for things they were credited for, yet this Corbin spoke at press conferences, personally investigated crime scenes, was quoted directly in other stories apart from the Crimson Run, and clearly had some judicial backing to his work.

Morgan doubted this Corbin character was the one behind all this, but he and the Crimsons were the only leads Morgan had. He had after all sabotaged both the Crimsons' and Corbin's reputations in his exploits. Could they be working together to take back what was theirs?

The coach rolled up to the city square, but Morgan instructed his coachman to park in the far back. The crowd gathered to see the local hero was alarmingly large. Morgan couldn't help the increasing knot forming in the pit of his stomach as he listened to what Chief Brighton had to say.

"I have nothing to say!" Chief Brighton roared. "And I ain't saying nothing. I have no bloody idea where the bloody Crimsons are! And the next one of you what asks is going to have his rump arrested for bothering me with damn fool questions!"

Standing beside Chief Brighton, dominated by the stout man's presence, Constable Corbin rested his hands on his cane in front of him, doing his best to look handsomely heroic. He was, frankly, doing a pathetic job of it, but the considerable crowd gathered to hear the "hero of the Crimson Run column" implied Isabelle's plan was working nonetheless.

Isabelle herself attended this press conference disguised as a lowly maiden—it took all her willpower to ignore Monty's word's—positioning herself to the far left of the dais, allowing her to blend in *and* have a proper vantage point to observe the crowd.

The message was simple. They were close to cracking the case. Imply heavily that evidence—provided by the hero, Constable Corbin—was currently under examination that would reveal the culprit without a doubt. The hero—Constable Corbin—wouldn't let the public down. The public should care because it was their intellectual property being stolen, their fortunes being denied, their right to the truth being revoked, and their lives at stake.

Ok maybe their lives weren't at stake, but with how beautifully intense Brighton delivered his speech, the citizens no doubt felt the danger anyway. To confirm the story in the public's minds, Brighton gestured to Corbin every time he was mentioned. The unlikely hero. Someone the people could relate to. And cheer for.

Isabelle rolled her eyes at Chief Brighton's outburst, but she granted that fellow was the fourth person to ask after the Crimsons' whereabouts. Funny how a couple of unpredictable miscreants could incite an entire population to borderline worship. These people relished the prospect of catching a glimpse of the notorious siblings. And Isabelle's work here was definitely pushing it into sycophantic territory.

But Isabelle had to admit, the duration of the Crimsons' absence these last few weeks was conspicuous.

Brighton took more questions, and a gentle drizzle began to fall upon the square, umbrellas popping up one by one. Citizen questions began with predictable curiosities, but Isabelle couldn't contain her surprise when one young man asked after joining the constabulary. Brighton was equally stunned as he said they were in fact accepting applications. They weren't, but Isabelle agreed it was the appropriate response anyway. Next thing they knew, men cried out from every part of the crowd, expressing their zeal about joining the constabulary.

While Brighton began instructing the new recruits on what to do and where to go to apply—all of which he made up on the spot, bless the man—Isabelle swept her gaze over the crowd, idly noticing a foul stench making its way to her section of the square. This was most definitely not part of the plan, but she couldn't help a note of pride at the accomplishment. The constabulary was all but incapacitated after the circus debacle, and yet here was their opportunity to rebuild it.

Many of the upper crust of Liverpool had quietly rolled in to listen to Chief Brighton's speech as well, though Isabelle couldn't tell from this distance how they were taking the show. To be fair—*what a god-awful stench*—not a few people in the crowd looked worried. That fellow over there kept trying to insert some sort of political agenda, though his following was small enough not to be a problem.

That—*has to be the worst thing I've ever had the displeasure of inhaling*—that ghastly woman's obvious disdain was likely directed at the constabulary, and she spat toward Chief Brighton before ushering her hundreds of kids away. In one building to Isabelle's left, there was that fellow who had managed to climb up to a precarious position. He—*must be on the verge of vomiting from this foul smell*—perched comfortably up there, but completely uninterested in anything Chief Brighton was saying. To her right, a couple—

Isabelle's eyes darted right back to the building on her left, blinking at the slim climber dressed in a long black coat, a wide-brimmed hat atop his head.

WHAT. IS. THAT. STENCH?

He was a bit far away, and though his eyes were shaded by his hat, Isabelle could tell his attention was held by something in the back of the crowd, where the affluent audience parked their coaches.

Isabelle eyed him with a frown. It couldn't be. Of all places, of all times, after hearing nothing from them for weeks, the Crimsons show up here? Now? And if that was indeed Jasper Crimson, where was his sister?

AND WHAT ON EARTH WAS THAT HORRID SMELL?!

Morgan was furiously writing out a letter to the magistrate, petitioning for more rules and regulations around the constabulary, when someone rapped at the door to his coach. He opened the door and Cleaver's intense face stared up at him.

"They're here."

"Who?"

"The Crimsons. They're here."

Morgan threw up his hands, and roughly leaned back in the coach. "Wonderful. Tell them I said good morning. Anything else?" Morgan sniffed the air, now that the coach door was open. "What is that awful stench?"

"You need to leave, sir."

"I'm aware!" He sucked in a breath, then coughed it right back out. He pulled out his handkerchief and covered his wrinkled nose in disgust. "Just find me my mousetrap, kill those infernal thieves, and get my plans back on track."

For a moment, Morgan thought Cleaver might actually defy him. His mouth tightened, and his shoulders tensed. After a moment, he nodded curtly. "I won't fail."

That would, of course, be the moment when all hell broke loose.

As Isabelle made her way to the side of the dais, where Corbin, Brooks, and Rivers stood, a sudden commotion toward the back of the crowd abruptly spun her around. A fishmonger's wagon, pulled by a very agitated horse came crashing into the square. A second, and then a third. Within seconds, the entire back area of the square was in chaos.

Panic spread quickly through the crowd, working its way to the people closest to Chief Brighton's podium, including where Isabelle stood. Droves (piles, floods, schools . . . I think its schools) schools of fish spilled into the square as the wagons crashed into buildings, coaches, or just overturned while the horses fled. That certainly wasn't going to help the terrible smell suffocating the square.

Chief Brighton leapt to help manage the chaos, while Corbin futilely tried to calm the crowd. Isabelle forced her way through the panicked crowd until she reached him. She grabbed his arm and pulled him away from his attempts to calm the frenzy. She managed to find a small patch of space at the back of the stage, where they could talk without risking being trampled.

"It's the Crimsons!" she shouted above the cacophony of screams, whinnying, crashes, shatters, and the epic music playing in the author's head making this scene way more dramatic than it actually is. She pointed up at the ledge where Jasper Crimson perched.

"Where's the sister?" Corbin asked. "And what's that smell?"

"I haven't seen her yet, but she likely caused the diversion. And I've not the faintest clue what that smell is. Head to where the horses came from and see if you can find her. I'll go after Crimson. Meet me back here."

Corbin nodded, eyes wide. Despite his injury, he managed to move fairly quickly. There was no way—and no time—for Isabelle to reach Chief Brighton. She left him to crowd control while she navigated around the chaos to the building where Jasper Crimson perched, surveying the chaos from his nest.

Isabelle drew closer, looking up at him. The chimneys jutting in the air behind him had steady streams of dark smoke curling into the chill air. That was odd. Why only a few? And why now? In the middle of the day? This wasn't the industrial district where the steam-powered technologies generated smoke all day long. Was that where the smell was coming from?

Holding her breath, she considered her options to catch Jasper Crimson. She would have to wait for him to make a move. But what was his target? If she could identify his mark, she could—

Crimson casually climbed his way down the edifice and went straight for the fish-covered street. With a click of her tongue, Isabelle quickly followed, shoving her way through the increasingly thinning crowd as more and more people escaped the chaos.

The once meticulous line of fine coaches was now in shambles. with some of them overturned. Others were pushed up against each other, a lamppost, or building. Their passengers were either trapped inside, attempting to climb out, or escaped with the rest of the crowd.

Crimson poked his head into one of the coaches, stepped in, then stepped back out, tucking something into his pocket. Moving on to the next coach, which was overturned, he climbed up on it, slipped down through the open window, then climbed back out a few moments later. No one in the absurdly hysteric crowd gave him a second glance.

Whenever there was someone still in one of the coaches, Crimson played it off as if trying to help them. He would offer his hand, snatch something off their person, then move on to the next. Amid the chaos of the crowd, Isabelle watched for an opening.

Crimson leaned into a coach wedged between two others, then slipped inside.

There!

Isabelle darted forward. Crimson would have to exit that coach the same way he entered it. Which meant Isabelle would be right in Crimson's face when he came out. Except someone else approached from the opposite side of the street, throwing a wrench in her plan.

Cleaver.

Dropping to one knee, Cleaver pulled out his pistol, aimed, and fired three shots into the coach. Crimson yelped as the shots missed, but there was no point in waiting for a better shot. Cleaver learned the hard way that if you had a shot at the Crimsons, you took it right then. You'd never get another one.

Cleaver darted toward the obsidian coach, and fired another shot through the door before throwing it open. He leveled his pistol inside, but no one was there.

Cleaver didn't even bother sparing a thought for how that blasted man got out. But he did, much to his own dismay, spare a moment of appreciation for the man's skill. He was just too good at this game. But Cleaver had a different plan this time. He was going to change the game entirely.

Isabelle threw herself to the ground as Cleaver fired rounds into the coach Jasper Crimson disappeared into. He opened fire in the middle of this crowd? Was he insane?

Furthermore, all that would accomplish was spooking Crimson into running.

Cleaver opened the coach doors.

"Of course he's not in there anymore," she muttered to herself, though she hadn't the foggiest idea how that would be possible.

The curse that leaked out between Cleaver's gritted teeth confirmed she was correct.

All right girl, Isabelle thought to herself. *What's your play?* She needed that mousetrap. But she couldn't take on Crimson and Cleaver together. She also couldn't reveal herself to Cleaver. Cleaver already made himself known to Crimson, and so now Crimson was already on high alert. Not that the thief needed any additional advantages. If Isabelle had any hope of besting him, she had to change the status quo.

A moment later, Isabelle caught sight of Jasper Crimson climbing out of the opposite side of a coach she hadn't even seen him enter. Instead of parkouring (pretend that's an actual verb) his way over the rooftops and into the sunset, Crimson climbed atop the coach, leapt to the next one, and simply continued his crime spree as though Cleaver wasn't even there.

Isabelle could've spat—except that was supremely rude. Of course Crimson wouldn't do the expected and go climbing over rooftops. She would've bet money—except gambling was supremely uncouth—that he would've stayed in the coach and waited for Cleaver. But oh no. Not him. There was always a third option Isabelle somehow missed.

She smiled as she got to her feet. Hopefully Cleaver missed it too.

Cleaver climbed into the coach after Jasper. The thief likely exited the other side, so Cleaver followed suit. With one foot out of the coach, Cleaver hesitated. That Crimson pretty boy and his punchable face were clever. On the train he had left the briefcase but took its contents. At the circus, he used his surroundings to staggering effect.

He never did what was expected.

He was still in the coach.

Any momentary triumph at his own cleverness was dashed a second later, when Jasper kicked at Cleaver's back with both feet, knocking him to the ground outside. Too pissed to notice the lack of pain between his shoulder blades—in fact the kick had been weaker than he would've expected from such a superb climber—Cleaver leapt to his feet and whirled on Jasper, ready for a rematch to their fight at the circus. Except Jasper wasn't there. The door to the coach closed, and he caught a glimpse of a woman inside.

Scarlet Crimson? No, he'd seen the sister up close. This wasn't her. But who else would've . . . and why did she look so . . . what the . . . .

Cleaver shook himself out of his momentary stupor. Jasper. That was his priority. Everything else could wait.

Jasper leapt over the tops of the coaches to Cleaver's right, and then swung his way down into one.

Gritting his teeth, Cleaver stomped toward Jasper, loading more rounds into his pistol. The game he was about to play was called Target Practice. Everyone who'd ever chased the Crimsons had only tried to catch them. But how clever and slippery were they against open fire?

"Excuse me," Alex said to a woman frantically running past him. She didn't seem to hear him. That was quite alright. Given the chaotic stampede of frightened citizens all around him, he could hardly blame her.

"Beg your pardon, sir," he said to a tall gentleman running past him. The man didn't seem to hear him either. Poor fellow was quite terrified.

"Excuse me, have you seen Scarlet Crimson per chance? I . . ." Nope. "Pardon me miss, but have you seen . . . Miss!" Not her either. "Sir, could I trouble you to tell me if Scarlet Crims—" Not only was that an emphatic no, but the fellow punched Alex in the face. Alex fell back like a knocked-over bookcase. As he struggled to his feet, relying heavily on his cane for support, Alex rubbed his cheek. What he had done to offend the irate gentleman? He would've liked to apologize for it. Shame.

People jostled Alex about as they scrambled in all directions. Odd, that. There was nothing dangerous happening now that the horses had all fled. The crowd wasn't running away from anything. They were just running in all directions with no apparent aim and for no apparent reason. Well, that sort of thing did happen when the Crimsons were involved.

Lady Viece had tasked him with finding the Crimson sister, but if he couldn't ask anyone if they'd seen her, and he couldn't see her himself, perhaps something else in the environment could point to her whereabouts.

He scanned the area. Standing on a cane in the middle of the cobblestoned street, wearing his most impressive pensive expression with people running frantic all around him was hardly the most unusual thing Alex had done in his recent past.

The horses came from *that* direction. Which meant something over *there* had spooked them. It was enough that their caretakers couldn't soothe them in time to keep them from running.

That fish cart had spilled its aquatic cargo all over the street, filling the air with a distinctly nautical scent. Well maybe not quite so distinct. It was mixed with horse dung and . . . was that onions? There was actually quite the myriad of pungent smells floating about. Glancing to his left, he could see several chimneys nearby smoking more than they should be. Interesting.

Glancing to his left (wait, he was already looking left) . . . glancing to his other left, he could see a cart of moldy onions sitting conspicuously just inside an alleyway. No one would have bothered wheeling down a cart full of something they couldn't sell, and an entire batch of moldy onions like that indicated it was deliberately placed. Since no one had attended to the over-smoking chimneys, those were likely deliberate too.

That combined with the horses, and the aristocratic coaches all neatly lined up at the back of the square clearly indicated . . . that it smelled bad and people hate bad smells. Alex sighed. He really wasn't very good at this detective stuff. Why did he even bother?

Isabelle added "kicking large men in the back" to her mental list of skills she needed to learn. Kicking Cleaver, even with both feet, was likely more painful for her than it had been for him. It was like her legs connected with a brick wall rather than a man. But still, it had worked. He had been off balance enough that her kick pushed him right out of the coach. And, she hoped, he hadn't seen her.

She climbed back out of the coach, dropped to the ground and rolled underneath, hoping Cleaver would forget about her. Sure enough, he went after Crimson. Perfect.

Crawling back out from under the coach, her dress getting dirtier by the second, Isabelle crouched down and ran beside the line of coaches, following Cleaver's footsteps.

Her plan was simple. Keep Cleaver away from Crimson. As much as she wanted the mousetrap, it was better off in Crimson's hands than back with Lord Garnet.

"I got it!" Alex exclaimed to no one in particular. "This was their plan. The Crimsons are responsible for the smells. That's why everyone is all panicked and running around all crazy. It's completely psychological. They got spooked by the carts crashing and the horses bolting and they don't know which way to run because the smells are coming from everywhere and they can't breathe, which induces feelings of anxiety, and—"

"A very clever deduction, my good man."

Alex whirled around and came face to face with one of the welders.

"Y–y–you." Alex pointed at him. An older man, the short, squat, balding welder wore spectacles, smelled of soot and iron, and had multiple stains on his gray jacket, covering a frayed vest. Leather cuffs with small pouches clung to his upper arms, and he had leather straps clipped to his boots that led all the way up the sides of his trousers.

"Ah, so you do recognize me." He smiled. "They call me Gauge. Pleased to make your acquaintance officially."

"Why . . . why are you being so polite?"

"Well I'm not a barbarian, son," Gauge chuckled. "I'm an educated man, and I'm guessing you run that direction yourself."

"What . . . w–w–w–what makes you say that?"

"Well you seem to be unraveling the mysteries of our evil plan effectively enough. Besides, it's unusual for anyone to figure out a Crimson run while it's happening. You missed a piece though. Those coaches, all neatly lined up, in the back of the square, just waiting to be took . . . ."

Alex frowned. "You planned that part?"

Gauge shrugged. "We've been after the Crimsons same as you. We figured they couldn't resist such an inviting target."

"We've . . . um . . . tried that before. It d–d–didn't work."

Gauge shrugged again. "Only needed to work once."

Alex hesitated. "It don't matter. You won't catch them. No one ever has."

"There's a first time for everything."

"Well . . . yeah. But even if you do catch them. What then? You really think they'll just h–h–have my mousetrap on them?"

Gauge raised an eyebrow. "*Your* mousetrap?"

"Yeah. It's mine. I invented it."

"Did you now? Wouldn't have guessed you had that in you. Well done, lad."

Alex glowered at him. "Thank you . . . What d–d–do you want?"

"Let me explain. You see, you have been investigating my employer, Lord Garnet. And you've been spreading about some inaccurate rumors."

"I only know what's in–in–in–in the evidence. And it don't look good for your employer."

"Nor for you."

Alex swallowed. "Come again?"

"Look, you clearly aren't cut out for this line of work. And yet, there is clearly a very deliberate attempt to undermine Lord Garnet's exposition. Between you, the chief, the Informant . . . you all have taken quite a shining to the late Lady Viece's conspiracy theories. But what I want to know is,"—he stepped into Alex's personal space—"who's behind all of it?"

Alex forced himself to meet Gauge's gaze. "You stole my invention."

"Let's say, just for argument's sake, that I did. What are you going to do about it?"

Glare really hard at you. "I . . ." *I might even stick my tongue out!* "I'm g–g–going to prove it." Alex swallowed. "I'm going to get–get–get to the bottom of this scheme and expose you for the criminal you are."

"You can't do a damn thing if you're dead," Gauge replied evenly, tossing out that same apathetic shrug Alex was coming to loathe.

Alex swallowed again, and took a deliberate step out of the man's reach, leaning his weight on his cane. "You know . . . threatening me . . ." *might very well work.* "Ain't gonna get me to stop fighting for what's right." *But please don't test me on that.* "All I'm doing is trying to figure out what in God's good name is going on. I'm serving justice." *And trying not to soil my trousers.* "There's a patent scandal afoot and your employer is smelling guiltier by the minute. So if you don't want me to go straight to the press with this, you better be on your way."

Gauge scowled. "I am not leaving empty handed, Constable Corbin, so-called hero of the Crimson Run column. One way or another you will stop this senseless attack on poor Lord Garnet's honor."

"Bite me." *Please don't.*

"Those are fighting words, son."

"Y–y–yeah." *No!* "You want to fight, old man?"

"Let's do it."

Oh dear, what have I done? "You're on."

Alex and Gauge locked eyes.

They stared.

And stared.

AND . . . stared.

AND THEN FINALLY! Gauge laid his briefcase on the stage clicked it open and started setting up a chess board. "White or black?" he asked.

"Black." He always wanted to be the dark knight for a change.

"If I win, you rescind your accusations against Lord Garnet publicly and adamantly. I want it decried by every paperboy on every corner come tomorrow morning."

"And if I win, you have to answer one question for me. Your word of honor on it."

Gauge blinked, but ultimately shrugged. "All right. If that's what you want."

The duel began. (Now normally this would be where I'd place a terribly clever, intense, suspenseful scene that takes you step by step through the minds of our genius chess opponents, explaining why they made each move, how they read each other's body language to determine their strategies, and delve into the psychological warfare that is the brilliant game we know as chess. But here's the problem . . . I don't know a thing about chess.)

Cleaver fumed as he scrambled to his feet, searching around him once again for the Crimson rat. He had him! Cleaver had a clear shot, he'd aimed, and just as he was about to fire, he had suddenly tripped on . . . something. He had never tripped before in his life. There was nothing there for him to trip on. This was the third time he had Jasper in his sights only to be distracted by something. It had to be that blasted sister.

A movement to Cleaver's right drew his attention. It was Jasper climbing up the side of a two story shop as if there were a ladder. Cleaver cursed, barreling after him to get a clear shot before Jasper disappeared over the rooftops.

Once again, he had him in his sights. Pistol poised to shoot, he hesitated a moment before dropping it and pulling out his wicked mallet. He swung it all the way around himself in a circle. The sister yelped, dropping to the ground out of the way of his swing. He smiled. *I've got you, little girl.*

"Checkmate?" Alex asked.

"It can't be." Gauge frowned, leaning forward and squinting at the chessboard.

"I think it is. Um . . . checkmate. Checkmate!"

Gauge blinked, then cursed.

Alex punched the air in triumph.

Gauge stomped and cursed, half-heartedly claiming Alex cheated. He could've called Alex any name in the book and frankly he wouldn't have cared. He won! He *was* good at something!

Beaming, and out of breath, Alex waited for Gauge to finish throwing his best loser's tantrum. Once Gauge calmed down, Alex grinned from ear to ear. "So . . . our deal?"

With a scowl that could send a mutt scampering in fear, Gauge wilted. "Fine. I'm a man of my word. What do you want to know?"

"Do you have a piece of paper?"

Gauge scowled some more as he pulled out paper and pencil from his briefcase and shoved it at Alex. Alex wrote down his question. "What's your name?"

"Alvin. Alvin Moris."

"Thank you." He handed the paper to Gauge, who fortunately hadn't set any conditions for the manner in which Alex asked his question. He would realize any moment now exactly what he had just committed to.

Gauge read it and his eyes widened in horror. "You . . . you filthy, son of a—"

"Yes or no."

Gauge fumed. "You wanted this in writing. With my name on it. A signed confession. You . . . you!" He fumed some more, complete with steam coming out of his ears.

Alex smiled innocently.

Finally, Gauge furiously scribbled his response on the paper. He shoved it at Alex again, then stalked away. "Well played, my friend. Well played."

Alex looked down at the paper and to his relief, Gauge answered *yes*.

Isabelle did not consider herself particularly creative, so she was quite proud of how well she used her surroundings to thart (thort, thwort, thwart, yes that's the one!) to thwart Cleaver's single-minded determination to shoot Jasper Crimson.

It was actually a clever idea, Isabelle had to admit. Not being caught was one thing. But not being shot? Isabelle wasn't sure how many bullets the Crimsons had been called upon to dodge during their successful criminal careers.

Cleaver had a shot open.

Isabelle snatched some moldy onions from the abandoned cart at her side and started throwing them. One of them hit true and distracted Cleaver long enough to stay his shot.

Cleaver moved on and had another open shot. At this rate, Isabelle wasn't sure how Crimson had survived as long as he had. Without her there, surely Cleaver would've sealed the thief's coffin by now.

This time, she found one of the broken coach wheels lying flat on the ground. She set it upright and rolled it in Cleaver's direction. She actually managed to swipe the legs out from under him.

This last time, Isabelle had darted ahead of Cleaver on the opposite side of the row of coaches, ducked beneath one when Cleaver stopped to take his shot, and threw her legs out, tripping the brute.

Once again, Cleaver determinedly stood up and aimed at Crimson, who was now nimbly spanning up the side of a brick building, just as easily as one might stroll through a garden.

Isabelle frantically looked around from her position beneath the cart. She had nothing to throw. Nothing to distract.

Except herself.

Several logical reasons as to why she should let the murder before her unfold rattled off in her mind:

One: she couldn't risk exposing her survival, lest this whole endeavor be for naught.

Two: Cleaver would likely kill her and then still go after Crimson.

Three: she couldn't be certain Crimson had the mousetrap on his person, ergo it was not worth risking her life.

In the end, it wasn't any of the logic that decided her. Crimson had saved her life. She owed him. That was justice.

With that, Isabelle crawled out from beneath the cart, stood up, and was about to throw herself at Cleaver's back, when he suddenly dropped his pistol, pulled out his mallet and whirled around.

With a yelp, Isabelle dropped to the ground just in time to save herself a fractured skull, and . . . nothing. She scrambled onto her back, using her palms to scoot backwards away from Cleaver. Isabelle's fear was only overcome by her utter sense of failure.

She had come so close. The plan was working. Everything was in place. Everything except these infernal Crimsons! It was difficult to stomach that her attempt to save Jasper Crimson's life would be her undoing, but apparently she wouldn't have to stomach it after all.

Cleaver wasn't even looking at her.

Eyes wild with confusion, Cleaver deftly swung his mallet this way and that, as though trying to bat a fly out of the air. Confused, Isabelle scrambled back under the coach, watching Cleaver's frenzied display from relative safety.

What on earth?

Cleaver finally stopped, breathing heavily and looking around himself. "Show yourself, you little whore!"

Isabelle smothered her indignation at that. All the trouble she just caused him and that was the best insult he had for her? Unbelievable.

Suddenly, Cleaver grunted as if he'd been punched. The tiny booted feet of a child with tattered lace petticoats that were too short for her landed lithely beside Cleaver's massive boots. The girl dropped low and swiped Cleaver's legs from under him. Cleaver didn't fall down though. He fell *up*.

Cleaver yelped as he was yanked up into the air and to the side, though Isabelle couldn't see to where from her vantage point beneath the coach. A large crate full of fish crashed into the ground where Cleaver had been standing moments before. Standing atop the crate was another set of boots covered by the hem of a long black coat. The whole thing was like a pulley with Cleaver on one end of the rope, and the fish crate, along with the other man, holding on to the other end of the rope.

Crimson of course.

Both Crimsons.

Isabelle listened to the two of them laugh as they sprinted away.

"No!" she exclaimed as she scrambled out from under the coach. She couldn't allow them to disappear again.

She bolted after the siblings, though she was no match for their uncanny speed. They ducked down an alley between a bakery and a perfume shop—poor business planning in Isabelle's estimation. Indeed she inhaled the conflicting smells as she approached the alley, mixing in with all the other unappreciated smells.

She spared a glance upward as she ran by. Cleaver hung from the side of the building right where Crimson had been when Cleaver was poised for the shot. But that was all she could glean with the quick glance.

She caught sight of Crimson's coat as he turned a corner. She followed suit, rounded the corner, and . . . nothing.

Isabelle let out a frustrated scream and sank to the ground, leaning against the alley wall, heedless of the dirty puddles and grimy walls beside her.

Obviously, Crimson had never been in any danger. Had Isabelle not interfered, the sister would've been right there. She shook her head and had to let out an exasperated chuckle.

How did those fools do it? No matter what the circumstances, they always got what they wanted, and disappeared without a trace. One of them had to be such a supreme criminal mastermind, each heist executed with such precision, that it looked like an utter mess. Indeed leaving a mess in their wake was always part of their strategy. And it worked!

Wait. It worked.

So well in fact that Garnet himself staged Crimson runs to cover his scandal.

Isabelle smiled as the last bit of her plan clicked into place. Gracefully rising to her feet—because she had done more than enough undignified, panicked scrambling for one day—Isabelle took off running to find Constable Corbin and Chief Brighton. She had so much to plan and only one more week to get it done.

Chapter 27

CRIMSON RUN: ARTICLE 85 THROUGH A CRIMSON VEIL

AS THE FINAL PIECES OF THE PUZZLE CLICK INTO PLACE, THE CRIMSONS HOLD THE LAST KEY TO UNCOVERING THE TRUTH BEHIND THE LARGEST, MOST SINISTER SCANDAL IN MODERN HISTORY. A SCANDAL CAPABLE OF DISMANTLING THE NEW PATENT SYSTEM, LEGAL ORDER, AND CREATION AND OWNERSHIP OF STEAM TECHNOLOGIES. BUT WITH ONE DAY LEFT BEFORE GARNET INDUSTRIES DEFENSE EXPO, WILL CONSTABLE ALEXANDER CORBIN RECOVER THE KEY IN TIME TO SERVE JUSTICE?

"Thank you for seeing me today," Morgan said politely as he took a seat in the editor in chief's office at *The Times*. The editor in chief sat on the other side of his desk in a utilitarian leather chair, and promptly lit up a cigar. The man referred to himself as The Wolf.

"Of course, of course," The Wolf said with the cigar clenched between his teeth. "I expected you sooner, what with all the negative

351

press you've brought down upon your head in recent weeks. Haha! I swear every article I've had on my desk in the last month has your name plastered all over it. I've got to thank you, old chap. Business is booming thanks to all your shenanigans. Keep it coming, my good man. Keep it coming."

Morgan intended to be civil upon his decision to come here, but the candor with which this articulate, erudite dog launched this conversation quickly changed his mind. "I could not care less about your business, your stories, your papers, your family, your health, or you. I am here to get these preposterous fables you call 'news' removed from this idiotic gossip disseminator you call a 'newspaper.' It will stop, or I will end your entire enterprise. Any questions?"

"Just one." The Wolf leaned forward, taking the cigar out of his mouth and holding it between two long, thin fingers. "If I remove any besmirching mention of you from my papers, and promise to only pen your illustrious name alongside words such as 'saint,' 'angelic,' and 'pulchritudinous,' will you promise to never call my business an idiotic gossip disseminator again? It really hurts my feelings."

Morgan seethed, rifling through his mental ledger of witty insults, but in the end he mentally threw the whole ledger at The Wolf. He returned Morgan's glare with an even gaze, leaning back comfortably in his chair, and puffing on his cigar.

"Where are you getting your information from?"

"My neighbor, Sandy. She has a reputation as the most reliable gossip in Liverpool. She'll have her own paper opening soon, if you ask me. The Sandy Tribune."

"Do not patronize me, newsboy. Give me your sources."

"Ahem. That's news*man*, thank you very much."

"And why should I address you as *newsman*? That would imply you take your work seriously, and thoroughly vet any and all information you receive so as not to mislead the public or speak a word of untruth. Your quick and thoughtless acceptance of slanderous information would indicate a stronger interest in selling papers than serving the public."

"Well I did sell an obscene amount of newspapers this month. How's business been these days for you? Any new patents pending?"

Morgan chuckled, shaking his head. "Business is as strong as ever. I employ practically half the city now." *Let him stew on that thought while he prints his infernal papers.* "In fact, I am garnering quite a substantial support structure outside Liverpool. Outside England, as it were. My reach . . . is growing quite far indeed."

"Not far enough, it would seem, seeing as how you had to come all the way here to threaten my sources out of me."

"Do you think I'm bluffing? Do you think I won't ruin your entire enterprise if you fail to comply?"

"Well . . . do I get to keep my desk?" The editor in chief caressed the smooth wood of his desk with his fingertips. "I've grown quite fond of her."

"Consider yourself untouchable, do you?"

"Your wife doesn't think so."

Morgan blew a gasket. He stood up and swiped everything off the desk, pointing an aggressive finger in the editor's face. "I will kill you."

"Ooh! That story would make a great cover article."

"YOU HAVE NO IDEA—"

"*You* have no idea what to say right now, do you? *You* have never had your reputation under fire, your entire world threatened to be ripped from what you thought was your *iron* grip. *You* are a frightened little boy who got caught with your hand in your mother's cookie jar. After having done it so many times, you thought you would always get away with it. YOU—" The editor in chief leaned back again, softening his voice. He gestured toward Morgan with his cigar. "*You* are in trouble."

Morgan found himself at a loss for words, all the flare and ire wrung out of him with a single sentence. He was, indeed, in serious trouble.

"Anything else I can help you with, *Lord Garnet?*"

Morgan stood up with all the dignity he could muster, and took a deep breath. He hadn't intended to reveal this move, but it seemed the appropriate time.

"You have until the end of my expo to get your affairs in order," he declared darkly. "I've already put a business deal in motion to purchase *The Times's* Liverpool branch, which should be finalized after my expo. At which point you will step down from your post, or be fired from it. Your choice."

With that, he turned to leave.

"Lord Garnet," The Wolf called after a moment.

Morgan turned once more, with the hardest glare he'd ever given anyone. He was pleased to see a grimace on The Wolf's face after Morgan's revelation.

"Here's the headline for tomorrow's issue of The Crimson Run column," he said stiffly as he tossed an unofficial paper bundle at Morgan.

As Morgan read the headline, his grip on the bundle tightened. Firing this fool wouldn't be enough. After *The Times* became his, he'd find a most fitting way to skin himself a wolf.

Monty arrived at the docks late in the night. Having finished the last piece of Viece's plan, carried out exactly to her specifications, he had dismissed his men to enjoy what was left of the last night before the expo. He himself had . . . business to attend to.

In his bowler hat, dark green coat and matching cravat, he struck quite the figure on this dark, misty night. The light from the gas lamps cast an eerie glow across the wet wooden planks as he strode forward to board the *Transparency*.

"Mr. Monaghan?"

Monty grimaced at the sound of Viece's voice. He had expected her to be in bed considering what an important day tomorrow would be for her. Still, he couldn't say he was entirely upset to see her beautiful form glide gracefully toward him.

"Lady Viece," Monty said smoothly, giving her his best debonaire bow. "You're up rather late."

Viece groaned. "Hardly by choice, or have you forgotten what a tremendously important day tomorrow is?"

"I remember." He grinned.

"Everything went well I presume?"

Ah, she had been waiting for him then. Of course. "It did indeed. Exactly according to plan, you might say."

"Splendid." Viece stood silently for a moment, looking out over the ocean. "Thank you," she said finally. "Despite your previous grievances against my household, I dare say you've been a great help to me, and I wish only to convey my sincerest gratitude."

Monty looked into those dark, deep pools that were Viece's eyes. Their depths had always caught Monty's breath, in a way no other woman had ever managed. Perhaps that was precisely why he needed her out of his life.

"You're welcome," he said evenly, flashing her a grin.

"I assume you already have plans in motion for seizing Garnet's assets after tomorrow?"

Monty shoved his hand in his pocket, gripping the letter Lady Viece didn't know about. Garnet had finally asked him to move his illegal accounts to a secure location. But Monty had even bigger plans. "All I need is for him to be arrested."

Viece pursed her lips. "That'll freeze his assets. The magistrate will open his assets to the prosecutors for proper investigation."

"Which gives me the opening to have those assets *misplaced*."

"To a location of your choosing." Viece smiled smugly and Monty couldn't help but return it.

"We make a great team Viece, you and I. A sort of dynamic duo, you might say."

"I quite agree. 'Tis a shame I can't trust you."

"Likewise, Lady Viece. Likewise."

A silence followed. Not an awkward one. Monty thrived in awkward silences. People revealed so much in their haste to end silence. But not Viece. She stood there as comfortably as Monty himself.

"I doubt we shall see one another again, Mr. Monaghan. Take care of yourself."

"You too, Lady Viece. Best of luck to you tomorrow."

Viece nodded, gave him a semi, curt curtsy, then glided up the gangplank into the *Transparency*.

Monty watched her until she was out of sight. He waited a few minutes longer for good measure. It was time to make his final play. He made his way up the gangplank, into the ship's hull. This was a sign of good faith. Anyone who wished could see the ship's cargo directly, implying there was no possible way it was transporting illegal cargo.

Monty often used this design for his own smuggling ships because the constables rarely boarded them. This was a smuggler ship if he ever saw one, and one he had spied on while investigating Isaiah Viece for Garnet.

Rather than make his way above deck, he immediately turned into the main area of the hull and had a look around.

This was the ship that would transport the circus up and down the coast after the last Crimson run all but destroyed them. Cages full of exotic animals, large boxes and crates carrying God only knew what, and broken remnants of the circus tents and wagons filled the hull.

Viece opined the circus had been used to transport and hide the original inventions, and possibly the blueprints, Garnet had stolen, though she presumed it all to have been destroyed during the Crimson run and the now infamous circus fiasco he'd heard about. She also theorized the circus served as an inconspicuous meeting place for Garnet's fences, ensuring inventory passed hands without notice.

Monty disagreed. The original inventions would've been needed to create the new ones Garnet patented. Once the new ones worked, Garnet would have no reason to keep the originals. However, as a precaution against losing the technology itself, or losing one of the people responsible for recreating and expanding on the inventions, Garnet likely would've kept the original blueprints.

Corbin's theory was that Garnet used the circus to move the materials needed to create the new weapons, and also presumed them to have been destroyed during the Crimson run and the following disaster. Monty disagreed with that too. Transporting materials for a steel tycoon like Garnet wouldn't raise any suspicions. He likely already had all the materials he needed.

Monty stopped moseying around as he stood in front of a particular box that was in better condition than the rest of them. After Viece had explained what happened during her first trip to the circus way back at the beginning of this book, Monty's theory was that Garnet sponsored the circus to hide the blueprints, and transport completed inventory to prep for mass production and sales.

Looking at the box in front of him, he wasn't so sure any of their theories were correct any more.

"What are you doin' in here?"

Monty turned to see that massive Scottish ringmaster standing at the foot of the ladder that led up to the second deck of the ship.

"Good evening to you, ringmaster," Monty said smoothly.

"Evening? It's practically morning it's so late!" The ringmaster approached Monty. "What are you looking for?"

"Lady Viece had a sort of theory she asked me to investigate," he lied smoothly. "She thinks Garnet was using the circus to transport the original inventions undetected. I'm here to see if she's right."

This would undoubtedly be where the ringmaster offered to help.

"Aye, right. Well I packed a lot of this junk up myself. I could lend ya a hand if ya like, Irishman."

"Splendid. Let me know if you find anything out of the ordinary."

With a smile, Monty knelt down on the damp wood of the crate that had caught his attention, zoning out the sounds of the strange creatures caged around him. Inside the box was what he expected, permits to use the zoned fairgrounds, maps detailing the limits of those zones, permits to bring strange creatures into the country and into Liverpool, permits to conduct potentially dangerous feats on British soil, indemnity documents absolving the fairground landlord of any legal responsibilities should anything untoward happen, a permit allowing the performers to scratch their bums in public in the event of severe and chronic chafing, and so on. No blueprints. Well Monty never would've put such important documents anywhere so obvious. He would've hidden them in plain sight, but where no one would ever look. Somewhere like the nondescript wall of a ship's hull.

"You could at least tell me what tah look for!"

"No need," Monty said, frowning.

He knocked on the side of the box. One side sounded hollow. He stood up with the box held above his head and dropped it in a heap, splintering the wood just enough to open the false side. Inside were blueprints. Monty smiled. So at least half his theory was correct. He tucked the file under his arm and was about to leave when he noticed the bottom of the cage beside him. Was it a little too thick? Perhaps even thick enough to hide something substantial.

"Cedric, was it?" he asked, lighting up a cigar and taking a puff.

The ringmaster nodded. "Aye, that's me."

Monty coolly blew a smoke ring at the ringmaster. He just glared at him. Monty liked this fellow. He was the sort of no-nonsense, get-it-done, don't-take-any-lip-from-no-one types that Monty preferred to hire. Unfortunate he had to be a performing buffoon.

"What are you lookin' at, ya pansy Irish snow pea? You a'gunta ask me a question or not?"

Monty frowned in amusement at the odd insult. He nodded toward the gryphon cage beside him, it's prisoner asleep in the corner. "What do you think is in the bottom of those cages?"

"Shite."

Monty chuckled. "Inside the base. In that thick metal part." He bent down to inspect the cage bottom."

"Don't know. Garnet supplied those a'fore we even set sail for England."

Monty cocked his head. "You don't say?"

"I just did say. Ya callin' me a mute?"

Monty ignored the Scottish ringmaster and kicked the bottom of the cage.

"Oi! Ya tryin' tah kill us all? That beast is a gryphon! Bite yar head clean off yar shoulders if ya wake him from a good dream."

"Oh really? Sounds mighty unsafe. A sort of 'accident waiting to happen' you might say." He puffed his cigar as he stood to face the ringmaster. "Ensures no one would ever approach this here cage or get close enough to inspect the cages themselves, eh?"

Cedric frowned.

"Who handles the animals? Care to fetch him for me?" He slipped the cigar back in his mouth.

"Aye," Cedric replied, nodding knowingly. "Right."

Right indeed. Right on both of his theories, which he hadn't shared with Viece, Corbin, or anyone, of course. He'd play Viece's game—it was brilliant, he could admit that —and make the fortune he was promised. But he'd be damned if anyone—whether Lady Viece or those infernal Crimson siblings—would come out of this endeavor ahead of him.

Chapter 28

GARNET INDUSTRIES ARMS EXPO EXTRAORDINAIRE DEBUTS DESPITE RISING DISTRUST IN COMPANY

THE TIMES IS YOUR GUIDE TO ALL THINGS EXTRAORDINAIRE!
GET THE LATEST UPDATES ON SHOWCASES, NOTABLE FIGURES,
NEW FASHIONS, AND PREDICTED IMPACTS OF THE WORLD'S
LARGEST ARMS EXPO.

"LADIES AND GENTLEMEN!" The hired host of the evening announced from the considerably impressive stage. A brass band with timpani and military drums played an epic fanfare beside him. "GARNET INDUSTRIES PRESENTS THE MOST ADVANCED WEAPONS TECHNOLOGY EXPOSITION EVER TO GRACE THE SOIL OF ENGLAND!"

The crowd eagerly gathered, murmuring and pointing at the deep red curtain behind the sharply dressed host.

"WHILE THE NEW STEAM TECHNOLOGIES CONTINUE TO TAKE US TO EXTRAORDINARY HEIGHTS, THERE IS ONLY ONE MAN WHO HAS PROVEN TIME AND TIME AGAIN THOSE HEIGHTS CAN BE SURPASSED, MUST BE

SURPASSED, AND ALREADY HAVE BEEN SURPASSED! LADIES AND GENTLEMEN, I STAND BEFORE YOU TODAY WITH THE HONOR OF ANNOUNCING. NAY, DECLARING! THAT THE FUTURE. HAS. ARRIVED! LIMITS HAVE. BEEN. DEFIED! AND A NEW ERA. HAS. BEGUN!"

Cheers erupted around the event space, and Isabelle grimaced. That was quite the inspired speech.

"IT IS MY GREAT HONOR TO INTRODUCE TO YOU THE MAN BEHIND THIS MOMENTOUS, INDUSTRIOUS STEP FORWARD FOR ENGLAND, AND FOR HUMANITY ITSELF. LORD MORGAN GARNET!"

Another impressive round of applause accompanied Garnet's emergence from behind the curtain. Streaks of sunlight from the side wall made entirely of windows cast a dramatic lighting effect across the path he walked as he waved to his adoring sycophants.

Isabelle clapped politely along with the other journalists standing beside her—The Crow had even given her an alias, The Raven. The rest of the crowd consisted of society's business elite, dressed in their finest fashions. Isabelle found it somewhat strange not to be among them. This would be the first time she'd ever experienced an event through someone else's eyes and she felt . . . ignored. Forgotten. Like she didn't matter.

"Thank you all so much for attending my exposition," Garnet said graciously. He did an admirable job exciting the crowd as he thanked all the appropriate people, laid out the evening's agenda, and cracked lame jokes that everyone laughed at anyway.

Isabelle scanned the room and spotted Chief Brighton. She made eye contact with him, and he motioned for her to meet him. She made her way through the crowd and met Brighton toward the back, near the firing range.

"We have a bit of a problem," he muttered to her while Garnet continued his speech. "Take a look to your right, at the back of the warehouse."

Isabelle casually glanced over, clapping along with the crowd after Garnet said something clever. There, standing by one of the exits, was Cleaver.

"Think those welder fellows'll try and stop me and my boys if we try to enforce the law?"

"Oh I'm counting on it."

Brighton eyed her sideways, then smiled slightly. "You expected them to be here?"

"Of course. Garnet would've been politically obligated to invite you as the chief of the constabulary, a clear indication to the public that he values safety. Hiring his own minions was the logical move to ensure most of the security present would actually do his bidding."

Brighton grunted. "Would've been nice if you'd told us all that before. I'll get my boys on it."

"No. Keep to the plan."

Garnet's speech earned another round of applause.

"If they interfere, throw your title around. Treat them as though they are part of your security force. It'll look strange if they disobey and garner questions, confusion, mistrust. Which is what we want."

"AND NOW WITHOUT ANY FURTHER ADO," the host chimed in beside Garnet up on stage. "WE INVITE YOU TO VISIT EACH BOOTH AS YOU PLEASE. THE NEXT HOUR WILL BE OPEN FOR YOU TO EXPLORE. ENJOY YOURSELVES." The crowd dispersed, rushing to the most extravagant exhibits first, while trying not to look like a bunch of school children scrambling to be first in line for their favorite candy.

With a snort, Isabelle got to work. As she headed to her first target, she glanced around the room. No sign of Constable Corbin.

Well, this was not good. The magistrate's office was in complete shambles. Clerics, clerks, attorneys, marshals, janitors, pet sitters . . . everyone working at the courthouse frantically ran this way and that, yelling at one another, carrying bundles of paperwork, boxes, files, castanets and all the other office essentials one might expect. Standing awkwardly in the midst of the chaos, Alex had already deduced what had happened here.

"Ah! Constable Corbin," called the magistrate's assistant. She bustled over to Alex, brushing locks of escaped hair off her spectacles. "I apologize for the hullabaloo. You see, we've—"

"Crimson run?"

She sighed, nodding.

"Well you seem to have a lot of cleaning up to do, so . . . um . . . I'll ah . . . just snatch up those patents and be on my way."

"Oh bother!" She slapped her forehead. "Your warrant. You were . . ." She snapped her fingers repeatedly, trying to recall the words. "Mmm . . . you were . . . YOU WERE AFTER THE GARNET INDUSTRIES PATENTS. That's right. Mmm. I'm sorry, as you can see everything is a bit of a mess right now. I'll get you the files as soon as I can but my hands are tied at the moment. Sorry. Let let me—" She began hustling away mid-sentence. "Let me just go check, *oof*,"—she ran into a scurrying secretary—"check on that for you."

Alex was left in the lobby spluttering. Nope. Not good at all.

". . . and what would be the implications for your business endeavors should you purchase a Garnet weapon built from stolen designs?" Isabelle asked.

"I . . . well . . . I would never purchase stolen goods, of course, but—"

"So if you knew you were purchasing stolen property, how would you feel?"

"Well . . . I . . . would simply not have purchased the property in the first place. I—"

"Because your company is most reputable?"

"Yes, precisely."

"Yes, precisely what?"

"My reputable company would never be party to any such illegal purchasing of goods!" The poor middle-aged merchant huffed indignantly.

Isabelle wrote all of it down. "Thank you, good sir." With a smile, Isabelle smoothly moved on to her next prey. She spoke differently to the people she knew, keeping her head low and careful not to make eye contact while she carefully crafted their quotes for them. Apparently her disguise was foolproof. It was remarkable what a set of false teeth that jutted her jaw out, and carefully applied makeup that elongated her face could do to change her appearance. She was quite unfortunate looking indeed.

On and on she went, planting seeds of distrust in the whole expo, building off the negative press and gossip she'd built about Garnet in the last month, stirring the attendees suspicions one by one.

"This one," Morgan declared, "is my absolute favorite." He led a small group of particularly influential individuals to his favored exhibit. Displayed atop a specially designed metal stand rested a set of small onyx balls, with a single pin sticking out of each of them.

"This set, esteemed guests, may look innocuous, but each actually contains the explosive power of ten sticks of dynamite. Imagine a lone soldier, exhausted from days at the front, wounded beyond recovery, the last of his platoon. The battle is lost, you think. But this soldier, he carried this set on his belt, saved them for the opportune moment." Morgan plastered a distant look on his face. "The enemy closes in. They think they have him. They think England is theirs. But then, this soldier, nay this hero, reaches into his belt"—Morgan reached at his waist though there was nothing there—"snatches one of these puppies, pulls out the pin with his teeth, and throws it at the coming enemy." Pause for dramatic effect . . . "BOOM!"

Morgan's audience jumped.

"Eight enemy soldiers down in a single blast! The others hear the blow, and they come running. Our lone hero pulls the pin from another explosive and rolls it into the path of his approaching enemies. With nothing but grit, determination, an undying love for Queen and country! . . . And a set of but six of these explosives. A single hero vanquishes England's enemies . . . while sitting on the ground."

He let that last line hover in the air. His audience was enthralled, but something was off. Before he could continue to regale his audience, one gentleman chimed in.

"Lord Garnet, these products are exquisite, I dare say. If they indeed work as you claim. How ever did you appropriate such powerful and revolutionizing technology?"

His small audience held their breath, waiting for Morgan's response to the thinly veiled accusation. Morgan almost cursed. These rumors had been more troublesome tonight than he ever thought possible. This was the third potential buyer to bring it up. Fortunately, he and his wife—bless that woman—had prepared for the possibility that some of the buyers in attendance might believe the stories circulating. Especially considering they were true.

Morgan plastered on an amused smile. "You refer to these gossips about my technology being stolen, I presume?"

If his audience had been silent before, they were now practically dead with stiffness. They hadn't expected him to respond bluntly. That had been his wife's idea. Show them these accusations held no sway over him.

"I take great offense to these rumors on behalf of my brilliant team of engineers," he said as he casually walked around the exhibit, placing the explosives between him and his enemies, er, potential business partners. "It is they who are truly under attack. I have done what I can for their reputations, and can only hope once this cowardly fear monger who has so carelessly spread these rumors is caught and incarcerated, this ridiculous attempt to sabotage the work of Garnet Industries and its incomparable team of scientists and engineers will finally be laid to rest."

He ran a caressing hand over his explosives, as though thinking fondly of all he had created, then froze. All the screws on the backside of the exhibit stand were missing. "But ah . . . I suppose, with such rumors going about, one can only be safe. I understand your reluctance, and do respect your decision to pass on being the first buyer of my new explosives. I shall not elongate your discomfort. I'm sure there are other buyers."

Morgan smugly walked away, cane in hand. Three, two, one . . . .

"Lord Garnet, a moment."

Morgan smiled.

"Perhaps a demonstration would help ease my mind."

"Why of course. We've selected some of our more modest arms, designed for self-defense, not warfare mind you, to be demonstrated at the firing range just over there. If you'll kindly head that direction, I'll be along in a moment to personally show you what my protective devices can do."

As the gaggle of potential buyers headed toward the firing range, Morgan waved Cleaver over.

"Sir?"

"Double check this exhibit for me. It appears your boys were a bit sloppy assembling it." It was fortunate the explosives were inactive, considering the stand holding them remained upright by virtue of physics and a well-timed prayer.

Mr. Avery sighed. "What's it missing? Nails? A plank? Screws?"

Morgan frowned. "Screws."

"There are a few other exhibits missing pieces, sir. I think . . . I think the Crimsons might be here." He cringed as he said it. The man had once again failed to even mildly inconvenience those thieves.

Morgan cursed under his breath. "Find them. Find them and dispose of them. I will not have them ruining this expo. It's going poorly as it is."

"Understood, sir."

"Am I? Am I understood? Because it would seem every time I give you an order these days, it amounts to a failure, a fiasco, or an otherwise major inconvenience on my part."

Cleaver visibly seethed, clenching his fists at his sides.

"Failure is not an option today, Mr. Avery. Cleaver. Or whatever cute name you like to call yourself these days. Today, you beat the Crimsons, or today . . . you lose more than your job. Now. Do. You. Under. Stand?"

Oddly, Cleaver took a deep breath and stepped closer, looming over Morgan like the new high-rise buildings. He looked Morgan directly in the eyes, smiled, and nodded curtly.

Morgan cleared his throat. "Good. Very good. Now if you'll excuse me . . . ." Turning on his heel, the slightly perturbed Morgan went to the firing range, plastered yet another smile on his face—he'd be out of plaster before the night was over—and started his demonstration. "My lords and ladies," he declared, gaining his confidence back with every word. "You are going to love this."

Only an hour into the expo, and the fruit of Isabelle's labors over the past month were already evident. Her planted rumors, Crimson Run articles, and all the aspersions floating on the wind against Garnet were at the forefront of just about every conversation. Whispers of "stolen" and "conspiracy" and other words of that ilk were more numerous than business chatter.

Her staged Crimson run was building momentum with a few failed exhibits—one stand collapsed not thirty minutes into the expo; another weapon fell apart as soon as the exhibit host picked it up—and whispers that the Crimsons were present crept into a handful of conversations Isabelle passed.

She spotted Garnet at the firing range, and made her way in that direction, watching from a safe distance, through the sea of fine silks and gentlemen's top hats. Garnet delivered an impressive narrative about the double-barreled pistol he held in his hand, but Isabelle hardly paid attention. She glanced around the expo, looking for Constable Corbin. She frowned. He still had time according to Isabelle's plan, but still. What was taking him so long?

Garnet took a couple rounds of bullets from an assistant at the firing range, and Isabelle couldn't help the smile creeping onto her face. She made some extra plans for the firing range. For that pistol. Provided Mr. Monaghan executed her instructions properly.

With a flourish, Garnet opened the magazine chamber of the pistol and blinked. He didn't seem to know what to do with himself for a moment. Isabelle knew exactly what he was looking at. Nothing. Her instructions were for Monty to remove the magazines on all the weapons at the firing range. No one would even notice until it came time to demonstrate. It would look, hopefully, as though the Crimsons were present and on a stealing spree.

"Forgive me ladies and gentlemen. If you will excuse me for but a moment, I must check to ensure the range is ready for demonstration one last time before we get started. Standard protocols at the behest of the constabulary I'm afraid." He pulled the attendant aside and muttered intensely with him for a moment.

And Isabelle just couldn't help herself. This was going well. Too well. So well in fact that she marched right up to Garnet and pulled out her notebook from the satchel hanging over her shoulder. "Lord Garnet," she said meekly. "Why did you stop the demonstration so suddenly? Is there something wrong with the weapons? Are we safe? Is the expo safe?"

"Miss," he said through clenched teeth. "I would be happy to indulge your questions momentarily, if you would please just step aside for a moment and . . . ." He trailed off as he looked at her. Really looked at her. She raised her eyes to defiantly meet his. "Where would you like me to wait for your fall from grace, Lord Garnet?"

If eyes could produce heat from their intensity, Garnet would've lit the entire warehouse on fire. "Miss. Isabelle. Viece." He licked his lips and then clenched his jaw. "You survived. How wonderful to see you alive."

"Your care warms my heart," she sneered.

"This is *your* doing then? All of it? The Crimson Run column, the rumors, this—" He brandished the pistol. "It's all *your* doing?"

Isabelle smiled. "And it's not yet over."

"On that we agree. This is far, far from over." Suddenly, he stood up straight and his entire demeanor changed to reflect relieved shock. "Lady Viece!" he exclaimed loud enough to attract attention.

Oh no.

"Lady Isabelle Viece! It *is* you! You're alive! Oh praise God."

Within moments, whispers of "the Viece heir lives" spread like wildfire throughout the expo.

One by one, various dignitaries approached. "By God, is that really you child?"

"Lady Isabelle, you really are alive!"

"How can this be?"

"What dreadful clothing, child. What's happened to your hair?"

"How did you survive?"

The dissonance of concern threatened to drown Isabelle's frantic mind as she sought a way out of this. Surely this couldn't be it. This couldn't be how her carefully laid plans fell apart. Her family was counting on her. She could. Not. Fail!

"Now, now, everyone!" Garnet exclaimed, calming the crowd. "That's quite enough. Who knows what horrors poor Lady Viece has endured since the unfortunate events at her estate. She needs a moment of privacy. Mr. Avery!"

Cleaver came shoving his way through the crowd.

"Please escort Lady Viece somewhere private to recover."

Cleaver snatched the journal out of Isabelle's hand, wrestled her satchel away from her, and stuffed the notebook inside. He gave her a covert, knowing smile. He had no reason to take her satchel unless he presumed she was armed. Which she was.

With Isabelle disarmed, Cleaver ushered her toward a set of iron doors that led out onto the wharf, they passed one group after another chatting about the Viece heir, eyeing her excitedly. Journalists accosted her, demanding answers. People she knew came to get a closer look, some doubting it was her. Her peers, Sarah and Marion had tried to get to her, but Cleaver continued to shove Isabelle along through the midst of the chaos.

He nudged her a bit too close to one of the exhibits. She grabbed the opportunity and "stumbled" into the exhibit area. Cleaver came a second later, yanking her back into the crowd and toward the doors, but not before Isabelle had managed to snatch one of the new pistol designs, hiding it in the folds of her skirt, under the pretense of holding her skirts up to walk.

Cleaver shoved her through the double doors, slamming them closed behind him and the noise suddenly cut off. Despite her now precarious situation, Isabelle couldn't help but feel a wave of relief to be out of there. But now, she was alone with Cleaver.

She eyed him warily.

Her eyed her back.

Isabelle swallowed.

Cleaver just stood there.

Seconds passed.

More seconds passed.

AND THEN SUDDENLY . . . more seconds passed.

Isabelle frowned. This man harbored no reservations about hurting nor even killing her. She licked her lips and treaded carefully. But as soon as she opened her mouth, Garnet came striding out of the warehouse, his naturally regal bearing demanding attention and obedience as he approached. Steve and Cog, stood on either side of him as they approached.

"I dare say," Garnet declared as he stepped up to Isabelle, the sea breeze blowing his smart gentleman's coat behind him. "And I mean this with utmost sincerity, I am impressed. I am truly impressed. You faked your own death to continue patronizing me from the shadows, and I blind as to who my true opponent was. A very clever and devious plan, Lady Viece. I commend you."

"You speak as though your opponent is defeated."

"Are you not?"

Isabelle smiled with more confidence than she felt. "Do you think I would've revealed myself to you if I wasn't certain all was going according to my plan? I was, am, and continue to be your opponent if you wish to view this as a game."

"Oh don't mistake me, Lady Viece. Lives are at stake, and lives have been lost during this contest. It would be remiss of me to so crassly refer to it as a game."

"Lives didn't have to be lost. You murdered your way to this expo, and your hour of fame will be soon overshadowed by a lifetime of notoriety for the scandal you employed to achieve it."

"Eloquently put, Lady Viece. I should expect nothing less from the daughter of a traitor. Who better to understand a future of notoriety than one who faces such a future herself."

The comment stung more than Isabelle wanted to admit. She hadn't allowed herself to dwell on that truth yet, though much of what drove her zeal for this plan was the mistrial she was counting on after Garnet's crimes came to light.

For now, she swallowed the insult, ignored the truth, and cracked on. "My situation will not save you from yours, Garnet. Insult and goad me as you wish. I have deduced every minute detail of your game. I can trace the murders and smear campaigns of Thomas Brass, Tommy Addison, and all the rest back to your company. I have proof your blueprints are forged from *stolen* blueprints, of which the originals I now have in my custody. I have a search warrant to access your precious patents, which will clearly show plagiarism when compared to the original copies. Count Downey, your circus sponsorship, your staged Crimson runs, not to mention your failed attempt to murder me . . . I. Know. Everything! And you will hang for it."

To Isabelle's chagrin, Lord Garnet simply shook his head, disappointed.

"Oh Lady Viece. If you did actually know everything, you wouldn't be trying to stop me. You always did have a stronger code of honor than your degenerate parents."

Fuming, Isabelle tightened her grip on the pistol still hidden in the folds of her skirt.

"I am quite relieved at your survival, truly. Though I admit your timing is less than convenient."

"Shall I dispatch her for you, sir?"

While the devious snake actually considered, Isabelle glared the darkest glare she'd ever glared, heart racing and breathing labored. She had never felt such a deep seething hatred for anyone or anything. And oh how it terrified her.

"Bah! I can't be hastened to a decision right now. Mr. Avery, confine her somewhere out of my way. I'll deal with her later." He turned to leave, still muttering to himself about all the things he needed to do, and how inconvenient all this Viece trouble had been.

Inconvenient. That was the only word he had to describe Isabelle's carefully laid and executed plans.

Cleaver, Cog, and Steve remained.

"Well that's just great." Cog grimaced. "Confine her somewhere. Ok. Where? It's a bloody wharf, and a gigantic warehouse full of people."

Inconvenient. That was all her family was to Garnet. She had to beat him. For her family's sake, she had to. But once again, she found herself in a compromised position. *Buy yourself time,* Isabelle thought. *You need time to think, assess your surroundings. First, get these reprobates talking.*

"What does he expect us to do?" Cog continued. "Lock her in a cage and toss her into the sea? Sure, we can just fish her out later. Not like she'll be dead or anything."

Inconvenient! *Yes, Garnet. Justice is usually quite inconvenient for the guilty.* "Well you're a resourceful one, aren't you?" Isabelle said, still held tightly in Cleaver's iron arms. "Does someone have to provide detailed instructions before you venture to the privy as well? Or have you managed to figure out how to do that one on your own?" *Tools at my disposal: the pistol I stole, my dress and coat, false teeth . . . .*

Steve snorted out a laugh.

"Shut up, Steve," Cog glared at him indignantly. "I don't hear you throwing out any ideas."

"We could stuff her in a pantry?" Steve offered.

"The pantry!" Isabelle exclaimed. "Brilliant! The kitchen area is just inside these doors. You'll have to usher me through the crowd again, giving me the chance to call out for help. I rather like that idea." Potential escape routes:

Option one: jump into the sea. And swim where?

Option two: run back into the warehouse. They could easily find and subdue her again within seconds. She wouldn't get far and there was nowhere to hide.

Option three: the ladder leading up to the roof of the warehouse. And get stuck at the top with nowhere to go.

Option four: down the wharf. Would still likely require her to jump into the sea at some point, but it was her best bet at the moment.

"Shut up woman!" Cleaver shook Isabelle to drive the point home, but her words were already having the desired effect.

"It was just an idea," Steve grumbled.

"How about putting her in one of those fishing barrels over there?" Cog pointed down the walkway, at the foot of the next warehouse over, where a stack of barrels stacked atop each other were stacked in a stack.

"Excellent. Why don't you go retrieve one for us? I'm fairly certain my big toe will fit."

Cog looked toward the barrels. The walkways were not connected. And they did look only large enough to fit a child.

"Well . . . I mean . . . If we were to fold you up—"

"Fold me up? Like an accordion? I am pleased you think me so conditioned for the contortionist position at the circus. I was considering applying. I dare say you should apply for the Beardless Man. Or perhaps the Spineless Fool would suit you better."

"All right, all of you just shut up!" Cleaver roared.

"I'm just trying to be helpful, Cleaver." Cog pointed at Isabelle. "*She's* the one getting all prissy. Tell *her* to shut up."

"Don't blame her for the fact that you've never had a good idea in your life, Cog," Steve snapped.

"Oi now." Cog put his hands up defensively. "That's right unfair. We was never supposed to come up with ideas. That was Gauge's job."

Steve nodded his agreement. "You're not wrong about that. Where is that old fart when you need him?"

"Come on now Steve, have a heart. You don't just get up and walk after losing a chess match like that. Poor fellow's going to need some time to recover."

"And what about Strangler? He going to need some time to recover on account of his head being blown clean off? Oh! And how about Smithy? Eh? I suppose acupuncture ought to do the trick in reassembling all his exploded bits!"

"Now you're just being unreasonable, Steve. I know, we've all suffered lots during this . . . escapade. Lost a lot of good men, we did. But it'll all be worth it in the end."

"It better be!" Cleaver finally chimed in. He had been stewing in his own thoughts through the argument. Based on his thunderous expression, they weren't lovely thoughts.

He set Isabelle aside. Physically, "set her aside". Isabelle found herself standing outside the circle of welders who were determined to verbally snap each other's necks.

Cleaver shoved a finger in Steve's face. "I for one have had enough of your vendetta." He pointed to Cog's face. "And enough of your scattered emotions. And I've definitely had enough of losing! Losing men. Losing fights. Losing money. Losing sanity . . . This *will* be worth it in the end. I *will* come out of this victorious. And if either of you stand in my way, I *will*—"

"What?" Steve said darkly. "You'll do what? Finish that sentence. I dare you."

Clearly Isabelle had managed to agitate a festering wound. This crew was at a breaking point. She was partially responsible for the fate of one of their missing crew members, and directly responsible for the fate of the other.

If these men stopped squabbling among themselves for a moment, they might figure that out and Isabelle would be in even more serious trouble than she was already.

Now might be the only chance she'd have to escape. Isabelle took the opportunity to slip away while they continued arguing, though it was mostly Steve and Cleaver yelling in each other's faces. Step by careful step, she eased her way toward the door of the warehouse. It didn't take them long to catch on.

"Get her!" yelled Cleaver.

She wasn't going to make it. She'd never get the door open. But she refused to give up the space she'd managed to gain between them. Pulling out the pistol she had snatched from the expo, she whirled around, and leveled it right at Steve's forehead.

Chapter 29

VIECE HEIR BACK FROM GRAVE!

AS COURT NEARS DECISION ON FATE OF VIECE HOUSE, LADY ISABELLE VIECE, THE CONTROVERSIAL HEIR TO HOUSE NAME AND FORTUNE HAUNTS GARNET INDUSTRIES EXPOSITION, SURVIVING INFAMOUS VIECE ESTATE EXPLOSION, AND SENDING GARNET, EXPO SIX FEET UNDER.

"Great. This is just fantastic." Chief Brighton grumbled as he hurried about the expo. He had heard all of the chatter about the Viece heir being alive, but had not been able to actually locate her to let her know her cover was blown. That was a bad sign, and one Lady Viece's plan had not accounted for. He had Brooks and Rivers looking as well, to no avail.

"Chief Brighton!"

Brighton turned around and caught sight of the Mayberry heir approaching like a man on a life and death mission. "I demand to see her."

"See who, Lord Mayberry?"

"Lady Viece, of course."

"Son, Lady Viece is dead."

"If that woman your security took into custody wasn't Lady Viece, I still demand to see her."

"Look son, I know how hard it can be to . . . wait. *My* security?"

"Yes. I demand to see her."

"Where did you see my security take her?"

Lord Mayberry frowned. "Outside. On the wharf. Chief Brighton, what is—"

Brighton left the young man spluttering and headed toward the double doors leading out onto the wharf. A couple members of Lord Garnet's security guarded the doors, though Brighton didn't recognize them from any previous encounters. He put on his best mean, get-out-of-my-way face, strode right toward the fellows, but just happened to glance out the massive windows making up the bulk of the rest of the wall beside the doors. He caught sight of movement on the outside of the windows. Someone—two someones—climbed up the outside wall of the warehouse, and disappeared onto the roof.

Brighton rubbed his eyes and sighed. Why was he not surprised to see *those* two here?

Alex was still at the magistrate's office, waiting for his patents. It had been a full twenty-four hours now.

Only a weak man needs to sleep, he told himself.

His back ached something awful, his eyes desperately wanted to close, and he was not on speaking terms with his broken leg.

Hold strong, Alex. You have a job to do! You need to get those patents . . . you need to . . . you . . . zzzzzzzzzz.

"Constable Corbin?"

Alex jolted awake. "Patents!"

"I . . . mmm yes. I have them here for you."

Alex rubbed his eyes and sniffled, shaking himself awake. "Thank you." He snatched the patents and hobbled on his cane toward the exit. He glanced at the clock on his way out. 5:30 p.m. Perfect. He should arrive at the expo just in time. Rifling through the documents as he walked, he froze.

Nail polish.

Bird cage.

Inkwell.

Picture frame.

Ingot.

Bunny.

With an exasperated sigh, Alex turned around and called the secretary. "I um . . . well I don't think these are the right documents."

The secretary looked at them, then broke down into tears. "Oh, oh, oh! The magistrate asked for a list of what was missing. What did I give him, then? Oh, I'm such a mess. Two days on the job and I'm already proving to everyone that I can't do it. Mmm! Those blasted Crimsons! It's all their fault!"

"Um. . . yes, well. I still need my patents."

"If they hadn't shown up and ruined everything . . . mmmm! Oh if they show their faces to me I might just pop them in the mouth."

"Okay but . . . my patents?"

"Can't do anything right," she sobbed, and threw her face into Alex's shoulder.

Alex looked around him helplessly. He lamely patted her on the head as he tried to think of a plan B.

Now what? Isabelle thought, as she held her firearm up to Steve's face. It succeeded in maintaining the distance between them.

The welders remained where they were, eyes darting from the pistol to Isabelle's face.

With her eyes wide, and her jaw set, she must've looked like she meant to shoot. There was a time when she would've been horrified at the idea of killing someone. But in that moment, looking at each of these men who had caused her so much pain over the last few months, had killed poor Professor Brass and his coachman, had ruined so many lives, including Constable Corbin's . . . She wasn't so sure anymore.

"Relax Steve," Cleaver said, though he didn't make a move toward Isabelle himself. "She won't shoot."

"You don't think I'll do it? After everything you've put me through?"

"First, you put yourself through all this. Don't blame us for your own stupid meddling. Second, you ain't going to shoot because you can't. You snatched that weapon from the expo. No live rounds."

Steve and Cog relaxed, smug grins sliding over their faces.

Isabelle blinked. She hadn't accounted for that. This was not one of the weapons she had instructed Mr. Monaghan to tamper with. She opened the magazine of the weapon to check for rounds just in case. There were none. In fact, the entire magazine was missing.

Cleaver frowned at the empty weapon, then raised his eyes to meet Isabelle's. As realization washed over Isabelle, Cleaver simply rolled his eyes and cursed.

Before anyone could make another move, Isabelle threw the pistol at Steve's face, and darted for the ladder to the roof. She hated gambling, and she hated relying on others—especially a complete wild card—to do her bidding. But so far, without fail, the Crimsons had been her unintended, unplanned, and frankly unwanted ace-in-the-hole. She suspected their presence at each of the fiascos over the past few weeks was not coincidental. But she had long since given up trying to understand their motivations or goals.

For now, as she sprinted up the ladder, three welders right on her heels, she merely hoped that her gamble on the Crimson siblings would pay off one more time.

Brighton led Brooks, Rivers, Terry, and Constable #8 (that's actually the guy's name; it's not because the author was too lazy to come up with a name on the spot or anything) to the double doors leading out onto the wharf. "Terry, Constable #8, guard the door from inside. No one comes out. Brooks, Rivers, with me. Prepare for a possible Crimson run."

Brooks snorted. "How does one prepare for a Crimson run, sir?"

Brighton hesitated. "Point."

With that he strode out onto the wharf, and looked around. To his left, the welders climbed the ladder to the roof. He spotted Lady Viece leading the climb, nearly at the top now, but the welder at the bottom had barely gotten onto the ladder when Chief Brighton reached up and yanked the man by the ankle back down to the ground.

To his credit, he leaped right back to his feet in an instant, and had a knife in hand a second later. When he locked eyes with Brighton, the hatred was nearly palpable.

"Well," Chief Brighton drawled, as he drew his truncheon. "Fancy seeing you here, Steve."

Alex was *still* at the magistrate's office. He had pulled his hair out, it grew back, and he'd pulled it out again, and this poor secretary was *still* wailing on about how terrible she was at life. Good Lord! Was this what Alex sounded like to others? He vowed never to complain about anything ever again.

"Miss."

She cried.

"Miss."

She wailed.

"Miss!"

She wallowed.

"Look I'm sorry you, you know, ain't good at nothing, ahem, but you know . . . you can't just keep crying like this. Crying ain't never got anyone nowhere."

She whimpered.

The magistrate's office was still in utter chaos. Papers flew in every direction, people ran and yelled orders at each other, a fire blazed in one of the cubicles . . . and in the midst of it all emerged a prominent figure in a smart brown suit. "Here now!" he roared. "What's all this? What the blazes is going on?"

"A Crimson run, sir," one of the accountants said. "As you can see from these figures—"

"Yes, yes, yes. I believe you, Peter. Why isn't it handled? Clean up this mess! Ms. Lovely Assistant! Where are you? You're never around when I need you."

"It's Martha, sir," sobbed the young woman as she pealed herself off Alex's shoulder and sniffled.

"Yes, Martha. Why are my offices in such terrible shape? I hired you for your organizational skills and ability to keep calm under pressure. What do you call this?" He gestured up and down at her with a flippant hand.

She collapsed back down in tears with renewed vigor.

The magistrate raised an eyebrow, then looked askance at Alex.

Alex shrugged helplessly. "Maybe she's . . . um, overstressed. And um overworked? And maybe she needs support and encouragement. You know. Instead of . . . you yelling? At her? All the time? . . . Maybe?"

The magistrate blinked. "Well you're about as helpful as a dead fish in a knife fight."

"Um . . . okay. But I'm actually . . . I'm here for the patents. For Lord Morgan Garnet's p–p–patents. I have reason to believe that that that that. . ."

"Wait. I know you." He pointed at Alex, narrowing his eyes, then suddenly let out a whoop. "Why Constable Alex Corbin! The hero of Liverpool! Such a pleasure to meet you, my dear man." The magistrate strode over to Alex and shook his hand in a too-tight grip. "To what do we owe the honor?"

"Um . . . my . . . patents?"

"Oh yes, yes! Martha, get this man his patents. And get him a drink. Get this man whatever he desires. We've a hero in our midst!"

No one paid him any mind. The place was *still* in chaos, that fire *still* blazed over to Alex's left, Martha *still* sobbed on the ground, and Alex *still* didn't have his patents.

"You see what I have to deal with?" The magistrate sighed, shaking his head melodramatically, and resting his fists on his hips. "Incompetent the lot of them."

Something about that comment sparked an idea in Alex's weary mind. "Incompetent isn't the half of it," he said. "Is this how you run your office? Law and order is what s–s–separates us from the animals, and this is what you call order? You keep the law literally on the papers filed away in this building, and this is how you treat it? How you treat people's intellectual property?"

"I . . . well," the magistrate spluttered, but Alex plowed on, gaining more courage as he spoke.

"D–d–disgraceful! My constables have to go through your office to get arrest warrants and search warrants and–and–and–and warrants of an unusual size but what about you? How do I get a warrant to investigate *your* office and its malpractice? I should put that motion in court."

"You wouldn't."

"I serve justice, Magistrate. Justice doesn't discriminate."

"What do you want then?"

"I want all the Garnet patents you have on file. And I want them now."

"All right, all right. Just cool your britches. I'll get them for you personally."

"About bloody time." Did he seriously just curse? "Oh and Magistrate?"

The magistrate turned, jaw tight and back stiff.

"Bring me the late Thomas Brass's patents as well."

"Of course," he replied stiffly. "Anything else?"

Alex hesitated a moment. "Yes, an arrest warrant for Lord Morgan Garnet."

No sooner did Isabelle reach the warehouse rooftop than she spotted the Crimson siblings. A hope blossomed within her. *There is a God!* And no sooner did she spot them than they lowered themselves into the warehouse from one of the skylights in the roof, and hope seeped right out of her veins. *There is no God!*

Isabelle ran toward that skylight for all she was worth. Fortunately, the rooftop was wet and slick, what with its close proximity to the sea, and so she threw her legs ahead of her and slid toward the hole where the Crimsons had disappeared. As Cleaver and Cog converged on her, she slid into the hole and fell into darkness.

Brighton sent the rest of his constables up the ladder after Lady Viece, while he stood facing off with Steve, slapping his truncheon against his palm in a disciplinary manner.

Steve casually brandished his knife.

Brighton smiled. "Your friend ain't here to punch some sense into you this time, I see?"

"He ain't here to keep me from killing you either," Steve snarled.

"Out of curiosity, why are you so hellbent on killing me? What did I ever do to you?"

"You, the constables, the blasted parliament. All of you think you own us. You think you—"

"What?" Brighton roared. "What do I think? That the world is fair? That fat, spoiled rich boys don't dictate the pathetic lives of the common folk? What do I think, Steve? That terrible things don't happen to good people and justice isn't a pleasant fantasy only fools believe in? Who the bloody hell do you think I am? I know what a God-forsaken hellhole we live in, and I know my wages are paid by people who don't give a damn about justice. But none of this. *None* of this. Justifies you going around killing folks, stealing from folks, breaking the law in every way imaginable, and then having the gall to swear this was somehow *my* fault! That this was *anyone* else's fault except for yours."

Brighton leveled his truncheon at Steve. "Now lay down your weapon and come quietly. No fuss or funny business. And I'll treat you right fair, I will. My word of honor on it."

Steve blinked. For a brief moment, Brighton actually dared hope something in his stupid drivel had actually gotten through to Steve. The torment was plain on the man's face. He even dared feel a small pang of pity for the welder.

Whatever he had seen gave way almost immediately to an intense, iron-hot fury. With another snarl, Steve lunged at Brighton like a feral animal, knife aimed for his chest.

After falling for only a second or two, Isabelle plopped abruptly atop a stack of boxes backstage. This portion of the warehouse was poorly lit. Isabelle could barely make out a wide wooden ramp with mini train tracks running up to the stage. A vertical loading door dominated the far wall behind stacks of crates, large boxes, dollies, and wheelbarrows. Ropes and pulleys hung from the rafters overhead.

Above Isabelle, Cleaver and Cog peeked down at her. Where was Steve? Scrambling off the stack of boxes, Isabelle landed behind the backstage. It was dark, but she could hear all of the expo chatter just beyond the thick stage curtain in front of her. She dropped down to the lower section, as there were a few people moving about backstage. She could now see the beams beneath the stage, which had just enough crawl space to fit through.

Cleaver and Cog landed on the stack of crates, as Isabelle quietly hid on the other side of the loading ramp. She did her best to still her heart and breath, but it sounded much too loud to her ears. They'd hear her. Surely they'd see her. They'd know—

Crimson?

Close. She spotted the sister half of the criminal duo climbing atop a large crate. Considering the sudden absence of anyone else backstage, Isabelle presumed Jasper Crimson was busy distracting everyone else.

Cleaver motioned for Cog to check the other side while he approached the large crate.

Isabelle smiled.

The expo program was to have a big finale, a spectacular reveal of some kind. That large crate was positioned to be rolled onto the main stage atop the track system. That would mean whatever weapon Garnet wanted to showcase was likely in there.

Cleaver pulled out his mallet and climbed up onto the crate beside the Crimson girl. Her silhouette was child-like, but standing beside Cleaver's hulking figure, she looked especially tiny. Vulnerable. Fragile. Isabelle snorted. Cleaver had no chance.

"AND NOW LADIES AND GENTLEMEN! THE BIG FINALE YOU'VE ALL BEEN WAITING FOR!"

Isabelle leapt up onto the ramp and darted toward the tracks where the massive box rested. There would be a lever around here.

Cleaver held up his mallet to swing at the Crimson girl, then cursed as he realized who it was. During the moment of indignation Isabelle spared that Scarlet Crimson could inspire that sort of reaction out of a dangerous criminal, the crate cracked.

"Cleaver!" yelled Cog from the shadows off to the side. "The Crimsons!" *Grunt.* "The Crimsons are—" *Grunt.* "They're here!"

Cog expertly threw knives, darts, stars, and other random metal objects at the quickly moving silhouette of Jasper Crimson, his signature coat flapping in his wake as he dodged and danced around the metal objects coming his way.

"I know!" yelled Cleaver as he swung his mallet right over the head of the agile Scarlet Crimson, who bent and twisted with remarkable flexibility around Cleaver's attempts.

"I CANNOT EXPRESS ENOUGH MY EXCITEMENT AT SHARING WITH YOU MY GREATEST ACHIEVEMENT IN PUBLIC SAFETY."

Scarlet Crimson dropped low and kicked Cleaver's legs out from under him. The crate they stood on cracked further.

Isabelle eyed the track in the dim lighting. It was slightly inclined, which meant its cargo would slide forward naturally, and likely slowly, once released from whatever held it in place. Not a lever then. Something at the front of the crate, or rather at the front of the rusty wheeled pallet it rested on.

Cog screamed. "I'm hit, Cleaver! The bastard got me! Ahhhh! I die! Farewell cruel world!"

"Cog shut up, and come help me with—" He grunted as Scarlet Crimson whacked him in the gut with his own weapon several times in quick succession.

Crack.

How did she get that away from him, Isabelle vaguely wondered as she moved to the front of the box. Indeed, there were stoppers holding the wheeled pallet in place.

"THIS IS THE FUTURE OF OUR WONDERFUL ENGLAND. WITH ONE OF THESE PROTECTING EVERY ONE OF YOUR HOMES, THIEVES WILL BE A THING OF THE PAST."

Cleaver finally managed to grab the Crimson girl's hair and yanked. He grabbed his mallet from her hand and wrestled it away easily, just as Jasper Crimson leapt up beside him.

Crack. Crrrrack.

Isabelle grabbed the handle atop one of the stoppers and pulled for all she was worth. The stopper came loose and she landed on her backside with a grunt. The cart lurched, throwing Cleaver off balance. The Crimsons barely noticed.

"BRIGANDS ON THE STREETS WILL BE ERADICATED. EVEN THE CONSTABULARY WILL NO LONGER BE NECESS-ARY EXCEPT TO PERHAPS ENSURE THIS LITTLE FELLOW'S WHEELS ARE OILED."

Isabelle snatched up the rope on the other stopper and yanked. This one didn't budge at all.

Jasper Crimson kicked Cleaver off the box, opposite to where Isabelle wrestled with the stopper. But his mallet landed on the box, then bounce off to land next to Isabelle. Cog—who was apparently still very much alive—climbed up onto the massive box and tried to pull Crimson off, but the thief leapt up in the air and grabbed something over his head. A pipe or beam in the rafters. Hanging there, he swung his legs around Cog, picked the man up with his legs and promptly dropped him back down onto the box.

"AND NOW WITHOUT ANY FURTHER ADO . . ."

Cog's lower half crashed through the top of the box.

"I GIVE YOU THE ANSWER . . ."

Scarlet leapt up next to her brother, catching his hand, and he pulled her up the rest of the way to acrobatically climb into the rafters.

The curtains opened.

Isabelle reached for the mallet. She swung it at the stopper. Once. Twice.

"I GIVE YOU . . ."

At the third whack, the stopper came loose, and the box began to slide forward.

Alex burst into the warehouse. "I have the warrant!" he announced. No one turned around. His heart sank as he realized he'd made his grand entrance at the precise moment the big finale started. Everyone was gasping and exclaiming and . . . were they saying "Crimson run"?

Using his cane to hoist himself up, Alex scrambled onto a table to get a better view of the stage. A large wooden crate sat atop a wheeled pallet in the middle of the stage. It slid forward a little too fast for a proper performance.

As the crate rolled forward, Jasper Crimson dropped from midair, landing smoothly beside Cog. At least, Cog's upper half—the rest of him was stuck inside the crate.

Then the sister dropped with an impressive flip and landed in a crouch on the other side of Cog. Scarlet snatched something off of Cog, while the brother opened the front of the box with a crowbar.

The Crimsons leapt off the crate in unison just as the front panel fell off, revealing some kind of cannon. Jasper acted like he was going to fire it, which made everyone panic and just like that, chaos broke out.

But the weapon did not fire. In fact, the Crimsons took that moment to snatch a few things out of the crate—the brother hastily stuffing them into his coat, and the sister tucking them into a belt pouch—while Cog sat atop the weapon in a panic. The Crimsons leapt off the stage and headed toward the back of the warehouse while everyone else was running for the front. Toward Alex. Oh dear.

There was no way Brighton could get out of the way in time to avoid the knife. But he could avoid death. And so he maneuvered just in time to take the knife hit to the chest where it wouldn't hit a vital organ. Still hurt like hell.

He grunted, but held Steve's hand in place, forcing him to keep the knife embedded in Brighton's chest. This way he couldn't try to stab again. With his other hand, Brighton took out his own knife, and plunged it into the side of Steve's neck. Steve's eyes went wide, and neither man moved. Their eyes locked for some time, Steve's a blazing fire of hatred, and Brighton's a dull resolve. He had always hated this part of the job. Understanding why someone did what they did, but watching it destroy them as surely as if they'd put a gun in their own mouths.

The fire in Steve's eyes began to fade, as blood spilled down the corner of his mouth. He fell to the ground, leaving his knife in Brighton's chest.

Brighton knelt beside Steve to see if there was any hope of saving him, though he already knew the answer. He closed Steve's eyes, gritting his teeth against the pain of his wound, and holding the knife steady with an increasingly bloodied hand. He'd live. He always did. But perhaps that was what he hated most about this job. He had wanted to get away from war. Instead he'd traded the war between countries for the war between classes.

A sudden commotion from inside the warehouse broke him out of his reverie. He slowly got to his feet, wincing, and went to see what else could possibly go wrong today.

"Seize them!" screamed Garnet.

Members of the constabulary and Garnet's private security converged on the Crimsons.

While the Crimsons did what they do best and sowed chaos, Isabelle leapt up onto the main stage, scanning the crowd for Chief

Brighton. She leapt off the side of the stage, frantically shoving forward to—

Someone grabbed her ankles and yanked her to the ground. She screamed as she was pulled under the stage, clawing at the ground to no avail.

Twisting around, she realized it was Cleaver who held her ankles from the crawl space beneath the stage. It wasn't easy for him to maneuver under there, with his hulking muscle and height, which might be her only bet, considering no one heard her cry for help over the deafening roar of chaos.

Into the darkness, he pulled her, toward the backstage area. If he managed it, there would be nothing Isabelle could do. She had to escape him now.

"I am so tired of failing," Cleaver declared suddenly.

Isabelle felt the same.

"If I only get one thing from this entire infernal, cursed job, I'm getting you back to Lord Garnet."

NO! Isabelle tried to grab the numerous rafters beneath the stage.

NOT like this! She was done. Done letting this man frighten her. Done barely escaping more thanks to luck, and most definitely thanks to the Crimsons, than to her own capabilities. Done feeling like everything she did was ultimately for naught.

She glanced behind her to see if Cleaver still had her satchel over his shoulder. He did.

It was time to stop *pretending* to be in control, and actually *take* control.

Isabelle thrashed, screaming, as Cleaver pulled her further through the underbelly of the stage, her arms and legs whacking the metal beams along the way. She'd be painted with bruises if she survived this, but she didn't want Cleaver to realize she wanted him to get her to the edge of the stage. She had one shot at this.

"To hell with the Crimsons!" Cleaver roared. "To hell with the welders! To hell with it all!"

Cleaver's legs poked out from the beneath the stage as they arrived at the edge. Isabelle continued to fight, waiting for her moment.

Cleaver pulled her along a little further.

Almost there. She wouldn't have thought her heart could beat any faster.

Cleaver cleared the edge of the stage, his whole body now free of the interlocking metal and wood confines.

Now!

Isabelle stopped fighting, and Cleaver now had his full range of leverage to pull Isabelle the rest of the way out in one yank. The result slid Isabelle right underneath Cleaver, who was still bent down on hands and knees.

Seeing this man while they were both standing was intimidating enough, but lying beneath him, he appeared even larger, even stronger. Isabelle's throat went dry.

Cleaver grabbed her shoulders to try to haul them both to their feet, but not before Isabelle reached into her satchel, and wrestled out her pistol.

Cleaver noticed, immediately releasing her shoulders, and tried instead to snatch the pistol out of Isabelle's hand.

Panicked, Isabelle pulled the trigger prematurely. Cleaver recoiled with the blow, though Isabelle wasn't exactly sure where she had shot him. She wriggled herself out from beneath him, shaking, and scrambled back beneath the stage, pistol still in hand, but Cleaver crawled after her. Through the spider web of metal beams, Isabelle crawled, Cleaver on her heels, moaning and holding a hand to his side.

Eyes wide, Isabelle tried to fire another shot at him, but she couldn't get her arm steady enough. Her next shot missed. Her third shot hit metal and ricocheted.

Shooting wasn't working. She desperately crawled forward. Tears she didn't remember crying streamed down her face.

Just a few more feet.

Almost there.

Cleaver grabbed her ankle again.

"No!" she shrieked, trying in vain to kick him off of her. "No! No! NO!"

"Let her go, you," said a new voice evenly. "Or I'll plug you right between the eyes."

Isabelle's head had not yet peeked out from the side of the stage, but she could see someone crouched down, pistol trained on Cleaver.

Constable Brooks.

Cleaver released Isabelle's ankle and she dragged herself the rest of the way out. Rivers was right there to give her a hand. "You all right, Lady Viece?"

Isabelle nodded, still shaking and gasping for air, clothing and hair a disheveled mess.

"It's all right, Lady Viece. We'll take it from here." Brooks held his pistol steady as Rivers and Constable Terry subdued and arrested Cleaver.

Isabelle backed away, but she couldn't take her eyes off of him. She had shot him. He had tried to kill her multiple times, and she had shot him once. He killed Professor Brass. And she shot him only once. This wasn't justice. Not yet.

Cleaver looked up at her with the darkest expression she'd ever seen.

No. Justice was not yet served.

As Brooks, Rivers, and Terry towed the wounded welder away in cuffs, Isabelle took in the remnants of her staged Crimson run turned actual Crimson run. The exhibits she'd instructed Mr. Monaghan to tamper with were now collapsing, shooting off steam, had coils whipping up in the air, or otherwise just didn't work.

The Crimsons were having the time of their lives. They used each exhibit to their advantage, tossing weapons into the midst of the guards to distract them, leaping from table to table, climbing up the windowed wall, and exiting from a couple open ones at the top.

Just like that, they were gone.

In the midst of all the panicked, overly dressed, pampered upper crust scrambling to exit the warehouse, Isabelle wondered for the first time if she had ever actually been one of them. These last few weeks of being "dead" had afforded her a true glimpse of a different life. One that she now felt foolish for ever thinking she understood. She didn't know the half of it.

But perhaps that was a thought for another time. Instead, she took in one last observation from the chaotic scene before her. On the far side of the warehouse, facing down the affluent stampede, Constable Corbin handed a stack of papers to Chief Brighton. The chief was clearly injured.

Isabelle met Chief Brighton's eyes, worried. Had he been shot? Did he need medical attention?

But he simply smiled back at her.

He was well.

Corbin beamed beside the chief, gracing Isabelle with the biggest grin.

All was well.

With a triumphant smile of her own, Isabelle scanned the frenzied crowd for Lord Garnet. She frowned. Where was he?

Finally, her eyes landed on the stage, where it appeared Cog had already been arrested. The only person still on the stage was Garnet himself. He sat primly on a small staircase, resting his elbows on his knees as the chaos unfolded before him, his face a mask of grim resolve.

Isabelle moved gingerly over to him, wincing at the increasing pain all over her body. Remembering the acrobatics the Crimsons had on display today, Isabelle added *become a master acrobat* to her list of things she needed to learn.

Standing at the bottom of the short stair case, Isabelle looked up at Garnet, who refused to meet her gaze.

"A Crimson run," he said somberly, still not looking at her. "In the end, a Crimson run is what finally puts the nail in the coffin for my expo." He chuckled. "This is going to be quite the mess to clean up."

"That," Isabelle declared, "is frankly the least of your worries, Garnet."

"Everyone freeze!" screamed Chief Brighton.

Everyone froze—one did not disobey Chief Brighton. Utter silence and stillness displaced the craze that engulfed the warehouse moments before. Garnet raised an eyebrow.

"What is this?"

Chief Brighton held Corbin's papers in one bloody hand and handed his handcuffs to Constable Corbin with the other. "By order of the Magistrate of Liverpool," he said with a voice just as strong as ever. "You are under arrest for larceny, forgery, and,"—Brighton hesitated only a moment before adding—"and treason."

Garnet's eyes grew wide as saucers. Only then did he look at Isabelle. She had imagined this moment. Imagined what she would say. Something bold, and cleverly sarcastic. But in that moment, with tears dried on her cheeks, seeing Corbin's triumphant face, and Chief Brighton's resolve. Seeing the welders finally completely incapacitated, and now having everything she needed for her family's case to be dismissed as a mistrial, Isabelle found herself meeting Garnet's disbelief with a simple smile.

Epilogue

um. Bum. B–b–bum. That rhythm, cold and steady, bespoke of the inevitable. *Bum. Bum. B–b–bum.* Harsh and resolute, there was no escape. No more pleading. A verdict had been reached. *Bum. Bum. B–b–bum.* The penalty for high treason is death.

And nothing Isabelle had done to discredit the accuser had been enough to outdo the condemning evidence he had uncovered against her parents.

The steady beat turned into a drumroll, matching the drumming in Isabelle's chest. The hangman ushered his two prisoners up the wooden stairs and placed them next to each other at the center of the drop.

Lord Isaiah Viece, her dear father, stood tall and strong, dressed in his best, hands bound behind his back, as the hangman fitted the noose around his neck and pulled the white cloth over his face.

Confident but careful. Kind, yet stern. Bold, but not reckless. This was her father. In Isabelle's mind, she was five years old, covered in mud when Father found her in the gardens. She showed him the bug she had caught, and instead of chastising her, he tackled her into the mud and the two of them laughed as they threw mud at each other.

Lady Isadora Viece, a mother a girl could only dream of having, stood stiffly, resolved to her fate as the hangman fitted her noose next. Isabelle had visited her parents in London's Newgate prison not two days ago for what would be the last time, but the memory that seized Isabelle's mind and heart as she looked at her mother was of her thirteenth birthday, when she had asked for a pistol, and her house regarded her with such shock and disappointment that Isabelle didn't mention it again.

That night, after one of the most enjoyable birthday parties she'd ever had, her mother came into her room and sat down beside her, giving her the wisdom a mother does when her daughter comes of age. Isabelle had groaned and rolled her eyes at the entire speech, but she heard every word, and still took that wisdom to heart to this day. Her mother handed her a present, and said simply, "Welcome to womanhood, my dearest." Inside the gilded box was the pistol Isabelle kept in her satchel, and yet still didn't really know how to use.

Isabelle squeezed her eyes shut as the executioner stepped up to the lever. As the lever fell, Isabelle stumbled to her feet and tremulously, aimlessly ran out of the execution yard. Newgate Prison was eerily quiet and empty, even for a private execution. She took a single step out into the garden area as the executioner announced the end of the hanging.

Collapsing to the ground as though she herself had fallen through the drop, she clenched her black gloved hands into the gravel, and vomited.

Then she wept.

She wept for her parents whom she barely had time for over the last few years, pursuing her delusions of becoming a detective.

She wept for her failure, that she wasn't able to stop this from happening. That her plan, while successfully routing Garnet, had not been enough to prevent her parents' fate.

She wept that the execution was just. Her parents were guilty. Traitors. The evidence was clear, and had been right under her nose all her life.

It's curious how one would spend so much time digging up the muck surrounding others but conveniently blind oneself to their own family's unsavory dealings.

Garnet's words hit harder than ever. Rang truer than ever. She hadn't seen it. She hadn't even thought to look. Criminals were those other people, who lived in those other areas, and maintained those other acquaintances. They weren't in your own home. They weren't your own flesh and blood. They weren't your loved ones. And they certainly weren't good people.

She still believed that. Her parents were good people.

Today destroyed Isabelle's understanding of law, justice, right and wrong. Was there no way to know?

"Belle?"

Isabelle didn't move at the sound of her uncle's voice. He was the only one who called her Belle. She'd always hated that nickname, likely because this particular uncle used it.

"Come, my dear."

Isabelle didn't move.

"We must be strong, my dear. We mustn't let this tragedy destroy the Viece family. We have much work to be about to recover our reputation."

Isabelle leapt to her feet. "That was my father!" she shrieked. "That was my mother! How could you just—"

"And that was my brother!" her uncle roared back, taking her shoulders in a rough grip. "Do not presume to dismiss my own grief at this loss! And do not ever presume to raise your voice to me again. You are in my charge now, and you will behave properly. I will not be so lax as your parents were." He took a deep breath and recovered his decorum.

This uncle was everything her father was not. If she had suspected anyone in her family of treason, it would've been this self-important, conceited shark. Every bit as capable as her father, but in ways that garnered fear instead of respect.

"There will be a time to grieve," Uncle Isaac continued more calmly, but with a stiffness that did—Isabelle grudgingly admitted— imply emotional compromise. "But right now, we have work to do. I have work to do. *So* much work. . . ." He trailed off, then stalked off toward their carriage.

All the fight evaporated as quickly as it had risen. She just . . . didn't care anymore. She was so tired. She stumbled away, until she hit a garden lamppost. Hugging it for a moment, she broke down in tears again, dropping to her knees. She turned to lean her back against the post, curled her legs up, and cradled her knees like a child.

There were many things to hate about prison: the stench, the perpetual cold, the grimy walls, the rickety, lice-infested, piss-stained pad he was forced to sleep on . . . but Cleaver found that boredom took the cake. There was nothing to occupy his time but his depressing thoughts.

He was still recovering from his gunshot wound, which had been treated regularly since his incarceration, but he barely even noticed it anymore. He did menial chores, he ate in the mess hall, he laid in his bunk and listened to his cell mate's incessant and boring stories.

But mostly, he seethed. He seethed at the loss of his friends, at his own failure, at his replete embarrassment. He didn't hate Lady Viece, even though she'd foiled his plans. Or Lord Garnet, even though he'd misplaced his trust in the businessman to bring him success and notoriety. Or Chief Brighton, even though he'd killed Steve, arrested Cleaver and Cog, and represented the enemy of all criminals: law enforcement.

The ones he truly hated were the Crimson siblings and the Informant. They represented everything he wanted to be, had tried so hard to be, but just wasn't. He had long since worked it out during his numerous sleepless nights in this unforgiving prison.

How did these people get to where they were? People who lived life by their own rules, answered to no one, and always came out ahead? Cleaver was so sick and tired (because you can't be sick without being tired) of playing by other's rules. The system failed him, now the criminal life had failed him. Where else was he supposed to go?

There was little point in this line of reasoning now, considering he'd be in prison for the better part of his life. He hadn't had a trial yet, so the exact sentence remained to be seen.

A rap at the door to his cell called him out of his dark thoughts. For a moment, he thought it was just his cell mate, but the man was asleep in the bunk below. Cleaver jumped down off his bunk and went to the cell door, where a portly man with bright red hair, a receding hairline, and an overall jovial disposition smiled at him.

"Who the bloody hell are you?" Cleaver demanded, eyeing the man up and down through the bars of the cell door.

"Name's Rodger, hehe! Rodger Jolliman."

"Is something funny, Rodger?"

"Always something to laugh about, if you've the mind for it."

"Well I don't. So unless they're adding a third cellmate to this hellhole . . . ."

"You mistake me, friend. I come on behalf of my employer, who was quite impressed with your dedication and persistence while under Lord Garnet's employ."

Cleaver raised a bushy eyebrow, realizing how strange this man's presence was. How had he gotten in here? Where was the night guard? "What?"

"My employer has a proposition for you. He'll get you out of this *hellhole*, hehe, if you come work for him."

Cleaver leaned forward, resting an arm overhead on the cell door bars. "And who exactly is your employer?"

"The one who's actually going to succeed at bringing about the change you and your welder friends have been looking for."

"How does your employer know anything about me?"

"Matthias Monaghan, the Informant I believe you call him, isn't the only one with eyes and ears, Seth Avery."

Cleaver stiffened at hearing his real name. No one had called him Seth in a good long while. It also seemed a bad sign that this chuckling oaf knew the Informant's real name. But nevertheless, he continued to play it straight. "And why should I work for your employer?"

"Well, hehe, your alternative is to rot in this hellhole."

True. "I ain't interested. I'm done working for wealthy bastards what think they own me."

"How would you like to help take down the current government?"

Cleaver started. "You bloody serious?"

"Yes." All mirth and merriment gone, Rodger gave Cleaver such a straightforward, no nonsense stare, Cleaver actually gave this silly offer a moment of consideration.

"All right," Cleaver said finally. "I'm listening."

Hours after the public execution, Isabelle climbed out of her uncle's coach and followed him somberly up the stairs to his house in Grosvenor Square, in a wealthy part of London. She hesitated outside the imposing black door. She'd been living in this cold, uninviting prison for the last several weeks. She doubted she'd ever feel at home anywhere again.

Her uncle didn't live in an estate with private grounds the way her father had. His luxurious townhome was fashionable, connecting to both the neighboring homes beside it. A gentle rain fell upon the well-maintained street outside, and the gas lamps gave off an eerie glow on this dreary day. Trees and flowers placed in perfect rows along the sidewalk did their best to liven the place up, but for Isabelle it wasn't enough. Nothing would ever be enough again.

Inside, the butler removed Isabelle's damp black cloak, but she would not allow him to take her satchel. She kept that on her person at all times now. She would never be caught unarmed again. In fact, she had already started taking firearms training, without her uncle's knowledge of course.

Before she could make her way to her quarters, another of her uncle's house staff approached her in the foyer. "This came for you while you were away, Lady Viece."

Isabelle frowned, taking the letter. It was from Inspector Corbin. The more she read, the darker her expression.

"Miss?" the attendant asked. "Are you . . . all right?"

Isabelle snatched her cloak right back from the butler, and wrestled it on as she stalked back to the coach, heedless of propriety, which was becoming a more consistent state for her. Before her uncle could catch her, she ordered the driver to take her to the address Corbin indicated in his letter.

It wasn't far.

She rolled up to an estate even more lavish than her own had been. Isabelle hardly waited for the coach to stop before she leapt out and quickly glided up to the front door, the gentle rain seeping through her hood and dampening her hair.

No sooner did the butler open the doors than Isabelle barged her way in. "I'm here to see your *guest of honor*," she demanded, slipping her cloak off and simply dropping it on the ground.

"Forgive me, miss," the butler said as he bent to pick up her cloak. "Might I ask who—"

"I am Lady Isabelle Viece. I demand to see Lord Garnet."

"Is he expecting you?"

"He can hardly be surprised."

Isabelle didn't wait around for more silly questions. She hiked up her black skirts and glided her way up the grand staircase, ignoring the butler's protests. "Which way?" she demanded once she'd reached the top.

"Miss, you cannot be up here. I—"

Rustling from a room down the hall pointed Isabelle in *that* direction. The butler was right on her heels, still protesting the entire way as Isabelle reached the room at the end of the hall and stood in the open doorway. Sure enough, Lord Garnet himself stood by a dresser, packing belongings.

"So it's true," she demanded, placing her hands on her hips. "You've managed to worm your way out of formally facing your crimes, and now seek to gallivant off into exile to enjoy the rest of your worthless life in the lap of luxury."

Garnet spun around and stared at her.

"Forgive me, sir. I tried to stop her." The butler bowed.

"It's all right. You may leave us."

"Sir?"

"Leave us."

The butler hesitated. "As you wish." He reluctantly bowed again, and took his leave, closing the doors behind him.

The silence was so thick, you could cut it with a knife.

While Isabelle served up her best glare, never taking her eyes off Garnet, the man she had thought of as the Puppet Master, didn't look at her. In fact, he didn't acknowledge her presence as all. Dressed in a pristine gentleman's suit, complete with a dark green cravat and diamond cufflinks, he looked every bit the arrogant, obscenely wealthy lord with more authority than God. And yet, something wasn't quite right.

He looked old, worn, haggard. That gave Isabelle some small measure of comfort, but not enough to offset her already inflamed ire. He was free. Why should he look so defeated?

"Might I offer you a drink, Lady Viece?" Lord Garnet finally said, shattering the silence.

"You may offer me an explanation."

"Oh come now. You didn't really think you could sever *all* of my connections and resources, did you?"

Isabelle fumed. How? How was this possible? Failing to recover the mousetrap from the Crimsons had put her entire plan in jeopardy, but Inspector Corbin had blessedly acquired that written and signed confession from one of the welders, and they still had the blueprints from Count Downey, as well as the evidence Corbin had planted at the estate.

They had *some* evidence. Not rock-solid proof, but combined with her efforts to discredit Garnet, it should have been enough to warrant a trial. And yet Garnet stood free before her.

Morgan flashed her a patronizing smile. "Oh child," he said, as he carefully poured himself a rather generous glass of sherry. "You still don't understand. You are a tadpole, just introduced to the pool where the big fish swim. And you're completely unaware of the ocean that sits just beyond your little puddle, where the leviathans dominate."

"A cute analogy, I grant you," Isabelle said dryly. "But if you are tactlessly referring to the war conspiracy my parents were a part of—"

"And consequently, the one I was trying to prevent."

Isabelle froze. What?

He took a long swig of his sherry, and only then did Isabelle realize he was already inebriated. His cheeks were flushed, his eyes glazed. "It would seem, with the death of your parents, that I was at least successful in delaying it. I had hoped to actually arm my country's elite with the same weapons our would-be conquerors would seek to employ against us, but alas, plans have a way of going awry." He took another swig. "But I suppose, albeit in a rather pernicious way, it all worked out in the end. Wouldn't you agree?" He leaned back against the elegant bar that held an array of spirits in fine glass bottles.

Still frozen, her fists and her teeth clenched, Isabelle swallowed, and forced her thoughts into submission. "The blueprints," she said finally. "They weren't depictions of weapons of any kind. They detailed inventions, or materials for inventions, you used to fashion weapons. Those were your forged patents. But the blueprints, like the one Count Downey had in his briefcase, those were actual weapons. We caught Count Downey because the dates on his blueprints didn't align. Who did you steal the weapon designs from?"

"Very clever, Lady Viece. Very clever. Have you heard the name Condello?"

Isabelle shook her head.

"I'm sure you will some day. His weapons designs are nothing short of . . . catastrophic. And our enemies would otherwise have been building them had I not stolen them first."

"Who? Who are you talking about?"

"Unfortunately, I was never able to determine that. Your parents covered their tracks well. Took me years just to get evidence against them."

"So you knew? You always knew. You were never merely trying to discredit my parents. You were trying to stop their treason."

"Now you're getting it."

Isabelle didn't know what to think. Her whole body went numb. This made too much sense. It all fit together, and filled every gap in the equation Isabelle had built on her now incinerated bedchamber wall. Garnet was, of course, in it for his own profit, make no mistake. But this machination was much too elaborate and risky to waste an existing fortune.

Unless there was decidedly more at stake.

Garnet finished his sherry, then poured himself another. "Justice always prevails, Lady Viece," Garnet gloated. "One way or another."

Isabelle found herself slipping into a dark place, disconnected from reality. She'd never been there before. A place, deep within her heart, within her soul, that could only be accessed once a large part of you broke. And that part of Isabelle, her innocence, had shattered with the drop of the hangman's lever.

"You worked so hard to serve justice."

She worked all her life for justice.

"And in the end, the traitors were hanged, the patriot lived, the thieves acquired a devastating weapon, and the crime lord of the Liverpool underground ran away with a fortune in currency and weapons assets."

Isabelle's mind raced to piece that last part together. Mr. Monaghan was the Informant. And he had the blueprints. They survived the circus fiasco, and Monaghan stole them. She could've used that as the last piece to confirm Garnet's guilt. But Monaghan *stole* them! Of course he wouldn't be content with acquiring Garnet's wealth alone. She had been looking for the angle he'd play to get the better of her. To win.

It would seem he found it.

Garnet eyed her knowingly. "The cruel irony here, is that it's all thanks to you."

The very air threatened to choke Isabelle. For a moment, her entire world held its breath.

"Without your helping hand, your meddling, your infuriating persistence at the behest of justice and sheer, idiotic will, none of this would have come to pass. Well done, Lady Viece. Well done." He smiled that smug, victorious smile that always sent a shiver down Isabelle's spine. Today, right now, that shiver was cold, pure hatred.

Before she even knew what she was doing, she reached into her satchel, pulled out her pistol and leveled it at Garnet's forehead.

Garnet smirked. "Threats, Lady Viece? Is this what it's come to for you?" The patronizing look of disappointment on his face almost pushed Isabelle to squeeze the trigger.

Almost.

This man deserved to suffer, deserved death. This man had cost her everything she held dear. And yet she hesitated. Did ending one unscrupulous man's life change anything? Was this justice? Could she even pull the trigger if she wanted to?

As she held her pistol in a quivering hand, she locked eyes with Garnet as a chilling revelation settled over her. She could. The decision before her was not if she *could* kill this man, it was whether she *would*.

Trembling, Isabelle began to slowly squeeze the trigger.

Garnet froze.

"Lady Viece," he warned. "You don't want to do this."

Tears streamed gently down Isabelle's cheeks, her face contorted in agony.

Was this justice?

She squeezed the trigger a little more.

Garnet put out a cautious hand. "There is much more you don't yet know. About your family. About their alliances. I can help you, Lady Viece. I can—"

Isabelle pulled the trigger.

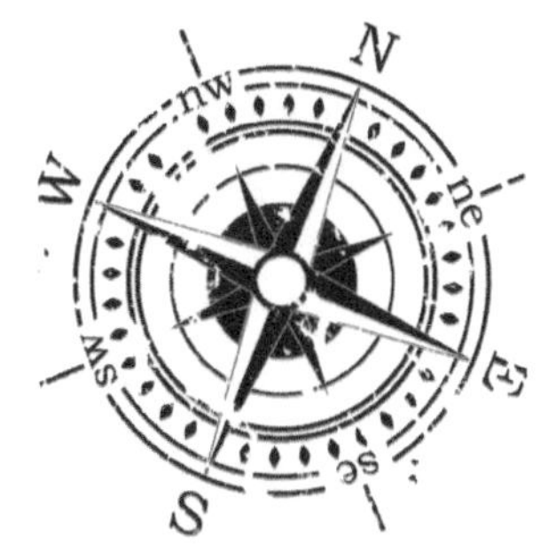

End of Book 1 of The Crimson Articles

To be continued in Book 2

(because every book worth reading has a sequel)